徐薇

教你背 新多益
單字(下)

NEW TOEIC

- **10** 種
  多益必考情境
- **1000** 個
  多益必背單字
- **2000** 組
  單字詞組搭配

4 小時徐薇老師精華單字教學

5 小時美籍、英籍雙口音朗讀MP3

記單字也學用法，多益單字再難都不怕！

《徐薇教你背新多益單字》序

從事英文教學二十多年，我深刻了解學習者在學英文和參加英文考試時會遇到的困難。尤其是年齡愈大的學習者，想要學好英文或是應考備戰，最需要的就是「快速而有效的方法」，這正是我們推出《徐薇教你背新多益單字》套書的目的，期望透過我一直推動的「徐薇UP學」，幫助眾多想挑戰多益測驗及加強英文能力的學習者，以最有效的方式學好英文，英文成績不斷UP、UP、UP！

《徐薇教你背新多益單字》套書，參考多益測驗官方所列出的主題情境及多益測驗常用字詞，同時對照全民英檢分級字表，套書分為(上)、(下)兩冊，共二十個單元，每單元皆有100個與多益測驗情境最相關的單字，並列出單字結構與記憶口訣方便理解，重點單字更有我的教學MP3，徐薇老師會透過英文部首、小故事及聯想記憶法，教你用最快的方式把單字牢牢刻進腦海裡哦！

針對多益測驗中一定會出現的不同口音，我們也聘請了專業美籍與英籍外師，為每個單字與例句錄製了朗讀音檔，透過聆聽不同口音，更能加深印象、增進聽力應考實力。

每單元結束前皆附有精選實力進階區，內容包括：易混字比較、與主題相關的補充字彙、實用片語、常用字根等，增強英文應用能力必不可少；而隨堂測驗區則可讓您在學習完一個單元後，還能自我檢測對單字的理解程度與學習成效。

《徐薇教你背新多益單字》不只是一套教你有效背單字的寶典，同時也是集結了多益考試、商用情境、日常生活溝通必備的英文學習秘笈。跟著徐薇老師學多益單字，收穫的不只是更漂亮的測驗成績，還有更扎實的語文實力喔！

預祝各位學習者

征戰考場，無往不利！

徐薇

目錄

目錄

頁面說明

頁面說明

對照全民英檢單字分級作為難易度參考。

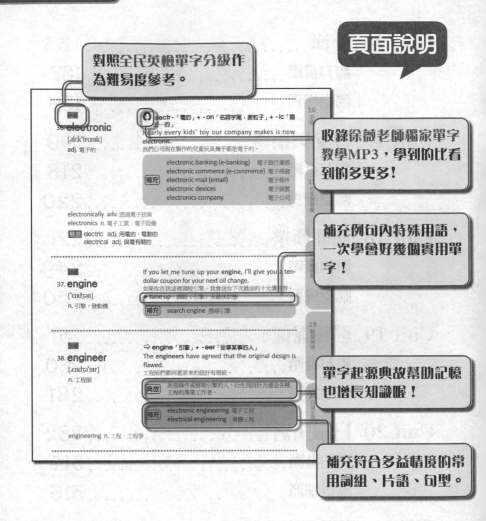

初級 electronic
[ɪlɛk'trɑnɪk]
36.
adj. 電子的

electr-「電的」+ -on「名詞字尾，表粒子」+ -ic「屬於…的」
Nearly every kids' toy our company makes is now electronic.
我們公司現在製作的兒童玩具幾乎都是電子的。

補充
electronic banking (e-banking)	電子銀行業務
electronic commerce (e-commerce)	電子商務
electronic mail (email)	電子郵件
electronic devices	電子裝置
electronics company	電子公司

electronically adv. 透過電子技術
electronics n. 電子工業；電子設備
易混 electric adj. 用電的，電動的
electrical adj. 與電有關的

收錄徐薇老師獨家單字教學MP3，學到的比看到的多更多！

初級 engine
['ɛndʒən]
37.
n. 引擎，發動機

If you let me tune up your engine, I'll give you a ten-dollar coupon for your next oil change.
如果你在我這裡調校引擎，我會送你下次換油的十元優惠券。
★ tune up：調節（引擎）至最佳狀態
補充 search engine 搜尋引擎

補充例句內特殊用語，一次學會好幾個實用單字！

初級 engineer
[ˌɛndʒə'nɪr]
38.
n. 工程師

⇨ engine「引擎」+ -eer「從事某事的人」
The engineers have agreed that the original design is flawed.
工程師們都同意原來的設計有瑕疵。
典故 原指操作或修理引擎的人，衍生為設計及建造各種工程的專業工作者。
補充 electronic engineering 電子工程
electrical engineering 電機工程

engineering n. 工程；工程學

單字起源典故幫助記憶也增長知識喔！

補充符合多益情境的常用詞組、片語、句型。

每單元精選實力進階課程，難字不混淆，實力更上一層樓！

 實力進階

Part 1. Savings account vs. Checking account

「bank account 銀行帳戶」，在台灣和在美國的用法有很大差異。美國的銀行帳戶主要分為 savings account 以及 checking account。通常 savings account 譯為「儲蓄帳戶」，而 checking account 譯為「支票帳戶」或「活期存款帳戶」。

savings account 是用來存款的帳戶，利率會比 checking account 高；通常開 savings account 的戶頭就是為了把錢放在裡面生利息，也很少會提錢出來。

checking account 的利率近乎零，這個帳戶的目的就在於機動性的使用，例如信用卡扣款、薪資的匯入款、支票的扣款、入款，都是和 checking account 相連結的。因為和支票使用有關，才有了 "checking" account 的稱呼。

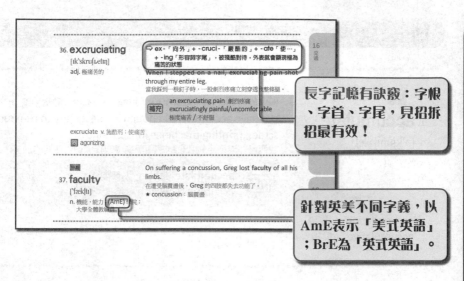

36. **excruciating**
[ɪkˈskruʃɪˌetɪŋ]
adj. 極痛苦的

⇨ ex-「向外」+ -cruci-「嚴酷的」+ -ate「使…」+ -ing「形容詞字尾」，被殘酷對待，外表就會顯現極為痛苦的狀態

When I stepped on a nail, excruciating pain shot through my entire leg.
當我踩到一根釘子時，一股劇烈疼痛立刻穿透過整條腿。

補充　an excruciating pain 劇烈疼痛
excruciatingly painful/uncomfortable
極度痛苦 / 不舒服

excruciate v. 施酷刑；使痛苦

同 agonizing

字尾

37. **faculty**
[ˈfæk̩ltɪ]
n. 機能，能力 (AmE) 學院；大學全體教職員工

On suffering a concussion, Greg lost faculty of all his limbs.
在遭受腦震盪後，Greg 的四肢都失去功能了。
★ concussion：腦震盪

> 長字記憶有訣竅：字根、字首、字尾，見招拆招最有效！

> 針對英美不同字義，以 AmE 表示「美式英語」；BrE 為「英式英語」。

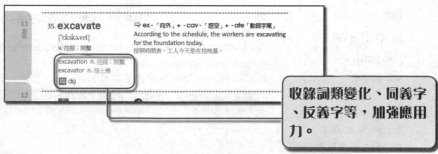

35. **excavate**
[ˈɛkskəˌvet]
v. 挖掘；開鑿

⇨ ex-「向外」+ -cav-「挖空」+ -ate「動詞字尾」

According to the schedule, the workers are excavating for the foundation today.
按照時間表，工人今天是在挖地基。

excavation n. 挖掘；開鑿
excavator n. 挖土機
同 dig

> 收錄詞類變化、同義字、反義字等，加強應用力。

> 每單元附隨堂練習，學完做檢測、記憶更深刻！

隨堂練習

★ 請根據句意，選出最適合的單字
(　　) 1. Everyone thinks that David is a(n)_____ to the company because he is both creative and diligent.
(A) boom　　　　　　　(B) peak
(C) asset　　　　　　　(D) deposit

(　　) 2. New policies need to be instituted to pull the country out of _____; otherwise, people will lose their confidence in the government.
(A) recession　　　　　(B) trend
(C) statistics　　　　　(D) expenditure

(　　) 3. Mark was arrested last night because he was caught selling _____ watches at the night market.
(A) redeemable　　　　(B) delinquent

Unit 11 製造

中高
1. accumulate
[əˈkjumjəˌlet]
v. 累積

⇨ ac-「to」+ -cumul-「堆積」+ -ate「動詞字尾」

We have **accumulated** enough ink necessary to run our screen printing machines for six months.
我們已經累積足夠我們的網版印刷機運作六個月所需的油墨。

補充　accumulate debts　累積債務
　　　accumulate wealth　累積財富

accumulation n. 累積
accumulative adj. 積累的

中級
2. accurate
[ˈækjərɪt]
adj. 精確的

⇨ ac-「to」+ -cur-「照料」+ -ate「形容詞字尾」，仔細照料就會精確沒有偏誤

The late shipment you received is not an **accurate** reflection of the type of company we are.
延遲交貨並不真的表示我們就是這樣的公司。

補充　accurate data　準確的資料

accuracy n. 精確
accurately adv. 精確地
同 exact / precise

---

3. adjustable
[əˈdʒʌstəbl]
adj. 可調節的；可調整的

 ad-「to」+ -just-「正確的」+ -able「可…的」，朝正確的方向去調整

We need to change our supplier for the **adjustable** straps we use on our backpacks.
我們得將提供我們後背包上可調式肩帶的供應商換掉。

補充　adjustable rate　機動利率

adjust v. 調整；調節；校正
adjustment n. 調整；調節

中高

4. **array**

[ə`re]

n. (排列整齊的) 一批，一系列

v. 排列，布置

Our most popular style of blouse for women comes in a wide **array** of colors.
我們最受歡迎的女上衣款式有眾多色系可供選擇。

補充
an array of... 一批…
a wide array of sth. 廣泛、大量的…

中級

5. **artificial**

[ˌɑrtə`fɪʃəl]

adj. 人造的

 - art - 「技術」+ - fic - 「做」+ - ial「形容詞字尾」，用技術做出來就是人造的

Most of our competitors use **artificial** sweeteners to enhance the flavor of their beverages.
我們大部分的競爭對手使用人工甘味劑來增強他們飲料的風味。

補充
artificial intelligence (AI) 人工智慧
artificial person 法人

artificially adv. 人工地；不自然地
artificiality n. 人為；矯揉造作

中級

6. **assembly**

[ə`sɛmblɪ]

n. 裝配；集合；集會

⇨ **assemble**「組裝，聚集」+ - y「名詞字尾」

This desk requires **assembly**.
這張書桌需要組裝。

補充
assembly line 裝配線
self-assembly 自己組裝的

assemble v. 組裝；聚集

中高

7. **barren**

[`bærən]

adj. 貧瘠的；不孕的；無成果的

barrenness n. 荒蕪；不孕；白費

Our biggest warehouse is out in the middle of the **barren** desert, so we produce all of our own solar power.
我們最大的倉庫遠在貧瘠的沙漠中央，所以我們全都自己生產太陽能。

同 infertile adj. 不能生育的
fruitless adj. 無成果的

8. **beware**

[bɪˋwɛr]

v. 小心

同 be wary

易混 aware adj. 意識到的

You should **beware** of the possibility of overload to the circuits in this room.

你應該要小心這間房間的電路有可能會超載。

補充 Beware of sth. 小心…（常用於警告標誌）

9. **blueprint**

[ˋbluˌprɪnt]

n. 藍圖；計畫

v. 將…製成藍圖；計畫

⇨ blue「藍色」+ print「印出的圖片」，印在藍色紙上的圖就是藍圖

If we just follow the **blueprint** that we created with our first restaurant, we should be successful.

如果我們按照第一間餐廳的藍圖去做的話，我們應該會成功。

補充 a blueprint for sth. 某事物的計畫
draw up a blueprint 繪製藍圖；起草一份計畫

10. **breadth**

[brɛdθ]

n. 寬度，幅度；廣泛性，廣度

broad adj. 寬的

同 width n. 寬度

易混 breath n. 呼吸

⇨ broad「寬的」+ -th「抽象名詞字尾」

Your overall **breadth** of knowledge in the IT field is unparalleled.

你對資訊科技產業了解的廣泛程度無人能及。

補充 market breadth 市場廣度
數字 + 單位 + in breadth 有…的寬度

16 交通

17 社交與用餐

18 休閒娛樂

19 醫療保健

20 日常生活

中高

11. **breakdown**

[ˈbrekˌdaʊn]

n. 故障；崩潰；分類

⇨ break「破裂」+ down「往下」

The **breakdown** of our conveyor belt means that parts will need to be passed down the line manually.
我們的輸送帶故障意味著零件需要用手動傳送。

補充	mechanical breakdown	機械故障
	nervous breakdown	神經衰弱
	cost breakdown	成本分析；費用明細

break down phr. 故障；失敗；弄壞；失控；分類

中級

12. **capacity**

[kəˈpæsətɪ]

n. 容納量；生產力，產量；
能力，才能

⇨ capacis「拉丁文，能拿很多的」+ -ty「名詞字尾」，
能拿很多表示容納量大、很有能力

The local high school contracted with us to build a state-of-the-art, high-**capacity** auditorium.
本地高中和我們簽約要建造一棟先進、容納量大的禮堂。

補充	a capacity of...	容量是…
	filled to capacity	客滿
	capacity crowd/audience	座無虛席
	work/operate at full capacity	全力工作、生產

capacious adj. 容量大的；寬廣的

中高

13. **clockwise**

[ˈklɑkˌwaɪz]

adv. 順時針方向地
adj. 順時針方向的

⇨ clock「時鐘」+ -wise「方式、方向」，依時鐘的方向
就是順時針

The machine is set only to run **clockwise** at a fairly low speed.
這台機器被設定只以相當慢的速度順時針方向運行。

反 counterclockwise adj. 逆時針方向的
adv. 逆時針方向地

中高

14. complement

[ˈkɑmpləmɛnt]

v. 補足，補充；與…相配

[ˈkɑmpləmənt]

n. 補充物

 com -「一起」+ -ple -「填滿」+ -ment「名詞字尾」，一起填滿就能補足事物使其完備

The dark color of the wood **complements** the glass surface of this desk.

木頭的深色和這張書桌的玻璃表面很相配。

補充　complement each other　相輔相成
complementary skills　互補的技能

complementary adj. 補充的；互補的

易混 compliment n./v. 讚美

中級

15. complicate

[ˈkɑmpləˌket]

v. 使複雜化；(疾病) 惡化

➪ com -「一起」+ -plic -「摺疊」+ -ate「使成為…」，摺在一起表示混亂複雜

Don't try to further **complicate** things by using overly technical language.

不要使用過度專業的術語，這會使事情更加複雜化。

complicated adj. 複雜的
complication n. 混亂；併發症

中級

16. compound

[ˈkɑmpaʊnd]

adj. 複合的
n. 複合物，化合物
v. 混合，合成

➪ com -「一起」+ -pound -「放置」，放在一起就是複合的

Although we initially invested a small amount, **compound** interest generated over the years tripled our money.

雖然我們最初只有投資一小筆錢，不過這幾年複利增長讓我們的錢成長了三倍。

補充　compound interest　複利
compound A with B　將 A 與 B 混和
compound substance　合成物質

中高

17. comprise

[kəm`praɪz]

v. 構成；包含；由…組成

Our sofas are **comprised** of fine cotton with a velvet exterior.

我們的沙發是以精棉外包天鵝絨所製成。

典故 源自法文 compris 表「抓在一起」的意思。

補充
be comprised of sth. 由某事物組成
= be composed of sth.
= be made up of sth.
= consist of sth.

同 constitute

中高

18. conservation

[ˌkɑnsɚ`veʃən]

n. 保存；(對自然資源的)保護；節約

⇒ con-「一起」+ -serv-「保護」+ -ation「名詞字尾」，把東西保護起來就是在保存

Conservation of resources is important to us, so we recycle everything we can at the plant.

節約資源對我們來說很重要，所以我們在工廠盡可能回收所有可以回收的東西。

補充
a conservation area 保育區
wildlife conservation 野生生物保育
energy conservation 節約能源

conserve v. 保存，保護；節約
conservative n. 保守的

中高

19. contaminate

[kən`tæməˌnet]

v. 弄髒；汙染；毒害

⇒ con-「一起」+ -tamin-「碰觸」+ -ate「使成為…」，碰在一起就弄髒了

One of our oil tankers was involved in an accident and the oil spillage **contaminated** the nearby stream.

我們有一輛油罐車發生事故，而灑出來的油汙染了附近的溪流。

contamination n. 弄髒；汙染；玷汙
contaminated adj. 弄髒的；受汙染的；受毒害的
contaminant n. 汙染物

同 pollute v. 汙染
poison v. 毒害

初級

20. control

[kənˋtrol]

v./n. 控制；支配；抑制

Tim lost his job as a quality **control** supervisor when a rat nest was found in the cooler.

Tim 丟掉了品管部主管的工作，因為冰箱裡面發現了老鼠窩。

補充

cost control	成本控制
quality control	品質管制
under control	在控制下
out of control	失控

controllable adj. 可控制的；可操縱的

中高

21. defect

[ˋdɪfɛkt]

n. 缺陷

[dɪˋfɛkt]

v. 脫離；背叛

 de - 「向下、分開」+ -fect - 「做」，愈做等級愈往下表示有缺陷

The customer is complaining of a **defect** in his DVD player, so I told him to ship it back to us.

那位顧客抱怨他的 DVD 播放器有缺陷，所以我請他把東西寄回來給我們。

補充

a product defect	產品缺陷
a design defect	設計缺陷
a manufacturing defect	製造缺陷
correct/remedy a defect	補救缺陷

defective adj. 有缺陷的

同 flaw n. 缺陷

中高

22. destructive

[dɪˋstrʌktɪv]

adj. 毀滅性的；有害的

 de - 「表相反的動作」+ -struct - 「建造」+ -ive「形容詞字尾」，建造的相反就是破壞毀滅

Those additives are banned because they are proved to be **destructive** to human bodies.

那些添加物因為證實對人體有害而被禁用了。

補充　be destructive to N. 對 N. 有害

destroy v. 摧毀
destruction n. 毀滅；破壞

同 devastating / ruinous / disastrous

中高

23. **deteriorate**
[dɪˋtɪrɪəˏret]
v. 惡化；質量下降

⇨ **deterior**「拉丁文，較差的」+ **-ate**「動詞字尾」，變得更差就是惡化

The machinery in the warehouse has **deteriorated** to the point where it is unsafe to operate.
倉庫裡的機器已經爛到無法安全使用的程度了。

 deteriorate into sth. 惡化成…

deterioration n. 惡化

回 worsen/degenerate

初級

24. **determine**
[dɪˋtɝmɪn]
v. 確定；決定；下決心

⇨ **de-**「完全」 + **-termine-**「設界限」，設定界限表示已做出決定

We have **determined** that we will discontinue the products.
我們已經決定要將這些商品停產了。

 determine that S. V... 確定…
determine to V... 下定決心去做…

determined adj. 下定決心的
determination n. 確定；決心

中級

25. **device**
[dɪˋvaɪs]
n. 設備，裝置；謀略，手段

There were all sorts of new **devices** at the trade show, although most will not be mass-produced.
貿易展上有各式各樣新的裝置，不過大多數都不會大量生產。

 electronic device 電子裝置
storage device （電腦的）儲存裝置
mobile / wireless / handheld devices
行動裝置 / 無線裝置 / 手持裝置

devise v. 想出，設計，發明

11 製造

中高

26. **diameter**

[daɪˈæmətɚ]

n. 直徑

⇨ dia -「穿越」+ -meter -「測量」，穿過圓所測量出來的就是直徑

The gaskets need to be exactly ten centimeters in **diameter** to fit properly.

這些墊圈必須剛好是直徑十公分才能妥善地密合。

> 補充
> 長度 + in diameter 直徑是…
> diametrically opposed/opposite
> 截然不同的，截然相反的

diametrically adv. 正好相反地，完全地

---

12 金融

中高

27. **disposable**

[dɪˈspozəb!]

adj. 可拋棄的；用完即丟的

 dis -「分開」+ -pos -「放置」+ -able「可…的」，可以分開放表示可以處理掉、用完後可以丟掉

The government has now insisted that we use **disposable** trash bags for all our perishable goods.

政府現在堅持我們要使用一次性垃圾袋來裝所有的易腐貨物。

> 補充
> disposable diapers/nappies 紙尿布
> disposable contact lenses 拋棄式隱形眼鏡
> disposable chopsticks 免洗筷

dispose v. 處置；處理；配置
disposal n. 處置；處理；配置

---

13 科技技術

中高

28. **distributor**

[dɪˈstrɪbjətɚ]

n. 經銷商；(電影) 發行商

⇨ dis -「分開」+ -tribut -「給予」+ -or「做…動作的人」，將東西分開配送的人就是經銷商

Our **distributors** have requested that we no longer send them our T-shirts in cases of 100.

我們的經銷商要求我們不要再將 T 恤以一百件一箱的方式寄給他們。

> 補充
> distributor of + 產品 某產品的經銷商
> local distributor 本地經銷商
> international distributor 國際經銷商
> exclusive distributor 獨家經銷商
> a film distributor 電影發行公司

distribute v. 分配；分發；配送 (貨物)
distribution n. 分配；分發
distributorship n. 經銷權

14 房屋地產

15 出差旅遊

中高

29. emission

[ɪˋmɪʃən]

n. 排出；排放；排放物

⇨ e-「向外」+ -miss-「發送」+ -ion「名詞字尾」，向外送出就是排放

Our factory **emissions** are checked annually by the EPA, and we always pass with flying colors.
我們的工廠排放物每年會由環境保護局進行檢核，而我們總是以很好的成績通過檢驗。

★ EPA = Environmental Protection Agency（美國）環境保護局

carbon dioxide emissions	二氧化碳的排放
emission credit	排放權
cut/reduce emissions of...	減少…的排放

emit v. 排放；排出

中級

30. enhancement

[ɪnˋhænsmənt]

n. 提高；強化；增強

⇨ enhance「提高；增強」+ -ment「名詞字尾」

We have made a few **enhancements** to our latest smart phone, including a brighter interface.
我們針對我們最新的智慧型手機做了一些強化，其中包含了更明亮的介面。

performance enhancement	性能增強
productivity enhancement	提高生產力
product enhancements	產品增強功能
make enhancements to sth.	強化某物

enhance v. 提高；增加；增進
enhanced adj. 增大的；強化的

中級

31. equipment

[ɪˋkwɪpmənt]

n. 設備；裝備

⇨ equip「裝配」+ -ment「名詞字尾」

When we started out, we only had second-hand **equipment** that barely functioned.
我們剛開始的時候只有勉強可以運作的二手設備。

a piece of equipment	一項設備
A be equipped with B	A 配有 B 的能力或裝備
be equipped to do sth.	被裝備能做某事
well/poorly equipped	設備良好的 / 差的

equip v. 裝備；使有能力；賦予

11 製造

中級

32. equivalent

[ɪˋkwɪvələnt]

n. 相等物

adj. 等值的；等同的

equivalence n. 相等

⇨ **equi** - 「相等」 + **- val** - 「價值」 + **- ent** 「具…性的」，具有同等價值就是相等的

The amount of work Tom gets done in two hours is the **equivalent** of a full day's worth for anyone else.

Tom兩小時內完成的工作量等同於其他任何人一整天所達到的。

be the equivalent to/of sth. 是某物的相等物
A be equivalent to B　　A 與 B 相等

---

33. evenly

[ˋivənlɪ]

adv. 均勻地；平等地；平靜地

even adj. 均等的；均勻的

⇨ **even** 「均等的；均勻的」 + **- ly** 「副詞字尾」

Be sure to spread each coat of icing **evenly** on all three layers of cake.

要確定將三層蛋糕的每一層上面都均勻地塗抹上糖霜。

evenly matched　勢均力敵的
evenly spaced　擺放整齊的

中高

34. expiration

[͵ɛkspəˋreʃən]

n. 期滿，到期；結束

expire v. 期滿，到期

★ 英：expiry ／美：expiration

⇨ **expire** 「到期」 + **- ation** 「名詞字尾」

Our closest competitor got into trouble for changing the **expiration** dates on their food cases.

我們最強的對手因為更改了他們食品包裝上的到期日而陷入麻煩。

expiration date (= expiry date)　保存期限，到期日
the expiration of visa　　　　　　簽證到期

中高

35. **external**

[ɪkˋstɝnl̩]

adj. 外部的；外面的；外表的

n. 外貌；外部

➪ **exter**「拉丁文，外面」+ **-al**「形容詞字尾」

Tom purchased a huge **external** hard drive to back up all our data.

Tom 購買了一個大容量的外接式硬碟來備份我們所有的資料。

補充　for external use only 僅限外用

externally adv. 在 (從) 外部；在 (從) 外面；外表上

同 exterior

反 interior/ internal adj. 內部的，內裝的

中級

36. **facility**

[fəˋsɪlətɪ]

n. 設施；能力；熟練；靈巧

 facile「容易，靈巧的」+ **-ity**「名詞字尾」，使動作更便利熟練的就是好的設施

Allergy Warning: This product was made in a **facility** that uses nuts.

[過敏警語]：本產品生產製程設備有處理含堅果之產品。

補充

shopping facilities	購物設施
medical facilities	醫療設施
sports facilities	體育設施
public facilities	公共設施

facile adj. 易做到的；熟練靈巧的

facilitate v. 使容易，使便利

37. **fertilize**

[ˋfɝtl̩͵aɪz]

v. 施肥

 fertile「肥沃的」+ **-ize**「使…」

Farmers have been using harsh chemicals to **fertilize** their fields.

農夫們一直在使用刺激性的化學物質來為田地施肥。

fertile adj. 肥沃的；能生育的

fertilizer n. 肥料

fertilization n. 施肥

11
製造

12
金融

13
科技技術

14
房屋地產

15
出差旅遊

38. **flammable**

[ˋflæməbl]

adj. 易燃的

⇨ **flame**「火焰」+ **-able**「可…的」，可生出火焰的表示
容易燃燒的

These gases are highly **flammable**, and must be kept in a cool, well-ventilated place.

這些氣體極度易燃，必須存放在陰涼且通風良好的地方。

flame n. 火焰

同 inflammable adj. 易燃的

反 non-flammable adj. 不可燃的；不易燃的

中高

39. **flaw**

[flɔ]

n. 瑕疵；錯誤
v. 使有缺陷

Because too many product **flaws** were found, customers have lost confidence in the manufacturer.

因為發現太多產品瑕疵，顧客對這間製造商已經失去了信心。

補充

a character flaw	性格上的缺陷
a fatal flaw	致命的缺陷
a flaw in sth.	某事物的缺陷

flawless adj. 無瑕的
flawed adj. 有缺點的

同 defect n. 缺陷

中高

40. **formulate**

[ˋfɔrmjəˌlet]

v. 制定，規劃；有系統地闡述

⇨ **formula**「公式，配方」+ **-ate**「動詞字尾」，制定規則
就是讓事物成為公式

You did not listen to the proposal long enough to **formulate** an accurate assessment.

你聽提案的時間不夠長無法制定出精確的評估。

補充 formulate a plan/policy 制定一個計畫／政策

formula n. 公式；配方
formulation n. 公式化；規劃

中高

41. framework

[ˈfremˌwɜk]

n. 架構，體系；（建築物的）骨架

⇨ frame「架構、框架」+ work「作品」

We need to put our heads together and construct a **framework** that can be a basis for our future partnership.
我們需要集思廣益來建立一個能成爲我們未來合夥基礎的架構。

★ put one's heads together：一起動腦，集思廣益

補充 a framework for N.　　N. 的架構 / 體系

frame n. 架構

---

42. futuristic

[ˌfjutʃəˈrɪstɪk]

adj. 未來的；有未來感的

 ⇨ future「未來」+ - istic「形容詞字尾」

We are going with a **futuristic** design for our latest headphones to make customers feel that they are trendy.
我們最新款的頭戴式耳機採用具未來感的設計，要讓消費者覺得自己很時髦。

補充 futuristic design/building/film
有未來感的設計 / 建築 / 電影

future n. 未來

 中高

43. generate

[ˈdʒɛnəˌret]

v. 產生；造成

⇨ -gener-「生產」+ -ate「動詞字尾」

The latest vacuum cleaners **generate** less noise than older models.
最新款的吸塵器產生的噪音比舊款的少。

 補充 generate revenue/income/profits
產生收益 / 收入 / 利潤
generate interest　引起興趣
generate electricity　發電

generation n. 產生；世代
generator n. 發電機

11 製造

12 金融

13 科技技術

14 房屋地產

15 出差旅遊

44. **goggles**

[ˋgɑg!z]

n. 護目鏡；蛙鏡

goggle v. 瞪大眼睛看

Wearing safety **goggles** is an absolute must to prevent eye injuries when you use the table saw.
在使用圓鋸機時配戴護目鏡預防眼睛受傷是絕對必要的。

補充　safety goggles 護目鏡，防護眼鏡

中高

45. **hazard**

[ˋhæzɚd]

n. 危險，危害物；風險

hazardous adj. 有危險的

Painting in an unventilated room is a health **hazard**.
在不通風的房間裡刷油漆是會危害健康的。

補充
fire/health/environmental hazard
火災隱患 / 健康危害 / 環境危害
potential hazards　潛在危險
be a hazard to...　對…造成危害
hazard light　危險警示燈
hazard pay　危險工作津貼

中高

46. **heighten**

[ˋhaɪtn̩]

v. 增強；升高

height n. 高度
同 intensify v. 加強
反 reduce v. 減少

⇨ height「高度」＋ - en「動詞字尾」，提升高度就表示加強、強化

Working overtime constantly will **heighten** the stress levels of all the employees.
不斷超時工作會增加所有員工的壓力。

補充
heighten sb's awareness of sth.
使某人更加了解某事物

47. horizontal

中高

[ˌhɑrəˈzɑntl̩]

adj. 水平的；橫向的

n. 水平線

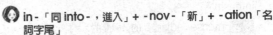

⇨ horizon「地平線」+ -al「形容詞字尾」

The success of our small company is due to a **horizontal** management structure where employees all consider themselves part of a team.

我們小公司能成功是因爲有橫向管理的體制，所有的員工都視自己爲團隊的一份子。

補充　horizontal 在商用情境可以指「橫向、平行、同階層的」，例如：horizontal management（橫向管理）。

horizon n. 地平線；眼界；視野

反 vertical adj. 垂直的

48. innovation

中高

[ˌɪnəˈveʃən]

n. 創新；革新；新方法

 in-「同 into-，進入」+ -nov-「新」+ -ation「名詞字尾」

For true **innovation** to take place, workers must be encouraged to think outside the box and not worry about conventionally accepted methods.

要有真正的創新，就必須鼓勵員工跳脫思想框架並且不用顧忌傳統上認定的做法。

補充
innovations in sth.	某事物的創新
product innovation	產品的創新
technological innovation	科技的革新

innovate v. 創新；革新
innovator n. 創新者
innovative adj. 創新的

49. instrument

初級

[ˈɪnstrəmənt]

n. 工具，器械；儀器；樂器

⇨ in-「同 on-，在上面」+ -stru-「建造」+ -ment「名詞字尾」，建造在上面表示把工具配置上去

The Internet has been the **instrument** by which we have quickly advanced technologically.

網路已經成爲我們在科技上能快速進步的工具了。

補充
| surgical instruments | 外科手術器械 |
| the instrument panel | 儀表板 |

instrumental adj. 對⋯起作用的，有幫助的

同 apparatus / device

中級

50. **intensive**

[ɪnˈtɛnsɪv]

adj. 密集的，加強的

⇨ intense「強烈的」+ -ive「形容詞字尾」，比強烈更加強烈表示集中了力道，也就是密集的

Energy-**intensive** industries make profits as the oil price drops.

油價下跌時，能源密集產業就會獲利。

intensive training / courses	密集訓練 / 課程
technology-intensive company	技術密集型企業
labor-intensive industry	勞力密集產業
intensive care	特別護理

intensively adv. 密集地
intensify v. 增強，強化；變激烈
intensity n. 強度；強烈

易混 intense adj. 強烈的，極度的

中級

51. **interval**

[ˈɪntəvl]

n. 間隔；(表演的) 幕間休息

⇨ inter-「在…之間」+ val「來自拉丁文 vallum，牆」

The factory machines need to be checked at regular **intervals** throughout the day.

工廠的機器每天都要定期做檢查。

典故 interval 原指壁壘之間的空間，引申為時間上的間隔。

| 補充 | at regular intervals | 定期，以固定的間隔時間 |
| | at intervals of ... | 每隔 (一段時間或距離) |

中級

52. **laboratory**

[ˈlæbrəˌtorɪ]

n. 實驗室；研究室

⇨ -labor-「工作」+ -tory「地方」，研究員工作的地方就是實驗室

The pharmaceutical company will build two more **laboratories** for future research.

為未來研究所需，這家藥廠將再蓋兩間實驗室。

a research laboratory	研究實驗室
a computer laboratory	電腦實驗室
a language laboratory	語言實驗室
laboratory tests	實驗室測試

 lab

53. lightweight
['laɪt'wet]
adj. 輕量的；膚淺的
n. (運動) 輕量級運動員

⇨ light「輕的」+ weight「重量」
Our company specializes in manufacturing **lightweight** furniture for college students.
我們公司專門為大學生製作輕巧的家具。

> 補充 | a lightweight jacket 薄外套
> a lightweight novel 膚淺的小說

中高
54. maintenance
['mentənəns]
n. 維修；維持；主張；生活費；扶養費

 - main -「手」+ - ten -「握住」+ - ance「名詞字尾」
The manufacturing facility began to fall apart after years of shoddy **maintenance**.
這台生產設備歷經數年的粗糙維護後開始解體了。

> 補充 | under maintenance　　　維修保養中
> maintenance checks　　　維修檢查
> routine maintenance　　　日常維護
> maintenance payment　　 贍養費

maintain v. 維持；維修；供養；主張

中高
55. manipulate
[mə'nɪpjə‚let]
v. 操作；操縱；竄改

 - mani -「手」+ - pul -「拉」+ - ate「動詞字尾」，用手拉就是在操作
This manufacturer designs wheelchairs that are easy to **manipulate**.
這家製造商設計容易操作的輪椅。
Franklin was let go after it was found that he was **manipulating** financial data.
Franklin 在被發現竄改財務資料之後就被解雇了。

> 補充 | manipulate the media 操弄媒體
> manipulate sb. into doing sth. 操縱某人去做某事

manipulation n. 操縱；竄改；操作

11
製造

中高

56. **manufacture**

[͵mænjəˋfæktʃɚ]

v. /n. 製造

manufacturer n. 製造商
manufacturing n. 製造業

 -manu-「手」+ -fact-「做」+ -ure「名詞字尾」，動手做就是在製造

We are the only company licensed to **manufacture** the latest microchip.
我們是唯一一間有執照能製造這種最新型微晶片的公司。

12
金融

初級

57. **material**

[məˋtɪrɪəl]

n. 材料
adj. 物質的；有形的

materialism n. 物質主義
materialistic adj. 拜金的；物質主義的
materially adv. 物質上

⇨ matter「物質」+ -al「形容詞字尾」，材料就是種物質

We will install any type of flooring **material** you would like, including tile.
我們會裝置任何你想要的地板材料類型，包含磁磚。

補充	building materials	建材
	teaching materials	教材
	raw material	原料

13
科技技術

初級

58. **measure**

[ˋmɛʒɚ]

v. 測量；評估
n. 措施

measurement n. 測量；尺寸
measurements n. 尺碼，特別指三圍

It is impossible to **measure** the true value of providing great customer service.
提供優質客戶服務的真正價值是不可能測量得出來的。

補充	made-to-measure adj. 訂做的
	measure up to N.　符合…的標準或預期
	measuring devices/techniques　測量裝置 / 技術

14
房屋地產

初級

59. **mechanical**

[məˋkænɪkl]

adj. 機械的

mechanic n. 技師
mechanically adv. 有關機械地；使用機械地

⇨ mechanic「機械工」+ -al「形容詞字尾」

Constant **mechanical** failures have caused great loss to the factory.
持續的機械故障已對工廠造成極大的損失。

| 補充 | mechanical failure | 機械故障 |
| | mechanical engineering | 機械工程學 |

15
出差旅遊

中級

60. mingle

[ˈmɪŋɡḷ]

v. (使) 混合；交往，往來

The two flavors did not **mingle** well, so we gave up on this formula.
這兩種口味沒有融合得很好，因此我們放棄了這個配方。

You are expected to **mingle** with all the other managers at the company retreat.
你應該在公司的度假會議中與其他所有的經理好好地認識交流。

★ company retreat：指公司以開會名義提供員工到外地休閒兼開會研習的活動。

補充 mingle A with B 混合 A 和 B

同 混合：mix / blend

中高

61. minimal

[ˈmɪnəmḷ]

adj. 最小的；極小的；極少的

⇨ minimum「極小」+ -al「有…性質的」
With only **minimal** effort, Greg meets his hourly quota after about thirty minutes.
只用了最小的努力，Greg 在大約三十分鐘後便達到他每小時的目標配額。

補充 at minimal cost 最少的花費

minimum n. 極小；最低限度
minimally adv. 極小地；極少地
反 maximal adj. 最大的

中高

62. minimize

[ˈmɪnəˌmaɪz]

v. 使降到最低限度；使減到最少；小看；有意淡化

⇨ minimum「極小」+ -ize「使…化」
In order to **minimize** employee fatigue, our manager has instituted a policy of a required break every two hours.
為了使員工疲勞狀況降到最少，我們經理已制定每隔兩小時就強制休息的規定。

補充 minimize the risk of sth. 將某事物的風險降至最低

minimization n. 減到最小
反 maximize v. 使最大化

中級

63. model

[ˈmɑdḷ]

n. 樣式，型號；模型；模範
v. 仿製；做模型，塑造；以…為榜樣

Our latest **model** features bigger screens and better reception.
我們最新款式的特色就是更大的螢幕以及更好的收訊品質。

補充
make and model	廠牌和型號
latest model	最新型產品
a scale/working model	比例模型 / 工作模型
business model	商業模式
role model	模範；行為榜樣

modelling n. 模特兒職業；模型製作

初級

64. operate

[ˈɑpəˌret]

v. 操作；運轉；動手術

⇨ opera「拉丁文，工作、勞動」+ -ate「動詞字尾」，工作就是要動手操作

You must have at least three years' experience of operating a forklift to be considered for this position.
你必須要有操作堆高機至少三年的經驗才有資格擔任這個職位。

補充	operating system	（電腦的）操作系統
	operating table	手術台
	operating room	手術室 (= operating theatre)

operation n. 運作；操作；手術；（有目的的）活動或行動
operator n. 操作員；（電話）接線生；圓滑精明的人
operative adj. 有效的；實施中的；使用中的

---

65. outdated

[ˌaʊtˈdetɪd]

adj. 舊式的；過時的

⇨ out-「越過」+ date「日期」+ -ed「形容詞字尾」，超過某個日期就是過期了

Our design team responded to our customers' complaints about the outdated fashions in our online catalog.
我們的設計團隊已回覆有關線上目錄款式過時的客訴。

補充	outdated equipment	老舊設備
	outdated technology	過時的科技
	outdated ideas	過時的觀點

同 old-fashioned / out-of-date / obsolete

中級

66. output

[ˈaʊtˌpʊt]

n. 產量

v. 生產；輸出

⇨ out「向外」+ put「放」，放到外面去就是輸出

I am shocked at the low output that was reported from our factory in Brazil for last month.
我對於我們巴西工廠上個月回報的低產量感到震驚。

補充	output of sth.	某物的產量
	net output	淨產出
	boost/increase/raise output	提生產量
	reduce/cut output	減少產量
	output falls/declines/is down	產量下降
	output rises/grows/is up	產量增加

同 production / yield n. 產量
反 input

16 交通

17 社交與用餐

18 休閒娛樂

19 醫療保健

20 日常生活

67. outsource

['aʊtsɔrs]

v. 外包

⇨ out「向外」+ source「從…取得」，向外取得工作上的協力就是外包工作

We made a commitment to the local community not to **outsource** any more jobs to India.

我們跟當地承諾了不會再外包任何工作到印度去。

補充
outsource jobs/work 外包工作
outsource sth. to... 外包某工作給…

outsourcing n. 外包；委外

68. particle

中高

['pɑrtɪkl]

n. 微粒；顆粒；極少量

⇨ part「部分」+ -i- + -cle「表小東西」，比一部份還更小的微粒

Each production line has a vacuum pump to prevent dust **particles** from floating into the air.

每條生產線都設有真空幫浦防止塵粒飄到空氣裡。

補充
dust particles　　　　　塵埃，塵粒
not a particle of truth　沒有一丁點真實性

69. patent

中高

['pætnt]

n. 專利

v. 取得…的專利權

adj. 獲專利的；有專利權的

Who is the true **patent** holder for this new type of video player?

誰才是這個新型影片播放器的專利所有者呢？

補充
apply for/file a patent　　　　　申請專利
be awarded/granted a patent 獲得專利

70. periodic

中高

[ˌpɪrɪˋɑdɪk]

adj. 定期的，週期性的

 period「時期，期間」+ -ic「與…有關的」

There are **periodic** checkups scheduled for each of our company vehicles.

我們每一台公司車都有安排定期檢查。

period n. 時期，期間
periodically adv. 週期性地，定期地；偶爾

71. perishable

[ˈpɛrɪʃəbl]

adj. 易腐爛的；容易變質的
n. 腐壞變質的東西（常用複數型）

⇨ perish「死去、腐爛」+ -able「容易…的」

The store will be fined one thousand dollars for each item of **perishable** food found to have expired.
只要有發現任何一件過期的生鮮或熟食產品，這家店就會被罰一千元。

★ perishable food：指保存期限不長的生鮮蔬果或肉類、乳製品或煮好的熟食，因此類食物容易腐敗，所以稱為 perishable food。

補充
perishable goods　易腐貨物
Perish the thought! 死了這條心吧！

perish v. 腐爛；死去

反 imperishable adj. 不朽的，永存的

初級

72. plant

[plænt]

n. 工廠

They used to manufacture steel at the **plant**, but it shut down when the company moved its operations offshore.
他們曾在這間工廠製造鋼鐵，但當公司將業務移至海外時它就關閉了。

補充
power plant	發電廠
assembly plant	組裝工廠
manufacturing plant	製造廠
plant closure	關廠
plant manager	廠長

同 factory

初級

73. pollution

[pəˈluʃən]

n. 汙染

⇨ pollute「汙染」+ -ion「名詞字尾」

The air **pollution** emitted by the factory is causing numerous respiratory illnesses.
這間工廠排放的空氣汙染引發許多呼吸道疾病。

補充
heavily/seriously/badly polluted	受到嚴重汙染
pollute A with B	用 B 汙染 A
pollute sb's mind	汙染某人的心靈

pollute v. 汙染
pollutant n. 汙染物
polluted adj. 受汙染的
polluter n. 造成汙染者；汙染源

74. **practice**

初級

[ˈpræktɪs]

n. 慣例；習慣做法；實行

The **practice** of reporting all factory injuries only became official in 2004.

所有工廠意外傷害皆需通報的做法是到 2004 年才正式開始的。

補充	common practice	常見的做法
	best practice	最佳方法
	standard practice	標準做法

---

75. **precaution**

中高

[prɪˈkɔʃən]

n. 預防措施；預防

➥ pre - 「在…前」 + caution「小心，謹慎」，事前小心做預防

We advise that you take **precautions** to safeguard against the possibility of this type of horrific accident.

我們建議你採取預防措施以防此類嚴重事故發生。

補充	a precaution against N.	預防 N. 的措施
	as a precaution	作為預防
	take precautions	採取預防措施

precautionary adj. 預防性的
🔲 safeguard

---

76. **precision**

中高

[prɪˈsɪʒən]

n. 精確性；嚴謹

➥ pre - 「在…前」 + - cis - 「切」 + - ion「名詞字尾」，事前先切好，東西才會精準明確

Drawing up the blueprints for the new facility requires **precision** and concentration.

繪製新設施的藍圖需要精準和專注。

補充	precision instrument	精密儀器
	with precision	精確地

precise adj. 精確的
precisely adv. 精確地
🔲 accuracy / exactness

---

77. **procedure**

中高

[prəˈsidʒɚ]

n. 程序；手續

🎧 pro - 「向前」 + - ced - 「走」 + - ure「名詞字尾」

Despite trying to help the customer, Jake did not follow the correct **procedure** and was therefore fired.

雖然 Jake 是在幫助顧客，但他沒有遵守正確程序所以被解雇了。

補充	procedure for...	做…的程序
	follow correct procedure	按照正確程序
	standard operating procedure (SOP)	
	標準作業程序	

proceed v. 繼續進行；前進
procedural adj. 程序的

11
製造

12
金融

13
科技技術

14
房屋地產

15
出差旅遊

初級

78. **produce**

[prə`djus]

v. 生產，製造

 pro -「向前」+ -duce -「引導」，向前引導表示使東西生產出來

We make it our mission to **produce** superior quality automobiles for a fair price.
生產價格實惠的高品質汽車是我們的使命。

補充 mass-produce v. 大量生產

producer n. 生產者，出產國
product n. 產品
production n. 生產；產量
productive adj. 有生產力的

中級

79. **progressive**

[prə`grɛsɪv]

adj. 進步的，先進的；逐漸的

 pro -「向前」+ -gress -「行走」+ -ive「形容詞字尾」，向前走就是進步的

I am assigning a committee to ensure that our policies are less conservative and more **progressive**.
我指派了委員會來確認我們的策略較不保守且較爲先進。

補充
progressive ideas　　先進的思想
progressive tax　　　累進稅
progressive disease　疾病進展；惡化中的疾病

progress n./ v. 進步；進展
progression n. 進展；前進

同 advanced adj. 進步的

中級

80. **proportion**

[prə`porʃən]

n. 比例

 pro -「表相關」+ portion「一部分」，表示各部份之間的關係就是比例

The number of male visitors to our sports web site is totally out of **proportion** with the number of female users.
來我們運動網站的男性訪客數量和女性訪客數量完全不成比例。

補充
the proportion of A to B　A 和 B 的比例
in proportion to N.　　　　與 N. 成正比
out of proportion with N.　與 N. 不成比例

proportional adj. 與…成比例的
proportionally adv. 比例上

初級

81. quality

['kwɑlətɪ]

n. 品質
adj. 優質的；優良的

Since we started to use oak instead of cedar in our tables, customers have been complaining about the **quality**.
自從我們開始用橡木桌取代杉木桌後，顧客就一直抱怨桌子的品質問題。

quality of life	生活品質
poor/low quality	品質差
high quality	高品質
quality control	品質管制（縮寫 QC）
quality time	（用於全心照顧某人的）寶貴時光，優質時間

qualify v. 使合格

易混 quantity n. 量；數量

中高

82. reinforce

[ˌriɪnˈfors]

v. 加強，強化；加固

➪ re-「一再」+ enforce「實施，執行」，一再執行就是強化

I want you to take the time to **reinforce** the safety regulations we have in place to avoid any future lawsuits.
我要你花點時間加強我們現行的安全法規以避免未來發生任何訴訟。

reinforced concrete 鋼筋混凝土
reinforce the message/idea/view that...
加強訊息／想法／觀點

enforce v. 實施，執行
reinforcement n. 加強

中高

83. reproduce

[ˌriprəˈdjus]

v. 複製；再生；繁殖

➪ re-「一再」+ produce「生產，製造」

We need you to **reproduce** the exact management model that you set up for all the restaurants in Kansas City.
我們需要你再製作一套你為堪薩斯市所有餐廳設計的相同管理模式。

reproduction techniques/methods
繁殖技術／方法

reproduction n. 繁殖；複製；再生；複製品
reproductive adj. 生殖的；生育的
reproducible adj. 可再生的；可複製的；可繁殖的

同 複製：multiply / copy / duplicate

84. restricted

[rɪˋstrɪktɪd]

adj. 限定的；被限制的

re - 「向後」+ -strict - 「拉緊」+ -ed「形容詞字尾」

Access to sensitive financial data is **restricted** to regional managers only.

敏感財務數據的存取權限只限於區經理。

補充 restrict oneself to N. 將自己限制在 N. 之內

restrict v. 限制
restriction n. 限制
restrictive adj. 限制性的；約束性的

中高

85. resume

[rɪˋzjum]

v. 重新開始；(中斷後) 繼續；
重返

re - 「再次」+ -sume - 「拿取」，再次把工作拿來做就是重新開始

All workers should **resume** production immediately as we are behind schedule.

由於我們進度落後，全體員工都應立即繼續進行生產工作。

補充 resume one's job/post 重返工作崗位

resumption n. 重新開始；繼續
易混 résumé n. 簡歷，履歷

中高

86. revolve

[rɪˋvɑlv]

v. (使) 旋轉

re - 「向後、一再」+ -volve - 「滾動，轉動」，一再地轉動就是在旋轉

The ceiling fan is **revolving** at a high speed.
天花板風扇正以高速旋轉。

補充 revolve around... 以…為中心
revolving door 旋轉門
think the whole world revolves around you
自以為了不起

revolving adj. 旋轉的
revolution n. 旋轉；革命

中高

87. specialist

[ˋspɛʃəlɪst]

n. 專家；專科醫生

special「特殊的」+ -ist「具專業技能的人」

Megan is our chief customer relations **specialist**, so all escalated cases will go to her.

Megan 是我們主要負責顧客關係的專家，所以所有高難度的客訴事件都會交給她處理。

補充 a specialist in N. N. 方面的專家

specialize v. 專門研究；專攻；專門從事
specialized adj. 專門的
specialty n. 特長；特產
同 expert / professional

88. **standard**

[ˈstændəd]

n. 標準；水準
adj. 標準的

⇨ stand「站立」+ hard「牢固地」

All workers in the factory are asked to follow the **standard** operating procedure to perform their job duties.
工廠全體員工都被要求按照標準作業流程執行工作。

| 典故 | standard 原指站穩的軍旗，並以此用來做爲軍隊的集合處，後來衍生爲眾人依循的標準。 |

補充	high/good standard	高水準
	low/poor standard	低水準
	set/meet a standard	設定 / 符合標準
	up to/below standard	達到 / 未達標準
	standard of living	生活水準

standardize v. 標準化

---

89. **stimulus**

[ˈstɪmjələs]

n. 刺激；促進

★ 複數：**stimuli**

The employee rewards program acted as a kind of **stimulus** to get a better effort from everyone.
員工獎勵制度扮演一種刺激大家更努力的角色。

| 補充 | economic stimulus | 經濟刺激 |
| | a stimulus to sth. | 促成某事物的刺激物或因素 |

stimulate v. 刺激
stimulating adj. 有啓發性的；增強活力的
stimulation n. 刺激；激勵
stimulant n. 刺激物；激勵物；興奮劑

---

90. **supplier**

[səˈplaɪə]

n. 供應者；供應商

⇨ supply「供應」+ -er「做…動作的人」

I'm sorry Sir, but our **supplier** does not have this particular model in stock.
先生，很抱歉，我們的供應商沒有這個特定型號的庫存。

補充	leading/main supplier	主要供應商
	first-tier supplier	一級供應商
	a supplier of N.	N. 的供應者或供應商

supply v./n. 供應

11 製造
12 金融
13 科技技術
14 房屋地產
15 出差旅遊

中高

91. **surpass**

[səˋpæs]

v. 超過；勝過

⇨ sur -「超越」+ pass「通過」

The company I founded twenty years ago has **surpassed** all of my expectations and made me a millionaire.
我在二十年前成立的這家公司超越我所有期望並讓我成為百萬富翁。

| 補充 | surpass one's expectations | 超出某人的期望 |
| --- | surpass oneself | 超越自我 |

surpassing adj. 出色的；卓越的

同 outshine / transcend

中高

92. **sustain**

[səˋten]

v. 維持；遭受；(感情) 支持

⇨ sus -「= sub -，在下方」+ -tain -「持、握」，在下方握住就能支撐維持不倒下

We are able to **sustain** a pace of about five hundred units produced per week.
我們可以維持每週生產約五百件產品的速度。

| 補充 | sustain damage/an injury/defeat/heavy losses |
| --- | 遭受破壞 / 傷害 / 失敗 / 嚴重損失 |

sustainable adj. 可持續的；能長期維持的
sustained adj. 持續的；持久的
sustenance n. 支持；支撐
self-sustaining adj. 自立的；自謀生活的

同 maintain v. 維持

中高

93. **synthetic**

[sɪnˋθɛtɪk]

adj. 合成的；人造的

 syn -「一同」+ -thet -「放置」+ -ic「形容詞字尾」，化學物質放在一起就是合成的

Over time, our **synthetic** men's briefs have surpassed our sales of cotton ones.
我們合成纖維製男用內褲的銷量隨著時間已超越棉質內褲的銷量。

補充	synthetic fabrics	合成纖維
---	synthetic drugs	合成藥物
	synthetic diamond	合成鑽石

synthetically adv. 合成地
synthesize v. 合成
synthesis n. 合成；綜合

中高

94. **toxic**

[ˋtɑksɪk]

adj. 有毒的

⇨ - tox - 「毒」+ - ic「形容詞字尾」

How to deal with the **toxic** waste is a challenge for this company.

如何處理有毒廢棄物對這間公司來說是一項挑戰。

	toxic waste	有毒廢料
補充	be toxic to N.	對 N. 有毒
	toxic chemicals	有毒化學物質

toxin n. 毒

同 poisonous / venomous

中高

95. **transformation**

[ˌtrænsfɚˋmeʃən]

n. 變化

⇨ trans - 「橫跨；轉變」+ form「形狀」+ - ation「名詞字尾」，形狀改變就表示有變化

The **transformation** of Frank from entry-level clerk to CEO was a thirty-year process.

Frank 花了三十年才從基層員工變成執行長。

	economic transformation	經濟轉型
補充	industrial transformation	產業轉型
	organizational transformation	組織變革
	undergo/go through a transformation	經歷改變

transform v. 轉變

transformer n. 變壓器

中高

96. **triple**

[ˋtrɪpl̩]

v. (使) 成三倍

adj. 三倍的

n. 三倍量

⇨ tri - 「三」 + - ple - 「摺疊」，摺三次表示三倍的量

Our production has **tripled** since the new equipment was installed.

從裝了新設備之後，我們的產量成長了三倍。

| 補充 | a triple blow/threat | 三重打擊 / 威脅 |
| | profits/sales triple | 三重利潤 |

triplet n. 三個一組；三件一套

中高

97. utilize

[ˈjutḷˌaɪz]

v. 利用

utilization n. 利用
utilizable adj. 可利用的
utility n. 效用；有用之物

同 make use of

⇨ utile「法文，有用的」+ -ize「動詞字尾」，使東西有用，表示去利用它

I suggest that we **utilize** Sharon's expertise in the area of contract negotiations.

我建議我們要利用 Sharon 在合約談判方面的專業。

中高

98. vertical

[ˈvɜtɪkḷ]

adj. 垂直的；頂點的
n. 垂直線；垂直面；垂直位置

vertex n. 頂點；頭頂
vertically adv. 垂直地

反 horizontal adj. 水平的

⇨ vertex「頂點；頭頂」+ -ical「形容詞字尾」

The mechanic adjusted the lever until it was in a totally **vertical** position.

技師調整槓桿直到它到完全垂直的位置。

 補充

| vertical structure | 垂直結構 |
| vertical merger | 縱向合併 |

中高

99. vibrate

[ˈvaɪbret]

v. 震動；共鳴；擺動

vibration n. 震動
vibrational adj. 震動的；搖擺的
vibrant adj. 活躍的；（光線或色彩）明亮的

⇨ vibrare「拉丁文，搖動」+ -ate「動詞字尾」

Heavy thunder made the entire building **vibrate**.

巨大的雷聲讓整棟大樓震動。

100. **waste**

[west]

n. 廢料；浪費
v. 浪費

Due to new regulations passed by the environmental agency, all of our **waste** will need to be packed into eco-friendly containers.

由於環保機構通過了新的法規，我們所有的廢棄物都必須裝在不會破壞生態的容器中。

補充

nuclear waste	核廢料
industrial/radioactive waste	工業 / 放射性廢棄物
household waste	家庭廢棄物
waste paper	廢紙
waste disposal	廢物處理機
a waste of money/resources/time	浪費金錢 / 資源 / 時間

wasteful adj. 揮霍的；浪費的

實力進階

Part 1. 常見貨品外箱標示

製造業者在出貨時會在外箱標示貨品性質或注意事項，以提醒經手的貨運公司小心搬運，常見的有：

Fragile	Fragile	易碎的
This way up.	This way up.	此面朝上
Handle with care	Handle with care.	小心輕放
Do not stack	Do not stack.	請勿堆疊
	Flammable	易燃物
	Non-flammable	不可燃物
	Toxic / Poisonous	有毒物
	Biohazard	會對環境產生危害
KEEP DRY	Keep dry.	保持乾燥
KEEP FROZEN	Keep frozen.	保持冷凍
PERISHABLE	Perishable	易腐壞生鮮產品

隨堂練習

★ 請根據句意，選出最適合的單字

(　　) 1. The factory was accused of _____ the river by discharging industrial sewage into it.
(A) generating
(B) contaminating
(C) fertilizing
(D) accumulating

(　　) 2. This company decided to recall all the strollers because of design _____ which might injure babies.
(A) defects
(B) devices
(C) precautions
(D) standards

(　　) 3. In an effort to fight global warming, China, the world's biggest emitter of carbon dioxide, announced that it will take immediate action to cut _____ by 40 to 45 percent per unit of GDP by 2020.
(A) particles
(B) hazards
(C) procedures
(D) emissions

(　　) 4. You had better apply for a _____ on any invention of yours because it helps you stop others from selling that product or claiming it as their own.
(A) patent
(B) diameter
(C) proportion
(D) framework

(　　) 5. My sister will _____ work after her baby is born at the end of this year.
(A) reproduce
(B) reinforce
(C) utilize
(D) resume

解答：1. B　2. A　3. D　4. A　5. D

Unit 12 金融

中級

1. account

[əˋkaʊnt]

n. 帳戶；帳目；會計部

⇨ ac-「to」+ count「計算」，算好錢記在帳目裡

You need to maintain a one-thousand-dollar minimum in your **account** to avoid any fees.

你的帳戶內需保留最低餘額一千元才不用繳交任何管理費。

 補充

bank account	銀行活期帳戶
(也直接稱作 account，縮寫為 a/c 或 acct.)	
open/close an account	開戶 / 結束戶頭
account book	帳簿，會計簿冊
pay/settle your account	付帳 / 結帳
buy/pay... on account	賒帳

accountant n. 會計師
accounting n. 會計學

2. accrue

[əˋkru]

v. 自然產生，增加

⇨ ac-「to」+ -cru-「同 -cre-，生長」，長出來表示有增加

Daily interest **accrues** on your checking account.

活期帳戶每天會產生利息。

補充

accrue to sb. 帶給某人（利益）
accrual of sth. 某事物的增加

accrual n. (常指錢的) 累積，增加

中級

3. adequate

[ˋædəkwɪt]

adj. 足夠的；適當的

⇨ ad-「to」+ -equ-「相等的」+ -ate「形容詞字尾」，與所需的相等就是足夠的

Before you think about a down payment for a house, you need an **adequate** amount in emergency savings.

在你考量購屋頭期款之前，你得先備好足夠的緊急預備金。

補充

be adequate to do sth. 足以做某事
be adequate for sth. 對某事物而言是足夠的

adequacy n. 足夠；適當

同 enough / sufficient

16 交通

17 社交與用餐

18 休閒娛樂

19 醫療保健

20 日常生活

中高

4. **allocate**

[ˈæləˌket]

v. 撥出；分配，配置

⇨ al -「to」+ -loc -「場所」+ -ate「動詞字尾」，將東西放到不同場所去就是去分配、配置

Barry **allocates** five percent of his salary to donations for charity.

Barry 撥出薪水的百分之五捐給慈善機構。

 補充

| allocate sth. to sb./sth. | 分配某物給某人 / 某單位 |
| asset allocation | 資產分配 |

allocation n. 分配；配給物，配給量

初級

5. **amount**

[əˈmaunt]

n. 數量；總額

v. 總計；等同

Craig lost a considerable **amount** of his retirement savings in the stock market crash.

股市崩盤讓 Craig 賠掉了相當大量的退休存款。

 補充

pay the full amount	付全額
a large/small/considerable amount 一大筆錢 / 一筆小錢 / 相當多的錢	
an amount of sth.	某物的數量
any amount of...	大量的…
amount to sth.	總計是；等同於

中級

6. **annual**

[ˈænjuəl]

adj. 一年一度的；按年度計算的

⇨ -ann -「年」+ -al「形容詞字尾」

I get a discount on my insurance premium because I make one large **annual** payment rather than smaller monthly installments.

我的保險費有折扣因為我是每年度繳一大筆而非每個月分期繳款。

 補充

annual sales	年度特賣
annual salary	年薪
annual leave	年假
annual bonus	年終獎金

annually adv. 一年一度地

中高

7. **assess**

[əˋsɛs]

v. 評估（財產價值）；
評定

assessment n. 估價；評價
assessor n. 財產估價人；估稅員；陪審法官

同 evaluate

 as-「to」+ -ses-「坐」，坐在一旁估算

Send someone out to the factory to **assess** the damage so we can get an estimate of the repair cost.

找個人去工廠評估損失的狀況，以便我們能估算維修的費用。

中級

8. **asset**

[ˋæsɛt]

n. 資產；有價值的物品；有
益的品質或才能；寶貴的
人才

Many consider your home to be an **asset**, but during a real estate market crash, it is a liability.

許多人認為你的房子是資產，但在房市崩盤期間，其實它是負債。

★ liability：（會計用語）負債

補充 liquid assets　流動資產
fixed assets　固定資產（不動產）

中高

9. **attain**

[əˋten]

v. 達到；獲得

attainment n. 達到，獲得；成就
attainable adj. 可達到的；可獲得的

同 achieve

It is quite possible to **attain** a high-quality education if your parents can pay all that tuition.

如果你父母付得起高額學費，你就非常有機會獲得高品質的教育。

典故 原意指「接觸」，引申為去碰到、達到目標的意思。

中高

10. audit
['ɔdɪt]
n./v. 稽核，查帳

Our senior financial experts will conduct a thorough **audit** of our books going back five years.
我們的資深財務專家會主持五年前至今的帳本稽核。

典故 audit 原意是「聽」，最早的稽核是用聽取報告的方式完成。

補充 an audit committee/firm
審計委員會 / 會計師事務所
complete/conduct/do/undertake an audit
從事稽核工作

auditor n. 查帳員，稽核員，審計員

中級

11. balance
['bæləns]
n. 結餘
v. 結算，使收支平衡

Sir, I have printed out this month's account statement with your **balance** at the bottom of the sheet.
先生，我已將本月帳戶明細印出，您的帳戶結餘在明細的最下方。

補充
bank balance	銀行存款餘額
check sb's balance	查詢帳戶餘額
balance sheet	資產負債表
balance the books/budget	使收支平衡

中高

12. banking
['bæŋkɪŋ]
n. 銀行業務

⇨ bank「存錢到銀行」+ -ing「名詞字尾」
There are now dozens of financial instruments available to you wherever you do your **banking**.
無論您要在哪裡處理您的銀行業務，現在有數十家財務機構可為您服務。

補充
international banking	國際銀行業
network banking	網路銀行業
banking industry	銀行業

bank n. 銀行 v. 存錢到銀行

13. bankroll
['bæŋkˌrol]
v. 提供資金
n. 資金；鈔票

⇨ bank「銀行」+ roll「一卷鈔票」，像銀行拿鈔票出來一樣表示提供資金
Tom made so much money playing professional football that he personally **bankrolled** all the start-up costs for my restaurant.
Tom 踢職業足球賺了很多錢，因此他個人提供資金給我當作餐廳的開店成本。

roll n. 一捲

11 製造

12 金融

14. bankrupt

中級

[`bæŋkrʌpt]

adj. 破產的；倒閉的

v. 使破產

n. 破產者

🔊 bank「銀行」+ -rupt-「打破」

The company was so good at hiding their debt that no one suspected that they were really **bankrupt**.

這家公司很善於隱藏債務，所以沒人懷疑他們真的破產了。

 補充

go bankrupt	破產；倒閉
declare sb. bankrupt	宣告某人破產
declare/file for bankruptcy	正式宣告破產
be on the brink/verge of bankruptcy	
在快要破產的時候	

bankruptcy n. 破產，倒閉

---

13 科技技術

15. belongings

中高

[bə`lɔŋɪŋz]

n. 所有物；財產，財物

⇨ belong「屬於」+ -ing「名詞字尾」+ -s「表名詞複數」，屬於自己的東西就是所有物

Please place all of your **belongings** in the small space under the seat in front of you.

請將您的個人物品放置於您前方座位下方的小空間。

補充 personal belongings 私人物品／個人物品

belong v. 屬於

同 property / possession

---

14 房屋地產

15 出差旅遊

16. bond

中級

[bɑnd]

n. 債券，公債；聯結聯繫；契約

With such low yields in the **bond** market, I suggest that you put all your money into stocks.

債券市場的收益這麼低，我建議您將您的所有資金投入股票。

 補充

buy/invest in/sell/trade bonds	
買進／投資／賣出／交易債券	
issue/hold bonds 發行／持有債券	

中高

17. **boom**
[bum]
v. 迅速發展
n. 繁榮

With business **booming**, the company hired thousands of new employees to fill orders.
由於生意快速拓展，該公司僱用上千名員工以達成訂單。

補充
boom in sth.	某事物蓬勃發展
property boom	房產業的繁榮
baby boom	嬰兒潮
experience/undergo a boom	經歷繁榮

booming adj. 景氣好的；大受歡迎的

中級

18. **bounce**
[bauns]
v. 支票跳票；彈跳
n. 彈跳

The company's account was frozen, so all of their checks **bounced**.
這間公司的帳戶被凍結了，因此他們所有的支票都跳票了。
The sales of retail shops **bounce** during the Christmas holiday season.
零售商店在聖誕假期間銷售驟升。

補充
a check bounces/is bounced	支票跳票
bounce back	恢復元氣，復甦，重新活躍

bouncing adj. 跳躍的

中級

19. **budget**
[`bʌdʒɪt]
n. 預算
v. 編預算
adj. 低廉的，收費公道的

I want the project coming in below **budget** so we have emergency funds leftover.
我希望這個計劃能以比預算低的方式執行，以便我們能留下急用資金。

補充
over/under budget	（支出）高於／低於預算
budget deficit	預算赤字
proposed budget	概算
balance the budget	保持收支平衡
be on a (tight) budget	預算吃緊，經濟拮据
budget for sth.	為某事計劃開支
budget airline	廉價航空公司

中級

20. **capital**

[ˋkæpətḷ]

n. 資金，資本；首都；大寫字母

adj. 資本的；大寫的

capitalist n. 資本家
capitalize v. 提供資金；利用

⇨ -cap- 「頭」+ -al「有關的」，像頭一樣重要的錢就是資金、本錢

In this city, even owning a small coffee shop requires millions of dollars in startup **capital**.
在這個城市即便是擁有一家小咖啡館也需要準備數百萬的開業資本。

補充	working capital	營運資本，周轉資金
	venture capital (VC)	風險投資，創業投資

中級

21. **check**

[tʃɛk]

n. 支票；打勾記號；餐廳的帳單

v. 開支票；(AmE) 作打勾標記

checkbook / chequebook n. 支票簿

★ 英：**cheque** ／美：**check**

Once your **check** clears at the bank, I will start working on your house.
一旦您的支票在銀行完成過戶，我就會開始處理您房子的事。

補充	write a check	開支票
	pay by check	用支票付款
	accept/take checks	接受支票
	cash a check	將支票兌現
	blank check	空白支票

中級

22. **collapse**

[kəˋlæps]

v./n. 崩盤，價格暴跌；失敗瓦解；倒塌

collapsible adj. 可摺疊的

 col- 「一起」+ -laps- 「滑，溜」，一起滑落表示東西倒塌了

We were prepared for a downturn in the market, but not a complete economic **collapse**.
我們對市場下滑做了準備，但我們沒有預期整個經濟崩盤。

補充	a price/market collapse	價格崩潰 / 市場崩潰
	talks/negotiations collapse	談判失敗

23. collateral

[kəˈlætərəl]

n. 擔保品，抵押品
adj. 擔保的，有擔保的

⇨ col - 「一起」+ - later - 「側邊」+ - al 「形容詞字尾」，在同一側表示是一起隨附的抵押品

We need you to put up something quite valuable as **collateral** if you're asking for such a huge loan.
如果您要申請數目這麼大的貸款，我們會需要您提供相當有價值的東西做為擔保品。

補充 put sth. up as collateral / pledge sth. as collateral
將某物作為抵押品

24. commission

[kəˈmɪʃən]

n. 佣金；委任，委託；委員會
v. 委任，委託

⇨ com - 「一起」+ - miss - 「傳送」+ - ion 「名詞字尾」，特別送來的工作就是委託；特別給的錢就是佣金

Paul gets a ten percent **commission** on every car he sells.
Paul 每賣出一部車都可以抽 10% 的佣金。

補充
get a commission on sth. 從某處得到佣金
on commission 根據銷售額抽成
commission agent 佣金代理商

commissioned adj. 受委任的，服役的

25. convert

[kənˈvɝt]

v. 轉變；兌換貨幣

⇨ con - 「一起」+ - vert - 「轉向」，金錢轉換就是指兌換貨幣

Amy saved on fees when she **converted** her standard checking account to a gold-level account.
Amy 將她的標準活期帳戶轉換成金級帳戶以省下一筆費用。

補充
convert sth. to/into sth.
將某物轉換成另一物；將某貨幣兌換成另一貨幣
cash conversion 現金轉換

conversion n. 兌換；轉換；換算
convertible adj. 可兌換的；可轉換的

26. counterfeit

[ˈkaʊntɚˌfɪt]

v. 偽造
adj. 偽造的
n. 仿製品

⇨ counter - 「反對」 + -feit - 「做」，做出與真實相反的東西就是偽造

The man was sued for **counterfeiting** credit cards and selling them online.
那男人因偽造信用卡並在網路上販售而被告。

Frank saved thousands of dollars by printing his own **counterfeit** coupons.
Frank 用自己印的假折價券省下數千元。

補充　counterfeit money　偽幣

同 adj. = fake / forged

初級

27. cover

[ˈkʌvɚ]

v. 支付，足夠付

I had to **cover** the hospital bill of the other driver's injuries since I was at fault for the accident.
由於我是事故中有錯的一方，我得支付另一位駕駛人受傷的醫療費用。

補充　cover the cost (of sth.)　支付成本或費用

同 pay for

中級

28. credit

[ˈkrɛdɪt]

n. 信用；信貸；帳面餘額
v. 把錢存入（賬戶）

⇨ -cred- 「相信」 + it

I had no access to **credit** after declaring bankruptcy for the second time.
在我第二次宣告破產後，我就無權使用銀行信貸了。

補充
credit card limit　　信用卡額度
buy/pay...on credit　以賒帳、掛帳方式買 / 付
interest-free credit　免息貸款（零利率貸款）
be in credit　　　　帳面有餘額
credit sth. with money (= credit money to sth.)
借貸給某帳戶某金額，在帳戶中存入某金額

徐薇教你背新多益單字（下）

16 交通

17 社交與用餐

18 休閒娛樂

19 醫療保健

20 日常生活

 中高

29. **currency**

[ˈkɝənsɪ]

n. 貨幣；流通，通用

⇨ -curr-「流動」+ -ency「抽象名詞字尾」

I suggest using US dollars in Africa rather than relying on the value of the local **currency**.

我建議在非洲使用美金而不要信賴當地貨幣的價值。

| 補充 | domestic/foreign/local currency
本國貨幣 / 外國貨幣 / 當地貨幣
currency exchange counter 外幣兌換櫃檯 |

current adj. 流通的；現行的

 初級

30. **debt**

[dɛt]

n. 負債；借款

Attending a private college was so expensive that the student loans left me heavily in **debt** when I graduated.

上私立大學是如此昂貴，以致於在我畢業時已經有一大筆學生貸款的負債了。

補充	be ($...) in debt	欠債；欠了多少債
	be/get out of debt	不欠債
	pay off/repay/clear your debts	償還債務
	run up a debt	積欠債務
	go/get/run/slip into debt	陷入債務之中
	be heavily/deeply in debt	債台高築

debtor n. 借方，債務人

中高

31. **deduct**

[dɪˈdʌkt]

v. 扣除，減去

⇨ de-「往下」+ -duct-「引導」，把錢往下帶表示使錢變少、扣掉了

Just **deduct** the amount you spent on gasoline this month from our monthly family budget.

從我們每月的家庭預算中扣掉你這個月所花的油錢吧。

| 補充 | deduct sth. from sth. 從某處扣除某物 |

deduction n. 扣除；扣除額；推論，演繹
deductible adj. 可扣除的；可減免的
deductive adj. 推理的，演繹的

11 製造

12 金融

13 科技技術

14 房屋地產

15 出差旅遊

中級

32. **deficit**

[ˈdɛfɪsɪt]

n. 差額；虧損，赤字

👩 de-「分離，表否定」+ -fic-「做」+ -it「名詞字尾」

Our department ran a **deficit** this month because we spent a large amount on office supplies.

我們部門這個月因為支付一大筆辦公設備費用而有虧損。

補充	a deficit of...	虧損某金額
	have/run/show a deficit	虧損
	a deficit in sth.	某方面的不足或虧損
	budget deficit	預算赤字
	in deficit	赤字

反 surplus n. 盈餘

中高

33. **delinquent**

[dɪˈlɪŋkwənt]

adj. 到期未付的，拖欠的

n. 違法者，不良青少年

👩 de-「分離」+ -linqu-「離開」+ -ent「形容詞字尾」

We are now a week **delinquent** on our utilities payments.

我們的水電瓦斯費已經逾期一週未繳了。

補充	delinquent accounts/payments	
	逾期帳戶 / 拖欠付款	
	delinquent borrowers/customers	
	拖欠借款 / 欠費用戶	
	delinquent in (doing) sth.	拖欠 (支付) 某款項
	juvenile delinquent	青少年罪犯

delinquency n. 違法行為；青少年犯罪

中級

34. **deposit**

[dɪˈpɑzɪt]

n. 存款；保證金，訂金

v. 存錢；付押金、保證金等

👩 de-「往下」+ -pos-「放置」+ -it「名詞字尾」

When this certificate of **deposit** matures, you will earn four hundred dollars.

這張定期存款到期時，你將可賺四百元。

★ certificate of deposit = CD：定期存款，定存單

補充	make a deposit	存款
	deposit account (BrE)	儲蓄帳戶
	deposit sth. in/into sth.	將某物存入某處
	security deposit	交易保證金
	put down/pay a deposit (on sth.)	付訂金
	ask for/require a deposit	要求付訂金
	refundable deposit	可退還押金

反 withdrawal n. 提款

35. depreciation
[dɪˌpriʃɪˋeʃən]
n. 跌價；貶值

⇨ de-「下降」+ -preci-「價值，價格」+ -ation「名詞字尾」

The **depreciation** of a new car after you first buy it can be thousands of dollars.
一輛新車在你購入之後的貶值幅度可達數千甚至數萬元。

 補充　the depreciation of... 某（貨幣或商品）的貶值

depreciate v. 降價，跌價；貶值；貶低重要性

反 appreciation n. 漲價；增值

 中級
36. depression
[dɪˋprɛʃən]
n. 不景氣；沮喪

⇨ de-「朝下」+ press「按」+ -ion「名詞字尾」，往下按表示給壓力、使事物陷入困境

When the public started a mass panic and pulled out of the stock market, the resulting economic **depression** destroyed the investments of many of my friends.
當大眾開始集體恐慌並從股市抽身時，所造成的經濟衰退毀了我許多朋友的投資。

 補充
Great Depression
經濟大蕭條（指 1929 年至約 1939 年期間的全球性經濟大衰退）
plunge/slide into depression　陷入不景氣狀態
economic depression　　　經濟蕭條

depress v. 使蕭條；降低（價格或工資）；使沮喪
depressed adj. 不景氣的；貧困的；消沉的

---

37. devaluation
[ˌdivæljuˋeʃən]
n. 貶值

⇨ de-「往下」+ value「價值」+ -ation「名詞字尾」

The **devaluation** of the dollar is necessary for us to compete with foreign companies.
對我們來說貨幣貶值有其必要性，以便我們能與外國公司競爭。

 補充　currency devaluation　貨幣貶值

devalue v.（使）貶值；降低價值，貶低

11
製造

12
金融

13
科技技術

14
房屋地產

15
出差旅遊

中高
38. discrepancy
[dɪˈskrɛpənsɪ]
n. 差異；不同；不一致

 dis-「分離」+ -crep-「爆裂，破裂」+ -ancy「名詞字尾」，雙方破裂分開的地方就是彼此有差異的點

There is a **discrepancy** between the figure you told me yesterday and the number I see on my spreadsheet today.
你昨天告訴我的數字和今天我在報表上看到的數目有差異。

| 補充 | discrepancy in sth. 某事物中出現的矛盾
discrepancy between sth. and sth.
某事物之間的不一致
account for/explain a discrepancy
說明出現的差異 |

discrepant adj. 有差異的，矛盾的

---

39. discretionary
[dɪˈskrɛʃənˌɛrɪ]
adj. 自由支配的；不受嚴格規定控制的

⇨ discretion「斟酌或行動的自由」+ -ary「形容詞字尾」

We should be able to cut back significantly on **discretionary** spending to bring down our operating costs.
我們應該能削減日常運作開支以壓低營運成本。

★ discretionary spending：可自由支配、運用的支出；美國聯邦政府預算中的 discretionary spending 則指聯邦政府需通過國會同意的日常運作開支，也可稱「裁量支出」。

discretion n. 斟酌或行動的自由；決斷能力；處理權，決定權；謹慎

中高
40. dispense
[dɪˈspɛns]
v. 免除；(以固定數額)分發；配藥

 dis-「分開」+ -pens-「秤重，衡量」

You can **dispense** with the pleasantries and just get down to business.
你的客套話可以免了，直接來談正事吧。

★ pleasantries：寒暄，客套話

| 補充 | dispense with sth./sb. 用不著，省去
water dispenser 飲水機 |

dispensable adj. 可分配的；可省去的，非必要的
indispensable adj. 不可或缺，不可避免的
dispenser n. 自動售貨機；自動櫃員機

中高

41. **disposable**

[dɪˋspozəbl]

adj. 可任意支配的

 dispose「處置，支配」+ **-able**「能夠…的」

It doesn't make sense for us to keep marketing to the working class since they have almost no **disposable** income.

我們一直對勞工階級做行銷活動是沒有意義的，他們幾乎沒有可任意支配的收入。

補充
disposable resources 可支配的資源
disposable income 可支配收入

dispose v. 處置，支配
disposal n. 處置，支配

中高

42. **diversion**

[daɪˋvɝʒən]

n. 轉移注意力的事物；轉移，轉用

 di-「離開」+ **-vert-**「轉向」+ **ion**「名詞字尾」

I need you to provide some **diversion** in your presentation away from the actual topic so Mr. Banks doesn't find out how far behind we are on the project.

我要你在報告中放一些東西轉移大家對實際主題的注意力，以免 Banks 先生發現我們的計劃進度落後了多少。

補充
the diversion of funds/money to...
將資金轉用於…用途

divert v. 轉向；轉移

中高

43. **dividend**

[ˋdɪvəˌdɛnd]

n. 紅利，股息；被除數

 divide「分配」+ **end**「最後結局」

Companies have been increasing their **dividends** in the desperate hope of attracting more investors.

公司紛紛提高它們的股息分紅，因為他們極度希望能吸引到更多的投資人。

補充 pay dividends 產生效益；有好處；有回報

divide v. 劃分；除

初級

44. double

[ˈdʌbl̩]

v./n. 加倍

adj. 兩倍的，加倍的；兩人
用的，雙人的

This new position will give you the chance to **double**
your salary.
這個新職位能讓你有機會使薪資加倍。

補充
double in size/price/value	
雙倍的大小 / 價格 / 價值	
double digits/figures	兩位數
double check	仔細檢查；複核
double-space	v. 隔行打字，設雙倍行距
double-minded	adj. 三心二意的

45. downturn

[ˈdaʊntɜ˞n]

n. 經濟衰退；降低

⇨ down「往下」+ turn「轉向，轉變」，轉往下方表示變差、
衰退

The **downturn** will force us to close several retail units.
經濟不景氣將迫使我們關閉幾個零售點。

補充
economic downturn	經濟衰退
a downturn in sth.	某事物的衰退

同 downswing

反 upturn n. 經濟好轉；回升

中級

46. due

[dju]

adj. 到期的；應支付的，
欠款的

Your payment is **due** in full by the end of the month,
and your service will be cancelled immediately if you
don't make the deadline.
您的應付款將在本月底全部到期，如果您未能趕在最後期限內
繳清，您的服務將會立刻被取消。

補充
due date	期限，到期日
become/come/fall due	（某筆帳目）到期了
due on/by sth.	在某時間（前）到期
pay sb's dues	繳會費

dues n. 會（員）費；應付款；稅金

47. **economic**

[ˌikəˈnɑmɪk]

adj. 經濟（上）的；產生經濟
效益的，合算的

⇨ -eco-「家」+ -nomy「希臘字尾，表管理」+ -ic「有
關…的」，管理家庭財物的就是經濟的

Germany has become an **economic** powerhouse in recent years by making sound, conservative financial decisions.

德國近幾年因做出穩健而保守的財政決定而成為經濟強國。

economic climate
經濟氣候（指影響貿易、工業和商業發展的條件）
economic growth 經濟成長

economy n. 經濟
economical adj. 經濟的；節約的

---

48. **exceed**

[ɪkˈsid]

v. 超過，超出；勝過

⇨ ex-「向外」+ -ceed-「走」，走到外面表示超過原來
的範圍

I strive to **exceed** your expectations.
我努力超越你的期望。

　exceed in sth. 在某方面超越了

excess n. 超過；超額量
exceeding adj. 過度的，非常的，極度的
excessive adj. 過度的，過多的

---

49. **exchange**

[ɪksˈtʃendʒ]

v./n. 交換；兌換

⇨ ex-「出去」+ change「更換」，向外做更換就是在交
換

We can **exchange** contact information, and hopefully we can put together a deal that suits both of us.

我們可以交換一下聯絡資訊，希望能安排出我們雙方都合意的交易。

to exchange sth. for sth.
將某一貨幣換成另一種；將某物換成其他東西
exchange of sth. 兌換某貨幣；交換某物
exchange rate 匯率
foreign exchange 外匯

中高

50. **exempt**

[ɪɡˋzɛmpt]

adj. 被免除的；豁免的
v. 免除，豁免
n. 被免除 (義務、責任) 者；
免稅者

exemption n. 免除；免稅

 ex-「出去」+ -empt-「拿」，拿出去表示不要了、免除掉

Susan was unemployed for all of last year, so she was **exempt** from paying taxes.
Susan 去年整年未就業，所以她可以免繳稅。

補充 | (be) exempt from sth. 免除某責任義務
tax exempt 免稅的

中高

51. **expenditure**

[ɪkˋspɛndɪtʃɚ]

n. 消費，開銷；支出額，
經費

expend v. 花費；消耗
expense n. 費用；支出
反 revenue n. 收益；稅入

 expend「花費」+ -ture「名詞字尾」

The first step in my financial help program is for you to list all your **expenditure** on a spreadsheet.
我的財務協助計劃第一步就是在試算表上列出你所有的開銷。

補充 | public/living expenditure 公共開支 / 生活支出
reduce/keep down/cut expenditure 減低開銷
expenditure on sth. 在某事物上的開銷

中級

52. **financial**

[faɪˋnænʃəl]

adj. 財務的，金融的

finance n. 財務；財政；金融 v. 提供資金；融資
finances n. 資金，財力
financially adv. 財政上；金融上

 finance「財務；金融」+ -ial「有關…的」

It makes no **financial** sense for me to continue to fund your project since I get no ROI.
我繼續提供資金給你的計劃是沒有財務意義的，因爲我得不到任何投資利潤。

★ ROI = return on investment：投資利潤，投資報酬

補充 | financial aid | 經濟資助；財政援助
| a financial success | 成功賺到錢
| corporate finance | 企業財務
| personal finance | 個人理財
| public finance | 公共財政

53. **fiscal**

[ˈfɪsk̩l]

adj. 財政的；會計的

 ⇨ fisc「國庫」+ -al「形容詞字尾」，與國庫有關的就是與財政相關的

The last **fiscal** year was an overwhelming success for us, as we were able to start to turn a profit.
上一個會計年度對我們來說是大獲全勝的一年，因為我們終於開始獲利。

補充		
	fiscal year	會計年度；財政年度
	fiscal crisis	財政危機
	fiscal restraint	財政緊縮

54. **fluctuate**

[ˈflʌktʃʊet]

v. 波動；起伏；漲落

 fluctus「拉丁文，波浪」+ -ate「動詞字尾」

Gasoline prices **fluctuate** so much that the price you pay at the pump is never the same.
汽油價格波動如此大，所以你每次加油時所付的價格都不一樣。

★ pay at the pump: 可提供自助加油及結帳的一種加油機系統。

補充		
	fluctuate between A and B	在 A 和 B 之間波動
	fluctuate wildly	起伏很大
	price fluctuations	價格波動
	fluctuations in sth.	某事物的波動

fluctuation n. 波動；變動
fluctuating adj. 波動的

55. **fraud**

[frɔd]

n. 詐騙；騙局；騙子

Mike scammed hundreds of investors out of millions of dollars, and he will now face thirty years in prison for **fraud**.
Mike 詐騙了數百名投資者達數百萬元，所以他現在將因詐欺面臨三十年的牢獄生涯。

補充	
	tax/share/bankruptcy fraud
	騙稅 / 股份詐欺 / 破產詐欺
	credit card fraud 信用卡詐騙

56. fund

[fʌnd]

n. 基金，專款；基金會
v. 提供資金

I began contributing to my child's college **fund** when he was only two years old.
我從我兒子兩歲起就開始投錢當孩子的大學基金。

補充
be short of funds	手頭拮据；經費不足
in funds	手頭有錢
pension fund	養老基金，退休基金
set up a fund	設立基金
raise/provide/generate funds	
籌募 / 提供 / 產生基金	

funding n. 資金；基金

---

57. gross

[gros]

adj. 總共的，全部的；
令人厭惡的
n. 總額，總量

Despite a fairly high **gross** income, I lose nearly half of it to taxes.
儘管我的總收入相當高，但我得拿幾乎一半的錢去繳稅。

補充
gross profit/gross margin	毛利
gross income	毛收入；總收入

---

58. impose

[ɪmˋpoz]

v. 徵稅；強加

⇨ im - 「在上面」 + -pos - 「放置」，把稅放在你身上就是向你課稅

The voters agreed to **impose** a higher city property tax to pay for their world-class school system.
選民同意徵收更高的城市房地產稅以支付他們世界級的學校系統。

imposition n. 規章、稅種、限制等的實施或徵收

---

59. income

[ˋɪnˏkʌm]

n. 收入；所得

Household **incomes** have been stagnating for the past ten years due to the economic crisis.
由於經濟危機，過去十年來的家戶所得一直停滯不前。

補充
be on a high/low income	高收入 / 低收入
live within your income	量入為出
take-home income	實得工資

同 returns / profits / earnings

反 expenditure n. 全部開支，花費

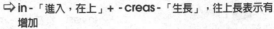

16 交通

17 社交與用餐

18 休閒娛樂

19 醫療保健

20 日常生活

60. **increase**

[ɪnˋkris]
v. 增加
[ˋɪnkris]
n. 增加，增強

⇨ in - 「進入，在上」 + - creas - 「生長」，往上長表示有增加

I want you to **increase** profits while decreasing labor costs.
我希望你能在減少勞工成本的同時也能增加獲利。

補充 be on the increase (= be increasing) 正在增加
increase in value/price/importance
價值 / 價格 / 重要性增加

increasing adj. 增加中的
反 decrease v./n. 減少

61. **inflation**

[ɪnˋfleʃən]
n. 物價飛漲；通貨膨脹

⇨ in - 「進入」 + - flat - 「吹氣」 + - ion 「名詞字尾」，氣吹進去就會膨脹

If we keep printing all these dollars, it could lead to **inflation**.
如果我們持續印鈔票，可能會導致通貨膨脹。

補充 control/curb/reduce inflation
控制 / 遏制 / 減低通貨膨脹

inflate v. 使 (物價 / 貨幣等) 膨脹；抬高物價
inflationary adj. 價格上漲的，引起通貨膨脹的

62. **interest**

[ˋɪntərɪst]
n. 借貸利息；存款利息

The **interest** rates skyrocketed, and I couldn't make my monthly mortgage payments.
貸款利率飆升了，我無法支付我每月的房貸。
★monthly mortgage payment：每月付的房貸

補充
interest rate	利率
interest charges/payments	利息費用
interest on sth.	某事物的利息
monthly/annual interest	月 / 年息
earn/pay interest	賺 / 繳納利息

中級

63. **investment**

[ɪnˋvɛstmənt]

n. 投資；投資額；投資物

invest v. 投資

⇨ invest「投資」+ - ment「名詞字尾」

Your **investment** in my coffee shop has paid off, and now I am ready to open several branch locations across the city.

你對我咖啡店的投資已經回本了，現在我已準備好要在全市開幾間分店。

★ pay off：取得成功、好結果

補充 make an investment in sth. (= invest in sth.)
投資某物

初級

64. **joint**

[dʒɔɪnt]

adj. 共同的，共有的

n. 關節；接合點

Since this is a **joint** account, I can't close it without the other party being present.

由於這是共同帳戶，沒有另一方到場我是不能關閉該帳戶的。

補充 joint account　聯合帳戶，聯名帳戶
joint effort　　共同努力

中級

65. **limitation**

[ˌlɪməˋteʃən]

n. 限制，限制因素；局限；限度

limit n. 界線；限制　v. 限制，限定

There are no **limitations** on how fast we could grow this business if we had access to a lot of capital.

如果我們有權動用一大部份的資本，我們讓生意成長的速度就不會受到限制了。

補充 limitation on/upon sth. 某事物的限制
impose/place limitations on sb/sth.
替某人 / 某事物設下限制
have/acknowledge/recognize sth's limitations
有其不足之處 / 承認其不足之處

66. **loan**

[lon]

n. /v. 貸款；借出

I need to take out a home equity **loan** to fund my child's college tuition.

我得拿房子去申請房屋淨值貸款以籌措我孩子的大學學費。

★ home equity loan：房屋淨值貸款

loan sb. sth.= loan sth. to sb.	借某物給某人
bank loan	銀行貸款
student loan	學生貸款
loan shark	放高利貸者

67. **null**

[nʌl]

adj. 無效的；沒有價值的

The contract is considered **null** and void if you miss the delivery deadline by more than three days.

如果你超過遞送期限達三天以上，這合約就被視為無效。

 null 源自拉丁文 nullus，同 none，意指「沒有，無」。

 null and void（法律用語）無法律約束力的；無效的

nullify v. 使無效；抵銷

68. **outnumber**

[aʊtˋnʌmbɚ]

v. 數量上超過

同 exceed

⇨ out「超過」+ number「數目」

That company's legal team **outnumbers** ours, but our lawyers are well-trained and experienced.

那間公司的法律顧問團數量超過我們的，但我們的律師都受過良好訓練且很有經驗。

69. **outstanding**

[ˋaʊtˋstændɪŋ]

adj. 未償還的；未解決的

The **outstanding** balance on your electricity account is still fifty dollars after your most recent payment.

在你付完最近一期的費用後，你的電費戶頭仍有五十元的待結清款項。

 outstanding balance 待結款項

70. overdraft

[ˈovɚˌdræft]

n. 透支；透支額

⇨ over-「超過」+ draft「匯款」，超過可匯出款項的額度就是透支

Your bank charges exorbitant **overdraft** fees, so give yourself a buffer of at least a few hundred dollars.

你的銀行收取過高的透支處理費，所以戶頭最少要留個幾百塊錢好給你自己一點緩衝。

pay off an overdraft　付清透支
an overdraft fee　　　透支處理費

draft n. 匯票，匯款單

71. overdue

[ˈovɚˈdju]

adj. 過期未還的；逾期的

⇨ over-「超過」+ due「到期的」，超過了到期時間就是逾期

Once your rent is five days **overdue**, there will be a charge of fifty dollars per day until it is paid in full.

一旦你的租金逾期未付達五天，每日將會另收取五十元的費用直到你付清為止。

overdue payment /bill　逾期未付款 / 帳單
overdue loan　　　　　逾期放款

同 past due

72. owe

中級

[o]

v. 欠錢

I **owe** Max a big favor after he bailed out my small company.

在 Max 緊急援助我的小公司後，我欠他一個大人情。

owe sb. (金額) = owe (金額) to sb.
欠某人多少錢
I owe you one. 我得報答你。

73. payment

中級

[ˈpemənt]

n. 支付，付款

⇨ pay「支付」+ -ment「名詞字尾」

You can make either thirty-six monthly **payments**, or one lump sum payment.

你可以選擇用三十六個月分期付款，或是一次付清。

make a payment　支付
installment payment (payment by installments)
分期支付
down payment　分期付款的頭款

pay v. 付錢
payable adj. 應支付的，到期的；可支付的

中級

74. **peak**

[pik]

n. 頂端，最高點
adj. 最高的，高峰的
v. 達到高峰

The market has not reached its **peak** yet.
股市尚未達到最高點。

Summer is the **peak** travel season, so ticket prices tend to be higher then.
夏天是旅遊季節高峰，所以票價此時都會比較高。

補充		
	be at one's peak	在巔峰時期
	hit/reach/rise to a peak	達到高峰
	peak hour/time	巔峰時刻，尖峰時間
	peak season	旺季

反 trough n. 低谷；低谷期
off-peak adj. 非尖峰的，非高峰的

75. **plummet**

[ˈplʌmɪt]

vi. 猛跌，驟然跌落；墜落

When the price of oil **plummeted**, we took advantage of the opportunity to corner the market and buy up as much as possible.
當油價暴跌時，我們就趁機壟斷市場並儘可能地全數買進。

典故	plummet 與 plumb「鉛錘」相關，原指測量物體是否垂直的工具，後來引申為「垂直墜落」的意思。

同 plunge

 中級

76. **profit**

[ˈprɑfɪt]

n. 利潤；收益；營利
v. 獲益；有益於

⇨ pro-「向前」+ -fit-「做」，不斷向前做就能獲利

We have to pay such a high rent in this mall that we can barely make a **profit**.
我們在這個購物商場得付如此高的租金，以致於我們幾乎沒辦法獲得利潤。

補充		
	make (a) profit	賺取利潤
	bring sth into profit	從…中獲利
	profit and loss	帳目盈虧
	profit by/from (doing) sth.	從做…中獲利

profitable adj. 有利可圖的；有益的
profit-making adj. 有利可圖的，營利的
nonprofit adj. 非營利的

11 製造

12 金融

13 科技技術

14 房屋地產

15 出差旅遊

77. **quarter**

[ˋkwɔrtɚ]

n. 一季；一刻鐘；四分之一

There was an upturn in sales during the fourth **quarter** due to holiday shopping.
第四季時由於假期購買潮使銷售額上揚。

典故 源自拉丁文 quartus「第四」。

補充 first/second/third quarter 第一 / 第二 / 第三季

quartered adj. 四等分的

---

78. **rate**

[ret]

n. 比率；速率；費率；等級

v. 定…的速率，費率；
對…作評估；被評價為…

My gas utility company informed me that my **rate** will increase ten percent after two months.
我的瓦斯公司通知我說兩個月後我家的費率要增加 10%。

補充
at a rate of... 以…的比率
exchange rate 匯率
birth/unemployment/divorce/crime rate
出生率 / 失業率 / 離婚率 / 犯罪率
the going rate 一般的收費

---

79. **recession**

[rɪˋsɛʃən]

n. 經濟衰退

⇨ re-「反向」+ -cess-「走」+ -ion「名詞字尾」，往回走表示退步

The Global **Recession** of 2008 will have long-lasting repercussions on unemployment.
2008 年的全球經濟衰退將對失業率產生長期、持續性的影響。

補充 recover from/pull out of (a) recession
從經濟衰退中復甦 / 走出經濟衰退

recede v. 退回；降低，縮減

---

80. **redeemable**

[rɪˋdiməbl]

adj. 可兌換成現金的；可贖回的

⇨ redeem「兌換；贖回」+ -able「能…的」

The coupon is not **redeemable** for cash, so use it before it expires.
這折價券不可兌換成現金，所以在過期前把它用掉吧。

補充 redeem a coupon/voucher
將優惠券等兌換成現金或物品

redeem v. 兌換現金（或物品）；贖回；付清
redemption n. 贖回；清償

中級

81. **reduce**

[rɪ`djus]

v. 減低；減少

⇨ re-「返回」+ -duce-「引導」，人事物被帶回較低的位置就是降級、減低了

You would need to **reduce** the interest rate of the mortgage loans you are offering so that I would be interested.

你得降低提供給我的抵押貸款利率我才會想跟你貸款。

> make a reduction　減價
> a reduction in sth.　某物減少了

reduction n. 減少；削減
reduced adj. 減少的

同 cut down / cutback

82. **remit**

[rɪ`mɪt]

v. 匯款；免除 (稅、罰)

⇨ re-「回去」+ -mit-「送」，把錢寄回給人就是在做匯款的動作

You must **remit** the original receipt to us in order to receive the rebate.

你必須將原始的收據匯寄給我們才能拿到退款。

> remit sth. to sb.　匯寄某款項給某人
> remit payment　匯款

remittance n. 匯款；匯款額

中高

83. **revenue**

[`rɛvənju]

n. 收益；歲入；稅收

⇨ re-「返回」+ -ven-「來到」，賺回來的東西就是收益

Our **revenue** is far below what it was at this time last year, so we need to cut back on the budget.

我們的收益比去年同期還要低很多，所以我們得削減某些部分的預算。

> revenue(s) from sth.　來自某事物的收益
> generate/bring in/raise revenue(s)
> 創造 / 帶來 / 提高收益

中高

84. **slash**

[slæʃ]

v. 大幅度削減；砍擊

n. 大幅降低；斜線符號

If you truly want to liquidate everything in the store, you will need to **slash** the prices by 70 % or more.

如果你真的想把店裡的每件東西都清倉處理掉，你得將價格砍到三折或是更低。

> slash prices/costs 削減價格 / 成本

中高

85. soar

[sor]

v./n. 猛增，暴漲；高飛翱翔

Sales of this new phone model will **soar** when people see how much better it is than the iPhone.

當人們知道這支新款手機比 iPhone 好太多時，它的銷售量將會暴增。

補充 soar from A to B 從 A 快速上升到 B

soaring adj. 急劇增加的

反 plummet v. 暴跌

中級

86. statement

[ˋstetmənt]

n. 財務報表，結算表，報告單

⇨ state「陳述，聲明」+ -ment「名詞字尾」，說出結果的東西就是報表

I've not been receiving my account **statements** since I moved a few months ago, but I've informed your company of my new address.

我從幾個月前搬家後就一直沒收到我的對帳單，但我之前就已經將我的新地址告知你們公司了。

補充 bank statement 銀行帳戶結算單

state v. 陳述聲明

中高

87. statistics

[stəˋtɪstɪks]

n. 統計，統計資料；統計學

⇨ status「狀態」+ -istic「形容詞字尾」+ -ics「學術名詞字尾」，去研究事物狀態的資料就是統計

The latest **statistics** show that our overhead costs are low, but sales have been poor.

最新的統計資料顯示，我們的經常性開支很低，但銷售額一直沒起色。

★ overhead costs：（公司的）經常性開支，營運成本

補充 crime/employment/economic statistics
犯罪統計 / 失業統計 / 經濟統計
government/official statistics
政府統計資料 / 官方統計資料
statistics show/indicate/suggest that...
統計資料指出…

statistic adj. 統計上的；統計學的
n. 統計量；數據

中高

88. **stock**

[stɑk]

n. 證券，股票；股份

The company is releasing a lot of positive PR information to boost up their **stock** price.

該公司持續發佈許多正面的公關資訊以提升他們的股票價格。

補充

stock market	股票市場；股票行情
stock exchange	證券交易所
stock rises/falls	股票上漲 / 下跌
invest in/buy/hold stock	投資 / 買進 / 持有股票
government stock	政府公債

stockholder n. 股東
stockbroker n. 股票 (證券) 經紀人
同 share

中高

89. **subsidy**

['sʌbsədɪ]

n. 津貼；補助金

⇨ sub - 「在下面」+ -sid - 「坐」+ -y「名詞字尾」，放桌子下以便隨時提供援助的就是補助金

Farmers are given a **subsidy** to encourage students to take up the profession.

農夫有補助金可支領，以鼓勵學生們從事農業。

補充

government /production subsidy
政府津貼 / 生產補貼
subsidy for sth. 為了某用途的補助金

subsidiary adj. 貼補的；拿津貼的
subsidize v. 給…津貼，補助，資助

中級

90. **sum**

[sʌm]

v. 算出總和；概述
n. 總和

I tried to **sum** up all of the comments by our management team on one page.

我試著將我們經營團隊的意見總結在一頁裡。

補充

sum up	計算；總結
in sum	簡言之
sum total	總計；合計
lump sum	一次性支付的金額
capital sum	本金總額

16 交通

17 社交與用餐

18 休閒娛樂

19 醫療保健

20 日常生活

69

11 製造

12 金融

13 科技技術

14 房屋地產

15 出差旅遊

初級

91. **target**

[`targɪt]

n. 目標

v. 以…為目標

This is the third month in a row that your team has missed the **target** sales goal, and I need you to give me a detailed reason why.

這是你們團隊連續第三個月未達目標銷售業績，我要你們說明詳細原因。

 補充

a target date/level/price	
預定日期 / 目標水平 / 目標價	
target client	目標客戶，目標顧客
hit/meet/reach a target	達到目標
be on target	按計畫順利進行

同 n. = aim / goal

中高

92. **tariff**

[`tærɪf]

n. 關稅，關稅表；收費表

v. 對…徵收關稅

With such high **tariffs**, no wonder only the rich can afford to buy imports in this country.

由於如此高的關稅，難怪這個國家只有有錢人才買得起進口商品。

典故 源自阿拉伯文 **arafa** 表「通知」，指通知你要付的款項清單，後來演變為「關稅」。

 補充 a tariff on sth. 某物的關稅

tariff-free adj. 免關稅的

中級

93. **tax**

[tæks]

n. 稅金

v. 向…課稅

I would suggest buying whatever you need in the suburbs since the city has a 9% sales **tax**.

我會建議去郊區買任何你需要的東西，因為城裡要多付 **9%** 的銷售稅。

補充

a tax on sth.	對某物課的稅
tax burden	納稅負擔
tax inspector	稅務稽查員，稅務員

tax-free adj. 免稅的，不付稅的

中高

94. **teller**

[`tɛlɚ]

n. 銀行出納員

⇒ **tell**「古英文，計算」+ **-er**「做…動作的人」

The bank **teller** informed me that they had no way to put together such a large cash withdrawal in just thirty minutes.

銀行出納員告知我說他們不可能在三十分鐘之內處理好這麼大筆的現金提款作業。

 補充 automated teller machine (= ATM) 自動櫃員機

同 bank teller / bank clerk / cashier

---

16 交通

17 社交與用餐

18 休閒娛樂

19 醫療保健

20 日常生活

初級

95. **total**

['totl]

adj. 總計的

n. 總額

v. 總計，合計

The estimated **total** cost of the project was only a fraction of what it turned out to be in the end.

相較於最終的支出，這項計劃原本估算的總成本只是其中的一小部份而已。

補充		
	a total of（金額）	總額是…
	in total	總共
	total number/amount/cost	總數 / 總量 / 總成本

totally adv. 完全地

中級

96. **trend**

[trɛnd]

n. 趨勢

Internet cafes used to be a hot **trend** several years ago, but that has changed since almost everyone has a smartphone.

網咖數年前曾是流行趨勢，但因為幾乎人人都有智慧型手機，那種情況就已經改變了。

補充		
	set the trend	開創潮流
	reverse a trend	使趨勢逆轉，扭轉趨勢
	underlying trend	基本趨勢，長期趨勢

trendy adj. 時髦的

中高

97. **trustee**

[trʌs'ti]

n. 受託人

trust v./n. 信任；委託

⇨ **trust**「信任；委託」+ **-ee**「被…的人」

The board of **trustees** determined that voting on the measure was not necessary yet.

董事會決定還不需要針對該項措施進行表決。

---

98. **undervalue**

[ˌʌndɚ'væljʊ]

v. 低估價值；看輕

⇨ **under-**「在下；不足」+ **value**「價值」

Ben obviously **undervalues** his employees since he replaces them for the smallest reasons.

Ben 以無關痛癢的理由替換掉他的員工，他顯然不重視他們。

undervaluation n. 低估價值；輕視

同 underestimate / underrate / look down on

反 overvalue v. 高估；過於重視

11
製造

12
金融

13
科技技術

14
房屋地產

15
出差旅遊

99. **wire**

[waɪr]

v. 電匯；連上電線

n. 金屬線；電線

For any **wire** transfers over $100,000 dollars, we are required to do an extensive security check before releasing the funds.

對任何一筆超過十萬元的電匯，我們都要在放款前先做大規模的安全檢查。

補充　wire transfer = telegraphic transfer　電匯

100. **withdrawal**

[wɪðˋdrɔəl]

n. 提款，提款額；收回，撤回

 with -「回來」+ draw「拉」+ -al「抽象名詞字尾」，把錢往回拉就是提款

You are now required to show a photo ID for any cash **withdrawal**, regardless of how small the amount is.

不論金額多寡，現在任何現金提款都要出示有照片的身份證。

補充　automatic withdrawal　自動提款
withdraw sth. from sale/from the market
從銷售／市場中收回某物；停止銷售

withdraw　v. 提款；收回，撤回；退出

實力進階

Part 1. Savings account vs. Checking account

「bank account 銀行帳戶」在台灣和在美國的用法有很大差異。美國的銀行帳戶主要分為 savings account 以及 checking account。通常 savings account 譯為「儲蓄帳戶」，而 checking account 譯為「支票帳戶」或「活期存款帳戶」。

savings account 是用來存款的帳戶，利率會比 checking account 高；通常開 savings account 的戶頭就是為了把錢放在裡面生利息，也很少會提錢出來。

checking account 的利率近乎零，這個帳戶的目的就在於機動性的使用，例如信用卡扣款，薪資的匯入款，支票的扣款、入款，都是和 checking account 相連結的。因為和支票使用有關，才有了 "checking" account 的稱呼。

Part 2. tax/duty/tariff

tax/duty/tariff 都有「稅」的意思，不過還是有些細微差異，說明如下：

tax	tax 的用途最廣，可以泛指任何稅金，通常是一國政府為了支付公共開支而向人民所徵收的錢。 tax 的形式有很多種，例如：income tax 是所得稅，sales tax 是顧客購物所支付的銷售稅，inheritance tax 是遺產稅，luxury tax 是奢侈稅。
duty	duty 主要有兩種用法： 一是購買某物所支付的稅，例如：the duty on cigarettes 香菸稅。 二是關稅，也就是 customs duty，是政府對進口或出口商品所課徵的稅。免稅商店叫做 duty-free shop。
tariff	tariff 和 duty 一樣同樣是指關稅；除此之外，tariff 還可以指「價目表」。

隨堂練習

★ 請根據句意，選出最適合的單字

(　　) 1. Everyone thinks that David is a(n)_____ to the company because he is both creative and diligent.
(A) boom　　　　　　　　　　(B) peak
(C) asset　　　　　　　　　　(D) deposit

(　　) 2. New policies need to be instituted to pull the country out of _____; otherwise, people will lose their confidence in the government.
(A) recession　　　　　　　　(B) trend
(C) statistics　　　　　　　　(D) expenditure

(　　) 3. Mark was arrested last night because he was caught selling _____ watches at the night market.
(A) redeemable　　　　　　　(B) delinquent
(C) disposable　　　　　　　(D) counterfeit

(　　) 4. I am short of money; I need to make a _____ from ATM.
(A) statement　　　　　　　　(B) withdrawal
(C) subsidy　　　　　　　　　(D) revenue

(　　) 5. The government decided to _____ tax on luxuries priced above 50 thousand dollars.
(A) impose　　　　　　　　　(B) soar
(C) dispense　　　　　　　　(D) fluctuate

解答：1. C　2. A　3. D　4. B　5. A

Unit 13 科技技術

中級

1. access

[ˈæksɛs]

v. 存取 (電腦資訊)

n. 通道，途徑；
(使用某物的) 權利

同 n. = entry / approach

⇨ ac -「to」+ -cess -「行進」，向前走就進入了

I need your password to **access** the database and search for the file I need.
我需要你的密碼進入資料庫搜尋我需要的檔案。

補充　access code　密碼；存取碼
access to sth. 進入某處；取得某物

中高

2. activate

[ˈæktəˌvet]

v. 啟動；加速…反應

activation n. 啟動；活性化
activator n. 催化劑；活化劑

⇨ active「活動中的；活躍的」+ -ate「動詞字尾」

Now that you have called to confirm your identity, we can **activate** your credit card.
因為您已經致電進行身分確認，我們可以開啟您的信用卡了。

中級

3. analyze

[ˈænḷˌaɪz]

v. 分析

analysis n. 分析；解析
analytical adj. 分析的；善於分析的

★ 英：analyse ／美：analyze

 ana -「完全」+ -lys -「鬆開；分解」，把原本綁在一起的事物鬆開來分析

Please **analyze** our competitor's marketing strategy and send me a summary.
請分析我們對手的行銷策略然後給我一份摘要。

補充　make an analysis of sth. 分析某事物

中高

4. **apparatus**
[ˌæpəˈretəs]
n. 儀器，裝置

 ap - 「to」+ -par - 「準備」+ -tus「表動作的拉丁字尾」，準備好裝置才能進行動作

Follow the instructions to use the electrical **apparatus** safely.
依照指示以安全使用此電氣設備。

補充　a piece of apparatus 一件裝置
breathing apparatus 呼吸裝置

同 equipment / device

中高

5. **applicable**
[ˈæplɪkəbl̩]
adj. 可應用的；合適的

apply v. 塗，敷；應用；申請
application n. 應用；申請

 apply「使用，應用」+ -able「能…的」

This tax deduction is not **applicable** to me since I don't have children.
這項減稅方案對我不適用是因為我沒有孩子。

補充　be applicable to sth./sb. 適用於某物 / 某人

中高

6. **astronomy**
[əsˈtrɑnəmɪ]
n. 天文學

astronomer n. 天文學家
astronomical adj. 天文學的

 astro - 「星球」+ -nomy「法則；學科」，研究星星運行規則就是天文學

Taking my students to the **astronomy** museum is always educational and entertaining.
帶我的學生去天文館總是能寓教於樂。

---

7. **automatically**
[ˌɔtəˈmætɪklɪ]
adv. 自動地

automatic adj. 自動的

 automatic「自動的」+ -ly「副詞字尾」

Once you place your online order, you are **automatically** added to our mailing list.
一旦您在網路上下了訂單，您就會自動被加進我們的郵寄名單。

8. automaton

[ɔˋtɑmətɑn]

n. 自動操作裝置；機器人

automation n. 自動化
automate v. 使自動化

同 robot

★ 複數：automatons／automata

⇨ auto -「自己」+ matos「希臘文，表思考活動」，會自己動的就是自動裝置

These **automatons** can only follow simple instructions.
這些機器人只能聽從簡單的指令。

---

9. beta

[ˋbetə]

n. 試用版

We are still in **beta** testing right now, and it may take two more months to finish this project.
我們現在還在測試階段，可能還要再多兩個月才能完成這項專案。

 beta 是希臘文的第二個字母，也可以指稱一系列元素或系統中占第二位者。

補充 alpha 是希臘文的第一個字母。

 中級

10. browse

[brauz]

v. 瀏覽；隨便翻閱

According to the survey, teenagers spend most of their time **browsing** the Internet.
根據這項調查，青少年大部分的時間都在瀏覽網路。
In my retail shop, customers are allowed to **browse** to their heart's content without being pressured to buy.
在我的零售店，顧客可以隨意瀏覽，沒有被迫購買的壓力。

 browse through sth. 翻閱某物
browse the Web　　瀏覽網路

browser n. 瀏覽器；只看不買的顧客
易混 brows n. 眉毛

中高

11. **buffer**

[ˈbʌfɚ]

n. 緩衝物；有緩衝作用的人
v. 緩衝，緩和

buff v. 減低力量；作緩衝器

⇨ buff「減低力量」+ -er「做…動作的人或物」

When you are thinking of a deadline, I suggest that you give yourself a few extra days as a **buffer**.

你在考量截止期限的時候，我建議你多給自己幾天緩衝的時間。

補充 serve as/act as/be a buffer 扮演緩衝角色
buffer zone 緩衝地帶，中立地區

中高

12. **capability**

[ˌkepəˈbɪlətɪ]

n. 性能，能力

capable adj. 能夠…的

易混 capacity n.（指人天生的）認知能力；（物品）容量

 capable「能夠…的」+ -ity「名詞字尾」

My small start-up company doesn't have the **capability** to complete such a large order in only one week.

我的小型初創公司沒有能力在僅僅一週內完成這麼大量的訂單。

補充 within/beyond one's capabilities
在能力所及範圍內 / 超過能力所及

初級

13. **chemical**

[ˈkɛmɪkl̩]

n. 化學製品
adj. 化學的

chemic adj. 鍊金術的；化學的
chemistry n. 化學

⇨ chemic「化學的」+ -al「與…有關的」

30 ml of this **chemical** should be diluted with 100 ml of water.

這種化學物質三十毫升要用一百毫升的水稀釋。

補充 the chemical industry 化學工業
chemical engineering 化學工程

中級

14. **click**

[klɪk]

v. 發出喀搭聲；點選
n. 喀搭聲

Be sure to right-**click** on the link and choose to open it in a new window.

在連結上面按右鍵並選取開啟新視窗。

補充 double-click 點選叫出程式
click on sth. 點選打開，啟動某物
one click away 點擊即可

初級

15. command

[kə'mænd]

n. 指令；命令；掌握
v. 命令

 com-「一起」+ -mand-「命令」

I had no idea why the operating system wasn't able to execute the specified **command**.

我不知道爲什麼作業系統無法執行這一項指令。

I would suggest that you take night classes to help you get a better **command** of English.

我會建議你晚上去上課使你對英語有更好的掌握能力。

補充 have a command of sth. 掌握，精通某能力

commander n. 指揮官；司令官

易混 commend v. 稱讚

中高

16. compatible

[kəm'pætəbl]

adj. 相容的

 com-「一起」+ -pati-「感受」+ -ible「可…的」，能一起感受表示有同感、能相互容納

Our software is not **compatible** with newer versions of Internet Explorer.

我們的軟體和較新版本的 IE 瀏覽器不相容。

補充 compatible blood 相容的血型

compatibly adv. 相容地；協調地
compatibility n. 相容性

---

17. compliance

[kəm'plaɪəns]

n. 服從，遵守；配合

 comply「順從」+ -ance「名詞字尾」

The company claims that it acts in **compliance** with environmental laws.

這家公司宣稱他們是依照環境法規經營。

補充 in compliance with 依照；遵守；符合

comply v. 順從，遵守
compliant adj. 順從的；符合標準的

中高

18. **component**

[kəm`ponənt]

n. 構成要素；成分；零件
adj. 組成的，構成的

➪ com - 「一起」+ -pon - 「放置」+ -ent「名詞字尾」，
被放在一起組成完整物品的東西就是零件

Some of the electronic **components** need to be replaced.
有一些電子零件需要更換。

The exam has two major **components**: listening comprehension and reading comprehension.
這個測驗分為兩個主要部分：聽力理解以及閱讀理解。

補充 electronic components 電子零件

同 n. = part / element

中級

19. **compute**

[kəm`pjut]

v. 計算

同 calculate

➪ com - 「一起」+ -pute - 「思考」，把所有事物一起考量進來就是在做計算

It's difficult to **compute** the final composite score of this test.
這項測驗的最後總成績是難以計算出來的。

中高

20. **computerized**

[kəm`pjutə,raɪzd]

adj. 電腦化的

➪ computer「電腦」+ -ize「使…化」+ -ed「形容詞字尾」

Within ten years, almost all of our daily chores will be **computerized**.
幾乎我們所有的日常雜務都會在十年內電腦化。

中高

21. **configuration**

[kən,fɪgjə`reʃən]

n. 電腦設備的配置；結構，構造

configure v. 安裝，配置（電腦設備）

➪ con - 「一起」+ -figur - 「形態；塑造」+ -ation「名詞字尾」，事物一起塑造出的形態就是構造、配置

We can't use this computer because there is a **configuration** problem.
因為有電腦配置的問題，我們無法使用這台電腦。

22. consecutive

[kənˋsɛkjʊtɪv]

adj. 連續的；連貫的

consecutively adv. 連續地

同 continuous / successive

⇨ con - 「一起」+ - secu - 「跟隨」+ - tive「有…性質的」，一起跟在後面表示連續沒有中斷

My supervisor has been working on this project for ten **consecutive** days.
我的主管已經做這項企劃連續十天了。

---

23. core

[kor]

n. 核心

Lack of sponsors is the **core** problem.
缺乏贊助廠商就是核心問題。

典故　core 是古字，表示心臟的意思。

補充	core value	核心價值
	to the core	徹底
	at the core of...	是…的核心所在
	multi-core processor	多核心處理器

同 center

---

24. cutting edge

[ˋkʌkɪŋ][ɛdʒ]

phr. 先鋒地位；尖端

I have heard that this course presents business strategies that are on the **cutting edge**.
我聽說這堂課會教具有領先地位的商業策略。
The employee we're looking for should possess **cutting-edge** technology skills.
我們在尋找的員工應該具備最先進的科技能力。

補充　意思相似的字詞還有：
leading edge　phr. 居領先優勢的
state-of-the-art　adj.（技術）最先進的

cutting-edge adj. 最先進的

25. database

[`detə͵bes]

n. 資料庫

⇨ data「資料」+ base「基地」，儲存資料的基地就是資料庫

As the senior **database** administrator, Mike must work overtime to ensure the security of our files.

身為資深資料庫管理員，Mike 必須加班以確保我們檔案的安全性。

| 補充 | a database for (doing) sth. 某事物的資料庫 |
| | database management 資料庫管理 |

中高

26. default

[dɪ`fɔlt]/[`dɪfɔlt]

n. 預設，默認；不履行，違約

v. 不履行，拖欠

 de-「遠離」+ fault「錯誤」

I never use the **default** ring tone on my cell phone because it's old-fashioned.

我從來不用手機的預設鈴聲因為它過時了。

| 補充 | win... by default 因對手棄權而獲勝 |

中級

27. delete

[dɪ`lit]

v. 刪除

⇨ de-「離開」+ linere「拉丁文，擦掉」，擦掉東西使其離開就表示刪除

I need you to **delete** any files which are over two years old to free up space on the company share drive.

我要你將公司共用硬碟裡超過兩年的檔案刪除以釋放容量。

| 補充 | delete sth. from sth. 從某處刪除某物 |

初級

28. design

[dɪ`zaɪn]

v./n. 設計

⇨ de-「完全」+ sign「標示」，將想法完全標示出來就是在做設計

The goal of **designing** display screens is to make them as flat and thin as possible.

設計顯示螢幕的目標就是要讓它們盡可能地平滑纖薄。

補充	web/product/job design
	網頁設計 / 產品設計 / 職位設計
	computer-aided design 電腦輔助設計 (簡稱 CAD)
	design patent 設計專利
	design brief 設計簡介

designer n. 設計師

中級

29. devise

[dɪˋvaɪz]

v. 設計；發明；策劃

deviser n. 設計者
device n. 設備

A new system has been **devised** to control the humidity of the room.
有一套新系統被設計來控制房間的溼度。

中級

30. digital

[ˋdɪdʒɪtl̩]

adj. 數位的；數字顯示的

digitally adv. 數位地
digitize v. 將資料數字化

反 analogue adj. 類比的

⇨ digit「數字」+ -al「具…性質的」
Why don't you buy a **digital** camera so you can stop buying all that expensive film?
你為什麼不買一台數位相機，這樣你就不用買昂貴的底片了？

補充 **digital native** 數位世代 (指成長於數位科技發達年代的人，對科技產品很容易上手。)

中高

31. dimension

[dɪˋmɛnʃən]

n. 尺寸；層面

dimensional adj. 尺寸的

 di-「拿開」+ -mens-「測量」+ -ion「名詞字尾」
Please specify the **dimensions** of the bookshelf.
請明確說明書架的大小。
Bob has that extra **dimension** of being able to think globally instead of just what local customers want.
Bob 的思考層面能顧及到全球顧客而非只是地區顧客的需求。

補充 產品說明中常用複數 dimensions 表示「尺寸」。後方會列出長 (length)、寬 (width)、高 (height)，有時候會列出重量 (weight)。

中級

32. disconnect

[ˌdɪskəˋnɛkt]

v. 使分離；斷開

 dis-「除去、拿開」+ connect「連接；連結」

This morning, all of the inbound customer calls were getting **disconnected** due to the storm.

今天早上所有的客戶來電都因為暴風雨的關係斷線了。

補充　be/get disconnected　網路斷線

disconnection n. 分離；切斷

反 connect v. 連接；連結

---

33. downgrade

[ˋdaʊnˌgred]

v. 降級

同 degrade

⇨ down「往下、向下」+ grade「等級；階級」

I have been told that the customer wants to **downgrade** to package C because he doesn't need cable TV.

我被告知客戶想要降級成 C 方案，因為他不需要有線電視。

中級

34. download

[ˋdaʊnˌlod]

v. 下載

反 upload v. 上傳

⇨ down「往下、向下」+ load「裝載」

If you **download** this app within the next 24 hours, you will get a special offer sent to your email.

如果您在接下來的二十四小時內下載此應用程式，您會收到我們寄給您的特別優惠。

中級

35. durable

[ˋdjʊrəb!]

adj. 耐用的

⇨ -dur-「持續」+ -able「可…的」，可持續使用就表示是耐用的

I guarantee you that this backpack is so **durable** that you can wear it in the worst of weather conditions.

我向你保證這一款後背包很耐用，就算是在最糟的天氣狀況下還是可以背。

補充　durable goods (consumer durables)
大件的耐用消費品（如汽車、家具等）

durability n. 持久性；耐用性

同 enduring / long-lasting

中級

36. **electronic**

[ɪlɛkˋtrɑnɪk]

adj. 電子的

 electr-「電的」+ -on「名詞字尾，表粒子」+ -ic「關於⋯的」

Nearly every kids' toy our company makes is now **electronic**.

我們公司現在製作的兒童玩具幾乎都是電子的。

補充	electronic banking (e-banking)	電子銀行業務
	electronic commerce (e-commerce)	電子商務
	electronic mail (email)	電子郵件
	electronic devices	電子裝置
	electronics company	電子公司

electronically adv. 透過電子技術

electronics n. 電子工業；電子設備

易混 electric adj. 用電的，電動的
electrical adj. 與電有關的

初級

37. **engine**

[ˋɛndʒən]

n. 引擎，發動機

If you let me tune up your **engine**, I'll give you a ten-dollar coupon for your next oil change.

如果你在我這裡調校引擎，我會送你下次換油的十元優惠券。

★ tune up：調節（引擎）至最佳狀態

補充	search engine 搜尋引擎

初級

38. **engineer**

[ˌɛndʒəˋnɪr]

n. 工程師

⇨ engine「引擎」+ -eer「從事某事的人」

The **engineers** have agreed that the original design is flawed.

工程師們都同意原來的設計有瑕疵。

典故	原指操作或修理引擎的人，衍生為設計及建造各種工程的專業工作者。

補充	electronic engineering 電子工程
	electrical engineering 電機工程

engineering n. 工程；工程學

中級

39. **expose**

[ɪkˋspoz]

v. 暴露

⇨ ex-「向外」+ -pos-「擺放」，放到外面去就暴露出來了

It is reported that the workers have been **exposed** to high levels of radiation.

根據報導，那些工人一直暴露在高劑量輻射之下。

You can't **expose** this company to such big risks by mishandling customer merchandise.

你不能因為不當處理顧客商品而讓公司陷入這麼大的風險。

補充
expose sb./oneself to sth.
使某人（自己）暴露於某事物中
expose A to B 將 A 暴露於 B 下

exposure n. 揭露；曝光

exposed adj. 無遮蔽的；易受攻擊的；有賠錢風險的

同 uncover / reveal

中高

40. **facilitate**

[fəˋsɪləˏtet]

v. 使容易；促進

🎙 facility「設備」+ -ate「動詞字尾」，有好的設備就使事物容易進行

We need a new structure to **facilitate** our work flow.

我們需要一個新的體系使工作流程更容易。

facilitation n. 促進；促動

facilitator n. 促進者；促動者

中級

41. **foresee**

[forˋsi]

v. 預見

⇨ -fore-「在⋯之前」+ see「看見」，事前先看見就是預見

I **foresee** disaster if you keep the machine running for a whole day.

如果你繼續讓這台機器跑一整天，我想災難是可以預見的。

foreseeable adj. 可預見到的

foreseer n. 有先見之明的人

同 foretell / predict

42. **fuel-efficient**

[ˈfjuəl][ɪˈfɪʃənt]

adj. 省油的

⇨ fuel「燃料」+ efficient「有效率的；效率高的」，有效使用燃料就是用更少量的燃料達到所需結果

This model is not only **fuel-efficient** but also capacious.

這一款型號不只省油還有很大的空間。

補充
fuel efficiency 　　燃油效率
fuel-efficient cars 節能汽車

 初級

43. **function**

[ˈfʌnkʃən]

v. 起作用

n. 功能

⇨ -funct-「執行，工作」+ -ion「名詞字尾」，事物執行出來的結果就是它的功能

You have an older version of PowerPoint, so many of the special features in my presentation won't **function** on your computer.

你的 PowerPoint 是舊版的，所以我的報告裡面有很多特效在你的電腦上是不能用的。

補充
function key 　　　　　　　　　功能鍵
carry out/perform a function 履行職責
to function as sth./sb. 　　　　當作…

functional adj. 功能的；機能的

---

44. **gadget**

[ˈgædʒɪt]

n. 小機件；小玩意兒

Bill just owns a few tools, but his brother Ted owns every **gadget** you can possibly find in a store.

Bill 那裡只有一些工具，但是他哥哥 Ted 有你在一家店裡頭所有可能找得到的零件。

 典故
gadget 據傳是從水手所用的俚語而來，指稱任何小型的機械物件，或船隻缺乏的零件。

 補充
kitchen gadgets 　廚房器具
electronic gadgets 電子產品

◎ widget / gizmo

中級

45. **generator**

[ˈdʒɛnə͵retə]

n. 發電機；產生器

 generate「生產」+ -or「做…動作的物品」

A portable home **generator** can be a big help when the electricity goes out.

在停電的時候有一台可攜式的家用發電機會有很大的幫助。

補充 income/revenue generator 收入來源

generate v. 產生；發生 (熱、電等)

---

46. **gigabyte**

[ˈɡɪɡə͵baɪt]

n. 十億位元組

 giga-「十億」+ byte「位元組」

Storing this movie on your flash drive will eat up half of the eight **gigabytes** of space.

在你的隨身碟上儲存這部電影會吃掉 **8G** 空間的一半。

補充 gigabyte 縮寫為 GB，也可簡寫為 G，為電腦硬碟容量或檔案大小常見的計量單位。

byte n. 位元組 (電腦資訊計量單位)
megabyte n. 百萬位元組 (縮寫為 MB)

中高

47. **hacker**

[ˈhækə]

n. 駭客

 hack「侵入電腦系統」+ -er「做…動作的人」

To prevent our website from attacks by **hackers**, we need to add some extra security.

為了防止駭客攻擊我們的網站，我們需要增加一些額外的保護措施。

典故 hack 原意是指「有技巧地修改電腦程式」。

補充 hack into sth. 侵入某電腦系統

hack v./n. 侵入電腦系統

48. hands-on

[hændz][ɑn]

adj. 實地操作的，親身體驗
的；躬親的

I prefer to take a **hands-on** approach when it comes to the training of all my employees.
談到訓練我的員工時，我比較喜歡採用實際操作的方式。

補充 hands-on education/learning/training
實務教育 / 學習 / 訓練

中級

49. hook

[hʊk]

v. 勾住；連結
n. 掛鉤

You can't print anything because the computer is not **hooked** up to the printer.
你印不出東西是因爲電腦沒有連接上印表機。

補充 hook up 連上網路，線路
hook up A to B = hook A up to B 將 A 連結到 B
a computer/internet/satellite hookup
電腦連線 / 網路連線 / 衛星連線

hookup n. 連接線路

---

50. hyperlink

[ˈhaɪpɚˌlɪŋk]

n./v. 超連結

link v./n. 連結

⇨ hyper-「超越…之上」+ link「環節；連結」
Just click on the **hyperlink** and follow the instructions on the web page to start using your new account immediately.
點選連結並依照網頁上的說明立即開始使用你的新帳號。

---

51. icon

[ˈaɪkɑn]

n. 圖示；記號

iconic adj. 畫像的；肖像的

Don't click on any of the **icons** in the ad on your screen or you will be inundated with pop-up windows.
不要在螢幕上點選廣告裡的任何圖示，否則你會不斷看到一大堆彈出視窗。

典故 icon 原意是指「相似的；相似性」，也指教堂中的聖像繪畫；在電腦領域則用來指電腦螢幕上代表特定檔案、目錄或應用程式等的「圖示」。

初級

52. **image**

[ˋɪmɪdʒ]

n. 形像；圖像

imagine v. 想像

Do an online search for the best background **image** to put our slogan over.
到網路上搜尋最適合放上我們標語的背景圖像。

補充　be the spitting image of... 酷似…

中高

53. **innovative**

[ˋɪnəˏvetɪv] / [ˋɪnəvətɪv]

adj. 創新的

⇨ innovate「創新」+ -ive「有…性質的」

I need **innovative** solutions to our dilemma, not the same old ideas being batted around.
我需要能解決困境的創新方法，不是我們一直在討論的舊想法。

★ bat around：討論

補充　innovative ideas/products/programs
創新的想法 / 產品 / 計畫

innovate v. 創立；創新；改革
innovation n. 創新

中級

54. **input**

[ˋɪnˏpʊt]

v. 輸入

n. 輸入；投入物

⇨ in-「進入」+ put「放置」

Miles has been **inputting** data into the computer since this morning.
Miles 從今天早上就一直在輸入資料。

Let's go around the conference table and ask each member of the team for **input**.
我們會議室找小組每位成員請他們給予一些意見。

補充　an input device 輸入裝置

反 output v./n. 輸出

90

中級

55. **insert**
[ɪn`sɝt]
v. 插入；加進
[`ɪnsɝt]
n. 插入物；夾在報刊中的插頁廣告

⇨ in - 「往裡面」+ - sert - 「放置」，往裡面放就是插入物品

When customers **insert** their cards into the ATM, they have to push them in really hard to get the machines to accept them.
顧客在將提款卡插入提款機的時候，必須要很用力推才能讓機器接受卡片。

補充　insert A in/into B 把 A 放入 B 裡面

inserted adj. 插入的
insertion n. 插入，放入

中級

56. **inspect**
[ɪn`spɛkt]
v. 檢查；審查；視察

⇨ in - 「進入」+ - spect - 「看」，往裡面仔細看就是在檢查

Please **inspect** each file carefully for data errors which may cause the uploads to be unsuccessful.
請仔細檢查每份檔案裏面有沒有會造成上傳失敗的數據錯誤。

補充　inspect (sth.) for sth.　檢查是否有某瑕疵
carry out an inspection　執行檢查

inspection n. 檢查
inspector n. 檢查員；視察員；督察員

同 examine

中高

57. **installation**
[ˌɪnstə`leʃən]
n. 安裝，安置；裝置設備

⇨ install 「安裝；設置」+ - ation 「名詞字尾」

The **installation** of two new servers should satisfy our customers' needs.
安裝兩台新的伺服器應該可以滿足客戶的需求。

install v. 安裝
uninstall v. 移除，卸載

58. **insulation**
[ˌɪnsə`leʃən]
n. 隔離；絕緣（或隔熱，隔音）

 - insul - 「島嶼」+ - ate「動詞字尾」+ - ion「名詞字尾」

You can save money on heating and cooling bills with good **insulation**.
有好的隔熱效果你就能省下暖氣費與冷氣費。

補充　insulate A against B 使 A 與 B 隔絕

insulate v. 隔離；使絕緣

初級

59. introduce
[ˌɪntrəˈdjus]
v. 介紹；引進

⇨ intro -「同 in -，裡面」+ - duc -「引導」，引到裡面來就是引進、介紹

We will formally **introduce** all the new employees at the company picnic this Saturday.
我們會在本週六公司野餐的時候正式介紹所有的新進員工。

introduction n. 介紹；引進
introductory adj. 介紹的；前言的；準備的

中級

60. inventor
[ɪnˈvɛntə]
n. 發明家

⇨ invent「發明；創造」+ - or「做…動作的人」

Bill started his career as an **inventor**, but now he advises others on how to improve their own inventions.
Bill 以發明家的身份創業，不過現在他建議別人如何改善自己的發明。

invent v. 發明
invention n. 發明

中高

61. know-how
[ˈnoˌhau]
n. 實際知識；技能

These young employees don't have enough **know-how** from real business experience.
這些年輕員工沒有從職場經驗學到足夠的技能。

 典故 know-how 來自 know how to do something，表示知道該怎麼做事的知識。

 補充 technical know-how 專業技能

 同 expertise

中級

62. machinery
[məˈʃinəri]
n. 機器；大型機械

⇨ machine「機器；機械」+ -ery「名詞字尾」

The **machinery** in your factory is in desperate need of an upgrade.
你們工廠的機器急需升級。

補充 office machinery 辦公用機械

63. **malfunction**

[ˌmælˋfʌŋkʃən]

v. 發生故障，機能失常

n. 故障

同 breakdown

⇨ mal -「不好的」+ function「功能；起作用」

The website is **malfunctioning**, so I can take your order over the phone if you wish.

因為網站故障了，所以如果您願意的話，我可以幫您透過電話來下訂單。

---

64. **mode**

中高

[mod]

n. 樣式；模式；方式

model n. 模型

Just start running your computer in safety **mode** for now until we can diagnose the problem.

在我們診斷出問題之前，你暫時用安全模式開啟你的電腦吧。

| 補充 | silent/vibrate mode （手機）靜音／震動模式
be the mode （服裝）風行，流行 |

---

65. **multimedia**

[ˌmʌltɪˋmidɪə]

n. 多媒體

adj. 多媒體的；使用多媒體的

⇨ multi -「多的；大量的」+ media「媒體」

I studied all forms of **multimedia** in college to prepare myself for any kind of work in the entertainment industry.

我在讀大學的時候研究過各種型態的多媒體，好讓自己做好在娛樂產業做各種工作的準備。

---

66. **network**

中級

[ˋnɛtwɝk]

n. 網絡系統；廣播電視網；電腦網路

同 Internet n. 電腦網路

⇨ net「網子」+ work「工作；工程」，如網子般密麻交錯的運作型態

The computer **network** is not working again. Please call the technician now.

網路又當掉了。請馬上聯絡維修人員。

初級

67. omit

[o`mɪt]

v. 忽略；刪除；疏忽

omission n. 省略；遺漏

同 neglect

⇨ o-「同 ob-，相對、反對」+ -mit-「送出」，往反方向送走就表示看不見、忽略了

None of the questions on this form may be **omitted**, or it will be considered an incomplete application.

這份表格上面的問題都不能漏答，否則它會被視為一份不完整的申請書。

---

68. on and off

[ɑn] [ænd] [ɔf]

phr. 斷斷續續地

同 off and on

I've been working on this project **on and off** for two months.

我斷斷續續進行這項企劃兩個月了。

---

69. online

[`ɑn͵laɪn]

adj. 線上的
adv. 網路連線地

反 offline adj. 離線的

⇨ on「在⋯上」+ line「線；網路線」

You can choose anything from the **online** catalog, but we may be out of some items in our retail shops.

你可以從線上目錄選擇任何商品，不過我們的零售店面那裡可能會有部分缺貨。

 補充
online shopping　線上購物
apply/book online　線上申請／訂購

---

70. outage

[`autɪdʒ]

n. 運行中斷；停電（期）

⇨ out「出去；沒有」+ -age「名詞字尾」，電源出去就會停電，機器沒電就不運作了

I'm shocked that the server **outage** has lasted for nearly all day, and we've lost tens of thousands of dollars in online sales as a result.

我很驚訝伺服器會斷線幾乎一整天，結果我們線上購物損失了好幾萬元。

補充　power outage 電力中斷，停電期

中級

71. portable

[ˈportəbl̩]

adj. 可攜帶的；輕便的
n. 手提式製品

⇨ - port - 「攜帶；運載」+ - able 「能…的」

Bring a **portable** generator to supply all of our power at the outdoor trade show.
帶一台攜帶式發電機好提供我們戶外貿易展所需的所有電力。

補充 | portable computer 可攜式電腦；手提式電腦
PDF = portable document format
PDF 檔案格式，便攜式檔案格式

portability n. 可攜性；輕便性

 初級

72. power

[ˈpaʊɚ]

n. 電力；能量
v. 給…提供動力
adj. 電動機驅動的

Always disconnect the **power** before attempting to repair electrical equipment.
維修電器之前務必要切斷電源。

補充 | power station/plant 發電站 / 發電廠
power cut/failure/outage 斷電
nuclear/wind/solar power 核能 / 風力 / 太陽能
power tools 電動工具

powered adj. 以…為動力的
high-powered adj. 高功率的

中級

73. predict

[prɪˈdɪkt]

v. 預測

⇨ pre - 「在…之前」+ - dict - 「說」，事前先說出來就是
　　預言、預測

I **predict** that in the next ten years, nearly all manual labor will be done by robots.
我預估在接下來十年內，幾乎所有的體力勞動工作都會由機器人執行。

prediction n. 預言
同 foretell / forecast

中級

74. **process**

['prɑsɛs]

n. 過程；步驟
v. 處理；加工

⇨ pro - 「向前」+ - cess - 「行進」，事物向前行進會有必經的過程和步驟

The **process** of converting all this data will take several weeks.

這些數據轉換的過程會花上數週。

> **補充**
> in the process of... 在…的過程中
> industrial process 工業生產流程

processor n. 處理器

75. **programmer**

['progræmɚ]

n. 程式設計師

⇨ program「寫電腦程式」+ - er「做…動作的人」

As a rookie **programmer** at this corporation, I need to code at least ten hours each weekend.

身為公司的菜鳥程式設計師，我每個週末都需要花至少十小時做編碼的工作。

program / programme n. 計畫；節目；電腦程式
v. 編寫電腦程式

中級

76. **protective**

[prə'tɛktɪv]

adj. 防護的；保護的

⇨ pro - 「向前」+ - tect - 「遮蓋」+ - ive「具…性質的」，向前蓋住以做保護

No one is allowed to enter without wearing full **protective** clothing.

未穿著全套防護衣不得進入。

I see why you would be so **protective** of the secret formula you use to make your world-famous soda.

我了解你為什麼會這麼保護你用來調製舉世聞名的汽水所使用的秘密配方。

> **補充** protective gear/clothing 防護衣

protect v. 保護
protection n. 保護

中級

77. **remote**

[rɪˋmot]

adj. 遠距的；遙控的

⇨ re-「返回」+ -mot-「移動」，移回去、移離開了，彼此間就有距離、就是遠距的

Remote control helps to administer our overseas data center.

遙控技術有助於管理我們的海外資料中心。

 補充
remote control 遙控
remote access ［電腦用語］遠端存取

remotely adv. 遠距離地；極少地
remoteness n. 遙遠；偏僻；細微

中級

78. **restore**

[rɪˋstor]

v. 恢復；修復；還原

⇨ re-「再次；回到」+ -sta-「站立」，讓東西再站回該站的地方也就是恢復了、還原了

I believe that if you gave me some of my money back for your failed product, it would **restore** my faith in your company's integrity.

我相信如果你們為你們出包的商品退還部分金額給我，這會使我對你們公司的誠信恢復信心。

 補充　backup and restore 備分與還原

restoration n. 恢復

 中高

79. **retrieve**

[rɪˋtriv]

v. 取回；檢索電腦信息

I have invented a search engine that **retrieves** difficult-to-find information from the Internet.

我發明了一個搜尋引擎可以從網路搜尋到很難找到的資訊。

 典故
retrieve 源自法文 retrouver，是指訓練獵犬啣回獵物的比賽，引申為找回東西的意思。

 補充
retrieve sth. from sth. 從某處取回某物
information retrieval （電腦資訊）檢索

retrieval n. 取回；檢索電腦信息

中高

80. **reverse**

[rɪˋvɝs]

adj. 相反的；顛倒的
v. 顛倒；反轉
n. 倒轉；反面

 re-「回去」+ -vers-「轉動；翻轉」，轉回去就變成方向相反的

To make it work, please reassemble the parts in **reverse** order.
要讓它正常運作，請以相反的順序重新組裝這些零件。

補充
reverse a car	倒車
quite the reverse	完全相反
reversal victory	逆轉勝

reversal n. 翻轉；逆轉
reversible adj. 可反轉的；雙面可用的

中高

81. **rigid**

[ˋrɪdʒɪd]

adj. 堅固的；精確的，嚴密的

rigidly adv. 嚴厲地；嚴格地
rigidity n. 堅硬；嚴格；剛直；死板
同 stiff

⇨ -rig-「僵直的；硬的」+ -id「具⋯性質的」，僵硬就表示是堅固的、無法輕易改變的

The company policies regarding the use of customer data are rather **rigid**.
有關使用客戶資料的公司規範相當嚴謹。

中級

82. **satellite**

[ˋsætḷͺaɪt]

n. 衛星

The broadcast program was transmitted around the world by **satellite**.
那個廣播節目透過衛星向全球轉播。

典故 satellite 的原意是「隨從；追隨者」。

補充
weather satellite	氣象衛星
communication satellite	通信衛星
spy satellite	間諜衛星
satellite TV	衛星電視
satellite dish	
碟形衛星信號接收器 (俗稱「小耳朵」)	

83. server

['sɝvɚ]

n. 伺服器

⇨ serve「服務」+ - er「做…動作的人或物品」

Our **server** is maintained by an off-site company.
我們的伺服器是由一間遠端的公司維持運作。

補充　web server 網路伺服器
server 在美式英語中也可指餐廳服務生，等同於
waiter/waitress。

84. shut down

[ʃʌt][daʊn]

phr. 使關閉；使停業

shut v. 關閉
down adv. 完全地

Shut down your computer before attempting to run
the program for the first time.
在第一次執行這個程式之前先將電腦關機。

85. simultaneously

[ˌsaɪmḷ'tenɪəslɪ] /
[ˌsɪmḷ'tenɪəslɪ]

adv. 同時地

⇨ simultaneous「同時的」+ - ly「副詞字尾」

Executing multiple programs **simultaneously** makes the
computer works more and more slowly.
同時執行多個程式讓電腦運作得越來越慢。

 源自拉丁文 simul，表示「一起、同時」。

 simultaneous interpretation 同步口譯

simultaneous adj. 同步的，同時的

同 synchronously

86. software

['sɔftˌwɛr]

n. (電腦) 軟體

⇨ soft「軟的」+ - ware「製品；用具」

The trial period on this unlicensed **software** has
expired.
這個未授權軟體的試用期已經到期了。

補充　相對於 software 的詞是 hardware，指「(電腦)
硬體；五金器具」，兩者都是不可數名詞。

中級

87. **solar**

[`solɚ]

adj. 太陽的；依太陽而運行的

⇨ - sol - 「太陽」+ - ar「形容詞字尾」

We can save fifty percent on electricity costs by installing our own **solar** panels on the roof.
我們在屋頂上自己裝太陽能板可以省下一半的電費。

補充　solar system　太陽系
　　　solar panel　太陽能板

中高

88. **sophisticated**

[sə`fɪstə,ketɪd]

adj. 複雜精密的；世故老練的

⇨ **sophisticate**「使複雜；使懂世故」+ - ed「形容詞字尾」

You need a highly **sophisticated** computer system to execute this software.
你需要高度精密的電腦系統來執行這項軟體。

補充　sophisticated weapons　尖端武器

sophisticate v. 使複雜；使懂世故
　　　　　　　n. 世故的人；(某方面的) 精通者

中高

89. **static**

[`stætɪk]

adj. 靜電的；靜止的，靜態的

⇨ - stat - 「使站立；使固定」+ - ic「…似的」，站著不動
就是靜止的

Do you know how to eliminate **static** interference?
你知道如何減少靜電干擾嗎？

Our profit margin has remained **static** over the last two years.
我們的利潤率在過去兩年維持不變。

同 still　adj. 靜止的
反 dynamic　adj. 動態的

中級

90. **switch**

[swɪtʃ]

v. 改變；轉換開關
n. 改變；開關

After weighing all of our options, we have decided to **switch** our Internet service provider.
評估了所有的選擇之後，我們決定換一間網路服務供應商。

補充　switch on/off　打開 / 關上電源

91. **synchronize**

[ˋsɪŋkrənaɪz]

v. 同步；顯示同一時間

⇨ **syn** - 「共同」 + - **chron** - 「時間」 + - **ize** 「使…」，使時間都相同就表示同步

Let's **synchronize** the time on all the computers in our office to avoid ambiguity.

我們把辦公室裡所有電腦上顯示的時間同步化以免造成混淆。

補充	synchronize your watches 校準鐘錶，對時 synchronize A with B 使 A 和 B 同時發生；使 A 和 B 的資訊同步

synchronization n. 同步

縮 sync

92. **technical**

[ˋtɛknɪk!]

adj. 技術的；專門性的；技巧的

⇨ **technic** 「技術；技巧」 + - **al** 「有…性質的」

Robert uses very **technical** language to describe the simplest ideas.

Robert 使用非常專業的術語來描述最簡單的想法。

補充	technical problem/hitch	技術性問題，機件故障
	technical support	技術支援
	technical terms	術語

technically adv. 技術性地；在專門技巧上

technician n. 技術人員；技師

93. **terminology**

[͵tɝməˋnɑlədʒɪ]

n. 專業術語；專有名詞

⇨ **term** 「專門名詞；術語」 + - **ology** 「名詞字尾，表學科」

For a better explanation of the **terminology** used in this report, please refer to our handy glossary.

如要更了解這份報告裡用的專業術語，請參考附上的詞彙表。

terminological adj. 術語的；專門名詞的

terminologist n. 術語學家

中高

94. **transmission**

[træns`mɪʃən]

n. 傳輸；傳送

transmit v. 傳送；傳輸

 trans -「橫跨」+ - mis -「寄送」+ - sion「名詞字尾」

The **transmission** of ideas through email is a good way for international companies to communicate across time zones.

透過電子郵件傳送訊息對國際企業來說是跨越時區溝通的一個好方法。

初級

95. **trial**

[`traɪəl]

adj. 試用的

n. 試用；試驗

⇨ try「嘗試」+ - al「名詞字尾」

I learn a lot about unfamiliar software by **trial** and error.

我在反覆試驗嘗試中對我不熟悉的軟體有了更多的了解。

> 補充
> trial and error　反覆試驗；不斷嘗試
> on trial　　　　　在試驗中

---

96. **troubleshooting**

[`trʌbḷˌʃutɪŋ]

n. 檢修；疑難排解

troubleshoot v. 疑難排解
troubleshooter n.（公司雇用的）處理難題的人

⇨ trouble「麻煩；故障」+ shoot「射擊」+ - ing「名詞字詞」，把麻煩都射擊掉就解決它了

Call the IT Help Desk and let them walk you through **troubleshooting**.

打電話給資訊科技服務中心請他們教你進行疑難排解。

★ walk sb. through sth.：耐心地為某人示範某事物

中高

97. **update**

[`ʌpdet]

n. 更新；最新資訊

[ʌp`det]

v. 更新

⇨ up「向上」+ date「標註日期」，標在最上面的日期就是最新的

If you want your software to run smoothly, you need to check for any available **updates**.

如果你希望軟體能順暢運作，你需要檢查有沒有可用的更新。

> 補充
> online update　　線上更新
> install an update　安裝更新

98. **upgrade**

中高

[ʌpˋgred]
n. 升級
v. 提升

⇨ up「向上」+ - grad -「行走；踩踏」，往上走表示升級了

After years of struggling with standard Internet service, we are ready to **upgrade** to the premium broadband package.

痛苦地用了幾年標準型網路服務之後，我們準備好要升級成優質寬頻方案了。

補充 an upgrade to sth. 升級至某狀態

反 downgrade n./v. 降級

---

99. **up-to-date**

中高

[ʌptəˋdet]
adj. 最近的；最新的

We can't afford to buy **up-to-date** computers. Let's find some used ones!

最新的電腦我們買不起。我們來找一些二手的吧！

補充 keep sb./sth. up-to-date
使某人得到最新消息；不斷更新消息

同 modern / latest
反 out-of-date adj. 過時的

---

100. **wireless**

[ˋwaɪrlɪs]
adj. 無線的

⇨ wire「電線」+ - less「缺乏…的」

Angie's house has such a weak **wireless** signal. Let's meet at a café instead.

Angie 家的無線訊號很弱。我們約在咖啡廳碰面吧。

補充
wireless communication 無線通訊
wireless signal   無線訊號
wireless network   無線網路

wired adj. 有連線的，有連網路的

實力進階

Part 1. 電腦及手機規格常見詞彙

購買電腦、筆電或智慧型手機等商品時，產品規格表上常見的字彙如以下範例：

英文	中譯	常見內容範例
Condition	產品狀況	used（二手） brand-new（全新）
Brand	品牌	
Product line	產品系列	
Model	型號	
Processor speed	中央處理器速度	3.10 GHz (★Ghz = Gigahertz)
Processor type	中央處理器類型	Intel Core i7
Memory	記憶體容量	8GB
Operating System	作業系統	iOS/Android/ Windows 8/ MAC
Hard Drive Capacity/ Storage Capacity	硬碟容量 / 儲存空間	16 GB/32 GB
Screen size/ Display size	螢幕尺寸	9.7" (★ 通常以 inch 吋為單位)
Internet Connectivity	網路連線	Wi-Fi / Ethernet
Hardware Connectivity	硬體連結埠	USB 2.0 / USB 3.0 / micro SD
Features	產品特色	Built-In Front Camera（內建前鏡頭） Touchscreen（觸控式螢幕） Bluetooth enabled GPS

隨堂練習

★ 請根據句意，選出最適合的單字

(　　) 1. All the employees have _____ to the gym as long as they show their employee ID card.
(A) access
(B) capability
(C) dimension
(D) command

(　　) 2. Don't be afraid to make mistakes. Only by _____ and error can we learn more.
(A) default
(B) design
(C) malfunction
(D) trial

(　　) 3. The reason for the power _____ is that the demand for electricity exceeds the supply.
(A) process
(B) transmission
(C) outage
(D) input

(　　) 4. If you can't make it to pay the bill before the deadline, the gas will be _____.
(A) disconnected
(B) switched
(C) synchronized
(D) inserted

(　　) 5. There is no denying that computers _____ language learning. In other words, learning a foreign language is easier by using computers.
(A) omit
(B) facilitate
(C) reverse
(D) analyze

解答：1. A　2. D　3. C　4. A　5. B

Unit 14 房屋地產

初級
1. alarm
[əˈlɑrm]
n. 警報，警報器；驚慌
v. 使恐慌

The **alarm** service company requires an activation fee and a forty-dollar monthly charge.
這家警報器服務公司會收取啓用費和每月四十元的月費。

fire alarm	火警警報器
smoke alarm	煙霧報警器
car alarm	汽車防盜系統

alarmed adj. 受驚的，驚恐的
alarming adj. 令人擔憂的；告急的
同 siren n. 警報器

2. amenity
[əˈmɛnətɪ]
n. 便利設施，文化設施，福利設施

Sir, this apartment is only five minutes away from all the **amenities** you could ever want.
先生，這間公寓離您可能需要的所有設施只需五分鐘的路程。

典故 amenity 與拉丁文 amore「愛」有關，amenity 原來是喜悅的意思。

補充
basic amenities	基礎設施
public amenities	公共設施
hotel amenities	旅館設施

中級
3. appliance
[əˈplaɪəns]
n. 設備；器具；家用電器

⇨ apply「應用」+ -ance「名詞字尾，表性質」，有可應用於生活中的性質就是應用設備、家用電器
All of the apartments come with standard **appliances**, but they don't include a microwave.
所有的公寓都附有標準的家用配備，但不包括微波爐。

補充 domestic/major appliances
大型家用電器或設備（如：冰箱）
small appliances 小型家電（如：微波爐）

apply v. 應用；請求

4. arcade

[ɑrˋked]

n. 騎樓，拱廊；電子遊樂場

⇨ arc - 「弓；弧形物」+ -ade「名詞字尾」

Thousands of people crowded the **shopping arcade** for the special holiday discount.

成千上萬的人為了假日特別折扣擠進了這個商店街。

Modern-day **arcades** include games for adults as well as children.

現代的電子遊樂場除了給小孩的遊戲也有給大人的遊戲。

補充	shopping arcade	長廊商場，商店街
	arcade game	街機，大型電玩
	amusement arcade	電子遊樂場

中級

5. architect

[ˋɑrkəˌtɛkt]

n. 建築師

 - arch - 「主要的；首要的」+ tect「源自希臘文 tekton，表建造者」

A world-famous **architect** was commissioned to design the King's mansion in Brussels, Belgium.

一位世界知名的建築師被委任設計國王在比利時布魯塞爾的官邸。

architecture n. 建築學；建築物
architectural adj. 建築學的；有關建築的

初級

6. brick

[brɪk]

n. 磚塊；積木
v. 用磚砌

I would suggest a **brick** exterior as opposed to stucco.

我會建議做一個磚砌的外牆而不是灰泥的。

補充	to brick sth. up 用磚堵住 (洞口)

bricklayer n. 泥水匠
brick-red adj. 紅磚色的

中高

7. **broaden**

['brɔdn̩]

v. 變寬

⇨ broad「寬闊的」+ -en「使變成…」

I would like all the trails that run behind this property **broadened** so that it can be used as a bike path and a jogging path.
我想要把這棟房子後方的小路都拓寬以便做爲腳踏車道和慢跑步道。

| 補充 | broaden sb's horizons | 開闊某人的視野 |
| | broaden the mind | 增廣見聞 |

同 widen / expand

中高

8. **bulk**

[bʌlk]

n. 體積；大多數
adj. 大量的，大批的

My roommate and I decide to buy household items in **bulk** to save on expenses.
我和我的室友決定大量購買家用品以節省開銷。

補充	in bulk	未包裝地；大量地
	the bulk of sth.	某物的主要部分
	bulk sale/buying	整批出售 / 大量購買

bulky adj. 龐大的；笨重的

中級

9. **burglar**

['bɝglɚ]

n. 竊賊；
　夜間入屋行竊的小偷

⇨ burgle「竊盜」+ -ar「表人」

Everyone in this neighborhood turns on their exterior lights at night to deter **burglars**.
本社區的每個人都會在晚上開啓室外燈以嚇阻竊賊。

| 補充 | burglar alarm | 防盜鈴 |

burglary n. 破門盜竊；闖空門
burgle v. (BrE) 竊盜

中高

10. **carpenter**

['kɑrpəntɚ]

n. 木工；木匠
v. 當木匠，做木匠工

carpentry n. 木工；木匠業

It's best to hire a professional **carpenter** to build that deck that you want outside your back door.
最好雇個專業木匠來建造後門外你想要的露臺。

| 典故 | 古代推車是用木頭做的，後來逐漸把推車和做木工的動作連結。 |

初級

11. **carpet**

[ˋkɑrpɪt]

n. 地毯；一層

v. 在…上鋪地毯

We've just laid a new **carpet** in our bedroom.
我們剛剛在臥室裡鋪了塊新地毯。

 carpet 源自拉丁文 carpere「扯、拔」，因為地毯的纖維多半是散亂像破布的樣子。

補充 the red carpet　紅地毯；隆重歡迎接待
a carpet of snow　一層積雪

同 rug

中高

12. **cellar**

[ˋsɛlɚ]

n. 地下室；地窖

 cell「小房間」+ -ar「拉丁名詞字尾」
The wine **cellar** in this older house is damp.
這間較舊的房子的酒窖很潮濕。

補充 wine cellar 酒窖
root cellar 建在地下或半穴式的蔬菜儲存室
salt cellar = saltshaker 頂部有孔的鹽罐

中級

13. **clay**

[kle]

n. 泥土，黏土

I prefer to mold the **clay** with my hands.
我比較喜歡用我的雙手捏黏土。

補充 clay 是指專門拿來做成磚或是做陶器的黏土。
mud 是指爛泥，泥漿。
soil 是泥土或土壤，強調是植物在上面生長的土壤。

初級

14. **closet**

[ˋklɑzɪt]

n. 壁櫥，壁櫃；儲藏室

⇨ close「關閉」+ -et「名詞字尾，表小東西」，可以關起來的小空間就是壁櫥
The master bedroom has a large walk-in **closet** with room for hundreds of outfits.
該間主臥房有一個能放數百套衣服的巨大衣帽間。

補充 walk-in closet 　（人可走進去的）衣櫃，衣帽間

15. community

[kə`mjunətɪ]

n. 社區；社群

⇨ common「共同的，共有的」+ -ity「名詞字尾」，共同生活的群體就形成一個社群、社區

This is a very tight-knit **community**, and we all look out for one another.

這是個很緊密團結的社區，而我們彼此都會互相照應。

補充		
	community center	社區活動中心
	business community	商業界
	online community	網路社群

中高

16. compartment

[kəm`partmənt]

n. 隔間

⇨ compart「分隔」+ -ment「名詞字尾」，分隔出來的空間就是隔間

We had a small **compartment** installed under this counter to hold our recycling and trash cans.

我們在這個櫃台下方安裝了一個小隔間，以放置回收桶及垃圾桶。

補充		
	storage compartment	儲存隔間

compart v. 分隔成幾部份

中級

17. concrete

[`kankrit]

n. 水泥，混凝土
adj. 具體的；混凝土的

 con-「一起」+ -cre-「生長」+ -te「拉丁字尾」，混凝土中有許多東西密切連結在一起

All of these buildings are made of **concrete** to withstand the frequent earthquakes.

所有這些建築物都以水泥建造，以承受經常性的地震。

補充		
	reinforced concrete	鋼筋混凝土
	a concrete floor/path	水泥地面 / 水泥路面

比較	cement n. 水泥 (粉)

中級

18. construction

[kən`strʌkʃən]

n. 建設

⇨ construct「建造；建設」+ -ion「名詞字尾」

The city council approved the **construction** of a pedestrian bridge over the busy highway.

市議會同意在忙碌高速道路的上方建造一條行人用陸橋。

補充		
	construction site	建築工地
	under construction	建設中

19. cookware

['kuk'wɛr]

n. 廚具，炊具

⇨ cook「烹調」+ -ware「製品；用具」

These college students don't have the necessary **cookware** to handle food preparation for large groups.
這些大學生沒有足夠的炊具來料理一大群人所需的食物。

常見的廚具說法：			
pot	pan	wok	kettle
罐；壺；鍋	平底鍋	中式炒鍋	煮水用水壺

補充

kitchenware n. 廚房用具

20. courtyard

 中高

['kɔrtjɑrd]

n. 庭院

⇨ court「庭院」+ yard「院子」

This property features a beautiful **courtyard**.
這棟房產的特色是有美麗的庭院。

補充 courtyard 也可簡稱為 court，指「四周被建築物或圍牆圍起來的庭院」，如 castle courtyard 城堡的庭院。

21. craftspeople

['kræftspipl]

n. 工匠

⇨ crafts「工藝；手藝」+ people「人們」

Hundreds of **craftspeople** met in the convention center for a seminar on new types of building materials.
數百名的工匠齊聚會議中心參加有關新式建築材料的研討會。

craft n. 工藝；手藝
craftsmanship n. 技巧，技術；手工藝品

 craftsman

初級

22. **damage**

[ˋdæmɪdʒ]

n./v. 破壞

⇨ dam「拉丁文，損害」+ - age「名詞字尾」

The tornado inflicted heavy **damage** on my house, flattening all of it except for the garage.

那龍捲風爲我家帶來嚴重破壞，除了車庫之外的其它地方都被夷爲平地了。

補充	do/cause damage to...	對…造成損害
	potential damage	潛在損害
	damage limitation	損失控制

damages n. 損害賠償金

同 harm

中級

23. **decoration**

[͵dɛkəˋreʃən]

n. 裝飾；裝飾品

⇨ decor「拉丁文，美麗」+ - ate「動詞字尾」+ - ion「名詞字尾」，裝飾使事物更美麗

During the holidays, you can see how the colorful **decorations** rejuvenate the entire neighborhood.

在假期中，你可以看到多彩多姿的裝飾讓我們鄰近社區整個重新恢復活力。

decor n. 裝飾風格
decorate v. 裝飾
decorative adj. 裝飾性的

---

24. **demolish**

[dɪˋmɑlɪʃ]

v. 毀壞，拆除

⇨ de -「往下」+ moliri「拉丁文，建立」，愈建造愈往下表示在拆毀

Let's call the city government to ask them to **demolish** these old vacant buildings.

我們打電話給市政府要他們把這些老舊空屋給拆除吧。

demolition n. 拆除房屋；毀壞

同 tear down

中高

25. **disposal**

[dɪˋspozl̩]

n. 處理；清除

 dispose「處理，清除」+ - al「名詞字尾」

The **disposal** of toxic substances into the general trash collection is not permitted.

將有毒物質丟棄到一般垃圾中是不被允許的。

補充	garbage disposal (waste disposal) 廢物處理機
	at one's disposal 供某人使用；供某人支配

初級

26. **distance**

[ˈdɪstəns]

n. 距離

⇨ dis-「分開」+ -sta-「站立」+ -ance「名詞字尾」，分開站立就會產生距離

Bob commutes a great **distance** each day to his office downtown.

Bob 每天通勤很遠的距離到市中心的辦公室。

補充 walking distance　步行可到的距離
go the full distance　堅持到底；勇往直前

distant adj. 遙遠的

中高

27. **distinctive**

[dɪˈstɪŋktɪv]

adj. 有特色的；特殊的

⇨ distinct「有區別的」+ -ive「有⋯性質的」，可以區別出來就表示很有特色

This house has a very **distinctive** floor plan; it has a huge kitchen but no formal dining room.

這間房子的平面設計很有特色；它有很大的廚房但沒有正式的飯廳。

補充 distinctive features　特點

distinct adj. 有區別的；與其他不同的
distinctively adv. 特殊地；區別地

中高

28. **dome**

[dom]

n. 圓屋頂，圓蓋

The architect mentioned that the museum will have a **dome**.

該名建築師說過博物館會有圓頂。

典故 dome 最早是指「房屋」，表示「上帝居住的地方」。

補充 dome 也可以指「巨蛋」，如：Tokyo Dome「東京巨蛋」。

domed adj. 有圓頂的

中高

29. **doorstep**

[ˋdor͵stɛp]

n. 門前的台階

⇨ door「門」+ step「台階」

A beautiful city park is just one hundred meters from my front **doorstep**.

從我家前門門台階出去不到一百公尺處就有一座美麗的城市公園。

補充
on the doorstep　在門口
on one's doorstep　離某人很近

中級

30. **drain**

[dren]

n. 排水管；排水設備

v. 排出液體；耗盡

drainage n. 排水系統
drainpipe n. 排水管

One of my tenants clogged a **drain** with all her hair in one of my apartments.

我的公寓其中一間有個房客，她的頭髮將整個排水管給堵住了。

補充
brain drain　　　人才外流
down the drain　付諸東流；前功盡棄

中高

31. **drape**

[drep]

n. 窗簾；布幕

v. 覆蓋，垂掛

同 curtain

The **drapes** are all brilliant, purple satin, and give the house a look of royalty.

所有布簾都是閃亮的紫色緞子，讓房子看起來很有皇家的尊貴感。

典故　drape 原來就是「布料」的意思。

補充　be draped in/with sth. 被某物覆蓋住

32. **dwelling**

['dwɛlɪŋ]

n. 住處，住宅

⇨ dwell「居住」+ -ing「名詞字尾」

This **dwelling** was unoccupied for ten years, so the renovation took nearly one year.

這間住宅已經十年沒有人住了，所以翻修花了將近一年的時間。

補充
permanent/temporary dwelling
永久住處 / 暫時住處
dwelling house 住宅房屋（相對於商店或辦公室）

dweller n. 居民；居住者

---

33. **entrance**

['ɛntrəns]

n. 入口

⇨ enter「進入」+ -ance「名詞字尾」

The **entrance** to my house is almost completely hidden behind some overgrown shrubs.

我房子的入口處被長滿的灌木叢幾乎全擋住了。

補充
front/back entrance 前門 / 後門
entrance fee   入場費
entrance exam   入學考試

反 exit n. 出口

---

34. **estate**

[ɪs'tet]

n. 財產；遺產；房地產

My brothers and I needed to sell my father's **estate** to pay off all his debts after he passed away.

在我爸爸過世後，我和我哥得把我爸的房產賣掉以償還他所欠的債務。

補充
estate 表示個人財產時，常用來指一個人死後留下的財產。

同 property

11
製造

12
金融

13
科技技術

14
房屋地產

15
出差旅遊

35. excavate

[ˈɛkskəˌvet]

v. 挖掘；開鑿

excavation n. 挖掘；開鑿
excavator n. 挖土機

同 dig

⇨ ex-「向外」+ -cav-「挖空」+ -ate「動詞字尾」
According to the schedule, the workers are **excavating** for the foundation today.
按照時間表，工人今天是在挖地基。

中高

36. extinguish

[ɪkˈstɪŋgwɪʃ]

v. 滅火

 ex-「向外」+ -stingu-「熄滅」+ -ish「動詞字尾」
We must completely **extinguish** our campfire before leaving a camp site.
在離開營地前，我們得完全撲滅營火才行。

補充　fire extinguisher 滅火器

中級

37. fertilizer

[ˈfɝtḷˌaɪzɚ]

n. 肥料

fertile adj. 肥沃的

⇨ fertilize「施肥」+ -er「做⋯動作的物品」
Spread a little **fertilizer** over your lawn in the spring, and by summer it will be green and lush.
春天時在草坪上撒一些肥料，那麼夏天時它就會長得又綠又茂盛。

中高

38. fixture

[ˈfɪkstʃɚ]

n. 房屋的固定裝置設備

Your new light **fixture** looks like a Victorian chandelier.
你的新照明設備看起來像是維多利亞時代的水晶燈。

補充　the fixtures and fittings 固定裝置和附加設備

中級

39. foundation

[faʊnˈdeʃən]

n. 地基；基礎；基金會

found v. 建造；創立

⇨ found「建造；創立」+ -ation「名詞字尾」，建造房子的基礎就是地基
The building has a major issue with its **foundation** which could cost tens of thousands to repair.
這棟建築物的地基有個大問題，可能得花好幾萬修理。

補充　lay the foundations 為⋯打下基礎

40. **furnish**

[ˈfɜnɪʃ]

v. 配置家具；提供

furnished adj. 備有家具的
furnishings n. 家具；室內陳設
furniture n. 家具

Not many of my university classmates have enough money to **furnish** their apartments.
我的大學同學裡沒幾個人有足夠的錢在公寓裡配備家具。

> 補充　fully furnished 配套齊全

41. **hedge**

[hɛdʒ]

n. 樹籬笆；防備措施
v. 用樹籬圍住；防止損失擴大

Todd is showing us how to trim **hedges** in a correct way.
Todd 正在把正確修剪樹籬笆的方法做給我們看。
I asked my financial advisor about how to **hedge** against currency risks.
我問了我的財務顧問關於如何避免貨幣風險的方法。

> 補充　hedge your bets　　多處下注以減少風險
> 　　　 hedge against inflation 防止通貨膨脹

42. **holding**

[ˈholdɪŋ]

n. 持有股份；私有財產

⇨ hold「握住；持有」+ -ing「名詞字尾」
The judge demanded that all of Ted's **holdings** be liquidated to pay all the people he scammed.
法官要求清算 Ted 的所有資產以償還給所有被他詐騙的人。

> 補充　holdings 常用複數形態，表示個人財產時常指土地。

43. **homebuyer**

[ˈhomˌbaɪɚ]

n. 購屋者

 housebuyer

⇨ home「房屋」+ buyer「買主；購買者」
Interest rates are so low that potential **homebuyers** are lining up to get a mortgage loan.
利率低到讓許多潛在買房客都排隊等著申請抵押貸款。

中級

44. **housing**

[ˈhaʊzɪŋ]

n. 住房，住房條件；
住房供給

house v. 居住；給…房子住

⇨ house「給…房子住」+ -ing「名詞字尾」

Those who are living on minimum wage are eligible for free government **housing**.

靠最低工資維生的人有資格申請政府提供的免費住房。

補充　public housing　公有住房

中級

45. **knob**

[nɑb]

n. 球形把手；旋鈕

doorknob n. 門把

Even the **knobs** on this chest of drawers are luxurious.
這個五斗櫃連把手都很奢華。

補充　control knob　控制旋鈕

---

46. **ladder**

[ˈlædɚ]

n. 梯子；(發跡的) 途徑

v. 在…上裝設梯子；成名，
發跡

易混 latter adj. 後者的

I would suggest buying a sturdier **ladder** before trying to paint the shutters on the second floor.
在漆二樓的百葉窗之前，我會建議買結實一點的梯子。

補充
ladder truck　　　雲梯車
career ladder　　　生涯階梯
kick down the ladder　過河拆橋

中級

47. **landlord**

[ˈlænd.lɔrd]

n. 地主；房東

landlady n. 女地主；女房東

⇨ land「土地」+ lord「君主；統治者」，土地的主人就是地主、房東

The **landlord** only allows a five-day grace period before the rent is due in full.
租金全額付清前，房東只容許五天的寬限期。

★ grace period：截止日之後的寬限期。

48. laundromat

[ˋlɔndrəmæt]

n. 投幣式自助洗衣店 (AmE)

 laundry「洗衣店」+ automat「自動售貨機」

Until we get a new washing machine, we'll need to make weekly trips to the **laundromat**.

在我們買一台新洗衣機之前，我們得每週去一趟自助洗衣店。

典故 laundromat 原來是洗衣機的商標名稱。

補充 do the laundry 洗衣服

laundry n. 洗衣店；待洗衣物

 launderette (BrE)

中級

49. lawn

[lɔn]

n. 草坪；草地

We host neighborhood badminton and volleyball tournaments on our **lawn** every week.

我們每週在我們家草坪上主辦羽毛球和排球比賽。

補充 mow the lawn 修剪草坪
lawn party 草坪派對

中高

50. lease

[lis]

n. 租約

v. 租用

Most apartments in this neighborhood have nine-month **leases** since the college students go back home for the summer.

這個社區的公寓大部份都有九個月形式的租約，因為大學生夏天會回家不在這兒。

補充 take out/sign a lease 簽租約

leasehold adj. 租賃的
leaseholder n. 承租人

中級

51. locate

[ˋloket] / [loˋket]

v. 使座落於

⇨ -loc-「地方」+ -ate「動詞字尾」，將建築物放在某地方就表示座落於此處

Our retail shops are conveniently **located** close to the major shopping malls.

我們的零售商店位於離主要購物中心很近的地方，非常便利。

補充 be located at/in/on... 位於，座落在…

location n. 地點

中高

52. lodge
[lɑdʒ]
n. (度假) 小屋；管理員室
v. 借住

When I go skiing at Mount Arlington, I always stay at the main **lodge** so I can have all the amenities I would ever need without going outside.
當我去阿靈頓山滑雪時，我總會待在渡假村的主屋，所以我不用走到外面也能使用各項設備。

補充　lodging house　宿舍；公寓
　　　 board and lodging　伙食和住宿，供應食宿

lodging　n. 寄宿處
lodger　n. 房客

中級

53. mansion
[ˋmænʃən]
n. 宅邸；大廈，大樓

⇨ -man- 「停留」+ -sion 「名詞字尾」

I would recommend that you buy a **mansion** in the country because you can get more space for half the price of living in the city.
我會建議你在鄉下買棟大房子，因為你可以用住在城市的一半價格享用更大的空間。

補充　mansion tax　豪宅稅
　　　 Mansion House　倫敦市長官邸

中高

54. mattress
[ˋmætrɪs]
n. 床墊

You need to flip your **mattress** over and rotate it every year so it doesn't get so worn down on one side.
每年你都要把床墊拍一拍轉個面，好讓它不會單邊磨損壞掉。

補充　air mattress　充氣床墊

中級

55. messy
[ˋmɛsɪ]
adj. 雜亂的；骯髒的

⇨ mess 「混亂」+ -y 「形容詞字尾」

The kitchen looked **messy** after we finished repairing the pipes.
我們修完水管之後，廚房看起來一團亂。

mess　n. 混亂

初級

56. **meter**

[ˋmitɚ]

n. 計量器，儀表；公尺

v. 用儀表測量

Go downstairs and read the electricity **meter** for me.
到樓下去幫我抄電表。
This incredible estate features a 50-**meter** Olympic-size swimming pool.
這間令人驚嘆的房產主打有座五十公尺奧運規格的游泳池。

補充 parking meter 停車收費器

中高

57. **modernize**

[ˋmɑdɚnˌaɪz]

v. 現代化

modernization n. 現代化

⇨ modern「現代的」+ -ize「…化」
I would like to **modernize** the color scheme and overall design of the interior of this house.
我想讓這間房子的內部色彩組合和整體設計更現代化。

中級

58. **mortgage**

[ˋmɔrgɪdʒ]

n./v. 抵押貸款

 -mort-「死亡，結束」+ gage「法文，承諾；抵押品」
I would suggest getting a fixed-rate **mortgage** because you never know when interest rates will surge.
我會建議採用固定利率的抵押貸款，因為你永遠不知道利率何時會突然飆升。

典故 mortgage 原指貸款或協議時為履行承諾而質押的房產，當貸款都付清或無法如期支付時，這個承諾也就死了、結束了。

補充
mortgage loan 房屋抵押貸款
take out a mortgage 辦理抵押借款
pay off a mortgage 清償抵押借款

中高

59. **mower**

[ˋmoɚ]

n. 收割機

lawnmower n. 草坪修剪機

⇨ mow「除草；割草」+ -er「做…動作的物品」
My neighbor rarely takes out his **mower**, so his lawn looks like a jungle.
我的鄰居很少拿出他的除草機，所以他的院子看起來像是座叢林。

11 製造

12 金融

13 科技技術

14 房屋地產

15 出差旅遊

中級

60. **neighborhood**

[`nebɚ,hud]

n. 街坊；住宅區；鄰近地區

⇨ neighbor「鄰居」+ -hood「名詞字尾」，鄰居住在附近的地區就是鄰近地區

We've just started a **neighborhood** watch program, and we take turns patrolling each night.
我們開始了鄰里守望相助計劃，而且我們會每晚輪流巡邏。

 neighborhood watch　　鄰里互守
the whole neighborhood　附近所有的鄰居

neighbor n. 鄰居
neighboring adj. 鄰近的

中級

61. **occupy**

[`akjə,paɪ]

v. 佔有；佔據

⇨ oc-「同 ob-，越過」+ -cup-「拿、取」，跨過去拿別人的東西佔為己有

The same family has **occupied** the house across the street for over forty years.
同一個家族已經住在對街的那間房子超過四十年了。

 be occupied in/with sth. 忙於做某事

occupied adj. 已佔用的；在使用的
occupancy n. 佔用；居住

中高

62. **ornament**

[`ɔrnəmənt]

n. 裝飾品

⇨ -orn-「裝扮，裝飾」+ -ment「名詞字尾」

The Christmas tree out front is decorated with hundreds of handmade **ornaments**.
大門外的聖誕樹裝飾了數百個手工製飾品。

同 decoration / adornment

中高

63. **outskirts**

[`aut,skɝts]

n. 郊區

⇨ out-「外側的」+ skirts「邊緣；外圍」，遠離城市的外圍區域就是郊區

The Parkers live on the **outskirts** of Chicago.
Parker 一家人住在芝加哥的郊區。

 in/on the outskirts (= in the suburbs) 在郊區

同 suburbs

64. parlor

[`pɑlɚ]

n. 會客室；店鋪

★ 英：**parlour** ／美：**parlor**

Amelia has her hair done once a month at her aunt's beauty **parlor**, where she gets a twenty percent family discount.

Amelia 一個月去她阿姨的美容院做一次頭髮，在那裡她可以享有家族成員打八折的優惠。

 源自法文 **parler** 表「說話」，引申為可談話的房間。

 pizza parlor 披薩店

65. patch

[pætʃ]

v. 補綴，修補

n. 一小塊；補丁

After years of neglect, Hank spent a week **patching** his driveway with a special sealant.

在忽視了好幾年後，Hank 花了一個禮拜用特殊的密封膠來修補他的車道。

 patch up　修補；暫時平息紛爭
eye patch （保護受傷眼睛用的）眼罩

patchy adj. 縫補的；拼湊而成的
patchwork n. 拼布工藝

66. pillar

[`pɪlɚ]

n. 柱子；棟樑

The main entrance of the house is between those two tall, elegant **pillars**.

那間房子的主要入口位在那兩根又高又講究的柱子之間。

 pillar of sth.　　　某組織的中堅分子
be a pillar of strength　給予幫助的精神支柱

 column

67. pipeline

[`paɪpˌlaɪn]

n. 管道，管線

⇨ pipe「管子；輸送管」+ line「線條」

Congress just passed a law granting permission to build a long oil **pipeline** from Canada down to Texas.

國會剛才通過一項法案核准建造一條由加拿大一路到德州的輸油管線。

 gas pipeline　　　天然氣管道
be in the pipeline　在籌劃中；在進行中

中級

68. **plumber**

[ˈplʌmɚ]

n. 水電工

plumb v. 給…裝水管
plumbing n. 管道系統

➪ plumb「給…裝水管」+ -er「做…動作的人」
A pipe burst and flooded my bathroom, so I called the **plumber** immediately.
水管破裂讓我的廁所淹水了，所以我立刻打電話叫水電工來。

中高

69. **porch**

[portʃ]

n. 門廊；走廊

I enjoy relaxing on the bench on my front porch and watching the sun set.
我喜歡坐在前門廊的長椅上放鬆並欣賞太陽西下。

 典故 porch 源自拉丁文 porta「通道」。

中級

70. **possession**

[pəˈzɛʃən]

n. 持有；所有物；個人財產

➪ possess「持有」+ -ion「名詞字尾」
You may take **possession** of the house immediately after the official closing paperwork has been signed.
在正式的文書作業簽名完成後，你就能持有這間房子。

 補充
take possession of sth.
持有、擁有某物（常指房地產）
personal possessions 個人物品

同 belongings n. 所有物

中級

71. **practical**

[ˈpræktɪk!]

adj. 務實的；實際的

➪ practice「實踐」+ -al「具有…屬性的」，有可以實踐的屬性表示實際的
I don't think it is **practical** to buy a house in the downtown area because the price is too high.
我認為在市中心買房子是不切實際的，因為房價太高了。

 補充
practical alternative 可行的其他方案
for/to all practical purposes 實際上，事實上

practically adv. 幾乎；實際上
practicability n. 實用性，可行性

72. presale

[`prɪsel]

n. 預售

 pre -「在前，在先」**+ sale**「銷售」，在正式銷售前就先賣表示預售

For more **presale** details and prices, visit our real estate agency.

想知道更多的預售詳情與價格，請造訪我們的房地產仲介公司。

補充　presale estimate/price　預售價

中級

73. property

[`prɑpətɪ]

n. 財產；房地產；所有權；特性

 proper「適合的」**+ - ty**「名詞字尾」

The **property** taxes for houses in this suburb are so high that only the super-rich can live here.

這個近郊住宅區房子的房產稅非常高，所以只有超級有錢人才會住在這兒。

補充
personal property　　個人財產
public property　　　公共財產
intellectual property　智慧財產權

proper adj. 適合的

---

74. real estate

[`riəl][ɪs`tet]

n. 不動產；房地產

There is nothing more thrilling than helping a client find exactly the kind of **real estate** they have been looking for.

沒有比幫客戶找到正是他們一直在找的不動產更令人興奮的事了。

典故　源自法語 royale，表示「皇家的」。因此 real estate 原指王室領土。

補充
a piece of real estate　一個房產
real estate agent　　　房地產經紀人
(AmE) real estate office = (BrE) estate agency
房地產代理，房地產仲介

同 realty / real property

75. **remodel**

[ri`madl]

v. 整修；改建

⇨ re -「再次」+ model「塑造」，把房子再塑造一次就是改建

We just bought a perfectly located storefront opposite the school campus, but the interior must be totally **remodeled**.
我們剛買了一間在學校校園對面、位置絕佳的店面，但它的內部必須整個重新改裝。

 be remodeled into... 整修成…

model v. 塑造

76. **renovate**

[`rɛnəˌvet]

v. 整修，翻新

⇨ re -「再次」+ -nov -「新的」+ -ate「動詞字尾」，把舊房子再次整理成新的樣子

If you don't **renovate** this dreary apartment complex, you won't get any new tenants.
如果你不把那間陰暗糟糕的公寓大樓好好整修一下，你是不可能找到任何新房客的。

renovation n. 修繕

同 repair / renew

77. **rental**

中高

[`rɛntl]

n. 租金；租賃；租用的東西

⇨ rent「出租；租用」+ -al「名詞字尾」

The sky-high storefront **rentals** made it difficult for young people to start up a store on their own.
昂貴的店面租金讓年輕人很難靠一己之力開店。
There are several ideal **rentals** for college students at the end of this street.
這條街的尾端有一些適合大學生的理想租屋。

rental agreement	租賃協議
car rental	汽車出租
fleet rental	車隊租賃

rent v. 出租；租用 n. 租金

78. **repairperson**

[rɪ`pɛrpɝsn]

n. 維修人員

⇨ repair「修理」+ person「人」

I'm not trained to handle furnace repairs, so let's call the **repairperson**.
我沒受過暖爐維修訓練，所以我們打電話請維修人員來吧。

補充 其他表示修理人員的字：
mechanic 機械工，修理工
如：car mechanic 汽車修理工
technician 技術人員
如：computer technician 電腦技術人員

同 repairman

中級

79. **resident**

[ˈrɛzədənt]

n. 居民

reside v. 定居；居住
residence n. 居住；住所
residential adj. 與居住有關的；住宅的

⇨ re-「一再，回返」+ -sid-「坐」+ -ent「做…的人」，
坐回原位的人表示是原來就住在這裡的居民

Several **residents** have complained of excessive noise coming from Mr. Smith's house.

數位居民已經在抗議 Smith 先生家傳出的巨大噪音。

中級

80. **rural**

[ˈrurəl]

adj. 鄉村的；田園的

反 urban adj. 城市的，都會的

⇨ -rur-「鄉村」+ -al「具…屬性的」

The disadvantage of living in a **rural** school district is the constant cancelling of school due to icy roads.

住在農村學區的缺點就是學校常會因路面結冰而停課。

初級

81. **sink**

[sɪŋk]

n. 水槽，洗滌槽
v. 下沉，沉沒

The **sink** in the lab is broken again, but the plumber won't get there to fix it until next Monday.

實驗室的水槽又壞掉了，但是水電工要到下週一才能來修。

 補充　sink 主要是指廚房的水槽；浴室裡的洗臉槽通常稱為 basin。sink unit 就是指流理台。

中高

82. **spacious**

[ˈspeʃəs]

adj. 寬敞的

同 roomy / capacious
反 cramped adj. 狹窄的

⇨ space「空間」+ -ous「充滿…的」，充滿了空間表示很寬敞

I want to upgrade to a more **spacious** floor plan than the cozy townhouse we have been living in.

比起我們一直住的小而舒適的市內連棟住宅，我想要升級成更寬敞的房型。

83. **sprinkler**

[ˋsprɪŋklɚ]

n. 灑水器；自動灑水滅火裝置

⇨ sprinkle「噴灑；撒落」+ - er「做⋯動作的物品」

A full fire **sprinkler** system inspection should be performed at least annually.
每年至少要做一次自動灑水系統的完整檢驗。

補充　在北美 sprinkle 一字還可以表示「下小雨」。

sprinkle v. 噴灑；撒落

---

84. **square meter**

[skwɛr][ˋmitɚ]

phr. 平方米，平方公尺

★ 英：square metre ／美：square meter

Could you live in a one hundred **square meter** apartment?
你能住一百平方米大的公寓嗎？

補充　歐美國家計算室內面積的單位是用 square meter 或 square foot（平方英尺）。

square adj. 平方的

---

85. **stairs**

[stɛrz]

n. 樓梯

同 stairway

Grandma lives in an apartment building with no elevator, so she has to climb five flights of **stairs** every day.
奶奶住在一間沒有電梯的公寓，所以她每天得要爬五層樓的樓梯。

---

86. **stripe**

[straɪp]

n. 條紋

My friend painted dark brown **stripes** on the walls to make the room look subtle and mature.
我朋友把牆漆上深棕色條紋，好讓房間看起來精緻而成熟。

補充　其他常見花紋 (pattern) 說法：
1. plaid n. 方格圖案
2. dot n. 圓點

striped adj. 有條紋的

16 交通

87. **structure**
[ˈstrʌktʃɚ]
n. 結構；建築物
v. 組織安排

structural adj. 結構上的

⇨ -struct- 「建造」+ -ure「名詞字尾」，建造出來的東西就是建築物

My friend built the entire **structure** all by himself.
我朋友自己動手蓋整棟建築物。

補充　structural damage 結構性損傷

17 社交與用餐

88. **studio**
[ˈstjudɪo]
n. 公寓套房；錄製室；
工作室

Dale constructed a recording **studio** in his basement and spent thousands on high-quality sound equipment.
Dale 在自己的地下室建了一個錄音室，還在高品質聲音設備上花了數千元。

補充
studio apartment (= studio flat) 單房公寓
film studio (= studios) 電影製片廠，攝影棚
TV studio 電視攝影棚

18 休閒娛樂

中高

89. **suburban**
[səˈbɝbən]
adj. 市郊的；近郊住宅區的

suburb n. 市郊；近郊住宅區

⇨ sub- 「接近」+ -urb- 「都市」+ -an 「拉丁文形容詞字尾」，接近都市的就是市郊的

All of the shopping malls in the metropolitan area are in **suburban** districts, which angers inner-city residents.
這個大都會區的購物中心都位在市郊區域，這讓住在城裡的居民很火大。

19 醫療保健

90. **surround**
[səˈraʊnd]
v. 包圍；圍繞

surroundings n. 環境；周圍事物
surrounding adj. 附近的，四周的

⇨ sur- 「在上，超越」+ unda 「拉丁文，波浪」

The building is **surrounded** by armed police.
這棟大樓被武裝警察團團包圍住。
The speakers in this room provide **surround** sound just like you would experience in a movie theater.
房間裡的喇叭會播放立體環繞聲，就像你在電影院感受到的一樣。

典故　surround 原指浪很大，使水滿出來讓東西浸泡在其中，就像水包圍住東西的樣子，因此引申出圍繞的意思。

補充　surround sound 環繞立體聲

20 日常生活

中級

91. tenant

['tɛnənt]

n. 房客；承租人；佃戶

⇨ - ten - 「持有」+ - ant 「做…的人」，憑租約持有房子的人就是承租人、房客

We charge the **tenant** in apartment 3C fifty extra dollars a month because he has a pet.

我們會向住在 3C 室的房客每月額外收五十元，因為他有養寵物。

tenancy n. (房地產) 租賃，租用；租用期限

反 landlord n. 房東；地主

中高

92. tile

[taɪl]

n. 瓦；瓷磚
v. 砌瓦，鋪瓷磚

Your kitchen would look better if you put **tiles** down on this floor instead.

如果你把廚房的地板換成瓷磚，你家廚房看起來會更棒。

 補充
roof/floor/ceramic tile 屋瓦 / 地磚 / 瓷磚
a tile floor　　　　　　瓷磚地

tiling n. 蓋瓦；貼磚
tiled adj. 瓦頂的

初級

93. unit

['junɪt]

n. 公寓大樓的單位，一戶

There are eight **units** in this apartment building, and all of them have been damaged beyond repair by the fire.

這間公寓大樓有八戶，它們全部都被火災破壞到無法修理了。

 補充
a public housing unit　　公共住房單位
a multiple-unit dwelling 多單位住宅

中高

94. utensil

[ju'tɛnsl]

n. 器具

Be sure to set the table with a cup, plate, and set of **utensils** on each place mat.

要讓每張餐墊上都擺好一個杯子、一個盤子和一套餐具。

 補充
kitchen utensils 廚房用具
cooking utensils 烹飪用具

同 tool

95. utility

中高

[juˋtɪlətɪ]

n. 公用事業，公共設施；實用性

⇨ utile「有用的；有益的」+ -ity「名詞字尾」，對大眾有益的東西就是公共設施

Our **utility** bills are always high in the winter.
我們冬天的水電費總是很高。

 補充
public utility	公用事業公司
utility bills	水電煤氣帳單，水電費
sports utility vehicle (SUV) 休旅車，多功能運動休閒車	

utile adj. 有用的；有益的
utilize v. 利用

96. vacuum

中高

[ˋvækjʊəm]

n. 真空；真空吸塵器
v. 用吸塵器清掃

Living with three dogs, Meg is constantly running the **vacuum** cleaner to keep all their hair out of the carpet.
由於和三隻狗住，Meg 得不斷用真空吸塵器吸地以維持地毯上不會有狗毛。

 補充
| vacuum cleaner | 吸塵器 |
| vacuum flask (= vacuum bottle) | 保溫瓶 |

vacuum-packed adj. 真空包裝的

97. ventilation

[͵vɛntɪˋleʃən]

n. 通風；流通空氣

Even having an excellent **ventilation** system in your home doesn't help much if you don't change your furnace filter.
如果你沒有更換暖爐濾網，就算你家有很棒的通風設備也是沒什麼幫助的。

 典故
源自拉丁文 ventus「風」，ventilate 原指拋動穀物到空中讓風將穀殼吹掉，引申有使通風、使空氣流動，名詞則為 ventilation。

 補充
| ventilation system | 通風系統 |
| well/poorly ventilated | 通風良好的 / 通風欠佳的 |

ventilate v. 使通風
ventilator n. 通風裝置；通風口

98. wardrobe

中高

[ˋwɔrd͵rob]

n. 衣櫥；（個人的）全部服裝

⇨ ward「保護；守衛」+ robe「長袍」，保護長袍大衣的地方就是衣櫥

Emily has three **wardrobes** in her bedroom, and two of them are overflowing with nothing but shoes.
Emily 在她臥房有三個衣櫥，其中有兩個光是放鞋子就已經塞到滿出來了。

 補充
| built-in/fitted wardrobe | 嵌入式 / 固定式衣櫥 |
| winter wardrobe | 冬裝 |

99. **withstand**

[wɪðˈstænd]

v. 抵擋；禁得起

⇨ with - 「反對」+ stand 「站立」，反對著某物站立表示抵抗、抵擋

These special, triple-pane windows are made to **withstand** winds of up to 150 kilometers per hour.

這些特別設計的三格式窗戶可以用來抵擋時速高達一百五十公里的強風。

 withstand the test of time 承受得起時間的考驗

同 resist

100. **wrench**

[rɛntʃ]

n. 猛扭；扳手
v. 扭緊

You need a large plumber's **wrench** to adjust those large water pipes in your basement.

為了調整地下室的大型水管，你需要一個水電工用的大型扳手。

 monkey wrench = adjustable spanner
活動扳手

同 spanner (BrE)

實力進階

Part 1. 國外租屋必學詞彙

要在國外租房子，一定要學會這些關鍵詞彙喔！

★ floor plan：房型

房型常見分類		房屋資訊範例
studio	套房，沒有客廳	2 Bed, 2 Bath, 977 sq ft, $6430/ mo, Deposit: $7300
1 bedroom	一房一廳	兩房、兩衛、977 平方英呎、每月租金 $6430、押金 $7300
2 bedroom	兩房一廳	

★ Amenities & Features：設施及特色
Amenities 是設備，可以指大樓的公共設備或是租屋內附的設備。Features 是指特點。有關住房的設備或特色，常見相關詞彙有：

1. full concierge service	提供大廈管理員服務 有時也只寫 Concierge 一字
2. individually controlled AC and Heat	獨立控制空調 (AC = air conditioning)
3. washer & dryer in unit	住房內附有洗衣機和烘衣機 ★in unit 表示住房內
4. on-site laundry facilities 或 laundry in building	附公共洗衣房 ★on-site 表示在大樓裡
5. fully furnished	家具全備 有時候也只寫 furnished 一字
6. partly furnished 或 partially furnished	只附部分家具
7. utilities included	包水電瓦斯
8. garage parking	提供車庫停車

★ Pet policy：寵物飼養規定
Pet policy 是養寵物的規定，有時也直接寫成 pets allowed 表示可以養寵物。有些會詳細寫出每戶規定能養的寵物種類及數量。值得注意的是，通常在公寓內養寵物是要另外付費 (pet fee) 的。

隨堂練習

★ 請根據句意，選出最適合的單字

( ) 1. Due to the political instability and lack of opportunities, many technically skilled people choose to emigrate to other countries, which leads to the so-called brain _____.
(A) sprinkle   (B) disposal
(C) possession   (D) drain

( ) 2. The mansion features the ability to _____ violent earthquakes and that's why it costs an arm and a leg.
(A) wrench   (B) furnish
(C) withstand   (D) renovate

( ) 3. Mutual respect and trust provides a solid _____ for their harmonious marriage.
(A) ornament   (B) foundation
(C) utility   (D) construction

( ) 4. If you have any question, don't hesitate to let me know; I am at your _____.
(A) disposal   (B) property
(C) alarm   (D) tenant

( ) 5. The only restroom is _____ at the moment; I am afraid that you might have to wait for another 10 minutes.
(A) broadened   (B) hedged
(C) surrounded   (D) occupied

解答：1. D   2. C   3. B   4. A   5. D

Unit 15 出差旅遊

中級

1. **accommodation**

[əˌkɑməˈdeʃən]

n. 適應；住所；膳宿

同 lodging

 accommodate「提供食宿」+ **-ion**「名詞字尾」
We can thank my boss, Ted, for such splendid **accommodations**– this hotel has everything!
我們要感謝我老闆 Ted 提供這麼棒的住宿，這間飯店真是應有盡有！

2. **acrophobia**

[ˌækrəˈfobɪə]

n. 懼高症

⇨ **-acr-**「高度，最高點」+ **-phobia**「恐懼症」
My cousin's **acrophobia** keeps him from enjoying my favorite pastime– mountain climbing.
我表弟的懼高症讓他無法享受我最愛的休閒娛樂—登山。

中級

3. **agent**

[ˈedʒənt]

n. 代理商；代理人；仲介

⇨ **-ag-**「行動」+ **-ent**「表人」，負責行動的人就是代理人
Our **agent** in Hong Kong is in charge of the sales in South East Asia.
我們在香港的代理商負責東南亞地區的銷售。
Give your passport to the immigration **agent** and, once he returns it to you, proceed to the baggage claim area.
把你的護照拿給移民官員，一旦他把護照還給你，就繼續前往行李提領區。

| 補充 | talent/sports agent | 演藝／體育經紀人 |
| | secret agent | 特務 |

agency n. 代理機構

初級

4. **airline**

[ˈɛrˌlaɪn]

n. 航空公司

⇨ **air**「空中」+ **line**「線」
The **airline** keeps changing their rules for how customers can use their frequent-flyer miles.
航空公司不斷修改他們提供給常客的里程使用規則。

| 補充 | budget/low-cost/no frill airlines 廉價航空 |

135

中高

5. **aisle**

[aɪl]

n. 走道，通道

Sir, kindly keep your feet out of the **aisle** so others don't trip.
先生，請不要將腳放在走道上，這樣別人才不會絆倒。

補充　aisle/window seat　靠走道 / 靠窗的座位
roll in the aisles　　捧腹大笑；笑得東倒西歪

同 passageway

中級

6. **alert**

[əˈlɝt]

n. 警報

adj. 警覺的

The government has issued an **alert** for all buildings in the downtown area due to the shooting at city hall.
由於市政廳的槍擊事件，政府向所有市中心的大樓發出警報。

補充　on the alert　警戒著；保持警覺

同 watchful　adj. 警覺的

反 unaware　adj. 未察覺到的

中級

7. **arrival**

[əˈraɪvl]

n. 到達；抵達

 ⇨ arrive「抵達」+ -al「表情況」
There won't be any charge for cancellation 3 days prior to the day of **arrival**.
在您抵達前三天取消，我們不會收取任何費用。

補充　New Arrival（廣告標語）新品上市

arrive v. 抵達

中高

8. **attendant**

[əˈtɛndənt]

n. 隨從；侍者

 attend「出席；服侍，照顧」+ -ant「做⋯動作的人」
The flight **attendant** instructed the man to return to his seat immediately due to the high turbulence.
因爲有強烈亂流，空服員指示那位男性立刻回到座位。

補充　flight attendant　飛機空服員

attendance n. 出席人數

中級

9. **baggage**

[ˋbægɪdʒ]

n. 行李

⇨ bag「袋子」+ -age「集合名詞字尾」，裝著大家東西的袋子就是行李

Any **baggage** weighing over 20 kilograms will result in an extra fee of NT$500 dollars per extra kilogram.

行李秤重超過二十公斤者將會被收取每公斤新台幣五百元的超重費。

 baggage claim （機場的）行李提領處
excess baggage 超重行李

同 luggage

---

10. **bellboy**

[ˋbɛLˏbɔI]

n. 旅館侍者

⇨ bell「鐘，鈴」+ boy「男孩」

There is no need to carry all those bags since the **bellboy** can just take care of them for you.

你們不需要拉著那些行李到處跑，因為旅館大廳的服務生可以為你們看顧行李。

典故 早期旅館櫃檯搖鈴叫侍者前來工作，因此得名。

同 bellhop

---

11. **boarding**

[ˋbordɪŋ]

n. 登機

⇨ board「登機，登船」+ -ing「名詞字尾」

Have your **boarding** pass ready to be scanned by the attendant when you reach the front of the line.

請備妥您的登機證，在到達隊伍前方時交給空服人員掃描。

 boarding pass 登機證
boarding gate 登機門

board v. 登上（交通工具）

中高

12. **booking**

[ˋbukɪŋ]

n. 預訂

同 reservation

⇨ book「預訂」+ -ing「名詞字尾」

My travel expenses were cut by twenty percent when I used a recommended **booking** agent.

當我使用建議的代訂服務，我的旅費支出就減少了 20%。

中高

13. **boundary**
[ˋbaʊndrɪ]

n. 邊界；界限

同 border n. 邊界

⇨ bound「界限」+ -ary「名詞字尾」
Giant tech companies are pushing the **boundaries** of what cell phones are capable of doing.
大型科技公司正在擴展手機所能涵蓋功能的範圍。

中高

14. **breathtaking**
[ˋbrɛθ͵tekɪŋ]

adj. 驚豔的；驚險的

同 astonishing / stunning

⇨ breath「呼吸」+ take「拿取」+ -ing「形容詞字尾」，拿走呼吸表示令人屏息的
She finds the views from this mountaintop cottage **breathtaking**.
她發現從這個山頂小屋看出去的景色令人讚嘆。

中高

15. **brochure**
[broˋʃʊr]

n. 小冊子

同 pamphlet / booklet

You don't need to decide your vacation destination now; just browse through these **brochures** and get back to me with your answer.
你不用現在就決定度假地點，只要瀏覽這些小冊子然後帶著你的答案回來找我。

典故 源自法文，原意是「裝訂紙張或書本」。

初級

16. **captain**
[ˋkæptən]

n. 機長；船長

同 chief / leader

⇨ -capit-「頭」+ -an-「表同族群的人」，一群人的頭頭就是長官
The ship's **captain** has advised that everyone return to their cabins - we are about to enter rough waters.
船長建議大家回到自己的船艙，因為我們將通過險惡的水域。

補充 captains of industry 產業龍頭

17. carry-on luggage

[ˈkærɪˌɑn] [ˈlʌɡɪdʒ]
phr. 隨身行李

Any extra **carry-on luggage** will need to be placed under the seat in front of you.
任何額外的手提行李必須放在您前方的座位底下。

 補充　carry-on case/bag 隨身手提行李

 中高

18. Celsius

[ˈsɛlsɪəs]
n. 攝氏溫度
adj. 攝氏溫度的

In desert regions, daily high temperatures can exceed 45 degrees **Celsius**.
在沙漠地區，日間高溫可以超過攝氏四十五度。

典故　Anders Celsius 為將水的冰點和沸點差距分為一百等分的計量方式發明者，後人為表彰他的貢獻，便將這個溫度計算方式以 Celsius 來命名，也就是我們今天常用的「攝氏溫度」。

補充　Fahrenheit n. 華氏溫度

同 centigrade

中級

19. checkout

[ˈtʃɛkˌaʊt]
n. 退房時間；結帳離開；結帳處

 ⇨ check「檢查」+ out「離開」
We need to get everything packed up because **checkout** is at 11:00!
我們需要把所有東西都打包好，因為退房時間是十一點！

補充　check out 辦理退房手續

反 check-in n. 住宿登記；辦理登機

中高

20. civic

[ˈsɪvɪk]
adj. 城市的；市民的

 ⇨ - civ -「城市」+ - ic「形容詞字尾」
It's time for the city council to approve some much needed **civic** improvements, like street lights!
市議會該通過一些像是路燈那樣更需要的市政改善建設了。

補充　civic center 市民展演中心
civic leader 公民領袖

16 交通

17 社交與用餐

18 休閒娛樂

19 醫療保健

20 日常生活

11 製造

12 金融

13 科技術

14 房屋地產

15 出差旅遊

21. climate
[ˈklaɪmɪt]
n. 氣候；風氣，趨勢

The **climate** in the southern region of Argentina produces some of the worst thunderstorms known to man.
阿根廷南部地區的氣候造就了一些有史以來最猛烈的大雷雨。

補充	climate change　　　　　　　氣候變遷
	political/business climate　政治 / 商業氛圍

climatic adj. 氣候的

---

22. cold front
[kold][frʌnt]
n. 冷鋒

反 warm front　暖鋒

The **cold front** moving toward us rapidly will bring torrential rain and high winds.
那道快速朝我們移過來的冷鋒將帶來狂風暴雨。

---

23. concierge
[ˌkɑnsɪˈɛrʒ]
n. 管理員；門房

Although he was quite demanding of his **concierge**, he was also very rewarding, tipping him thousands of dollars.
雖然他對門房相當嚴苛，他也給予相當好的報酬，給了他數千元的小費。

補充	在北美，concierge 也可指旅館服務人員，也稱 hotel concierge。

---

24. counter
[ˈkaʊntɚ]
n. 櫃台

⇨ count「計數」+ - er「= -tory，表地點」，計算數量與錢的地方就是櫃台
If you can't find what you want in the store, just ask the man behind the **counter**.
如果你在店裡找不到你要的東西就問櫃台人員。

補充	check-in counter　　報到櫃台
	under the counter　私下地；非法地

中級

25. **crew**

[kru]

n. 一隊工作人員

The flight **crew** made everyone on the flight relaxed by passing out hot towels and being generous with their drink service.

空服人員藉由發送溫熱的毛巾，以及慷慨的飲料服務來讓機上的每個人放鬆。

補充
flight crew　飛機上的空服人員
ground crew　地面工作人員

同 staff

中高

26. **cruise**

[kruz]

v./n. 巡航；乘船遊覽

cruiser n. 遊艇；巡洋艦

The **cruise** was cut short when a deadly virus was transmitted to dozens of passengers.

遊艇行程在許多乘客遭到致命病毒傳染後就中斷了。

---

27. **customs**

[ˈkʌstəmz]

n. 關稅；海關

custom n. 風俗習慣
customer n. 顧客

同 tariff

Customs agents seized a bag at the airport with five million dollars in cash inside from a suspected drug trafficker.

海關人員在機場從一名毒品嫌犯手中查扣一個裝有五百萬現金的袋子。

---

28. **deluxe**

[dɪˈlʌks]

adj. 豪華的；高級的

同 luxurious

 de - 「法文，同 of，表…的」+ - lux - 「過剩的，奢華的」

I recommend that you order the **deluxe** package.

我推薦你訂購豪華套裝行程。

補充　deluxe suite　豪華套房

11 製造

12 金融

13 科技技術

14 房屋地產

15 出差旅遊

中級

29. **depart**

[dɪ`pɑrt]

v. 啟程；離開

⇨ de- 「分離」 + -part- 「離開」

My flight is scheduled to **depart** at 10 a.m., so we had better get to the airport by eight to check in.

我的班機預計早上十點離開，所以我們最好在八點之前到機場報到。

| 補充 | depart from | 離開；出發 |
| | depart this life | 死亡；過世 |

departure n. 離開；啟程

同 leave

中級

30. **destination**

[ˌdɛstəˋneʃən]

n. 目的地

 destine 「註定」 + -ation 「名詞字尾」

For those with Tokyo as your final **destination**, make sure you fill out a customs form, which will be provided by the flight attendant.

目的地為東京的旅客，請確實填妥空服員提供給您的報關表格。

destine v. 註定；預定

31. **detector**

[dɪˋtɛktɚ]

n. 探測器

 detect 「偵測」 + -or 「做…動作的物品」

Every passenger must walk through a metal **detector** and all items must go through an X-ray machine.

每一位乘客都必須走過金屬探測器，而所有的東西必須經過 X 光機。

| 補充 | lie detector | 測謊器 |
| | metal/smoke detector | 金屬/煙霧探測器 |

detect v. 偵測

detective n. 偵探

中高

32. **drizzle**

[ˈdrɪzl̩]

n. 毛毛雨

v. 下毛毛雨

同 sprinkle

It is going to be cloudy with outbreaks of **drizzle** or light rain.
即將會是多雲偶有小雨的天氣。

中級

33. **drought**

[draʊt]

n. 乾旱；旱災

反 flood n. 洪水；水災

A severe **drought** has ruined all the crops.
嚴重的乾旱使所有的作物都損壞了。

34. **entire**

[ɪnˈtaɪr]

adj. 整個的

entirely adv. 完全地，徹底地

entirety n. 整體

同 whole / complete

反 partial adj. 部分的；局部的

The **entire** town showed up for the school board meeting to show their disapproval of the newly proposed policy.
整個城鎮的人都出席了學校理事會以反對新提出的政策。

中高

35. **escort**

[ˈɛskɔrt]

v./n. 護航；護衛；護送

同 convoy

ex - 「向外」+ correct「改正」

He arrived at the airport with a police **escort** at half past nine.
他在九點半時由警察護送至機場。

中高

36. **exotic**

[ɪɡˋzɑtɪk]

adj. 異國風情的；異國的

同 foreign / alien

👩 exo-「外部的」+ -ic「形容詞字尾」

Maria has filled her entire patio with **exotic** plants, some of which are poisonous.

Maria 將她的整個露臺擺滿了異國植栽，有一些還是有毒的。

補充 exotic species 外來物種

中高

37. **expedition**

[ˌɛkspɪˋdɪʃən]

n. 探險；遠征隊

expeditionary adj. 探險的；遠征的

👩 ex-「向外」+ -ped-「腳」+ -tion「名詞字尾」

Doctor Grant will lead the **expedition** into the Amazon Jungle to study a nearly-extinct species of monkey.

Grant 博士將率領遠征隊進入亞馬遜叢林去研究一種瀕臨絕種的猴子。

中級

38. **extraordinary**

[ɪkˋstrɔrdṇˏɛrɪ]

adj. 不尋常的

同 unusual / uncommon

⇨ extra-「向外；沒有」+ ordinary「尋常的」

Barring **extraordinary** circumstances, the football game will still be played tomorrow noon.

除非有異常的狀況，這場足球賽仍會在明天中午舉行。

★ barring = except for：除…之外

初級

39. **flight**

[flaɪt]

n. 飛行；航班；航程

in-flight adj. 飛行中的

Due to rough weather at my destination, my **flight** was rerouted to a different city.

由於原先目的地天候惡劣，我的班機改變路線降落在另一個城市。

補充 domestic/international flight 國內／國際航班

中級

40. **foggy**

[ˈfɑgɪ]

adj. 有霧的；多霧的

⇨ fog「霧」+ -y「多…的」

It tends to get **foggy** when you drive through these mountains, so you will need to take precautions and slow down when visibility is low.

當你在這些山間開車時很容易遇到起霧，所以你要小心並在能見度降低時放慢速度。

| 補充 | fog lamp （交通工具上的）霧燈 |
| | not have the foggiest idea 一點都不了解 |

中級

41. **freezing**

[ˈfrizɪŋ]

adj. 結冰的；極冷的

⇨ freeze「冷凍」+ -ing「形容詞字尾」

We drove through **freezing** rain and sleet, and when the temperature dropped, the road turned into a sheet of ice.

我們驅車穿過凍雨和雨夾雪，而當氣溫急速下降時，路面就結了一層薄冰。

| 補充 | freezing rain 凍雨 |
| | freezing fog 冰霧 |

中級

42. **frequent**

[ˈfrikwənt]

adj. 頻繁的

As a **frequent** guest at this hotel, Mr. Hoffman enjoys certain perks, like free room service.

作為這家飯店的常客，Hoffman 先生享有特定的禮遇，像是免費的客房服務。

| 補充 | frequent flyer 飛行常客 |
| | FAQ = Frequently Asked Questions 常見問題集 |

frequency n. 頻率
frequently adv. 頻繁地；經常地

43. **frigid**

[ˈfrɪdʒɪd]

adj. 嚴寒的；冷淡的

⇨ -frig-「冰冷的」+ -id「形容詞字尾」

Despite the **frigid** conditions, we stayed at the football stadium to watch the game to the bitter end.

儘管天氣酷寒，我們還是留在足球場觀看比賽直到最後。

★ to the bitter end：堅持到底

frigidity n. 寒冷；冷淡
frigidly adv. 寒冷地；冷淡地

11 製造

12 金融

13 科技技術

14 房屋地產

15 出差旅遊

44. **gate**

[get]

n. 大門；閘門

All passengers for flight KH105, please proceed to **gate** 12.

欲搭乘 KH105 班機的乘客請前往 12 號登機門。

補充　boarding gate 登機門

---

45. **hail**

[hel]

n. 冰雹

v. 下冰雹

同 hailstone

The **hail** was the size of golf balls.

冰雹就跟高爾夫球一樣大。

補充　hail 也可指招計程車或公車的動作，hail a taxi 就是指招計程車。

---

46. **high pressure**

[haɪ][ˈprɛʃ ɚ]

n. 高氣壓

反 low pressure n. 低氣壓

As a **high pressure** system moved into the city, the skies cleared and temperatures dropped.

因為高壓系統移入這個城市，天氣轉晴，溫度也下降了。

---

47. **historic**

[hɪsˈtɔrɪk]

adj. 歷史性的

⇨ **history**「歷史」+ **-ic**「與…相關的」

The town is celebrating the 200th anniversary of the **historic** battle.

這座城鎮正在慶祝一場歷史性戰役的兩百週年紀念。

補充　historic 指有重大歷史意義的，例如 historic site 就是「古蹟，歷史遺跡」。

historian n. 歷史學家

historical adj. 歷史的；史學的

48. hospitality

中高

[ˌhɑspɪˋtæləti]

n. 熱情好客；款待

I am grateful for the **hospitality** of my brother, who let us stay at his place for a week while our electricity was out.

我很感謝我哥哥的款待，他讓我們家裡停電時住在他家一個禮拜。

> **典故** 好客 (hospitality) 和醫院 (hospital) 兩字其實都和主人 (host) 來自同一字源。hospital 原指主人提供來客庇護的場所，而 hospitality 則是指主人接待客人的動作，也就是款待、招待。

> **補充** hospitality area（活動會場的）招待區

hospitable adj. 好客的；招待周到的

---

49. housekeeper

中級

[ˋhausˌkipɚ]

n. 管家；（飯店或醫院的）
　女傭

⇨ house「房子」＋ keeper「維持者」，維持房子整潔的人就是管家、傭人

I phoned the front desk to make sure if the **housekeeper** had stopped by our room this afternoon.

我打了電話給櫃檯確認今天下午飯店的女傭是否有來過我們的房間整理。

---

50. humid

初級

[ˋhjumɪd]

adj. 潮濕的

humidity n. 濕度

同 moist

It is not easy to work in the hot and **humid** weather.
在悶熱潮濕的天氣下工作並不容易。

---

51. imposing

中高

[ɪmˋpozɪŋ]

adj. 壯觀的；莊嚴的；
　令人印象深刻的

同 impressive / spectacular

impose「施加壓力」＋ -ing「形容詞字尾」
The skyline of New York City is quite an **imposing** sight for the tourists.
紐約市的天際線對遊客來說是一種很令人印象深刻的景色。

52. inclement
[ɪnˈklɛmənt]
adj. 氣候嚴酷的

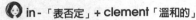 in - 「表否定」 + clement 「溫和的」
Due to **inclement** weather, the company picnic will be postponed until next Saturday.
因為天氣險惡，公司野餐將會延後到下個星期六。

> 補充　clement 表「溫和的」，通常用來指人的個性很溫和、仁慈。17 世紀時，這個字開始用來形容天氣溫和，反義的 inclement 也只會用在形容天氣嚴酷，所以 inclement weather 已是英文中固定的搭配詞組。

inclemency n. 天氣險惡；氣候嚴酷
反 clement adj. 溫和的

53. intensity
[ɪnˈtɛnsətɪ]
n. 強烈；強度

⇨ intense 「強烈的」 + -ity 「名詞字尾」
The storm hit with such **intensity** that a tree fell through the roof.
暴風雨強烈襲擊以致於有棵樹掉落撞穿屋頂。

intense adj. 強烈的
同 strength

54. itinerary
[aɪˈtɪnəˌrɛrɪ]
n. 行程；旅程計劃

⇨ -itiner- 「旅行」 + -ary 「名詞字尾」
We stuck to the **itinerary** until heavy rain forced us to skip the beach completely and we spent the rest of the day at the museum.
我們緊跟著行程走，直到大雨迫使我們整個跳過海灘的部分，然後那天剩下的時間我們都在博物館度過。

同 journey / route

55. jet lag
[dʒɛt][læg]
n. 時差

After catching a late flight across the Atlantic Ocean, Greg played tennis poorly due to **jet lag**.
在搭乘夜班飛機飛越大西洋後，Greg 因為時差的關係網球打得很糟糕。

lag v./n. 落後；遲滯
jet-lagged adj. 有時差的
同 time lag

16 交通

56. landing

初級

[ˈlændɪŋ]

n. 降落

⇨ land「降落」+ -ing「名詞字尾」

The **landing** was a bit bumpy because of the thunderstorm, but the pilot did the best he could under the circumstances.

降落時因爲大雷雨有點顛簸，但是飛員在這樣的情況下已經盡力了。

補充 crash landing n. 迫降

反 takeoff n. 起飛

17 社交與用餐

57. landmark

中高

[ˈlændˌmɑrk]

n. 地標

⇨ land「土地」+ mark「標示」

The huge, rainbow-colored fountain is the town's central **landmark**, and is the backdrop for many wedding photos as well.

那個巨大的七彩噴泉是這個鎮上的地標，而且也是許多婚紗照的背景。

18 休閒娛樂

58. last-minute

[læst][ˈmɪnɪt]

adj. 臨時的；最後的

The **last-minute** change of our vacation destination turned out to be for the best since we got a great deal on our hotel room.

我們臨時更改渡假地點終究是有好處的，因爲我們在住宿上得到很棒的優惠。

19 醫療保健

59. life vest

[laɪf][vɛst]

n. 救生衣

同 life jacket (BrE)

Hank's **life vest** kept him afloat until a passing ferry spotted him hours later.

Hank 的救生衣讓他能持續在海上漂浮，直到一艘經過的渡輪在數小時後發現他。

20 日常生活

60. local

初級

[ˈlokl]

adj. 地方的；當地的

localize v. 使在地化

⇨ -loc-「地方」+ -al「與…有關的」

A **local** guide agreed to take us thirty miles down the river, but no further.

一位當地的嚮導答應帶我們沿著河流下行三十英里，但是就不能再往前了。

中高

61. lounge

[laʊndʒ]

n. 休息室；候機室

The student **lounge** is on the first floor.
學生休息室在一樓。

補充	staff/transit lounge	員工／轉機用休息室
	lounge car	火車上提供餐飲空間的餐車
	lounge music	沙發音樂、輕音樂的一種

中級

62. luggage

[ˈlʌgɪdʒ]

n. 行李

⇨ lug「使勁拉」+ -age「集合名詞字尾」，要使勁拉的就是行李

I'm looking to purchase some expensive **luggage**.
我計劃要買個昂貴的行李箱。

| 補充 | luggage cart 行李推車 |
| | luggage rack 車廂行李架；車頂行李架 |

同 baggage

中級

63. luxurious

[lʌgˈʒʊrɪəs]

adj. 奢華的；非常舒適的

同 deluxe

反 poor adj. 貧窮的；低劣的

⇨ luxury「奢華」+ -ous「充滿…的」
These shops specialize in **luxurious** clothing.
這些店家專門賣奢華的衣服。

中高

64. metropolitan

[ˌmɛtrəˈpɑlətn̩]

adj. 大都市的

n. 都市人

 -metro-「母體，主體」+ -polit-「城市」+ -an「表同族群的人」
Houses in the New York City **metropolitan** area are so overpriced that many people commute to work from hundreds of miles away.
紐約市都會區的房價過高，所以很多人都從幾百英里外通勤到紐約工作。

| 補充 | metro 在美國通常指 metropolitan 的縮寫，即「都會區」。但在非英語系國家，metro 一字通常表示地鐵。例：the Paris Metro 巴黎地鐵。 |

metropolis n. 大都會；首都；首府

同 adj. = urban

16 交通

65. migrant

中高

[ˈmaɪgrənt]

n. 移居者；移民

⇨ -migr- 「移動」 + -ant 「表動作執行者」，移動遷徙的
人就是移民

Thousands of **migrants** work in the orchards of California, moving from place to place wherever they can find work.
數以千計的移民在加州的果園工作，哪兒有工作機會就往哪兒去。

 migratory bird 候鳥

migrate v. 移居，定期的遷移
emigrant n. 移出者
immigrant n. 移入者

17 社交與用餐

66. mileage

中高

[ˈmaɪlɪdʒ]

n. 總英里數

⇨ mile 「英里」 + -age 「集合名詞字尾」

I keep a log book of all the **mileage** that my vehicle incurs from having to drive to business conferences, and I am compensated for fifty cents per mile.
我記錄了所有為參加商務會議的行車總里程數，而且每英里我可以得到五十分錢的補貼。

18 休閒娛樂

67. municipal

中高

[mjuˈnɪsəpl̩]

adj. 市政的；地方自治的

⇨ -muni- 「職責」 + -cip- 「拿取」 + -al 「形容詞字尾」

In addition to already high prices for food and clothing, we also pay a **municipal** sales tax.
除了負擔高額的食物與服飾，我們還要負擔城市稅。

典故 拉丁字 municipalis 原指在羅馬以外的地區城市公民，他們享有羅馬公民的權利，但受各自地區的法令管理。municipal 就是各地方拿取各自的權責，也就是地方自治的。

同 civic

19 醫療保健

68. out of town

[aut][əv][taun]

在城外

We are opening a B & B **out of town**.
我們要在城外開一家民宿。

★ B&B = bed and breakfast，提供床位和早餐的民宿

 out-of-town 為形容詞，表示在城外或市郊的，如 an out-of-town shopping center 市郊購物中心。

20 日常生活

69. overseas

初級

[`ovɚ`siz]

adv. 在海外，在國外
adj. 在海外的；國外的

同 abroad adv. 在國外

⇨ over「超越」+ sea「海」+ s，超越到海的另一邊表示在國外

I lived half of my life **overseas** before finally returning to my homeland for my retirement.
在我最後退休回鄉之前，我在海外住了大半輩子。

---

70. packing

初級

[`pækɪŋ]

n. 包裝；打包

⇨ pack「包裝」+ -ing「名詞字尾」

I always do my own **packing** the night before I leave.
我總是在我動身前一晚打包自己的行李。

補充 send sb. packing 撐走某人

---

71. patience

中級

[`peʃəns]

n. 耐心

⇨ patient「有耐心的」+ -ence「名詞字尾」

Eric does not have the **patience** for a layover of more than three hours, so I would suggest that you book a different flight for him.
Eric 對於中途停留要超過三個小時會沒有耐性，所以我會建議你替他訂不同的班機。

補充 out of patience (with...) 不能再容忍 (某人事物)

反 impatience n. 不耐煩；沒有耐心

---

72. percent

中級

[pɚ`sɛnt]

n. 百分比

★ 英：per cent ／美：percent

There is about a fifty-**percent** chance that our flight will be delayed due to ice on the runway.
我們的班機有百分之五十的機會將會因機場跑道上的結冰而延誤。

典故 源自拉丁文 per centum，表「每一百」。

補充 low/high percentage 比例很低 / 高

percentage n. 百分比；比例

---

73. pickup

中高

[`pɪkʌp]

n. 接送

Please arrange an airport **pickup** service for me.
請幫我安排機場接送服務。

補充 片語 pick up 指接某人或取某物。

中高

74. picturesque

[ˌpɪktʃəˋrɛsk]

adj. 如畫般美麗的

⇨ picture「圖畫」+ -esque「具…風格的」

Taking a stroll through **picturesque** wine country, we stopped at a few vineyards.

散步經過如詩如畫的葡萄酒莊園，我們在一些葡萄園停留。

中高

75. porter

[ˋportɚ]

n. 搬運工；門房 (BrE)

⇨ -port-「搬運」+ -er「做…動作的人」

Be sure to tip the **porter** after having him carry those oversized suitcases.

在搬運工搬好那些超大的行李後一定要給他小費。

 補充 porter 常指在車站及機場的行李搬運工人。

中級

76. proceed

[prəˋsid]

v. 前進

⇨ pro-「向前」+ -ceed-「行進」

Shoppers with credit cards may **proceed** to checkout lanes 8 and 9.

持有信用卡的顧客可以往前到 8 號和 9 號櫃台結帳。

 補充 proceed to do sth. 接著做某事

proceeds n. 收入；收益

初級

77. region

[ˋridʒən]

n. 地區

⇨ -reg-「管理；治理」+ -ion「名詞字尾」，固定管理的地方就形成一個地區

In the northernmost **region** of Canada, the sun never sets in the summer.

在加拿大最北邊的地區，夏天時太陽從不落下。

 補充 in the region of... 大約是…

11 製造

12 金融

13 科技技術

14 房屋地產

15 出差旅遊

中級

78. **reservation**

[ˌrɛzɚˋveʃən]

n. 預約；預訂；保留

 re - 「回來」+ -serv - 「保存」+ -ation「名詞字尾」

I made a **reservation** for this famous restaurant one month ago.

我一個月前就跟這家知名餐廳訂位了。

> 補充　make a reservation 訂位；訂房

reserve v. 預約；保留

同 booking

中高

79. **resort**

[rɪˋzɔrt]

n. 名勝；渡假旅館

 re - 「再次」+ -sort - 「出去」，讓人一再想去的地方就是渡假名勝景點

I think it was worth every penny to stay at the theme park **resort** and enjoy the hotel, park, and beach for one package price.

我認為住在主題樂園渡假飯店，然後以套裝價格享受飯店設施、遊樂園和海灘是非常值得的。

> 補充　resort 當動詞用指「訴諸、採用」，如：
> resort to law　　訴諸法律途徑解決
> resort to violence 採取暴力手段

---

80. **round-trip**

[raʊnd][trɪp]

adj. 來回的；雙程的

⇨ round「完整繞一圈」+ trip「旅程」

Since a one-way ticket was almost as expensive, I just bought a **round-trip** ticket.

由於單程票價幾乎和來回票一樣貴，我就買了一張來回票。

> 補充　(AmE) round-trip ticket = (BrE) return ticket
> 來回票

反 one-way adj. 單程的

初級

81. **separate**

[ˋsɛprɪt]

adj. 分開的；各自的

[ˋsɛpəˌret]

v. 分離，分開

⇨ se - 「分離」+ -par - 「準備」+ -ate「動詞字尾」

May we have **separate** checks, please?

請問我們可以分開結帳嗎？

separation n. 分離；分開

separately adv. 各自地，單獨地

中級

82. sightseeing

['saɪtˌsiɪn]

n. 觀光；遊覽

sightsee v. 觀光；遊覽
sightseer n. 觀光客；遊客

⇨ sight「景色」+ see「看」+ -ing「名詞字尾」，看景色就是指觀光

We have set the whole day aside to go **sightseeing** at all the famous landmarks around Paris.
我們已經撥出一整天在巴黎周邊所有著名的地標景點觀光。

初級

83. single

['sɪŋgl]

adj. 單人的

The triple rooms are all booked up, but we can arrange a double room and a **single** room for you at the same price.
三人房全都訂滿了，但我們可以相同價格為您安排一間雙人房和一間單人房。

 single bed　單人床
single room　單人房

中高

84. spectacular

[spɛk'tækjələ]

adj. 壯觀的；驚人的
n. 壯觀場面；盛大演出

⇨ spectacle「壯觀的場面」+ -ar「具…性質的」

The fireworks looked **spectacular**.
煙火看起來很壯觀。

 a spectacular success 驚人的成就

初級

85. stay

[ste]

v./n. 停留

Do you prefer **staying** at a hotel or at a B&B?
你比較喜歡住飯店還是住民宿？

 stay behind　　　仍留在原地
stay up　　　　　熬夜
an overnight stay 只待一晚

86. stopover

['stɑpˌovɚ]

n. 中途停留

Our three-hour **stopover** in Japan turned into a two-day ordeal when a blizzard kept us snowed in at the airport.
暴風雪將我們困在機場，讓我們原本在日本三小時的中途停留變成兩天的苦難。

 片語 stop over 指「中途停留」。

 layover

11
製造

12
金融

13
科技技術

14
房屋地產

15
出差旅遊

中高

87. **suite**

[swit]

n. (旅館的) 套房；一套家具

The famous Hollywood couple spent $500,000 on a honeymoon **suite** at the exclusive hotel.
那對有名的好萊塢夫婦花了五十萬在專屬的旅館蜜月套房上。

補充 C-suite：公司高階經理人 (因高階經理人頭銜多以字母 C 開頭，如：執行長 CEO、財務長 CFO、營運長 COO 等。)

初級

88. **temperature**

[ˈtɛmprətʃɚ]

n. 氣溫；體溫

⇨ temperate「溫和的」+ -ure「名詞字尾」
I was shocked at how the **temperature** dropped rapidly after the sun went down out in the desert.
我很驚訝沙漠裡的氣溫會在太陽下山後這麼急速的下降。

補充 have/run a temperature 發高燒
take sb's temperature 量體溫

中級

89. **thunderstorm**

[ˈθʌndɚˌstɔrm]

n. 大雷雨，雷暴

thunderclap n. 雷鳴；霹靂；晴天霹靂的消息
thundershower n. 雷陣雨

⇨ thunder「雷」+ storm「暴風雨」
The violent **thunderstorm** blew down several trees and knocked out the power to half of the city.
這起強烈雷雨將幾棵樹吹倒，也讓大半個城市電力中斷了。

中高

90. **token**

[ˈtokən]

n. 象徵；紀念品；代幣

Please accept this handmade silk scarf as a small **token** of our friendship.
請收下這條手工絲巾做為我們友誼的紀念。

補充 as a token of gratitude/appreciation 以表謝意

16 交通

17 社交與用餐

18 休閒娛樂

19 醫療保健

20 日常生活

中級

91. **tourist**

[ˈtʊrɪst]

n. 旅客

⇨ tour「旅遊」+ -ist「做…動作的人」

This world-famous theme park is actually a **tourist** trap-once inside, you are forced to overpay for everything.

這個世界知名的主題樂園實際上是個遊客陷阱，一旦進去，你就得被迫為每樣東西多付錢。

 tourist attraction　觀光景點
tourist season　　旅遊季節

初級

92. **travel**

[ˈtrævl̩]

v./n. 旅行

Being a novice at world **travel**, Sheila used an agent to arrange everything for her European tour.

身為一名世界旅遊的新手，Sheila 找了位旅遊仲介為她安排歐洲旅行的大小事。

 travel agency　　旅行社
travel expense　　旅費
traveler's check　旅行支票

traveler n. 旅客；遊客

中高

93. **undo**

[ʌnˈdu]

v. 解開；消除

⇨ un-「表相反的動作」+ do「做」，做出相反動作表示消除原來的動作

Can someone help me to **undo** my seat belt?

有人可以幫我解開安全帶嗎？

Once you confirm your order, you will not be able to **undo** it, as all transactions on these discounted items are final.

一旦你確認了訂單，你將無法取消，因為這些特價品的所有交易是不可以更改的。

同 unfasten　v. 解開

中高

94. **unlock**

[ʌnˈlɑk]

v. 開…的鎖

同 open

⇨ un-「表相反的動作」+ lock「鎖」

Ask Grandma for the four-digit combination to **unlock** her suitcase.

跟奶奶問那四位數密碼好打開她的手提箱。

11 製造

12 金融

13 科技技術

14 房屋地產

15 出差旅遊

中高
95. unpack
[ʌnˋpæk]
v. 打開（包裹）取出東西

⇨ un-「表相反的動作」+ pack「打包」
You will find an empty wardrobe and chest of drawers in your room if you would like to **unpack**.
如果你要開行李整理，房間裡有一個空的衣櫥和五斗櫃。

中高
96. via
[ˋvɪə] / [ˋvaɪə]
prep. 經過；透過，經由

We flew to Athens **via** Paris.
我們經由巴黎飛往雅典。
Parents will receive notification **via** text message if classes are canceled.
如果停課，家長會經由簡訊收到通知。

初級
97. view
[vju]
n. 景色；觀點
v. 觀看；看待

I will pay extra for a hotel room with a perfect **view** of the snowcapped mountains.
我會為了住進能看到絕佳雪山景色的旅館房間付額外費用。

補充	sea/mountain view	海／山景
	a room with a view	景觀房
	point of view	觀點
	in view of	考慮到；有鑑於

viewer n. 觀眾
viewpoint n. 觀點

中高
98. visa
[ˋvizə]
n.（護照上的）簽證

Americans may stay up to 14 days in Taiwan without a **visa**.
美國人可以免簽證在台灣停留最多十四天。

補充　transit visa n. 過境簽證

中級

99. **voyage**

[ˈvɔɪdʒ]

n. 旅行；航行

⇨ **- voy -**「道路，途徑」**+ - age**「集合名詞字尾」

The **voyage** around the African continent will last around two months, and dozens of crew members will be needed.

這趟繞行非洲大陸的旅程將持續約兩個月，而且會需要很多名船員。

 補充
Bon voyage! （祝福語）旅途愉快！
maiden voyage 處女航

voyager n. 航行者；航海者

中級

100. **warning**

[ˈwɔrnɪŋ]

n. 警報

⇨ **warn**「警告」**+ - ing**「名詞字尾」

Without **warning**, the boat capsized, and we were flung into the ocean.

在沒有警報的情況下，船翻覆了，而我們都被拋進大海中。

 補充
oral/verbal warning 口頭警告
warning bell 警鐘；警訊

實力進階

Part 1. 常見旅館房型

旅館房型通常依人數或所附設備分類，常見的有：

single room	單人房，通常為一張單人床和簡易的書桌和衣櫃
double room	雙人房，通常為一張雙人床的房型
twin room	雙人房，為兩張單人床的雙人房型
triple room	三人房，通常為三張單人床或一大床一小床的房型
quad room	四人房，通常為四張單人床，有時也會是兩張雙人床的房型
suite	套房，通常房間內會包含數個隔開的房間和床，還有獨立的沙發客廳，一些商務飯店的套房還會附小型廚房或會客室以利商務旅客使用。常見的飯店套房形式有：business suite(商務套房)、honeymoon suite(蜜月套房)、presidential suite(總統套房)或 royal suite(皇家套房)

Part 2. 飯店旅館基本設施 (basic amenities)

(1) 客房內設施：

TVs	電視。雖然多數飯店都有電視及免付費的頻道，但一些商務型飯店都會提供可另外付費的有線電視頻道 (cable) 或隨選視訊 (VOD) 的服務。
Internet access	網路使用。許多具一定規模的飯店多半會提供免費網路給房客使用，最常使用的上網方式是無線網路 (wi-fi)，其次則為有線網路 (hard-wired)，一些飯店也會在飯店大廳提供住客免費使用電腦。
Kitchen facilities	廚房設備。為讓長住型旅客方便，一些週租公寓旅館或商務飯店會在客房內配置小型廚房 (kitchenette)，並附有微波爐及小型冰箱，此類型設施通常稱為 MicroFridge。
Dryers & Irons	吹風機和熨斗，一些飯店也有提供自動熨衣板，只要將衣物依指示套掛夾好即可自動加熱熨燙衣物。
Personal care amenities	個人保養用品，包含毛巾、洗髮精、潤髮乳、沐浴乳、洗面乳及可拋式的牙刷、牙膏和刮鬍刀及梳子等用品。

(2) 飯店公用設施：

Vending machines	自動販賣機，最常見的就是各種飲料的販賣機，一些飯店也會提供投幣式的零食或冰淇淋販賣機。
Laundromat	自助洗衣機，商務飯店多半會提供投幣式洗衣機以方便住客換洗衣物。
Restaurants	餐廳，多半為提供旅客可吃早午晚餐的餐廳。
Gym & Sauna	健身房及三溫暖，許多商務型飯店會提供住客使用健身房或三溫暖以舒解商旅疲勞。
Other recreations	如游泳池、室內或室外球場，一些渡假中心甚至還包含高爾夫球場等設備。

Part 3. 常見飯店早餐型式

飯店住房通常含早餐與不含早餐兩種，若為含早餐，多以自助餐 (buffet) 形式供應，常見的西式早餐有：

Continental breakfast	歐陸式早餐，內容通常為簡單的吐司、可頌等麵包配起司、肉片、果醬或奶油，以及水果、果汁和咖啡等飲料。
American-style breakfast	美式早餐，內容包括吐司、麵包，並有培根、蛋、肉或香腸，有時也提供早餐穀片，另搭配咖啡、牛奶或果汁。
English breakfast	英式早餐，傳統英式早餐的內容主要有炒蛋、煎蛋或水煮蛋佐炒培根、香腸、香菇或番茄，還會搭配炸麵包、布丁或吐司。

16 交通

17 社交與用餐

18 休閒娛樂

19 醫療保健

20 日常生活

161

隨堂練習

★ 請根據句意，選出最適合的單字

(　　) 1. Since the Ebola outbreak continues to spread, our health ministry has issued a travel _____.
(A) alert
(B) boundary
(C) expedition
(D) checkout

(　　) 2. David and Amy decided to hold their wedding at a famous ski _____ in Korea because both of them have a mania for skiing.
(A) cruise
(B) lounge
(C) landing
(D) resort

(　　) 3. These travel _____ may help you have some ideas about where to spend your vacation.
(A) escorts
(B) customs
(C) brochures
(D) porters

(　　) 4. If you don't have time, you can ask the travel agent to plan your _____.
(A) itinerary
(B) visa
(C) intensity
(D) token

(　　) 5. It is a good idea to make a(n) _____ well in advance since this restaurant is always the top choice during the holiday seasons.
(A) warning
(B) accommodation
(C) reservation
(D) landing

解答：1. A　2. D　3. C　4. A　5. C

Unit 16 交通

中高

1. accelerate
[æk`sɛləˌret]

v. 加速；促進；前進

acceleration n. 加快；加速
accelerator n. 加速器，油門

同 speed up

🙎 ac-「to」+ -celer-「加速」+ -ate「使…」
The train **accelerates** from zero to two hundred kilometers per hour in just 35 seconds.
列車會在三十五秒內由時速零加速到時速兩百公里。

中高

2. accessible
[æk`sɛsəbl]

adj. 容易進入的；易懂的

access v. 進入

⇨ access「進入」+ -ible「可…的」
Each floor of your building must be **accessible** by wheelchair, so an elevator will need to be installed along with ramps.
你們大樓的每一層都應讓輪椅方便進入，所以除了坡道外也要安裝電梯。

初級

3. aircraft
[`ɛrˌkræft]

n. 飛機；航空器

同 airplane n. 飛機

⇨ air「天空」+ craft「工藝」
At our National Aviation Museum, you can see actual **aircraft** which have been decommissioned and restored to mint condition.
在我們的國家航空博物館，你可以看到已經退役的實體飛機，並且被完好如初地保存著。
★ in mint condition：完好無缺，像新的一樣

中級

4. automobile
[`ɔtəməˌbɪl]

n. 汽車

同 car

⇨ auto-「自動的」+ mobile「可移動的」
Owning an **automobile** is expensive, with insurance, taxes, and maintenance all adding up.
擁有一輛汽車要花很多錢，包括保險費、稅金和維修費用。

補充 automobile industry 汽車產業

11 製造

12 金融

13 科技技術

14 房屋地產

15 出差旅遊

中高

5. **aviation**

[ˌevɪˈeʃən]

n. 飛行；航空學

 - avi - 「鳥」 + - ation「名詞字尾」

The **aviation** industry is looking to hire thousands of new pilots over the next ten years.
航空業正思考在未來十年內要雇用數千名新機師。

補充　aviation insurance　航空保險

中級

6. **barrier**

[ˈbærɪr]

n. 障礙；障礙物；隔閡

Strong **barriers** have been erected on either side of the train tracks to prevent derailments.
在鐵道兩側已豎起堅固的屏障以防止出軌。

補充　barrier-free　　　無障礙的
　　　no-tariff barrier　無關稅障礙

---

7. **bicyclist**

[ˈbaɪsɪklɪst]

n. 單車騎士

⇨ bicycle「自行車」 + - ist「具專長的人」

A **bicyclist** was knocked off his bicycle by a hit and run driver.
有一名駕駛撞倒一位單車騎士後逃逸。

★ hit and run：指汽機車肇事逃逸

初級

8. **block**

[blɑk]

n. 街區；(BrE) 大樓；一組
v. 阻塞；封鎖

blockage n. 堵塞，阻塞物

To get to the library, go straight down this road for about six **blocks**.
要去圖書館，你要往這條路尾直走約六個街區。

補充　an office block　　　(BrE) 辦公大樓
　　　make block booking　訂購團體票

中高

9. **boulevard**

[ˈbuləˌvɑrd]

n. 林蔭大道

同 avenue
縮 Blvd.

The glamorous star likes to stroll down the **boulevard** uptown, stopping at all the high-end boutiques.
那位大明星喜歡沿著高級住宅區的林蔭大道逛街，並在所有高級精品店走走看看。

典故　源自法文和荷蘭文，原意指「堡壘」，後演變指堡壘拆除後所留下的大馬路。

中高

10. **buckle**

[ˈbʌkl̩]

n. 皮帶釦，扣環
v. 扣住；扣緊

Although the child was in the car seat, the **buckle** on the seat belt was not fastened, so the mother received a hefty fine from the police officer.
雖然小孩有坐在安全椅上，但安全帶上的扣環沒綁好，所以那位媽媽被警察開了張鉅額罰單。

 補充
buckle up　　　扣上安全帶
buckle down　　積極投入

中級

11. **cabin**

[ˈkæbɪn]

n. 客艙，機艙；小屋

The seats in first class **cabin** are ten centimeters wider than those in economy class.
頭等艙的座椅比經濟艙的還要寬十公分。
We can drive up to my parents' **cabin** by the lake this weekend and spend all our time fishing.
我們這個週末可以開車到我爸媽的湖邊小屋，然後釣魚釣個夠。

 補充
cabin crew　機艙服務人員
log cabin　　木屋

中級

12. **canal**

[kəˈnæl]

n. 運河；渠道

同 waterway

Brad proposed to Rachel while floating on a gondola on Venice's Grand **Canal**.
當乘坐平底船在威尼斯大運河上遊覽時，Brad 向 Rachel 求婚了。

 比較　channel n. 水道；海峽；頻道

中級

13. **cargo**

[ˈkɑrgo]

n. 貨物

同 freight

The United States sent twenty **cargo** planes filled with supplies to Africa to combat the Ebola epidemic.
美國派遣了二十架裝滿補給品的貨機飛往非洲以對抗伊波拉疫情。

 補充　cargo ship/plane 貨船 / 貨機

11
製造

12
金融

13
科技技術

14
房屋地產

15
出差旅遊

中高
14. **cautious**
['kɔʃəs]
adj. 小心的；謹慎的

caution n. 小心；謹慎
cautiously adv. 小心地；謹慎地

同 careful

😊 caution「謹慎」+ -ous「充滿…的」
You need to be overly **cautious** when driving on the highways during winter due to black ice.
冬天在高速公路上開車時因為有路面結冰，你得要特別小心。
★ black ice：路面結冰，因冰是透明的，結冰後路面還是原本的黑色，但表面卻是一層冰，因此得名。

中高
15. **chaos**
['keɑs]
n. 混亂

chaotic adj. 混亂的
chaotically adv. 混亂地

Chaos ensued when the state government told citizens to evacuate and move further inland.
州政府要求市民撤離並移至較內陸地區時引發了混亂。

補充 be in chaos 凌亂不堪，一團亂

中高
16. **circuit**
['sɜ˙kɪt]
n. 環道；電路迴圈

😊 circum -「環繞」+ -it -「走」
The drivers are testing their cars and tires on the racing **circuit**.
駕駛們正在賽車環道上測試他們的車子和輪胎。

補充 circuit board 電路板

初級
17. **coach**
[kotʃ]
n. 遊覽車，長途巴士

The coach tour is a great way to see the sights.
搭長途巴士旅遊是觀光的一個好方法。

補充 a railway coach 火車車廂

中高

18. **commute**

[kə`mjut]

v./n. 通勤

⇨ com-「表加強語氣」+ -mut-「改變」

Bob **commutes** to work on the elevated train since the parking fees near his downtown office are sky high.

Bob 搭高架鐵路通勤上班，因為他市中心辦公室旁的停車費根本就是天價。

★ elevated train：高架鐵路列車

典故 commute 原指付款方式改變，19 世紀時的 commutation ticket 指坐火車或電車所用的季票，季票改變了每次搭乘都要付錢的付款方式，且用季票的乘客多為每日往返住家和工作地的通勤族，後便引申出以 commute 表「通勤」的意思。

補充 within commuting distance
在可通勤往返的範圍內

commuter n. 通勤者

中級

19. **conductor**

[kən`dʌktɚ]

n. 列車長，車掌

⇨ conduct「指揮」+ -or「做…動作的人」

The train **conductor** informed us that there would be an extended stopover in the next city due to maintenance issues.

火車列車長通知我們，由於維修因素，我們在下個城市暫停的時間會拉長。

同 guard (BrE)

中高

20. **convertible**

[kən`vɝtəbl]

n. 敞篷車

adj. 可轉換的

 convert「轉換」+ -ible「可…的」

I haven't been able to put the top down on my **convertible** all year due to all the heavy rain we've been having.

由於我們這一直在下大雨，所以我一整年都還沒辦法把我的敞篷車頂蓋放下來。

convert v. 轉換

同 n. = cabriolet (BrE)

中高

21. **crooked**

[`krukɪd]

adj. 彎曲的；歪的；變形的

⇨ crook「使彎曲」+ -ed「形容詞字尾」

The car door was knocked **crooked** due to the accident.
車門因為車禍被撞凹了。

補充 crooked roads/streets 彎曲的路 / 街道

反 straight adj. 直的

中高

22. **crossing**

['krɔsɪŋ]

n. 交叉口；穿越道；
河流的渡口

cross v. 穿越

⇨ cross「穿越，交叉」+ - ing「名詞字尾」

A car broke through the barrier at the railroad **crossing**.
有一輛汽車闖越了在鐵路平交道的柵欄。

補充

railroad crossing 鐵路平交道
zebra crossing 斑馬線
pelican crossing
自控式人行穿越道 (行人可自按紅燈令車輛停下以
過馬路)

中高

23. **crossroad**

['krɔsˌrod]

n. 十字路口；重大的抉擇時刻

⇨ cross「穿越，交叉」+ road「馬路」

The nearest **crossroads** to our store is Main and Spring
Streets; just remember to park in the lot at the back of
the store.
離我們商店最近的一個十字路口是 Main Street 和 Spring
Street 的交叉口，記得把車子停到我們商店後方的停車場。

補充 at the crossroads 處在抉擇的緊要關頭

中高

24. **cruiser**

['kruzɚ]

n. 遊艇；巡邏艦；巡邏車

⇨ cruise「巡航」+ - er「做…動作的事物」

A police **cruiser** circles this block twice a day looking for
signs of mischief.
一輛警察的巡邏車每天在這個街區繞行兩次以搜尋是否有傷害
發生。

中高

25. **curb**

[kɝb]

n. 路邊，高於路面的人行道
邊欄

★ 英：kerb ／美：curb

You can park right next to the **curb** on most streets in
this city for free, but on Main Street you need to pay at
a parking meter.
你可以免費將車停在本市大部份地區的路邊，但在 Main
Street 上你得要付停車費。

16 交通

26. 初級 **delay**

[dɪˋle]

v./n. 耽擱；延遲

Ladies and Gentlemen, white-out blizzard conditions are causing a four-hour **delay** to Flight 254 to Detroit.

各位女士及先生，暴風雪使飛往底特律的第 254 號班機延遲四小時起飛。

★ white-out：指因大雪或雲霧造成能見度為零的天候狀況。

補充　without delay　刻不容緩

---

17 社交與用餐

27. **detour**

[ˋditʊr]

v./n. 繞道；繞行路線

 de -「離開」+ -tour -「轉彎」

Road construction on Main Street forced traffic to be **detoured** through Long Street.

Main Street 上的道路施工使車流繞行到 Long Street 上。

補充　to make/take a detour　繞道而行

---

18 休閒娛樂

28. 中級 **downward**

[ˋdaʊnwəd]

adj. 向下的

downwards adv. 向下地

反 upward adj. 向上的

 down「向下」+ -ward「朝…方向」

There is a **downward** slope crossing under the highway.

有一個向下的斜坡穿越高速公路的下方。

---

19 醫療保健

29. 中高 **driveway**

[ˋdraɪˌwe]

n. 私人車道；社區馬路

⇨ drive「駕駛」+ way「道路」

Parking your car on the **driveway** is fine until December.

到十二月之前，把車子停在社區道路上是沒關係的。

---

20 日常生活

30. 中高 **enclosure**

[ɪnˋkloʒə]

n. 圍住；圍籬，圍欄

enclose v. 圈起；隨信裝入

⇨ enclose「圍住」+ -ure「名詞字尾」

Our exotic pets are kept in an **enclosure** in the back yard.

我們的稀有異國寵物都被關在後院的圍欄裡。

中級

31. **escalator**

[ˈɛskəˌletə]

n. 電扶梯

escalade「用梯子攀爬」+ elevator「電梯」

The airport renovation includes an **escalator** that runs from the baggage claim area to the parking garage on the top level.

機場整修工程包括增建由行李提領區直達頂樓停車場的電扶梯。

中級

32. **explore**

[ɪkˈsplor]

v. 探索；探究

➡ ex-「向外」+ -plor-「喊叫」

We need to **explore** all the possible options for diverting traffic out of this congested area.

我們需要探究所有可使這個塞車區域的車流改道的選項。

典故 explore 原指獵人間的術語，源起於打獵出發前的吆喝，因此向外喊叫 explore 就成爲去探險、探索。

explorer n. 探險家
exploration n. 探查；探索

33. **expressway**

[ɪkˈsprɛsˌwe]

n. 快速道路

➡ express「快速的」+ way「道路」

With the opening of the new **expressway**, I can commute to downtown in less than half the time it took me before.

隨著新的快速道路啓用，我只需花比以往一半還要少的時間就可以通勤到市中心。

補充 highway 與 expressway 都是美式用語。highway 指公路或翻譯爲「高速公路」；expressway 則指城市內的快速幹道。

中級

34. **fare**

[fɛr]

n. 交通工具的票價；車資

If you add up all the **fares** you spend taking public transportation for a month, it is small compared with the costs associated with driving your car everywhere.

如果你將一個月內花在大眾交通工具上的車資加總起來，比起你自己開車到各處的費用絕對少很多。

補充 half-fare/full-fare ticket 半票 / 全票

中級

35. **fasten**

[ˈfæsn̩]

v. 繫緊；扣上

fastener n. 扣件；鈕扣

反 unfasten v. 解開；鬆開

The children's car seats need to be **fastened** securely to the seats they rest on or they will fly forward if there is an accident.

兒童汽車安全座椅需要牢牢繫在孩子們坐的位子上，不然發生意外時他們會往前飛。

中級

36. **ferry**

[ˈfɛrɪ]

n. 渡輪

同 ferryboat

⇨ **- fer -** 「載運」 + **- ry** 「名詞字尾」，載客的船就是渡輪

The only way to get your car over to the private island is to drive it onto the **ferry** and take it across.

要將你的汽車送到那座私人島上的唯一方法，就是把它開到渡輪上然後運過去。

中級

37. **forbid**

[fɚˈbɪd]

v. 禁止

forbidden adj. 被禁止的
forbiddance n. 禁止

⇨ **for -** 「離開」 + **bid** 「命令」，命令人離開某行為表示去禁止

I **forbid** you to drive while intoxicated.

我禁止你在酒醉的狀況下開車。

 補充 God/Heaven forbid.
拜託不要。(期望事情不會發生的感嘆詞)

中級

38. **fuel**

[ˈfjuəl]

n. 燃料

biofuel n. 生質燃料
fuel-efficient adj. 節能的

Research has shown that hydrogen has been a viable alternative car **fuel**.

研究顯示氫氣是可行的汽車替代燃料。

 補充 add fuel to the fire/flames　火上加油
alternative fuel　　　　　　替代性燃料

11 製造

12 金融

13 科技技術

14 房屋地產

15 出差旅遊

39. gondola
[ˋɡɑndələ]
n. 纜車

My commute time to the mountain-top university has been cut to just twenty minutes thanks to the opening of the **gondola** sky lift.

幸好空中運輸纜車開始運行，我通勤到山頂大學的時間縮短到只要二十分鐘就到了。

補充　gondola 也指威尼斯特有的平底小船，這種船的船伕就叫做 gondolier。

同 gondola lift / cable car

---

40. helicopter
[ˋhɛlɪkɑptɚ]
n. 直升機

⇨ helicon -「螺旋」+ pteron「拉丁文，翅膀」，以螺旋槳當機翼飛起的就是直升機

The ambulance driver called in a **helicopter** to quickly transport the victims of the head-on car crash on the highway to a hospital.

救護車駕駛呼叫直升機將高速公路上汽車對撞車禍的傷患迅速送到醫院去。

補充　helicopter pad　直升機起降場
helicopter parent 直升機家長(喻過度保護或處處干預孩子行動的父母)

---

41. immense
[ɪˋmɛns]
adj. 廣大的；無限的

⇨ im -「表否定」+ -mens -「測量」，大到無法測量

An **immense** amount of money and time has been put into the construction of the subway system.

大量的金錢和時間被投注在建造地下鐵系統。

immensely adv. 廣大地；無限地；非常地
immensity n. 無限；廣大；巨大

---

42. impact
[ˋɪmpækt]
n. 衝擊
[ɪmˋpækt]
v. 衝擊

⇨ im -「進入」+ -pact -「打擊」，打進去就造成衝擊

The **impact** of the newly-opened subway line was immediate, with freeway traffic being reduced by 40% in the first week of the line's operation.

這條剛開始營運的地鐵線所產生的衝擊是很直接的，在營運第一週就讓高速公路的車流量減少了百分之四十。

補充　have an impact on　對…造成衝擊

中高

43. intersection

[ˌɪntɚˈsɛkʃən]

n. 路口

 inter-「在…之間」+ section「區域」

The **intersection** of Broad Street and Fourth Street is the most dangerous one in the city.

本市最危險的十字路口在 Broad Street 和 Fourth Street 的交會處。

intersectional adj. 交集的；區間的

中高

44. jaywalk

[ˈdʒeˌwɔk]

v. 亂穿越馬路

 jay「(謔) 鄉下人」+ walk「走路」

Although he was only ten meters away from a crosswalk, Gary tried to **jaywalk** instead.

儘管 Gary 離行人穿越道只有十公尺，但他還是想穿越馬路。

| 典故 | jay 原指「松鴉」，松鴉是鄉下才有的鳥類，20 世紀時被拿來做為鄉下人、鄉巴佬的代稱，因鄉下人不清楚都市馬路規則，常無視指揮或號誌闖越馬路，造成交通問題，後來就出現以 jaywalk 來稱呼鄉下人隨意行走、穿越馬路的動作。 |

jaywalker n. 亂穿越馬路的人

---

45. jeopardy

[ˈdʒɛpɚdɪ]

n. 風險；危險；危難

Walking around in this part of town wearing such flashy clothes could put your life in **jeopardy**.

穿著如此花俏的服裝在城裡這個區域走動可能會讓你有生命危險。

| 補充 | in jeopardy　處於危險之中 |

jeopardize v. 危及；冒…的危險

jeopardous adj. 危險的；冒險的

同 danger / risk

中級

46. lane

[len]

n. 車道；通道；巷弄

Traffic on the expressway was finally alleviated when the road was widened from three to five **lanes** in the downtown area.

市中心馬路由三線車道變五線後，快速道路上的車流量終於紓解了。

| 補充 | bus lane　　　　　　公車專用道
life in the fast lane　節奏快速、緊張忙碌的生活
It is a long lane that has no turning.
[諺語]：否極泰來。 |

11
製造

中級

47. lean

[lin]

v./n. 傾斜

Do not **lean** on the doors of the subway.
請勿倚靠在地鐵車門上。

補充	lean down	彎下腰
	lean on	依賴；施壓
	bend/lean over backwards	竭盡全力

12
金融

中級

48. load

[lod]

v./n. 裝載

The truck ahead is carrying a wide **load**.
我們正前方的卡車載滿了東西。

補充	get/take a load off one's feet 坐下；放鬆
	get/take a load off one's mind
	因擔憂或問題解決而鬆一口氣
	a load of N. 很多 N.

13
科技技術

overload v./n. 超載
upload v./n.（網路）上載，上傳
download v./n.（網路）下載

14
房屋地產

中高

49. navigate

[ˈnævəˌget]

v. 航行；導航

 - nav - 「船」 + igate 「源自拉丁文 agere，表駕駛」
Before GPS systems were built into car dashboards to **navigate** the route to your destination, people had to actually know how to read road maps!
在可做目的地路線導航的 GPS 系統成為汽車儀表板的內建功能前，人們得知道如何看懂道路地圖！

navigator n. 領航員；航海家
navigation n. 航行；航運

15
出差旅遊

50. overcrowd

[ˌovəˈkraud]

v. 過度擁擠

⇨ over - 「超過」 + crowd 「擠，塞滿」
The bus was so **overcrowded** that the driver did not allow any new passengers to get on.
公車太擁擠了以致於司機不讓任何新乘客上車。

overcrowded adj. 過度擁擠的

初級

51. **overpass**

[`ovɚpæs]

n. 天橋

⇨ over「在上方的」+ pass「通過」，可以讓人從上方通過的就是天橋

There is a pedestrian **overpass** which connects all four corners of this intersection, keeping those who commute on foot safe from the dangerous drivers below.

有一座行人天橋連結這個交叉路口的四個角落，讓行人能避掉下方的危險駕駛以確保自身安全。

 中級

52. **parallel**

[`pærəlɛl]

adj. 平行的

v. 與…平行

 para -「在…旁邊」+ -allel -「另一個」

The construction boss pointed out that the workers had not painted **parallel** lines to mark the different lanes on the road.

工頭指出工人還沒在馬路上漆上區隔不同車道的平行線。

補充 parallel imports 平行輸入品；水貨

 中高

53. **paralyze**

[`pærəlaɪz]

v. 使癱瘓

★ 英：paralyse ／美：paralyze

 para -「在…旁邊」+ -ly -「鬆開」+ -ize「使…」

A head-on collision between two motorcycles **paralyzed** both of the riders.

兩輛機車對撞使兩名騎士都癱瘓了。

The airport is still **paralyzed** by the snowstorm.

因爲暴風雪的緣故，機場仍舊是癱瘓的狀態。

paralysis n. 麻痺；癱瘓

---

54. **parking lot**

[`parkɪŋ][lat]

n. 停車場

同 car park

This **parking lot** is full. We have to park our car somewhere else.

停車場沒位子了。我們得到其他地方去停車。

55. **passenger**

['pæsndʒɚ]

n. 乘客；旅客

⇨ passage「通行」+ - er「做…動作的人」

This seven-**passenger** vehicle still has enough room in the back to carry everyone's luggage.
這輛七人座客車後方還有足夠空間可載運每個人的行李。

補充　a passenger train　客運火車

56. **passageway**

['pæsɪdʒ͵we]

n. 通道

同 passage

The hikers groped their way along the pitch-black **passageway,** hoping to somehow find an exit.
登山者沿著漆黑的通道摸索著前進的路，希望能找到個出口。

57. **path**

[pæθ]

n. 小路；步道

All the signs in the park warn visitors to stay on the **path** so as not to disturb the natural habitat.
公園裡所有的標示都警告訪客要待在步道上，以免破壞了動植物的天然棲息地。

補充　flight path　飛行路線

58. **pedestrian**

[pə'dɛstrɪən]

n. 行人

⇨ pedester「拉丁文，以腳走路」+ - ian「表同族群的人」，以腳走路的族群就是行人

Crosswalks at each intersection need to be widened in this part of town to accommodate increased **pedestrian** traffic.
城裡這一區的每個路口的行人穿越道都需要加寬，以符合日益增加的行人往來需求。

中高

59. **petroleum**

[pə'trolɪəm]

n. 石油

 -petr- 「石頭」 + oleum 「拉丁文，油」

Our dependence on **petroleum**-based fuels is dangerous; we need to start using alternative sources of energy more.

我們倚賴以石油爲主的燃料是很危險的，我們得開始多使用替代性能源才行。

補充	unleaded petrol/gasoline	無鉛汽油
---	diesel	柴油
	kerosene	煤油

petrol n. 汽油 (AmE= gasoline)

易混 patrol v. 巡邏

中高

60. **pier**

[pɪr]

n. 碼頭

同 wharf

You can get your river bus ticket at the **pier** ticket office before boarding.

你可以在登船前先到碼頭售票處購買你的水上巴士船票。

中級

61. **pilot**

['paɪlət]

n. 飛行員

autopilot n. 自動駕駛

co-pilot n. 副駕駛飛行員

同 aviator

The **pilot** locked the cockpit door when he was warned of a possible terrorist on board.

當被警告有疑似恐怖份子在飛機上時，飛行員就將駕駛艙門鎖上。

初級

62. **platform**

['plæt,fɔrm]

n. 平臺；月臺；講臺

 plat 「古法文，平的」 + form 「形狀」

There should be safety gates at the edge of the **platform**

月臺邊應該要設置安全門。

| 補充 | an oil platform | 海上鑽油平臺 |
| --- | a trading platform | 貿易平臺 |

中高

63. precede

[prɪ`sid]

v. 在…之前（發生）；處在…前面

precedent n. 先例

preceding adj. 在前的

易混 proceed v. 繼續做；持續進行

pre-「在…前」+ -cede-「前進」

A terrible blizzard **preceded** what turned out to be the wettest winter on record for our city.

先前一個可怕的暴風雪發生，緊接著就變成了本市有史以來最溼冷的冬天。

中高

64. procession

[prə`sɛʃən]

n. 行列；隊伍

processional adj. 隊伍的；列隊行進的

⇨ pro-「向前」+ -cess-「行進」+ -ion「名詞字尾」

You have to take another route because there is a carnival **procession**.

因為有嘉年華遊行隊伍，你必須改道而行。

中級

65. prohibit

[prə`hɪbɪt]

v. 禁止

prohibition n. 禁止；禁令

⇨ pro-「向前，離開」+ -hibit-「保持」，離開並保持一段距離就是禁止你靠近

During the epidemic, many countries are **prohibiting** travel to or from the most heavily affected regions of Africa.

在疫情蔓延期間，許多國家會禁止旅行往返非洲受重度感染的地區。

補充　be prohibited by law 受法律禁止

中級

66. prominent

[`prɑmənənt]

adj. 著名的；重要的；卓越的

prominence n. 突出；顯著；傑出

prominently adv. 顯著地；重要地

pro-「向前」+ -min-「突出」+ -ent「形容詞字尾」

The most **prominent** form of travel in Tokyo might be the subway system since cars are so expensive to park in the city.

在東京最重要的旅遊方式就是地鐵系統，因為在市內停車非常昂貴。

中高

67. **rail**

[rel]

n. 欄杆；扶手；鐵路；鐵軌

Hold onto the **rail** so that you won't fall.
握住扶手，這樣你才不會跌倒。
Thousands of people were injured when the train went off the **rails**.
火車出軌的時候上千名人員受傷了。

 補充

| rail consignment note | 鐵路托運單 |
| go off the rails | 行為越軌、不正常 |

railing n. 欄杆
handrail n. 扶手

中級

68. **rear**

[rɪr]

n. 後面；背後
adj. 後面的

Younger, healthier passengers should move towards the **rear** of the bus and leave the front seats for elderly and handicapped people.
年輕健康的乘客應移至公車後方，並將前方座位禮讓給年長及行動不便的人。

補充 | a rear-view mirror 汽車後照鏡

 中級

69. **restriction**

[rɪ`strɪkʃən]

n. 限制；約束

re- 「回來」 + -strict- 「拉緊」 + -ion 「名詞字尾」
There are speed **restrictions** on this part of the road.
這一段路有行車速限。

補充 | speed restrictions 速限

restrict v. 限制
restrictive adj. 限制的；約束的
同 limit

中級

70. **route**

[raut] / [rut]

n. 路徑；路線

Although buses 45 and 47 follow a similar **route**, they split off in opposite directions once they get closer to their terminal stops.
儘管 45 路和 47 路公車走的是差不多的路線，但在接近終點站時它們是分別往兩個不同方向行駛。

 補充

| en route (= on the way) | 在去…的路上 |
| route march | 行軍 |

router n. (網路) 路由器

11
製造

初級

71. **row**

[ro]

n. 排；列

v. 划船

Every **row** in the parking lot is filled with cars now.
停車場每一排都是滿滿的車子。

A fisherman **rows** down the river to catch fish every day.
一位漁夫每天在這條河上划船捕魚。

補充
get/have one's ducks in a row　讓事情井然有序
a hard/tough row to hoe　　面臨困難
in a row　一個接著一個；接續地

12
金融

72. **runway**

[ˈrʌnˌwe]

n. 飛機跑道；（停車場的）車道；伸展台，延伸舞台

易混 runaway adj. 逃跑的

⇨ run「奔跑」+ way「路」

My flight was delayed three hours while crews de-iced and cleared the **runways** of snow after the blizzard.
因為暴風雪後機場人員必須將飛機跑道除冰並將積雪清理乾淨，所以我的班機延遲了三個小時。

13
科技技術

73. **seat belt**

[sit][bɛlt]

n. 安全帶

同 safety belt

⇨ seat「座椅」+ belt「腰帶」

There is a huge recall on the most popular car brand for all 2013 models due to faulty **seat belts**.
該家最受歡迎的汽車廠牌，因安全帶有瑕疵而大規模召回 2013 年的車款。

14
房屋地產

中級

74. **shortcut**

[ˈʃɔrtˌkʌt]

n. 近路；捷徑

⇨ short「短的」+ cut「切」，切到較短的路線就是抄近路

With traffic on Main Street at a standstill, Craig quickly turned right and discovered a **shortcut** to Park Road through the back alleys.
由於在 Main Street 上的車流完全不動，Craig 馬上右轉並發現從後面小巷可以直通 Park Road 的捷徑。

15
出差旅遊

中級

75. **shuttle**

[ˈʃʌtl̩]

n. 來回穿梭的車子或物品

v. 穿梭

A **shuttle** bus runs between the MRT station and the shopping mall every twenty minutes.
來回捷運站及購物中心的接駁車每二十分鐘一班。

An elevated train **shuttles** travelers back and forth between Terminals One and Two in this huge airport.
這個大型機場的第一航廈與第二航廈間有高架鐵路來回載運旅客。

補充
shuttle bus　　接駁車
space shuttle　太空梭
shuttlecock　　羽毛球

16 交通

17 社交與用餐

18 休閒娛樂

19 醫療保健

20 日常生活

76. **speed**

[spid]

n. 速度

v. 快速移動

speedy adj. 迅速的；快的

speeding n. 超速行駛

You should lower your **speed** as you approach a junction.
接近交叉口時你應該減速。

補充	speed bump	減速路障
speed trap	超速偵測照相機
speed up	加速

---

77. **station**

[`steʃən]

n. 車站；電臺

⇨ - sta - 「站立」＋ - tion「名詞字尾」

A new central transportation hub is designed to alleviate the traffic congestion around the main subway **station**.

一個新的中央交通轉運站是設計用來紓解主要地鐵站週邊的交通堵塞。

| 補充 | station agent/master | 站長 |
| petrol/gas station | 加油站 |

---

78. **stationary**

[`steʃənɛrɪ]

adj. 靜止不動的

⇨ station「車站；駐紮地」＋ - ary「關於…的」

The train has remained **stationary** for thirty minutes.
火車已經停下來三十分鐘了。

| 補充 | stationary 是指原來應該在動的東西停下來的狀態，常用來描述交通工具。 |

易混 stationery n. 文具；信紙

---

79. **steer**

[stɪr]

v. 駕駛；操縱

She carefully **steered** the car through the narrow street.
她小心翼翼地駕駛經過那條狹窄的路。

| 補充 | steer clear of N. | 避開 N. |
| steering wheel | 方向盤 |

80. **street lights**

[strit][laɪts]

n. 路燈

同 street lamps

The installation of **street lights** throughout our neighborhood has nearly eliminated break-ins.
整個社區裝設路燈已讓闖空門事件幾乎絕跡了。

81. **stuck**

[stʌk]

adj. 卡住的

The icy roads caused me to crash into a snowdrift, and I was **stuck** there for almost an hour.
路面結冰讓我撞進雪堆中，而且我被卡在那裡快一個小時。

 補充　be stuck on sth. 在某事物上被卡住
be stuck with 被…纏身；受…困擾

stick v. 黏住，固定住

初級

82. **subway**

[ˈsʌbˌwe]

n. (AmE) 地下鐵；
(BrE) 地下道

⇨ sub-「在下方」+ way「道路」

All the **subway** cars undergo a thorough examination every night to ensure the safety of passengers.
所有地鐵車廂每晚都會經過徹底檢查以確保乘客的安全。

 補充　英國的地鐵叫做 underground。Tube 則專指倫敦的地鐵系統。

中級

83. **suspend**

[səˈspɛnd]

v. 暫停；中止

⇨ sus-「在…之下」+ -pend-「懸掛」，把許可證掛下方不讓你用，就是中止你的權利

Due to his arrest for drunk driving, the truck driver's manager decided to **suspend** him for one year.
由於卡車駕駛酒駕被逮，他的經理決定讓他停職一年。

 補充　be suspended from school 被勒令退學
suspended sentence　緩刑
suspension bridge　吊橋

suspense n. 懸而未決；提心吊膽
suspension n. 懸掛；暫停

---

84. **take off**

[tek][ɔf]

v. 起飛；快速成長

take-off n. 起飛

反 land v. 降落

Just as the pilot was preparing to **take off**, the co-pilot told him that one of the engines would need emergency repairs.
就在機長要起飛時，副機長告訴他有一顆引擎需要緊急維修。

初級

85. taxi

[ˈtæksɪ]

n. 計程車

Maria aggressively hailed a **taxi** and told the driver to step on it, as she was already late for a meeting at the office.

Maria 快速地叫了輛計程車並要司機加速，因為她去公司的會議已經遲到了。

中級

86. terminal

[ˈtɝmənl̩]

adj. 終點的；末端的

n. 終點；（機場）航廈

 - termin - 「界限，邊界」+ -al「屬性」，到邊界就表示到終點了

This newly-renovated airport **terminal** has cushioned recliners and over thirty restaurants to choose from.

這個重新改裝的機場航廈有柔軟的可調式靠椅，以及超過三十間餐廳可供選擇。

補充	terminal station（公車或火車的）終點站

terminate v. 結束；終止
terminator n. 終結者

初級

87. ticket

[ˈtɪkɪt]

n. 票；罰單

Kimberly cashed in her frequent flyer miles for a free airplane **ticket** to Malaysia.

Kimberly 將她的飛行常客哩程數兌換了一張免費飛往馬來西亞的機票。

★ cash in：將…兌換成獎品或現金

補充	a one-way/round-trip ticket	單程／來回票
	a ticket office	售票處
	a ticket to/for sth.	某事物的門票

中高

88. tilt

[tɪlt]

v./n. 傾斜

After the terrible earthquake, the entire apartment building was **tilted** to the east and needed to be torn down.

在強烈地震後，整棟公寓向東傾斜，因此需被拆除。

補充	at full tilt 全力地

 slant
易混 tile n. 瓦片

11 製造

12 金融

13 科技技術

14 房屋地產

15 出差旅遊

 中級

89. timetable

[ˈtaɪmˌtebl̩]

n. 時間表；時刻表

同 schedule

⇨ time「時間」+ table「表格」

What is our **timetable** for getting our entire fleet of jets in proper condition to fly?

我們整個飛航機隊要準備好能出發的時間表是何時？

 中高

90. toll

[tol]

n. 過路費；通行費

I have purchased a transponder to automatically pay the **toll** when I drive past this **toll** booth twice a day.

我已購買了感測器能在我每天行經兩次收費站時自動扣繳通行費。

補充	toll booth	收費站(亭)
	toll bridge/road	收費橋樑 / 道路
	take a heavy toll on sth.	
	對某事物造成嚴重影響 / 損失	

toll-free adj. 免付電話費的

 初級

91. track

[træk]

n. 軌道；行蹤

v. 追蹤

Passengers must not walk across the **tracks**.

乘客不得穿越鐵軌。

The police **tracked** down the robbery suspect by looking up his license plate number.

警方透過嫌疑搶匪的車牌號碼追查到他的行蹤。

補充	keep track of	追蹤記錄
	track down	追查到
	track and field	田徑運動

 中高

92. transit

[ˈtrænsɪt]

n. 運輸

v. 通過

trans-「穿越」+ -it-「行走」，穿越各處行走就是在運行

I used to drive my car to work, but taking public **transit** saved me a lot of money, both in fuel costs and parking fees.

我以前是開車上班，但搭乘大眾運輸後，我的油錢和停車費都省很多。

According to the online tracking system, bus 78 is in **transit** to this stop, and should be arriving in about twenty minutes.

根據網路追蹤系統，78 號公車正朝本站運行，在二十分鐘內應可到本站。

補充	public/mass transit	大眾運輸
	rapid transit	地鐵；捷運
	in transit	運送中

16 交通

17 社交與用餐

18 休閒娛樂

19 醫療保健

20 日常生活

中級
93. transport
[træns`port]
v. 運輸
[`trænsport]
n. 運輸

 trans-「穿越」+ -port-「攜帶」，帶著在各處穿梭來回就是在運輸

This metro system was constructed to **transport** passengers living in the suburbs.
這個地下鐵系統是為了運送住在郊區的乘客而建造的。

補充
public transport/transportation 公共交通運輸
a transport/transportation hub 交通轉運站

中級
94. upwards
[`ʌpwədz]
adv. 向上地

upward adj. 向上的
反 downwards adv. 向下地

 up「向上」+ -wards「朝…方向」

The bus fare has been revised **upwards** again this year.
公車車資今年又再度往上調了。

補充
onward and upward 步步高升

中級
95. vehicle
[`viɪkl]
n. 交通工具；車輛

 vehere「拉丁文，載運」+ -cle「名詞字尾」

Motor **vehicles** are not allowed to enter this area.
機動車輛不得進入此區域。

補充
RV = Recreational Vehicle 露營車
SUV = Sport Utility Vehicle 休旅車

中級
96. vessel
[`vɛsl]
n. 船艦；血管；容器

Our cargo **vessel** has returned to the port.
我們的貨船已經回到港口了。

補充
(almost) burst a blood vessel 爆血管、震怒
Empty vessels make the most noise.
[諺語]：空桶響叮噹。無知者卻愛高談闊論。

中高

97. **wharf**

[hwɔrf]

n. 碼頭；停泊處

★ 複數：wharfs ╱ wharves

There are some people fishing at the **wharf**.
有一些人在碼頭釣魚。

中高

98. **whirl**

[hwɜl]

v. 旋轉；急駛

n. 旋轉

A sports car just **whirled** down the street.
一台跑車剛剛快速飆過這條街。

 補充

a tilt-a-whirl	（遊樂園設施）大轉盤
be in a whirl	思緒一片混亂
give it a whirl	嘗試

中高

99. **windshield**

[ˈwɪndʃild]

n. 擋風玻璃

同 windscreen (BrE)

⇨ wind「風」+ shield「盾牌」

Make sure your **windshield** is clean before you drive.
開車前要確認你的擋風玻璃是乾淨的。

補充　windshield wiper 雨刷

中高

100. **yacht**

[jɑt]

n. 遊艇

I have been dreaming of traveling by **yacht** for a long time.
我夢想著搭遊艇旅遊很久了。

 補充

| a luxury yacht | 豪華遊艇 |
| a yacht club | 遊艇俱樂部 |

yachting n. 駕駛遊艇巡遊；帆船運動 ╱ 比賽
yachtsman n. 遊艇駕駛者

實力進階

Part 1. 搭乘飛機常見句型及用語

機場或機內廣播與設施描述是多益考試常出現的情境，常出現的句型或搭配詞有：

機場內	常用詞	check-in counter 報到櫃台 check-in luggage 託運行李 carry-on baggage 隨身行李 boarding pass 登機證 boarding call 登機廣播 regular boarding 一般旅客登機 baggage claim 行李提領處 customs 海關
	常用句型	Flight OOO to (place) at (time) is now boarding at gate XX. …點飛往 (某地) 的班機現在開始登機。 Flight OOO from (place A) to (place B) has been delayed. Please contact your carrier for further information. 由 A 飛往 B 的 OOO 航班延遲。詳情請洽您的航空公司。
機艙內	常用詞	cabin crew 機艙內服務人員 emergency procedures 緊急情況步驟 emergency exit 緊急逃生門 oxygen mask 氧氣面罩 life raft 救生衣
	常用句型	Fasten your seatbelts. 繫好您的安全帶。 Turn off all personal electronic devices. 關閉所有個人電子裝置。 Keep the tray and the seat at the upright position. 小桌及座椅保持在直立狀態。 Secure all baggage underneath the seats or in the overhead compartments. 請將座位下或頭頂上置物櫃中的行李固定好。 We will take off/be landing in (time). 班機將在…(時間) 後起飛 / 降落。 Smoking is prohibited. 禁止吸菸。

16 交通

17 社交與用餐

18 休閒娛樂

19 醫療保健

20 日常生活

Part 2. 常見交通標誌用語

馬路如虎口，行車走路要注意各種交通警示標誌，常見的有：

禁止標誌	警告標誌	指示標誌
No Entry. 禁止進入	Road Work Ahead. 前有施工	Single Lane./One Way. 單行道
No Parking. 禁止停車	Slippery Road. 小心路滑	Fast/Slow Lane. 快 / 慢車道
No Vehicle Allowed. 車輛禁止通行	Double Bend/ Winding Road. 連續彎道	Exit./Entrance. 出 / 入口
No Horn. 禁鳴喇叭	Landslide/ Falling Rock Ahead. 前有坍方 / 落石	Toll Station. 收費站
Keep in Lane. 禁止越線	Road/Bridge Closed. 道路 / 橋樑封閉	Parking Lot/Zone. 停車場
Keep Right/Left. 靠右 / 左行駛	Bumpy Road. 路面顛簸	Walking Area. 徒步區
No U-Turn. 禁止迴轉	Children Crossing. 小心兒童	Sidewalk./Pavement. 人行道

Part 3. 常見汽車種類

Microcar/bubble car	迷你車
compact car/compact	小型車
hatchback	掀背車
sedan	大型房車
sports car	跑車
convertible	敞篷車
off-roader/off-road vehicle	越野車
camper van/recreational vehicle = RV	露營車
sport utility vehicle = SUV	休旅車

隨堂練習

★ 請根據句意，選出最適合的單字

(　　) 1. Although the tourist resort is beautiful, it is _____ only by boat because it is located on a small island.
(A) convertible　　　　　　(B) accessible
(C) cautious　　　　　　　(D) immense

(　　) 2. His driving license was _____ because he was caught driving under the influence.
(A) suspended　　　　　　(B) preceded
(C) impacted　　　　　　　(D) accelerated

(　　) 3. There is no _____ to mastering a foreign language, which means one has to be patient and persistent to have a good command of a language.
(A) escalator　　　　　　　(B) expressway
(C) terminal　　　　　　　(D) shortcut

(　　) 4. This country is considering lifting _____ on U.S. beef imports.
(A) restrictions　　　　　　(B) routes
(C) tolls　　　　　　　　　(D) tracks

(　　) 5. The government introduced a law which _____ fast food restaurants from offering free toys with unhealthy kids' meals.
(A) tracks　　　　　　　　(B) loads
(C) steers　　　　　　　　(D) prohibits

解答：1. B　2. A　3. D　4. A　5. D

Unit 17 社交與用餐

1. a long shot

[ə][lɔŋ][ʃɑt]

phr. 希望不大的嘗試；沒把握的猜測

The chance of that model actually going out with you on a date is **a long shot**.
你能和那位模特兒出去約會的機會不大。

補充　not by a long shot/chalk　沒什麼希望
take a shot at N.　試試看 N.

中級

2. academy

[əˈkædəmɪ]

n. 學院

Even after so many years of attending a prestigious **academy**, Mary still didn't fit in with the other rich kids.
即便在貴族學院上了好多年的課，Mary 仍無法融入其他有錢人家孩子的圈子。

典故　academy 來自古雅典城北邊的地名 Akademia，意思是希臘守護神雅典娜 (Athena) 的庇護所。西元前四世紀，柏拉圖在 Akademia 設立了第一所哲學學院，教授哲學思考，演變到後來就有以 academia、academy 指高等學院的用法。

補充　Academy Award　學院獎，奧斯卡金像獎

academic adj. 學術的

中級

3. acceptance

[əkˈsɛptəns]

n. 接受；贊同

 accept「接受」+ -ance「名詞字尾」
The chef's new recipe has received wide **acceptance**.
主廚的新食譜受到廣泛的認同。

補充　acceptance speech　得獎感言
customer/consumer acceptance　顧客接受度
confirm acceptance of N.　確認接受 N.

accept v. 接受
acceptable adj. 可接受的

同 approval

反 refusal n. 拒絕

4. acquaintance

[əˋkwentəns]

n. 相識，瞭解；相識的人

⇨ **acquaint**「使認識、了解」**+ -ance**「名詞字尾」

It's a pleasure to finally make your **acquaintance** after so many years of hearing about you.

在聽聞您的事蹟這麼多年後，終於能和您相識真讓我倍感榮幸。

 have a nodding/passing acquaintance with N.
對 N. 只知道一點點皮毛

acquaint v. 使認識，了解

---

5. adjacent

[əˋdʒesn̩t]

adj. 相鄰的；毗鄰的

⇨ **ad-**「to」**+ -jac-**「放靠近」**+ -ent**「形容詞字尾」，
放很靠近就是相鄰的

I've just bought the property **adjacent** to yours and I just wanted to come over to introduce myself.

我剛買下和您毗鄰的房子，我想過來做個自我介紹。

 be adjacent to N. 在 N. 的旁邊

---

6. alcohol

[ˋælkəˌhɔl]

n. 酒精

There is just a hint of **alcohol** in this cocktail beverage.
這雞尾酒飲料裡只有微量的酒精成份。

 alcohol 來自阿拉伯語，原指當時阿拉伯人用來做化妝品的一種粉末，這種粉末中有酒精成份，人們便以 alcohol 來稱呼這種成份，後來人們就以 alcohol 泛指含有酒精成份的飲料。

補充
alcohol-free	無酒精的，不含酒精成份的
low-alcohol	低酒精成份的
alcoholic beverage	含酒精飲料

alcoholic adj. 含酒精的；酗酒的 n. 酗酒者
alcoholism n. 酒精中毒

中級

7. **anniversary**

[͵ænə`vɝsərɪ]

n. 週年紀念日

⇨ - anni - 「年」+ - vers - 「轉動」+ - ary 「與⋯有關」

Our restaurant is a hotspot for people celebrating their wedding **anniversaries** with a fancy dinner.

本餐廳對許多以豪華大餐慶祝結婚週年的人來說是個超夯地點。

 to celebrate the anniversary 慶祝週年紀念

中高

8. **antique**

[æn`tik]

n. 古董
adj. 古代的

⇨ ant - 「在之前」+ - ique 「具⋯風格的」，具以前風格的東西就是古董

That coffee table is a refurnished **antique** made of cherry wood.

那張咖啡桌是由一件桃木古董翻修而成。

 an antique dealer　古董商
antique furniture　古董家具

antiquity　n. 古代；古代的遺物、風俗

中級

9. **appetite**

[`æpə͵taɪt]

n. 食慾；胃口

⇨ ap - 「to」+ petere 「拉丁文，尋找、渴望」，尋找食物、對食物的渴望就是胃口

The twenty-four ounce steak is only for those who have huge **appetites**.

這二十四盎司的牛排只適合提供給那些有大胃口的人。

補充	give sb. an appetite	讓某人胃口大開
	spoil sb's appetite	減少某人的胃口
	have a good appetite	食慾旺盛
	Bon appetite.	祝你胃口大開。

appetizer　n. 開胃菜；開胃小吃
aperitif　n. 餐前酒

中高

10. **apprentice**

[ə`prɛntɪs]

n. 學徒

v. 使人當學徒

 ap-「to」+ prehendere「拉丁文，去抓、去學」+ -ice「名詞字尾」，去學習的人就是學徒

Instead of going to classes all day, David earned most of his college credits as the **apprentice** electrician.

David 以當電工學徒身份取得大部分的大學學分，而非去學校上一整天的課。

補充 an apprentice chef/baker/electrician/technician
廚師 / 烘焙師 / 電工 / 技工學徒

prentice n. 徒弟

中級

11. **associate**

[ə`soʃɪt]

n. 同事；夥伴

adj. 副的

[ə`soʃɪet]

v. 和…有關聯

association n. 協會；聯盟

 n. = coworker / partner

 as-「to」+ -soci-「友伴」+ -ate「使變成…」

Will is a former **associate** of mine from our days at the Wright Brothers Firm.

Will 是我之前在萊特兄弟公司時期的同事。

補充 business associate 生意夥伴

---

12. **assorted**

[ə`sɔrtɪd]

adj. 各種各樣的；混雜的

assort v. 把…分類，把…分級

 as-「to」+ sort「挑選」+ -ed「形容詞字尾」，挑出各種類型放在一起就是混雜的

All employees are asked to bring a box of **assorted** desserts to the company potluck party.

所有員工都要帶一盒不同種類的甜點來參加公司的百樂餐派對。

★ potluck party：百樂餐、各自帶菜赴宴的派對。

補充 ill-assorted adj. 不搭的

中級

13. **atmosphere**

[`ætməsˌfɪr]

n. 氣氛；大氣

 atmo-「空氣」+ sphere「球形的表面」，地球表面的空氣就是大氣

This café offers a laid-back **atmosphere** along with a picturesque view of downtown.

這間咖啡館提供悠閒的氣氛，還可以欣賞如畫般的城市美景。

中高
14. auditorium
[ˌɔdəˈtorɪəm]
n. 禮堂；會堂

auditor n. 審計員；聽眾

🗣 -audi-「聽」+ -or「做…動作的人」+ -ium「表地點」，聽眾聚集的地方就是禮堂

This school **auditorium** has seating for two thousand people and incredible lights and sound.
這間學校的禮堂有可容納兩千人的座位和極佳的燈光音響設備。

中高
15. banquet
[ˈbæŋkwɪt]
n. 酒席；正式的宴會

feast n. 盛宴；筵席

🗣 banco「義大利文，表長椅」+ -et「表小東西的名詞字尾」

Although a little pricier than most, our **banquet** hall offers a huge facility along with impeccable service.
雖然比大多數的貴了點，我們的宴會廳提供非常大的場地和無懈可擊的服務。

中高
16. batter
[ˈbætɚ]
n. 麵糊；打擊手

bat n. 球棒；球拍 v. 打擊

Be sure to coat the chicken breasts in **batter** before coating the outside with the flour mixture.
要先將雞胸肉裹一層麵糊，然後在最外面再沾一層混和好的麵粉。

 補充
to coat with batter　裹上麵糊
batter's box　　　（棒球）打擊區

中高
17. beverage
[ˈbɛvərɪdʒ]
n. 飲料
同 drink

I am opening up a **beverage** stand on the east side of the campus next to the dormitories.
我要在校園東邊宿舍的旁邊開一間飲料攤。

18. **bland**

[blænd]

adj. 淡而無味的；溫和的；
無刺激性的

同 flavorless / gentle

Let's use some garlic to liven up these **bland** pork chops.
我們用一些大蒜來爲這些沒味道的豬排添風味吧。

19. **blend**

[blɛnd]

n. 混合物

v. 使混合；攪拌；混合調製

blender n. 攪拌器

同 n. = mixture
v. = mix / combine

Our company sells prepackaged **blends** of herbs and spices in grocery stores.
我們公司在雜貨店有販售預先包裝好的香草香料混合物。

	a blend of A and B A 與 B 的融合
	blend into N. 混進 N. 裡面去
	blend in with N. 混入 N.；與 N. 十分協調

20. **broth**

[brɔθ]

n. 高湯；清湯

An entire pot of this chicken **broth** should last us a week.
這一整鍋的雞高湯應該夠我們吃一個禮拜。

| | Too many cooks spoil the broth. |
| | [諺語]：人多手雜礙事。 |

21. **buffet**

[bəˈfe]

n. 自助餐

All the **buffets** downtown are overpriced, but they offer a better seafood selection than the big chains in the suburbs.
雖然市中心的自助餐都太貴了，但它們卻提供比市郊大型連鎖店更多更好的海鮮選擇。

| | buffet 來自法文的 bufet，原指長椅、邊桌。以前歐洲人因家中空間有限，發展出將食物放邊桌，讓客人端盤自行取用的宴客方式，後來廣爲流行，於是法文的 bufet 就被引進到英語世界成爲 buffet。 |

	buffet car （火車上的）行動餐車
	finger buffet 站著以手取用食物的自助餐
	all-you-can-eat buffet 吃到飽自助餐

22. **cafeteria**

[ˌkæfəˈtɪrɪə]

n. (公司或學校的) 自助餐廳

⇨ café「咖啡」+ teria「西班牙文，做生意的地方」

What I like about my company's **cafeteria** is that it is buffet style instead of charging by the weight of your plate.

我喜歡我們公司自助餐廳的地方就是它是自助式的而非秤重的計價方式。

補充 cafeteria plan = flexible benefit plan
選擇性福利計劃

23. **canteen**

[kænˈtin]

n. (學校 / 工廠的) 販賣部，小吃部；鐵水壺

Every Thursday at lunch, a live band plays at the university **canteen**.

每週四午餐時間，在大學的小吃部有樂團現場演奏。

補充 a staff canteen 員工餐廳

24. **cater**

[ˈketɚ]

v. 為…提供飲食，承辦宴席；提供所需

Our waiters are trained to **cater** to the customers' every need.

我們的服務生都被訓練為能為顧客們的每一項需要提供服務。

補充 a catering business
承攬宴席的生意 (如：總鋪師、外燴公司)
cater for sb./sth. 迎合；滿足某人 / 某事物
cater to N. 滿足 (令人難接受的需求)

caterer n. 餐飲服務公司

25. **chain**

[tʃen]

n. 連鎖店；連鎖；鏈子，項圈
v. 鎖上鏈子

Thomas has built up a **chain** of 100 clothing stores across the country.

Thomas 創立了一家在全國有一百間連鎖通路的服裝店。

補充 chain restaurants/stores/hotels
連鎖餐廳 / 商店 / 飯店
chain reaction 連鎖反應

26. **charity**

[ˈtʃærətɪ]

n. 慈善；慈善團體

The proceeds from today's company bake sale go directly to **charity**.

今天的公司烘焙特賣收益將直接捐給慈善團體。

補充　N. go to charity　將 N. 捐給慈善機構
　　　a charity shop　二手義賣商店

charitable adj. 慈悲爲懷的；仁慈的

---

27. **chef**

[ʃɛf]

n. 主廚；大廚

易混　chief [tʃif] n. 首領

The **chef** was the understudy of a French master for five years before opening his own restaurant.

在成立自己的餐廳之前，該名主廚曾擔任一位法國大師級廚師的替角長達五年。

---

28. **comedian**

[kəˈmidɪən]

n. 喜劇演員

 comedy「喜劇」+ - ian「從事…的人」

Being such a natural **comedian**, Robert is the life of every party.

身爲天生的喜劇演員，Robert 是每個派對的靈魂人物。

補充　a stand-up comedian　獨角喜劇演員
　　　a stand-up comedy
　　　獨角喜劇（類似東方的單口相聲、對口相聲）

comedy n. 喜劇

---

29. **comfortable**

[ˈkʌmfɚtəbl̩]

adj. 舒服的

⇨ comfort「安慰」+ - able「可…的」，能令人感到安慰就是舒適的

The seats in this movie theater are **comfortable** and spacious.

這間電影院的座位既舒適又寬敞。

補充　comfortable as an old shoe　像舊鞋一樣舒適
　　　make oneself comfortable　讓某人自己放鬆
　　　be comfortable with N.　對 N. 放心

comfort v. 安慰　n. 安逸；舒適

同　comfy

11 製造

12 金融

13 科技技術

14 房屋地產

15 出差旅遊

中高

30. **commemorate**

[kəˈmɛməˌret]

v. 慶祝；為…舉行紀念活動

 com - 「一起」+ memor「拉丁文，想著的」+ - ate「使變成…」

To **commemorate** the birthday of this famous late actor, there is a twenty-four hour film festival downtown showing his best performances.

為紀念這位已故知名演員的冥誕，在市中心有一場二十四小時影展播映他最棒的演出作品。

commemoration n. 慶典，紀念節日
commemorative adj. 紀念性的

中高

31. **companionship**

[kəmˈpænjənˌʃɪp]

n. 友誼；交往；伴侶關係

⇨ com - 「一起」+ pan「源自拉丁文 panis，指麵包」+ - ion「表狀態」+ - ship「表關係」，可以一起吃麵包的關係就是友伴、伴侶關係

Amy was only seeking **companionship**, but Rob turned out to be her true love.

Amy 原本只是想要找個伴侶，但 Rob 卻變成她的真愛。

companion n. 同伴；友伴
同 fellowship

中高

32. **complexion**

[kəmˈplɛkʃən]

n. 氣色，膚色；性質

⇨ complex「複雜的」+ - ion「狀態」，複雜的身體狀態會影響人的氣色

Kathy had always had a fair **complexion** until her entire face broke out with acne when she was 17.

Kathy 原本有著白皙的膚色，直到她十七歲後整個臉竟冒出了青春痘。

補充	a healthy/clear complexion	健康的 / 清爽的氣色
	a fair/dark complexion	白皙的 / 深的膚色
	wheat complexion	小麥色皮膚

complex adj. 複雜的；複合的
　　　 n. 複合物；(情緒) 情結
同 skin color

中級

33. **compliment**

[`kɑmpləmənt]

n. 讚美；恭維

 com - 「一起」+ -pli - 「填滿」+ -ment「名詞字尾」，
一起用讚美填滿你的心

Greg paid me the nicest **compliment** when he commented on my recent weight loss.

Greg 在評論我最近的減重成果時給了我最棒的讚美。

補充
return the compliment 報答；回謝
compliments slip
贈禮便箋（贈送禮品上附的小紙條、名片）

complimentary adj. 讚美的；恭維的；免費的

同 admiration / praise

中高

34. **conspiracy**

[kən`spɪrəsɪ]

n. 陰謀

 con - 「一起」+ -spir - 「呼吸」+ -acy「名詞字尾」

This author's novels are all about **conspiracy**.

這位作者的小說都和陰謀有關。

補充
conspiracy against sb. 針對某人的陰謀行動
a conspiracy theory 陰謀論

conspire v. 密謀；共謀

同 plot / scheme

中級

35. **courtesy**

[`kɝtəsɪ]

n. 禮貌；禮儀

Each of our hotels has a workout room as a **courtesy** to our guests.

我們的每一間飯店都免費提供了一間健身房讓我們的客人使用。

補充
a courtesy call 禮貌性電訪
to exchange courtesies 禮貌性寒暄、招呼
common courtesy 基本禮節
(by) courtesy of N.
承蒙 N. 的允許（用來表示感謝）

courteous adj. 有禮貌的；殷勤的

同 politeness

36. **crack**

[kræk]

v. 砸開；使破裂；破解（密碼）

n. 裂縫；裂痕

Please **crack** these eggs into a bowl and mix them together.
請將這些蛋打到碗裡並混合。
Rick fell down the stairs and **cracked** a bone in his leg.
Rick 從階梯上跌下，一隻腳的骨頭裂了。

| 補充 | crack a joke | 說笑話 |
| | crack the code | 破解密碼 |

cracker n. 鹹餅乾；蘇打餅

---

37. **crave**

[krev]

v. 渴望獲得；迫切需要

The hungry child **craves** for food.
那饑餓的小孩渴望食物。

| 補充 | crave for N. | 渴求 N. |
| | crave to V. | 渴望做… |

craving n. 渴望

同 desire

---

38. **criticize**

[ˈkrɪtɪˌsaɪz]

v. 批評；批判；評論

⇨ critic「評論家」+ -ize「使…化」
Although many major magazines and newspapers **criticize** the author's works, his novels are all best sellers.
儘管許多主流雜誌和報紙都批評該名作家的作品，但他的小說都是暢銷書。

| 補充 | criticize sb. for sth. | 針對某事批評某人 |

critic n. 批評家，評論者
criticism n. 評論，指責
critical adj. 吹毛求疵的；危急的；關鍵的

---

39. **cuisine**

[kwɪˈzin]

n. 料理；菜餚；烹調法

She only knows how to prepare Japanese-style **cuisine**, so she now visits an online recipe site.
她只知道如何準備日式料理，所以她現在都會參看線上食譜網站。

| 補充 | French cuisine | 法國菜 |
| | Italian cuisine | 義大利菜 |

40. **delicacy**

[ˋdɛləkəsɪ]

n. 佳餚；精美

delicate adj. 鮮美的；脆弱的；易碎的

同 savory n. 佳餚

In some regions of Asia, insects are a **delicacy** for the natives.
在亞洲一些地區，昆蟲對當地人來說是美味佳餚。

中高

41. **descendant**

[dɪˋsɛndənt]

n. 子孫；後裔

 descend「向下」+ - ant「表人」，一代代向下的人就是子孫
I am a **descendant** of one of the founding fathers of this country.
我是這個國家開國元老之一的後代子孫。

補充 direct descendant 直系子孫

中高

42. **devour**

[dɪˋvaʊr]

v. 吃光；狼吞虎嚥；吞沒

 de -「向下」+ - vour -「吞」
Mark is able to **devour** several plates of food at the buffet.
Mark 有辦法在自助餐廳吃光好幾盤。

補充 be devoured by N. 被 N. 吞沒

同 swallow / gulp / gobble up

中級

43. **digest**

[daɪˋdʒɛst]

v. 消化；領悟、領會

 di -「分開使成碎片」+ - gest -「運送」，將食物切碎運送就是消化的過程
According to experts, you need to allow one hour for your food to **digest** before attempting to do heavy exercise.
據專家所說，在開始重度運動之前，你最好先保留一小時的時間讓食物先消化。

補充 digestive system 消化系統

digestion n. 消化作用；吸收；領會
digestible adj. 容易消化的
digestive adj. 消化的

同 comprehend / absorb v. 領會

中級

44. dine

[daɪn]

v. 用餐

I used to **dine** out five days a week before I learned how to cook.

在我學烹飪之前，我曾經一週有五天在外用餐。

補充	dine out	外出用餐
	wine and dine sb.	招待某人吃飯
	dining room	飯廳

中級

45. distinguished

[dɪ`stɪŋgwɪʃt]

adj. 卓越的；傑出的；
著名的

⇨ distinct「有區別的」+ -ish「動詞字尾」+ -ed「形容詞字尾」，有別於他人就是卓越傑出的

Several **distinguished** professors are speaking at the luncheon today.

幾位傑出的教授將在今天的午餐會中致詞。

補充	a distinguished writer/director 傑出的作家 / 導演

distinguish v. 區別，識別

 outstanding

中高

46. donation

[do`neʃən]

n. 捐贈

⇨ -don-「給予」+ -ate「使…」+ -ion「表情況」，給出去的情況就是捐贈

We are accepting **donations** of any amount to help fund cancer research.

我們接受任何金額的捐款以募集資金協助癌症研究。

補充	a generous/large/small donation 慷慨的 / 大筆的 / 小筆的捐贈	
	make a donation	進行捐贈
	charitable donation	慈善捐贈
	organ donation	器官捐贈

donate v. 捐贈
donor n. 捐贈者；贈送人

47. drop in

[drɑp] [ɪn]

phr. 順道拜訪；非正式的
拜訪

We have several appointments this evening, but we would be happy to **drop in** to have a few drinks.
我們今天傍晚有幾個約訪，但我們會很高興能順道來拜訪一下喝點飲料。

補充　to drop in on sb. 順道拜訪某人

同 drop by

中高

48. eloquent

[ˋɛləkwənt]

adj. 雄辯的；有說服力的；
清楚表明的

⇨ e - 「向外」+ -loqu - 「說」+ -ent「形容詞字尾」
Your receptionist's **eloquent** pronunciation makes me wonder whether she has worked in radio before.
貴公司接待人員清晰的發音讓我很好奇她以前是否做過廣播工作。

補充　an eloquent speaker 具說服力的演講者

eloquence n. 雄辯；說服力

中級

49. encounter

[ɪnˋkaʊntə]

v. 相遇；遭遇；面臨

⇨ en - 「進入」+ counter「對著」，一進來就對著瞧就是
遭遇到了
That is the rudest waiter I have ever **encountered**.
那是我遇過最無禮的服務生了。

補充　encounter group 會心團體；討論團體

同 meet with / run into / come across

---

50. entrée

[ˋɑntre]

n. (AmE) 主菜；(BrE) 前菜；
（進入上流場合的）入場資
格

同 main course　n. 主菜

Each family is supposed to bring one **entrée** and a side dish to the potluck dinner party.
每一家都要帶一道主菜和一道配菜來參加這個百樂晚餐派對。

中高

51. **episode**

[ˋɛpəˌsod]

n. 一集（演出）；一個事件；
插曲

The next **episode** will be shown on Friday.
下一集週五會上映。

🎧

52. **etiquette**

[ˋɛtɪkɛt]

n. 禮節；規範

I was shocked at your boyfriend's poor **etiquette** when the whole family went out for a fancy dinner.
當全家人都一起出去吃豪華晚餐時，我對你男友的差勁禮儀感到很驚訝。

| 典故 | **etiquette** 來自古法文，最早指寫有法庭注意事項的標籤或小卡片，後來也指給士兵的書面命令，上面載明士兵駐紮時要注意的行為規範，後來就泛指在各種場合該有的行為舉止，也就是「禮節、禮儀」。 |

| 補充 | office etiquette　　辦公室禮節
business etiquette　商界禮節
medical etiquette　　醫界規範 |

同 manners

中級

53. **extend**

[ɪkˋstɛnd]

v. 延伸，延長

⇨ **ex** - 「向外」 + - **tend** - 「伸出」，向外伸出就是延伸、延長

Due to high demand, the restaurant has decided to **extend** the special family discount for another month.
由於反應熱烈，該餐廳決定將家庭特別折扣再延長一個月。

| 補充 | **extend** an agreement/contract/visa
延長協議 / 合約 / 簽證的效期 |

| 比較 | **extend** 常指時間上延長，而 **expand** 常指體積或量擴大。 |

extension n. 延長；延期；電話分機
extensive adj. 廣泛的

16 交通

17 社交與用餐

18 休閒娛樂

19 醫療保健

20 日常生活

 中級

54. farewell
[ˈfɛrˈwɛl]
interj. 一路平安；再見
n. 告別；送別會

⇨ fare「旅程，費用」+ well「好好地」

To show our appreciation, all of us students would like to treat you- our beloved professor- to a farewell dinner.

為表達我們的感謝，我們所有學生想要請您－我們敬愛的教授－來參加惜別晚宴。

 典故　fare 是費用，最早指旅程、行走，行走會經過各種地方，有的地方會提供吃喝，就會向你收費，後來就有 fare 指費用的意思；well 是好的，farewell 就是好好地走、好好地出發，會請人好好地走就是要跟人告別、說再見了，所以 farewell 就有告別、再見的意思。

補充　golden farewell = golden goodbye　高額離職金

回 good-bye

 中高

55. fiber
[ˈfaɪbɚ]
n. 纖維

★ 英：fibre ／美：fiber

The fibers in this sweater are really soft!
這件毛衣的纖維真的好柔軟。

 補充　natural/artificial/synthetic fiber
天然／人造／合成纖維
optical fiber　光學纖維，光纖

 中級

56. fragrance
[ˈfregrəns]
n. 香氣；芳香

I like to spray a light fragrance all over the house before guests arrive to mitigate the smell of my dogs.

我喜歡在客人來之前把整個屋子到處都噴上一點香水以蓋掉我們家狗狗的氣味。

 補充　frangrance-free　adj. 無香料的
the fragrance of N.　N. 的香氣

fragrant adj. 有香味的；有香氣的
回 aroma

205

57. **fundraising**

[ˈfʌndˌrezɪŋ]

n. 募款

⇨ fund「資金」+ raise「提高，增加」+ -ing「名詞字尾」，讓資金增加要靠募款

Thanks to some strong **fundraising**, our community was able to do a complete renovation of the playground.

由於強力募款，我們社區終於能針對遊樂場進行全面整修。

| 補充 | fundraise for N. | 為 N. 募款 |
| | a fundraising drive/campaign | 募款活動 |

fundraise v. 募款
fundraiser n. 募款人

中高

58. **garment**

[ˈgɑrmənt]

n. 服裝，衣服

同 clothing / wear

April tried on several types of **garments** before deciding on a strapless black evening dress.

在決定穿這件無肩帶黑色晚宴服之前，April 試了幾種不同的服裝。

中級

59. **generosity**

[ˌdʒɛnəˈrɑsəti]

n. 慷慨，大方

⇨ generous「寬容的」+ -ity「名詞字尾」

Although I can never repay my uncle for his **generosity** over the years, I do treat him to lunch as often as I can.

儘管我永遠無法回報我叔叔這些年來對我們的慷慨給予，但我的確盡我所能地經常請他吃午餐。

| 補充 | treat sb. with generosity 以慷慨的態度對待某人 |

generous adj. 大方的；寬容的；大量的

同 kindness

60. **get-together**

[ˈgɛtəˌgɛðɚ]

n.（非正式的）聚會

This Friday, I want to host our weekly **get-together** since I just bought a house with a swimming pool.

由於我才剛買下一間有游泳池的房子，本週五我想要主辦我們的每週聚會。

| 補充 | a family get-together 家庭聚會 |

同 reunion

61. gossip

中級

['gɑsəp]

n. 閒話；流言
v. 說閒話

Maria is the queen of **gossip** around our neighborhood and is constantly prying into everyone's private affairs.
Maria 是我們這附近的八卦女王，她總是一直打探每個人的家務事。

補充	a gossip column	八卦專欄
	to gossip about N.	說有關 N. 的閒話

---

62. gratuity

[grə'tjuətɪ]

n. 小費；離職金；慰勞金

同 tip n. 小費

Be sure to leave a 20% **gratuity** for this waiter.
要留兩成的小費給這位服務生。

補充	to leave a gratuity	留下小費
	a retirement gratuity	退職金
	one-off gratuity	一次領的離職金

---

63. greeting

中級

['gritɪŋ]

n. 致敬；問候

⇨ greet「迎接」+ -ing「名詞字尾」
When meeting anyone from Japan, be sure to bow in **greeting** and try not to keep looking at them directly in the eye.
和從日本來的人見面時，要鞠躬致意而且不要一直盯著對方的眼睛看。

補充	greeting card	禮卡；賀卡
	birthday/Christmas greetings	生日 / 聖誕問候
	to exchange greetings	彼此打招呼問候

greet v. 歡迎、迎接
greetings n. 賀詞，問候

同 salutation

---

64. hilarious

[hɪ'lɛrɪəs]

adj. 極可笑的；令人捧腹的；歡鬧的

 hilarity「歡喜，高興」+ -ous「多…的」
I find it **hilarious** to watch little Katie mash cake icing all over her face when she eats.
我覺得小 Katie 吃蛋糕時弄得滿臉都是蛋糕糖霜真的很好笑。

典故	hilarious 源自古羅馬人一項崇拜希栢利女神的慶典 Hilaria，人們會狂歡慶祝持續數日，後來就從 Hilaria 這個名稱衍生出 hilarity，用來指歡喜、高興。

hilarity n. 歡喜

同 funny

中級

65. informal

[ɪnˋfɔrml]

adj. 非正式的；不拘禮節的

⇨ in -「表否定」+ formal「正式的」

Don't wear such **informal** clothes to the opera house.

別穿這麼不正式的服裝去歌劇院。

補充
informal settlement
臨時居所（如：鐵皮屋）

an informal meeting/visit 非正式的會議 / 拜訪

同 casual
反 formal adj. 正式的

中級

66. ingredient

[ɪnˋgridɪənt]

n. 成分；原料；要素

⇨ in -「進入」+ - gred -「步入」+ - ent「名詞字尾」，
放到物品內部的東西就是組成的原料

I'm not going to divulge all the secret **ingredients** of my homemade fried chicken.

我不會洩露我們家傳炸雞的祕密成分。

補充
the ingredient of/for/in N.　N. 的成份
basic/key ingredient　基本 / 關鍵的成份
food ingredient　食物原料

同 element / factor

中級

67. intrude

[ɪnˋtrud]

v. 侵入；闖入；侵擾

⇨ in -「進入」+ - trud -「推入，刺入」

The children noisily **intruded** on the adults' private meeting.

那些孩子們吵吵鬧鬧地闖入大人們的私人聚會。

補充 intrude on/upon + N. 打擾到 N.

intruder n. 侵入者；闖入者
intrusion n. 侵入
intrusive adj. 侵擾的

同 break in

68. lavish

中高

[ˈlævɪʃ]

adj. 過分大方的；浪費的；
豐富的

v. 揮霍；浪費

 lave「洗浴」+ -ish「有…性質的」

Gary surprised Jenny with a date to a **lavish** restaurant for their twenty-fifth wedding anniversary.

Gary 帶 Jenny 去一間豪華餐廳慶祝他們結婚二十五週年讓 Jenny 受寵若驚。

典故 洗浴時會耗費大量的水，而水在古時是很珍貴的資源，所以 lavish 就有了「浪費的、過分大方的」意思。

補充 | a lavish lifestyle | 奢侈的生活
| lavish costumes/celebrations | 奢華的服裝 / 慶祝

同 adj. = extravagant

69. leftovers

[ˈlɛftovɚz]

n. 剩飯菜；廚餘（必用複數）

 left「被留下的」+ over「剩餘地，額外地」+ -s「複數名詞字尾」

All my guests left all their dishes at my dinner party, so I ate **leftovers** for lunch for the entire following week.

我所有賓客都把晚餐派對的菜留下來給我，所以我接連吃了一整個禮拜的剩飯菜。

leftover n. 殘餘物；剩飯菜
adj. 殘餘的；吃剩的

70. linen

中級

[ˈlɪnən]

n. 亞麻布；亞麻布製品
（如：內衣、床單等）

adj. 亞麻布的

Hang all the **linen** on the clothesline to dry in the sun.

把所有織品掛到晒衣繩上好讓太陽晒乾。

補充 | bed linen | 床單
| table linen | 餐桌布
| linen basket | 洗衣籃
| to wash sb's dirty linen in public | 家醜外揚

71. liquor

中級

[ˈlɪkɚ]

n. 酒，(BrE) 含酒精飲料；
(AmE) 烈酒

It's best to buy shot glasses if you're going to be drinking hard **liquor** as opposed to beer.

如果你要喝烈酒而非啤酒，最好買些一口杯。

補充 | hard liquor 烈酒

11
製造

12
金融

13
科技技術

14
房屋地產

15
出差旅遊

72. luncheon
['lʌntʃən]
n. 午餐會

I would like to invite you to a **luncheon**.
我想邀你共進午餐。

 補充
business luncheon　午間商務餐會
luncheon voucher　午餐券
luncheon meat　　　午餐肉

中級

73. modest
['mɑdɪst]
adj. 謙遜的；適度的；樸實的；
　　端莊的；不大（多）的

Although Chris is one of the top actors in the world, he remains **modest**, and that has earned him many true friends.
儘管 Chris 是全球頂尖演員之一，但他仍然很謙遜，而且這也讓他得到許多真正的朋友。

 補充
modest increase/improvement
些許的增加 / 進步

modesty　n. 謙虛；樸實；端莊

同 humble　adj. 謙虛的

---

74. munch
[mʌntʃ]
v. 用力嚼；大聲咀嚼

All the finger food is on the back table for everyone to just grab a plate and **munch** on until the main course arrives.
所有的小點心都放在後面的餐桌上，大家在主菜上來前都可拿個盤子先吃一點。

★ finger food：指可以用手指拿起來吃的食物，通常為一口大小，也就是小點心。

中高

75. notable
['notəbl]
adj. 值得注意的
n. 名人；重要人物

⇨ note「留意」+ -able「可…的」，可以留意表示是值得關注的
Many **notable** celebrities attended the awards ceremony.
許多知名人物都出席了這場頒獎典禮。

 補充　be notable for N. = be famous for N. 以 N. 聞名

同 adj. = remarkable / noteworthy

16 交通

17 社交與用餐

18 休閒娛樂

19 醫療保健

20 日常生活

76. **overflow**

[͵ovɚˋflo]

v. 溢出；滿出

[ˋovɚ͵flo]

n. 過多的人或物

⇨ over-「超過」+ flow「流出」

The restaurant is **overflowing** with people ready to take advantage of their special grand opening prices.

該間餐廳擠滿準備來搶開幕特惠價的人們。

補充　overflow with N.　N. 多到滿出來
　　　overflow into N.　多到分佈到 N. 去

---

77. **palatable**

[ˋpælətəbl̩]

adj. 美味的；怡人的；
　　可接受的

palate n. 上顎；味覺

同 delicious

反 unpalatable　adj. 難吃的；味道差的

⇨ palate「味覺」+ -able「可…的」，可產生怡人味覺的
　就是美味的

The chicken panini was not **palatable** at all since it had been burned to a crisp.

這份雞肉三明治不好吃，因為它的肉都烤焦了。

---

78. **pastry**

[ˋpestrɪ]

n. 酥皮；脆皮點心

paste n. 糊狀物；漿糊

⇨ paste「麵糊」+ -ry「名詞字尾」

There is nothing more rewarding than being a **pastry** chef and taking care of everyone's sweet tooth.

沒有任何事比當個點心師傅，照顧每個人的甜點胃來得更有意義了。

---

79. **philanthropic**

[͵fɪlənˋθrɑpɪk]

adj. 仁慈的；慈善的

⇨ -phil-「愛」+ -anthrop-「人類」+ -ic「形容詞字
　尾」，有對全人類的愛就是慈善的

After a long career in medicine, Dr. Thomas began his first **philanthropic** venture in Africa.

在長年的醫療生涯後，Thomas 醫生開始到非洲進行他的第一次慈善義診。

補充　philanthropic organization/project
　　　慈善機構 / 計劃

philanthropy n. 慈善；仁慈
philanthropist n. 慈善家

初級

80. **photographer**
[fəˋtɑgrəfə]
n. 攝影師

⇨ **photograph**「攝影」**+ - er**「做…動作的人」
As a wedding **photographer**, I have to work on the weekend.
身為一個婚禮攝影師，我週末得要工作。

 a fashion/wildlife photographer
時裝 / 野生動物攝影師

photograph v. 攝影　n. 照片

中級

81. **portion**
[ˋporʃən]
n. 一部分，份量

Please buy a cake large enough to split into twenty generous **portions** to ensure that everyone will have some.
請買一個足夠切成二十人份大份量的蛋糕，以確保每個人都可以吃得到。

 a generous/small portion of N.
大份量 / 小份量的 N.
portion control　份量控制

 share / part

---

82. **preservative**
[prɪˋzɝvətɪv]
n. 防腐劑
adj. 防腐的

⇨ **pre -**「在…前」**+ serve**「保存」**+ - tive**「具…性質的」，具事前保存起來的性質就是防腐的
The jam is heavily laced with **preservatives** to ensure freshness.
這果醬掺入了大量的防腐劑以確保新鮮。

 artificial/natural preservatives　人工 / 天然防腐劑
No added preservatives.　　　無添加防腐劑。

preserve v. 保存，保留；醃漬（蜜餞、果醬）；禁獵
　　　　　 n. 蜜餞；禁獵區
preservation n. 保護；保存；防腐

中級

83. prompt

[prɑmpt]

adj. 迅速的；立即的；準時的

v. 激發；促使；提詞、提示

n. 提示台詞

I expect a **prompt** reply from you on this matter as too much time has been wasted already.
這個問題我期望能得到你的快速回覆，因為已經浪費了太多時間了。

The recession has **prompted** consumers to spend less.
經濟不景氣促使消費者減少花費。

補充

prompt delivery/payment	立即運送 / 付款
prompt attention/treatment	即時的注意 / 治療
be prompt for N.	準時參加 N.
to prompt sb. to V.	促使某人做某事
to prompt a line/to give a prompt	提詞

unprompted adj. 未受提示的；自動自發的

同 immediate adj. 迅速的
punctual adj. 準時的

中級

84. rack

[ræk]

n. 架子；衣架

v. 把⋯放架子上；使受痛苦

Despite all the online shops, I would still rather buy all my clothes directly off-the-**rack**.
儘管有那麼多線上商店，我仍舊可直接去買現成的成衣來穿。

補充

off-the-rack / off-the-peg / ready-made 現成的
rack rate 牌價；飯店的標準房價
go to rack and ruin 情況變糟
be on the rack 十分痛苦

---

85. ravenous

[ˈrævənəs]

adj. 饑餓的；貪婪的

ravenously adv. 饑餓地

同 starved

The teenagers with **ravenous** appetites will be here, so you will need to order a huge quantity of food.
有胃口極大的青少年會來這，所以你得點大份量的食物。

中級

86. recipe

[ˈrɛsəpɪ]

n. 食譜；烹飪法；訣竅；醫師處方

Gina has a new **recipe** for fried chicken.
Gina 有一個做炸雞的新食譜。

補充

a recipe for N. 做 N. 的食譜
be a recipe for disaster 可能會造成災難發生

中高

87. refreshment

[rɪˈfrɛʃmənt]

n. 茶點；提神飲料或點心

refresh v. 使恢復精神
refreshing adj. 提神的，讓人神清氣爽的

⇨ refresh「使恢復精神」+ -ment「名詞字尾」，吃茶點就可以恢復精神

You can help yourself to the ice-cold **refreshments** which are in the coolers on the patio.
你可以自己取用在露台冰桶裡的冰涼茶點。

中高

88. salute

[səˈlut]

v. 行禮，致意；讚揚；
　向…表示敬意
n. 敬禮，致敬

I want to **solute** John for the backbreaking years of work he put in to get us to where we are now.
由於 John 這麼多年的辛勤投入才使我們達到目前的狀態，所以我想向 John 致敬。

 典故　salute 來自拉丁文 salvus 指平安 (safe)，salutare 就是迎接某人、祝福某人健康，到了 14、15 世紀時，這個字就被用來指軍人對長官行舉手禮，也就是「敬禮、行禮」了。

 補充　raise sb's glass in salute 某人舉杯致意

中高

89. seasoning

[ˈsiznɪŋ]

n. 調味料

season v. 調味
　　　 n. 季節

⇨ season「調味」+ -ing「名詞字尾」

While the vegetables are simmering in the pan, add some bold **seasoning** instead of just a little salt.
當蔬菜還在鍋裡悶煮時，大膽地加些調味料，不要只放一點點鹽。

中高

90. serving

[ˈsɝvɪŋ]

n. 服務；食物或餐飲的一份

serve v. 提供餐食；侍候飲食

⇨ serve「提供飲食」+ -ing「名詞字尾」

The caterer says that each entrée pan is ten **servings**, but I could eat half a pan by myself.
宴會承辦人說每一份主餐鍋是十人份，但我自己一個人就可以吃掉半鍋！

91. **silverware**

[ˈsɪlvəˌwɛr]

n. 銀器；銀餐具

⇨ silver「銀的」+ -ware「製品」

Be sure to wrap each set of **silverware** in a napkin and place one to the right of each plate.
要確定把銀餐具用餐巾包好並在每個盤子右邊擺放一組。

中高

92. **socialize**

[ˈsoʃəlaɪz]

v. 從事社交活動，交際；
使社會化

★ 英：socialise ／美：socialize

⇨ social「社交的，社會的」+ -ize「使…化」

I'm glad to see that you're studying hard, but taking no time to **socialize** is bad for your mental health.
我很高興你努力用功，但沒時間社交對你的心理健康不好。

補充	socialize with sb.	和某人往來
	social life/skills	社交生活 / 社交技巧
	social class/issues	社會階級 / 社會議題

social adj. 社交的；社會的
sociable adj. 好交際的；友善的

中高

93. **specialty**

[ˈspɛʃəltɪ]

n. 專業；特產

★ 英：speciality ／美：specialty

⇨ special「特別的」+ -ty「表狀態」

Manning the grill at barbecues is Tom's **specialty**.
在烤肉餐會中負責處理烤肉是 Tom 的專長。
★ man：當動詞用指負責處理或擔任某工作

| 補充 | local specialties | 當地特產 |
| | a specialty store | 特色商店，專賣店 |

中級

94. **spice**

[spaɪs]

v. 使增添趣味

n. 香料；調味品

I have decided to **spice** up our monthly get-together by hosting a card tournament.
我已決定主持卡牌競賽來為我們的每月聚會增添一點樂趣。

| 典故 | spice 來自拉丁文 specie，原指「種類」，後來衍生出指各種商品、製品或香料的種類，到 14、15 世紀就逐漸被用來指「香料」。 |

補充	add some spice to N. 為 N. 增加一些趣味
	to spice sth. up 將某物調味；為某事增添趣味
	Hunger is the best spice.
	[諺語]：肚子餓，什麼都好吃。
	Variety is the spice of life.
	[諺語]：變化乃生活的調劑。

spicy adj. 有加香料的；辛辣的

中高

95. spotlight

[ˈspɑtˌlaɪt]

n. 聚光燈

v. 聚光照明；使大家注意

⇨ spot「點」+ light「燈光照射」，光線照射在一個點上的燈就是聚光燈

Alicia was suddenly thrust into the **spotlight** when the low-budget movie she was in became a smash hit.

Alicia 在她演的低成本電影一炮而紅後，她突然成為大家注目的焦點。

 be in the spotlight　　成為注目焦點
turn the spotlight on N.　吸引大家對 N. 的關注

中級

96. starve

[stɑrv]

v. (使)挨餓，餓死；缺乏，渴望

starvation n. 饑餓；餓死

This crowd is just **starving** for excitement, and you're just the person to provide some.

這群人渴望刺激，而你就是能提供一些刺激的人。

 starve to death　饑餓而死
starve for N.　渴望 N.
be starved of N.　缺乏(所需的)N.

中高

97. stew

[stju]

n. 燉煮的食物

v. 燉煮，熬煮

Our restaurant serves the best beef **stew** in town.
本餐廳供應全城最棒的燉牛肉。

 stew 是中世紀英文 stewen 的縮寫，原指「泡熱水澡」。燉煮的菜都是泡在熱水或熱湯中不斷用小火煮，就像食材在泡熱水澡一樣，所以 stew 就是烹飪中的「燉煮」，用這種料理方式煮出來的食物也稱為 stew。

 stew over N.　　　　仔細思考 N.
stew in one's own juice　自作自受

98. **steward**

[ˈstjuwəd]

n. 服務員；管理員；總管

 stig「古英文，廳室，欄舍」+ **-ward**「朝…方向」

While I was working overseas, you were such a good **steward** of all my finances.

當我在海外工作時，你真是我財務上的好管家。

| 典故 | steward 就是朝著屋內各個廳室或欄舍前進，最早指在家中掌管大小事、忙前忙後的管家，後來便衍生出在交通工具上處理乘客餐食與日常生活需求的人。 |

| 補充 | wine steward 侍酒員 |

stewardess n. 女服務員

同 attendant

99. **vegetarian**

[ˌvɛdʒəˈtɛrɪən]

n. 素食者
adj. 素食的

 vegetable「蔬菜」+ **-arian**「表執行某主義或信條的人」

Remember that about a quarter of your guests tonight will be **vegetarians**, so have plenty of healthy meal options available.

記得今晚你的客人中有四分之一是素食者，所以要準備大量健康餐食讓他們選用。

| 補充 | vegetarian meal 素餐
lacto-vegetarian 吃奶素的素食者 |

100. **volunteer**

[ˌvɑlənˈtɪr]

n. 志願者；義工
v. 自願做…；自願服務

⇨ **-vol-**「意願」+ **-ent**「形容詞字尾」+ **-eer**「做…的人」

It's more rewarding to spend your time in retirement as a **volunteer** instead of watching TV all day.

退休後花時間當志工比整天看電視更有意義。

補充	volunteer staff/worker	志工；義工
	a volunteer doctor/lawyer	義務性質的醫生/律師
	to volunteer to V.	自願做…
	to volunteer for N.	自願…

voluntary adj. 自願的；志願的

實力進階

Part 1. entrée/main course/appetizer/starter/side dish

常飛來飛去的商務人士一定要很熟悉常見的一些菜單英文用語，同一個字在不同的國家可能是不同的意思，一定要注意自己身處的國度才不會產生誤會喔！

entrée / main course	entrée 這個字在使用上要特別注意，因為在美國和英國就有意思上的差異。在美國，entrée 指的就是主菜，也就是 main course 的意思。但是在英國，entrée 指的是主菜前的小菜，就是前菜。
appetizer/starter	appetizer 和 starter 都是開胃菜，appetizer 是美式用法，starter 是英式用法。
side dish	side dish 又叫做 side order 或 side item，很多美國人甚至直接說是 side，指的是主菜旁的配菜，可以和主菜放在同個盤子上，有時也會放在獨立的盤子上。

Part 2. beverage/drink/liquor/soft drink

beverage	beverage 泛指任何一種飲料，若要特別指含有酒精的飲料要說 alcoholic beverage。
drink	drink 除了同樣可以表飲料外，另外也可以直接表「酒」。
liquor	liquor 一般是指烈酒，也可以說是蒸餾酒，英文稱為 distilled beverage。
soft drink	soft drink 字面上叫做軟性飲料，指的是不含酒精的飲料，通常是指含有碳酸水、增甜劑及調味香料的飲料，汽水就是屬於這一類，所以也可以稱為 soda。

Part 3. 常用來形容食物味道的各種說法

酸的	sour/acid
甜的	sweet/sugary
苦的	bitter/acrid
辣的	hot/spicy/peppery
油膩的	greasy
多汁的	juicy
鹹的	salty/savory/saline
令人垂涎欲滴的	mouth-watering
美味可口的	delicious/yummy/palatable/toothsome/tasty

隨堂練習

★ 請根據句意，選出最適合的單字

(　　) 1. What makes this company a success is that it does its best to _____ to special requests.
    (A) cater   (B) volunteer
    (C) extend   (D) rack

(　　) 2. It is rude of you not to leave a _____ for the waiter since he did provide good service.
    (A) delicacy   (B) fragrance
    (C) generosity   (D) gratuity

(　　) 3. No matter how successful you are, you have to be _____ so that you can win the respect of others.
    (A) distinguished   (B) eloquent
    (C) modest   (D) hilarious

(　　) 4. Many employees in this company think that their employers should not _____ into their private lives by calling them after work.
    (A) crack   (B) intrude
    (C) digest   (D) crave

(　　) 5. Eating between meals will spoil your _____.
    (A) appetite
    (C) refreshment   (B) garment
                           (D) portion

解答：1. A   2. D   3. C   4. B   5. A

Unit 18 休閒娛樂

1. acclaim
[əˈklem]
n. 歡呼；稱讚
v. 為…歡呼、喝采

⇨ ac -「to」+ claim「聲稱」，聲稱某人是有功勞的就是一種稱讚

The famed actress has received much critical **acclaim** over the years.
該位知名女演員這些年來已得到許多好評。

 a highly acclaimed novel/movie
受到高度推崇的小說 / 電影
be acclaimed for N. 因 N. 而受到讚揚

acclaimed adj. 受到讚揚的；廣受推崇的
acclaimation n. 歡呼；喝采
同 praise

---

2. activity
[ækˈtɪvətɪ]
n. 活動

⇨ active「有活力的」+ -ity「名詞字尾」

There is a different community **activity** going on each night at the recreation center.
休閒中心裡每晚都有不同的社區活動。

outdoor/leisure activity	戶外 / 休閒活動
commercial/marketing activity	商業 / 行銷活動
to boost economic activity	促進經濟活動

active adj. 有活力的；積極的

---

3. admission
[ədˈmɪʃən]
n. 准許進入；入場費；門票

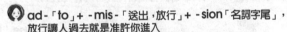 ad -「to」+ -mis -「送出，放行」+ -sion「名詞字尾」，放行讓人過去就是准許你進入

To pay for the renovation, the cost of **admission** to the stadium has gone up.
因為要整修，體育場門票的費用調高了。

補充
the admission to N.
獲准進入 N.，成為 N. 的成員之一
apply for/deny admission to N.
申請 / 否決進入 N. 的許可
free admission to N. 參加 N. 的免費入場券
admission charge/fee 入場費

admit v. 准許…進入；容許；承認
admittance n. 入場許可
同 access n. 入場；進入
ticket n. 門票

4. aerobics

[ɛ`robɪks]

n. 有氧運動

 - aero - 「空氣」+ - bio - 「生物」+ - ics 「名詞字尾表學術」

Taking an **aerobics** class is a great way to stay in shape.
上有氧運動的課是保持身材的好方法。

> **典故** 二十世紀有位美國醫師庫柏 (Dr. Cooper) 發現許多肌力很好的人做長時間運動時無法持久，便開始研究人體提高氧氣利用的方法，並將研究出版成 Aerobics 一書，從此帶動 aerobics 有氧運動的流行。

> **補充** do aerobics　　做有氧運動
> go to aerobics　上有氧運動課

aerobic **adj.** 有氧的；需要氧氣的

初級

5. affect

[ə`fɛkt]

v. 影響

 ⇨ af - 「to」+ - fect - 「做」，對著你做動作就會影響你

Dramatic movies always **affect** me deeply due to my sensitive character.
由於我敏感的個性，激動人心的電影總是會深深地影響我。

> **補充** be affected by... 受到…的影響

affection **n.** 影響；感情、情愛

同 influence

中級

6. amuse

[ə`mjuz]

v. 使歡樂；使愉快；使發笑

 a - 「to」+ Muse 「繆斯女神」

This comedian **amuses** me, but he doesn't make me laugh like some others do.
這個喜劇演員是讓我笑了出來，但他並沒有讓我像其他人一樣捧腹大笑。

> **典故** Muse 是古希臘神話中掌管藝術音樂的繆斯女神，amuse 就是指為你提供音樂和藝術讓你身心感到愉悅、愉快，也就是「使愉快、使歡樂」。

> **補充** amuse A with B 以 B 讓 A 歡樂開心

amusement **n.** 娛樂、樂趣、休閒
amusing **adj.** 有趣的；好玩的

同 entertain

7. **anecdote**

[ˋænɪkˏdot]

n. 軼事；祕聞

⇨ an - 「表否定」+ ec - 「= ex - ，向外」+ dote 「源自希臘文，表給予」，不能給出去的祕密

Mr. Ross has used several personal **anecdotes** to illustrate how debt has destroyed people he loves.

Ross 先生用幾個親身的奇聞軼事舉例說明債務如何毀了他所愛的人們。

>
> 典故
> 這個字來自東羅馬帝國的歷史學家普羅科彼厄斯 (Procopius)，他曾寫了一本自稱「充滿醜聞而無法寫入正史」的 anecdote(秘史)，意思就是不能給外人知道的，也就是軼事、祕聞。

中級

8. **applaud**

[əˋplɔd]

v. 鼓掌；讚許

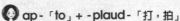 ap - 「to」+ -plaud - 「打，拍」

The crowd **applauded** so loudly for Taylor Swift that she did three encores.

群眾如此用力地為 Taylor Swift 鼓掌，所以她唱了三首安可曲。

> 補充
> applaud N.　　　讚許 N.
> applaud sb. for sth.　為某事讚許某人

applause n. 掌聲，鼓掌

同 clap

中高

9. **artifact**

[ˋɑrtɪˏfækt]

n. 手工藝品

★ 英：artefact ／美：artifact

⇨ art 「藝術，技術」+ i + -fact - 「做」，用技術做出的就是手工藝品

The downtown museum exhibits the most Medieval-era **artifacts** in one location.

市中心博物館有一區展出許多中世紀時期的手工藝品。

---

10. **audition**

[ɔˋdɪʃən]

n. 試鏡，試演，試唱會

v. 試鏡，試演

 -audi - 「聽」+ -tion 「名詞字尾」

Ang Lee is holding open **auditions** for small parts in his upcoming movie.

李安正在為他即將開拍新片中的小角色進行公開試鏡。

> 補充
> to audition for N.　為 N. 進行試演 / 唱
> to audition sb.　　為某人進行試鏡

中級

11. author

[ˈɔθɚ]

n. 作者

v. 著作；編寫

➡ - auct - 「增大」+ - or「做…動作的人」，增加作品產量的人就是作者

Although Eric is a best-selling **author**, he still gets writer's block from time to time.

儘管 Eric 是位暢銷作家，但有時他仍會遇到文思不順的狀況。

★ writer's block：作家的障礙，指作家遇到沒有靈感或文思不順暢的狀況。

中級

12. ballet

[ˈbæle] / [bæˈle]

n. 芭蕾舞

In the off-season, some football players will take part in the **ballet** to stay agile.

在非球季時，一些足球選手會跳芭蕾舞以保持敏捷的身手。

補充

ballet dancer	芭蕾舞者
ballet shoes	芭蕾舞鞋

13. billboard

[ˈbɪlˌbord]

n. 大型廣告看板；（美國唱片）排行榜

 bill「帳單」+ board「板子」

I'm thinking about running a **billboard** ad for our company.

我正考慮要幫我們公司做個大型看板廣告。

補充

an advertising billboard	大型看板廣告
digital billboard	電子看板

🔄 hoarding (BrE)

14. billiards

[ˈbɪljɚdz]

n. 撞球

➡ bille「古法文，木桿」+ - ard「名詞字尾」

Please show me the tips about how to play **billiards** well.

請教我如何能打好撞球的訣竅。

🔄 snooker/ pool

15. box office

[bɑks][ˈɔfɪs]

n. 票房；售票處

Doing well at the **box office** does not necessarily mean that a movie is of high quality.

票房表現亮眼不見得表示它就是部高品質的電影。

補充

a box office bomb 票房很差的電影

a box-office success = a blockbuster
賣座的電影

box-office adj. 受歡迎的；叫座的

16. **broadcast**

[ˋbrɔdˏkæst]

v. 播送；廣播

n. 電視節目；廣播節目

★ 動詞變化：broadcast, broadcast, broadcast, broadcasting

⇨ broad「寬廣的」+ cast「擲出」，廣播就是將訊息電波廣泛投射出去

Our local news is only **broadcast** at six and seven o'clock at night.

我們的地區新聞只有在晚間六點和七點播出。

補充

to broadcast A on B 在 B(頻道) 上播出 A(節目)

a radio/television broadcast 收音機 / 電視播出

a live broadcast 現場直播

---

17. **cable**

[ˋkebl̩]

n. 有線電視

I love a few **cable** channels, but the cable companies force you to buy an entire package.

我喜歡一些有線電視頻道，但有線電視公司會逼你買一整個套裝組合。

補充

a pay cable channel 付費有線頻道

cable company 有線電視公司

---

18. **capture**

[ˋkæptʃ⋅]

v. 拍攝；捕捉；取得

n. 捕獲；俘虜；佔領

⇨ - cap -「抓」+ - ture「名詞字尾，表結果」

I **captured** some breathtaking images of the sunset last night.

我昨晚捕捉到一些令人驚豔的夕陽影像。

補充

capture a large share of the market 取得大部份的市場

data capture 數據收集

captive n. 俘虜；受控制的人

---

19. **carnival**

[ˋkɑrnəvl̩]

n. 嘉年華會；狂歡

 - carn -「肉」+ val「源自拉丁文，表減輕，去掉」

The Smith family goes to the local **carnival** every year.

Smith 一家人每年都去當地的嘉年華會。

典故

carnival 原指「把肉拿掉、丟棄」，因基督教中有所謂的齋戒期，齋戒時不可辦派對活動，也不可吃肉或乳製品，所以齋戒前必須將所有此類食物丟棄，古時人們會在齋戒前舉辦大型狂歡活動將這些食物吃掉，後來就用 carnival(把肉丟掉) 來稱呼齋戒前的這個活動，也就是今天的 carnival 嘉年華會。

20. **cathedral**

[kəˋθidrəl]

n. 大教堂

⇨ cat-「向下」+ hedra「希臘文，座位」+ -al「名詞字尾」

The historical **cathedrals** around Paris have the most intricately crafted figures I have ever seen done by hand.

在巴黎週邊具歷史性的大教堂，有我所見過最精緻複雜的手工打造雕像。

 cathedral 原指古時各區主教在教堂內所坐的座位，後來就用來指各區主教所在的教堂。

21. **celebrity**

[səˋlɛbrətɪ]

n. 名人；名聲

⇨ celeber「拉丁文，有名的」+ -ity「名詞字尾」

What your small company needs in order to get noticed is a **celebrity** spokesperson.

你的小公司想要吸引人注意，就需要找名人做代言人。

22. **ceremony**

[ˋsɛrəˌmonɪ]

n. 儀式；典禮

The wedding **ceremony** cost nearly $100,000.

這場婚禮花了快十萬塊。

 ceremony 來自拉丁文的 caerimonia，最早指「不可侵犯的、聖潔」，據說這個字源起於義大利遠古時期伊特魯里亞人在 Caere 所舉行的神秘神聖儀式。

 stand on ceremony
講究禮節，拘謹地（常用於否定句）
without ceremony　粗糙地，隨便地

ceremonial adj. 儀式的，慶典的

同 rite

23. **chorus**

[ˋkorəs]

n. 合唱團；齊聲

v. 合唱，合奏；齊聲說

choir n.（教堂）唱詩班

A **chorus** of boos rained down upon the comedian for making such offensive remarks.

那名喜劇演員說了很冒犯人的評論，引來一片噓聲。

 a chorus of sth. 一致、一片的某種聲音或意見
in chorus　　　異口同聲地

16 交通

17 社交與用餐

18 休閒娛樂

19 醫療保健

20 日常生活

24. **cinema**
['sɪnəmə]
n. 電影院

同 movie theater

Due to the high cost, I only go to the **cinema** when the critics praise a movie.
由於看電影所費不貲，我只去看影評有正面評價的電影。

 cinema 源自 cinematography 指拍攝動作影像的技術。

 go to the cinema = go to the movies 去看電影

---

25. **concert**
['kɑnsət]
n. 音樂會；演奏會

The rock star is going to hold a **concert** at the downtown arena in April.
那名搖滾明星四月時要在市中心小巨蛋舉辦演唱會。

 concert-goer 演奏會常客；常聽演奏會的人
act in concert (with sb.)（和某人）一起行動

---

26. **costume**
['kɑstjum]
n. 服裝

You are expected to be in **costume** and in position backstage by no later than 6:30 pm.
你最晚得在六點半前著裝並在後台就位。

 Halloween costume 萬聖節服裝
costume jewellery 人造珠寶
costume party 化妝舞會

---

27. **cue**
[kju]
n. 暗示；提示
v. 給提示，給暗示

Your **cue** to speak is when Mary sneezes.
Mary 打噴嚏時就是暗示你可以說話了。

 cue card 錄影現場的提示字卡
(right) on cue 立即，就在此刻
take your cue from sb./sth. 照著別人的樣子做

11
製造

12
金融

13
科技技術

14
房屋地產

15
出差旅遊

中高
28. culminate
[ˋkʌlmənet]
v. 以…告終；最終

⇨ culmin「拉丁文，頂端」+ -ate「使…」，到達頂端表示結束了

The show **culminates** in a fantastic pyrotechnic display with a roaring orchestra.
這場表演以燦爛的煙火伴隨雄壯的管弦樂音做為結尾。

補充 culminate in N. 以 N. 做為結束

culmination n. 頂點，終結

初級
29. curtain
[ˋkɝtn̩]
n. 窗簾；幕

We are waiting for the **curtain** to rise.
我們正等待簾幕拉起。

補充 curtain call　　　　　（表演）謝幕
bring down the curtain on N.　N. 結束了

中高
30. debut
[deˋbju] / [ˋdebju]
n. 首次登台
v. 首演；首次登台；首次亮相

Harriet will **debut** her new line of designer dresses on the catwalk tomorrow.
Harriet 明天將在伸展台上首次展示她最新設計的一系列服裝。

典故 源自法文 début，原意指「開球、開始」。

補充 make one's debut 某人首次登台
to debut N. 　　　首次發表 N.

初級
31. drama
[ˋdrɑmə]
n. 戲劇；劇本

Tammy enjoys watching TV **dramas** in her free time.
Tammy 喜歡在休閒時看電視劇。

補充 a drama critic　　　戲劇評論者；戲評
a drama queen　　　小題大作的人
drama documentary 由真實事件改編的戲劇

dramatic adj. 戲劇性的；劇烈的
同 play

中級
32. **editorial**

[ˌɛdəˈtɔrɪəl]

n. 社論
adj. 編輯的

⇨ editor「編輯」+ -ial「有關…的」，編輯寫在報紙中的文章就是社論

After years of reporting, I got the chance to write **editorials** and divulge what I really feel.

在報導新聞數年後，我終於有機會撰寫社論透露我真正的想法。

補充   editorial staff 編輯人員

edit v. 編輯
editor n. 編輯者

中高
33. **enrich**

[ɪnˈrɪtʃ]

v. 使豐富；使富裕

⇨ en-「使…」+ rich「富含…的」

I love teaching my son to do home improvement projects that **enrich** his education outside of school.

我喜歡教我兒子做一些家居修繕，以豐富他在學校課業以外的學習。

補充   enrich A with B 用 B 來增強 A

enrichment n. 豐富；增強營養

中高
34. **enroll**

[ɪnˈrol]

v. 把…記入名冊；將…登記起來

★ 英：enrol ／美：enroll

⇨ en-「使放入」+ roll「名單」，放到名單裡就是登記註冊了

Even older adults are now choosing to **enroll** at colleges again to have a better chance of getting promoted.

即便是年紀較大的成年人現在也選擇再到大學註冊就讀以得到更多升遷的機會。

補充   enroll sb. for/in/on N. 將某人納入 N. 中

enrollment n. 登記；入會；註冊登記
同 register

11 製造

12 金融

13 科技技術

14 房屋地產

15 出差旅遊

中級

35. entertain

[ˌɛntəˋten]

v. 使娛樂，使歡樂；招待，款待

entertainer n. 藝人；表演者
entertainment n. 娛樂

同 amuse / delight v. 使歡樂

⇨ enter「進入」+ -tain-「留住」，招待你讓你進來留下

I won't be home for a while, so you'll need to **entertain** your parents by yourself.
我有段時間會不在家，所以你得自己招待你爸媽。

 entertain sb. with sth. 用某物來娛樂某人

中級

36. exhibit

[ɪgˋzɪbɪt]

v. 展示；表示（情緒）
n. 展示品；展覽會

exhibition n. 展覽；展示會；表現出

同 display

The company's latest products will be **exhibited** at the annual trade fair.
該公司最新的產品將在年度貿易展覽會展出。

exhibit (N.) at/in... 在…中展示 N.
sth. be on exhibition 某物在展出中

中高

37. fidelity

[fɪˋdɛlətɪ]

n. 準確性，精確性；忠貞，忠誠

It is disappointing that the film lacks **fidelity** to the original novel.
令人失望的是電影並沒有忠於原著小說。

典故 源自拉丁文 fides 表「信念、信仰」。有信念、信仰就會對所相信的事物很忠誠。fidelity 原本就指對信仰或配偶的忠貞，後引申也可指翻譯確實、影像逼真的意思。

the fidelity to N. 對 N. 的忠實度
high fidelity (hi-fi) 高傳真，高保真度

同 loyalty

初級

38. film

[fɪlm]

v. 拍攝影片
n. 軟片，膠捲；電影

When the director is shooting on location, he likes to **film** for eighteen hours straight each day.
那導演在拍外景時，他喜歡一天連續拍十八小時。

CF= commercial film 電視廣告；商業影片
silent film 默劇
filmmaker 電影製作人；電影導演
film-goer = moviegoer = cinema-goer
電影迷（經常看電影的人）

39. **finale**

[fɪˋnælɪ]

n. 結局；樂曲的最終章

On New Year's Day, the fireworks shows around the world always have a huge, explosive **finale**.
在新年時，全球的煙火秀都有大型且具爆發力的結尾。

補充　grand finale　（演出的）大結局
the finale of N.　N. 的最終章

final adj. 最後的　n. 決賽；期末考

中級

40. **fireworks**

[ˋfaɪrˌwɝks]

n. 煙火

⇨ fire「火」+ work「作品」+ -s「複數名詞字尾」
People got together at the square to watch the **fireworks**.
人們聚集在廣場上看煙火。

補充　a firework display　　　　煙火大會
set off/let off the fireworks　施放煙火

中級

41. **gallery**

[ˋgælərɪ]

n. 畫廊，藝廊；（大廳或劇場的）樓座

I'm having a showing at the local art **gallery**, and I hope you'll have time to stop by.
我在本地藝廊有展覽，希望你們有空可以來順道參觀。

補充　an art gallery　　　藝廊
press gallery　　　國會議堂上的記者旁聽區
shooting gallery　射擊練習場

中級

42. **headline**

[ˋhɛdˌlaɪn]

n. 標題；（報紙）大標題

⇨ head「頭」+ line「字詞，話語」，放在新聞最前頭的字就是標題
It made **headlines** when the movie star rented out an entire hotel just for his entourage.
那電影明星租了一整棟旅館只為了給隨行人員住，這件事就上了新聞版面。

補充　the headlines　　　　　新聞大標
a banner headline　報紙橫幅大標
grab/make/hit the headlines
上新聞版面；成為新聞話題

headliner n. 主演；重頭戲；壓軸

43. **heritage**

[ˋhɛrətɪdʒ]

n. 遺產；繼承物；傳統

 inherit「繼承」+ -age「名詞字尾」

This ancient temple has been listed in the World **Heritage** Sites.

這間古廟已被列為世界遺產。

| 補充 | the cultural heritage 文化遺產 |
| | World Heritage Site 世界遺產所在地 |

中高

44. **hockey**

[ˋhɑkɪ]

n. 曲棍球

⇨ hoc「古法文，鉤子」+ -ey「表小東西」

The best thing about winter in Canada is playing ice **hockey** on a frozen pond.

在加拿大，冬天最棒的事就是在結冰的池塘上玩冰上曲棍球。

補充	ice hockey 冰上曲棍球
	field hockey 草地曲棍球
	street hockey 直排輪曲棍球

中高

45. **holder**

[ˋholdɚ]

n. 持有者；支架

⇨ hold「持有」+ -er「做…動作的人或物」

Official members and season ticket **holders** can buy up to an extra five tickets for family and friends for this season.

正式會員及季票持票人在本季可額外為親友購買最多五張票。

補充	a ticket holder 票卡持有人
	a property holder 財產所有人
	a record holder 紀錄保持人
	a cup holder (交通工具上的)杯架
	a candle holder 燭台

同 owner n. 持有者

中級

46. **indoor**

[ˋɪndɔr]

adj. 室內的

⇨ in「在…裡面」+ door「門」

There are plenty of **indoor** activities for us to do at my house, such as table tennis and pool.

在我家我們可以從事許多室內活動，像是桌球和撞球。

| 補充 | indoor sports/activities 室內運動/活動 |
| | an indoor swimming pool 室內游泳池 |

indoors adv. 室內的，在室內

反 outdoor adj. 戶外的

中級

47. **inspiration**

[ˌɪnspəˈreʃən]

n. 靈感；啟發

 inspire「激發，啟發」+ -ation「名詞字尾」

Steve Jobs was my **inspiration** to start inventing some of the electronic gadgets that I sell online.

我之所以開始發明一些電子玩意兒並在網路上販售都是受到 Steve Jobs 的啟發。

補充

spark of inspiration　靈光一閃
A be an inspiration to B
A 是 B 所仰慕、仿效的對象
the inspiration for N.　做出 N. 的靈感
Genius is ten percent inspiration and ninety percent perspiration.
[諺語]：天才是九分努力加一分的靈感。

inspire v. 激發，啟發
inspired adj. 受到啟發的，被鼓舞的
inspirational adj. 具啟發性的

中級

48. **intellectual**

[ˌɪntʃˈɛktʃʊəl]

n. 知識份子
adj. 智力的，動腦筋的

⇨ inte-「在…之間」+ -lect-「選擇」+ -al「形容詞字尾」，要動腦筋才能在事物間做選擇

You need to be quite an **intellectual** to join our neighborhood book club.

你得是名知識份子才能參加我們社區的讀書會。

補充

intellectual property rights　智慧財產權
intellectual property law = IP law　智慧財產法
intellectual asset　軟資產 (智慧資產)
intellectual challenge　智力挑戰

中級

49. **journal**

[ˈdʒɝnl̩]

n. 日誌；期刊

I kept a daily **journal** of my exploits in Africa three years ago.

我三年前在非洲拓荒時每天都有記日誌。

典故

journal 來自法文，最早指教堂進行儀式或禮拜的紀錄。

補充

keep a journal　記錄日誌
a medical/trade/scientific journal
醫學 / 貿易 / 科學期刊

journalism n. 新聞業，新聞工作
journalist n. 新聞工作者；記者
同 diary n. 日記

中級

50. landscape
['lænd‚skep]
n. 風景，景色

🙂 land「陸地」+ -scape「表狀態」
Tonight as the sun sets, we can gaze out on the desert **landscape** and marvel at its beauty.
當今晚太陽落下時，我們可以凝望沙漠風景並讚嘆它的美麗。

補充

seascape	海景
cityscape	城市風景
townscape	城鎮風景
streetscape	街景
landscape painting	風景畫

中級

51. league
[lig]
n. 體育聯賽；聯盟

Who do you think will win the **league** championship?
你覺得誰會贏得聯賽冠軍？

補充

Major League Baseball (MLB)	美國職棒大聯盟
Little League Baseball (LLB)	世界少棒聯盟
the big league	
重要的組織；有頂級水準的活動	
in league with sb.	和某人密謀

同 聯盟：union / alliance

中級

52. lecture
['lɛktʃɚ]
n./v. 演講；授課；教訓

➡ -lect-「選擇」+ -ure「表結果」，挑選後發表的東西就是演講
The famous speaker is giving a **lecture** at the auditorium this afternoon.
那位知名演說者今天下午在大禮堂有一場演講。

補充

deliver/give a lecture on N.	進行關於 N. 的演講
lecture series	系列講座
give sb. a lecture (= to lecture sb.)	
教訓，訓斥某人	

lecturer n. 演講者；講師

同 speech / address n. 演說

中級

53. leisure

[ˈliʒɚ]

n. 閒暇；空閒時間

Instead of going to movies, I enjoy buying DVDs and watching them at my **leisure**.

我喜歡買 DVD 並在空閒時觀賞，而不是上電影院去看電影。

補充	leisure activities/facilities	休閒活動／設施
	the leisure industry	休閒娛樂產業
	at sb's leisure	某人空閒時，有空時

同 spare time / free time

中級

54. marathon

[ˈmærəˌθɑn]

n. 馬拉松；耐力賽

adj. 馬拉松式的；長時間的

I love to run in **marathons** that raise funds for cancer research.

我喜歡參加為籌募癌症研究基金而舉辦的馬拉松。

補充	do/run a marathon	跑馬拉松
	marathon negotiations	長時間的談判
	ultramarathon n. 超級馬拉松	
	telethon n. (為募款而舉辦的) 馬拉松式電視節目	

中高

55. massage

[məˈsɑʒ]

n. 按摩術

v. 幫…按摩

It's been a stressful day, and you deserve a long **massage** to take a load off.

今天是壓力很大的一天，你應該要來個時間長一點的按摩放鬆一下。

★ take a load off：坐下或躺下放鬆

補充	a massage parlor	按摩院、按摩店
	deep tissue massage	深層組織按摩
	give sb. a massage	幫某人按摩
	to massage sb's ego	奉承、討好某人

中級

56. masterpiece

[ˈmæstɚˌpis]

n. 傑作；名作；代表作

⇨ **master**「大師」+ **piece**「一件物品」

Of all the poems you've ever written, I believe this one is your **masterpiece**.

在你所有寫過的詩篇中，我相信這一篇就是你的代表作。

補充	a masterpiece of N.	N. 的最佳例證、最好的示範

同 masterwork

11
製造

12
金融

13
科技技術

14
房屋地產

15
出差旅遊

中高

57. **media**

[ˈmidɪə]

n. 傳播媒體

You shouldn't believe everything the **media** tells you about this news story since they often exaggerate.

因為媒體常常會誇大，關於這個消息你不應該盡信他們告訴你的每件事情。

補充
mass media	大眾傳媒
media attention/coverage	媒體的注意 / 普遍報導
a media baron/tycoon	媒體大亨

---

58. **mountaineering**

[ˌmaʊntəˈnɪrɪŋ]

n. 爬山；登山運動

⇨ mountain「山」+ -eer「從事…活動的人」+ -ing「名詞字尾」

I am taking a survival class where they teach you about **mountaineering** on your own and living off the land.

我正在上一門野外求生課程，他們教你如何獨自登山並在野地生存下去。

補充　go mountaineering 去登山

mountaineer n. 登山者

中級

59. **musical**

[ˈmjuzɪk!]

n. 音樂劇
adj. 音樂的

⇨ music「音樂」+ - al「與…有關的」

My cousin Jack is playing the lead role in the school's winter **musical**.

我表哥 Jack 在學校冬季音樂劇中擔任主角。

補充
musical instruments 樂器
musical chairs
音樂椅，音樂結束時所有人要搶有限座位的遊戲
to play musical chairs（職場）職位調動

中高

60. **newscast**

[ˈnjuzˌkæst]

n. 新聞廣播，新聞播送

⇨ news「新聞」+ cast「投擲」，將新聞對外送出就是在播送新聞

I am waiting for the eleven o'clock **newscast** so I can check on tomorrow's weather forecast.

我正在等十一點整的新聞播報，那樣我才能看一下明天的天氣預報。

newscaster n. 新聞播報員；新聞主播

61. orchestra

[ˋɔrkɪstrə]

n. 管弦樂隊

Mary is first chair viola in the school **orchestra**.

Mary 是學校管弦樂團的第一中提琴手。

 原指古劇院中保留給重要人士的座位區，後漸演變為劇院中音樂演奏者所在的區域，十八世紀後便用來指專司演奏的管弦樂團。

symphony orchestra	交響樂團
chamber orchestra	小型管弦樂團
scratch orchestra	倉促成軍的樂團

orchestrate v. 編管弦樂曲；精心（祕密）策劃

---

62. participate

[pɑrˋtɪsəˌpet]

v. 參加；參與

⇨ part「分開」+ -cip-「拿」+ -ate「動詞字尾」，拿了分出來的一部分就表示你也參與其中了

Each child must pay a small fee to **participate** in school sports.

每個孩子必須付一點費用以參加學校的體育活動。

 participate in sth. 參與某事

participation n. 參與；分享
participant n. 參與者；參加者

同 take part in

---

63. pastime

[ˋpæsˌtaɪm]

n. 消遣；娛樂

Online shopping seems to be the most popular national **pastime** now.

網購現在似乎是最風行全國的休閒活動了。

同 recreation / amusement / hobby

---

64. performer

[pɚˋfɔrmɚ]

n. 表演者

⇨ perform「演出」+ -er「做⋯動作的人」

I'm impressed that your production is stacked with top **performers**.

你的演出作品裡盡是頂尖表演者，這點讓我印象深刻。

 the star performer（團體中）表現最搶眼的人

perform v. 演出，表現
performance n. 演出；表演

中高

65. periodical

[͵pɪrɪˋɑdɪkl̩]

n. 雜誌；期刊
adj. 週期的；定期的

⇨ **periodic**「定期的」+ **-al**「名詞字尾」，定期發行的刊物就是雜誌、期刊

To properly research your report topic, I suggest going to the **periodicals** section on the second floor of the main library.
為好好研究你的報告主題，我建議到圖書館總館的二樓期刊區看看。

period n. 時期；期間
periodic adj. 週期的、週期性的；定期的

初級

66. positive

[ˋpɑzətɪv]

adj. 正面的；積極的；確定的
n. 正面；正向

⇨ **-posi-**「放置」+ **-tive**「具…性質的」，放著讓人看得到就是明確的

Our presentation before the Board generated a **positive** response.
我們給董事會做的報告得到了正面的回應。

 補充

positive review/note	正面的評價
a positive impact/effect	正面的影響 / 效果
positive response/feedback	正向的回應 / 回響
a positive attitude	積極的態度

反 negative adj. 負面的；消極的；否定的

初級

67. press

[prɛs]

n. 新聞界；出版社 (常大寫)

Whatever happens, we can't leak any information to the **press** about this embarrassing incident.
不論發生什麼事，我們都不能洩露關於這件糗事的任何訊息讓媒體知道。

 補充

freedom of (the) press	新聞言論自由
press conference = press briefing	記者會
press release	新聞稿
go to press	送印；付梓

68. preview

[ˋprɪˏvju]
n. 試映；預習
[prɪˋvju]
v. 預習；試演

⇨ pre-「在…前」+ view「觀看」，事前先看就是預習或影片的試映

Many celebrities attended the sneak **preview** of Karl Lagerfeld's winter collection.

很多名人出席了 Karl Lagerfeld 的冬裝發表會。

★ sneak preview：在時裝界指新款上市前所舉行的走秀、發表會，讓消費者可預先看到新的款式。

補充
print preview （電腦）預覽列印
a press preview （只對媒體公佈的）媒體試映會

反 review n./v. 複習

---

69. prime

[praɪm]
n. 全盛時期，黃金時期
adj. 主要的；最好的

The TV series will be broadcast during **prime** time.
該齣電視劇將會在黃金時段播出。

補充
in sb's prime 在某人的黃金時期／全盛時期
prime time （電視或廣播的）黃金時段
prime cost = direct cost 主要成本
prime minister 首相

primary adj. 主要的；初級的

---

70. production

[prəˋdʌkʃən]
n. 生產，製作；出品

⇨ pro-「向前」+ -duct-「引導」+ -ion「名詞字尾」，往前引導做出成品就是在進行生產製造

If you want this **production** to be top-notch, we're going to need a lot more funding.

如果你想要這個產品是最棒的，我們需要更多的資金。

★ top-notch：一流的

補充
production cost/target 生產成本／目標
batch production 批次生產
go into/out of production 開始／停止生產

produce v. 生產，製作
product n. 產品

11 製造

初級

71. **recreation**

[ˌrɛkrɪˈeʃən]

n. 娛樂；消遣

⇨ re - 「再次」+ create「創造」+ - ion「名詞字尾」，休閒使人有再次創造的動力

Leave some time for **recreation** so you don't get burned out.

留點時間休閒一下免得累壞了。

補充 recreation center 休閒中心

recreational adj. 休閒的；娛樂的

同 pastime / amusement

---

12 金融

中高

72. **referee**

[ˌrɛfəˈri]

n. (足球、籃球等的) 裁判
v. 仲裁，審閱、鑑定

 refer「參考、查閱」+ - ee「被…的人」，提供人參考、讓人詢問求助的就是裁判

The **referee** seems to have a bias towards the home team.

裁判似乎有偏袒地主隊的傾向。

補充 assistant referee = referee assistant 助理裁判
be sb's referee 當某人的推薦人

縮 ref.

同 umpire / judge

---

13 科技技術

14 房屋地產

中級

73. **rehearsal**

[rɪˈhɜsl]

n. 排練，預演

⇨ rehearse「排練」+ - al「名詞字尾」

With less than two weeks of **rehearsals** until opening night, we have our work cut out for us.

距離開幕之夜只有不到兩週的預演時間，我們要做的事真的是很棘手。

★ have work cut out for sb.：比喻事情很棘手、很困難

補充 be in rehearsal 在排演中
dress rehearsal 彩排

rehearse v. 排練，排演、練習

同 drill / practice

15 出差旅遊

16 交通

17 社交與用餐

18 休閒娛樂

19 醫療保健

20 日常生活

中級

74. **relaxation**

[ˌrilæksˈeʃən]

n. 放鬆；休閒娛樂；放寬

⇨ relax「放鬆」+ - ation「名詞字尾」

The holiday weekend is meant for **relaxation**, not the backbreaking work you are doing.

週末假日是用來放鬆的，而不是做你正在做的辛勞工作。

補充
for relaxation	做爲休閒娛樂
a relaxation of travel restrictions	寬鬆的旅遊限制
a relaxation of currency controls	寬鬆的貨幣管制

relax v. 放鬆
relaxed adj. 輕鬆的；悠閒的

初級

75. **remind**

[rɪˈmaɪnd]

v. 提醒；使想起

⇨ re -「再次」+ mind「注意」，提醒使你再次注意

The speech you gave **reminds** me of one of your father's when he had just founded this company.

你剛才的演說，讓我回想起你父親在他剛創立這間公司時所進行的一次演說。

補充
remind sb. of N. 提醒某人 N.
remind sb. to V. 提醒某人做…

reminder n. 提醒者，提醒物

中高

76. **renowned**

[rɪˈnaʊnd]

adj. 有名的；有聲譽的

 re -「一再」+ known「已知的」+ - ed「形容詞字尾」，一再讓人知道就是有名的

This comedian is **renowned** for getting audiences to roll in the aisles after just a few minutes.

這名喜劇演員以短短數分鐘就能讓觀眾捧腹大笑而聞名。

★ roll in the aisles：觀眾開懷大笑，形容觀眾笑到在座位旁的走道上打滾的樣子。

補充
be renowned for N. 以 N. 知名
world-renowned 全球知名的

renown n. 名聲；聲望

同 celebrated / noted / well-known / famous / famed

77. resounding

[rɪˋzaʊndɪŋ]

adj. 極大的；響亮的；
徹底的

⇨ re-「一再」+ sound「聲音」+ -ing「形容詞字尾」，
一再聽到聲音表示很響亮的

When asked about the possibility of starring in the Broadway production, the actress gave a **resounding** "yes".

當被問到在百老匯演出的可能性時，那名女演員大聲地回答說「會」。

[補充] a resounding victory/failure 極大的勝利 / 失敗

resound v. 充滿聲音；聲音迴蕩

[初級]

78. role

[rol]

n. 角色

Although she was only offered a small **role**, Anita took it due to the quality of the musical.

儘管 Anita 只被分配到音樂劇裡的一個小角色，但因爲該劇的品質好，她還是願意演出。

[補充]
play a key/important/major role in sth.
在某事物上扮演關鍵 / 重要 / 主要角色
leading/supporting role   主角 / 配角
role play   角色扮演
role model   模範；榜樣

[中級]

79. scenery

[ˋsinərɪ]

n. 舞台布景；風景

⇨ scene「場景」+ -ry「表地點或事物的總稱」

All **scenery** for the film consisted of set pieces on the studio lot.

這部片子的所有場景都是用片場裡的立體布景搭出來的。

[補充]
blend into the scenery
融入背景中，表現與大家一致以免被注意

scene n. 場景；景色
scenic adj. 舞台場景的；風景秀麗的

[初級]

80. screen

[skrin]

n. 螢幕；屏障；紗窗；電影界
v. 以…遮蔽；播映（影片）

Greta lights up the **screen** with her charming presence.

Greta 以她迷人的風釆讓影視圈爲之一亮。

[補充]
off-screen   真實生活的；螢光幕下的
the silver screen   電影圈
a touch screen   觸控螢幕
to screen sb. from N.   保護某人以免 N. 的傷害
to screen sth. off   把某物隔起來

81. scriptwriter

[ˋskrɪptˏraɪtɚ]

n. 編劇；劇作家

⇨ script「劇本」+ writer「作者」

Everyone is giving credit to the actors, but the movie won an Oscar due to the efforts of the **scriptwriter**.
所有人都將功勞給了演員，但這部片贏得奧斯卡獎是因為編劇的努力。

script n. 劇本，腳本

同 dramatist / screenwriter / playwright

82. sculpture

[ˋskʌlptʃɚ]

n. 雕塑品

⇨ sculpt「雕刻」+ -ure「表結果」

It took a lot of trial and error before I could finally create a **sculpture** worthy of being displayed.
在最終創作出值得展示的雕塑品之前，我花了很多嘗試和修正錯誤的時間。

a life-size sculpture
與實物相同大小的雕刻品
to install/place a sculpture in/on/at N.
在 N. 上安置雕塑品

sculpt v. 雕刻
sculptural adj. 雕刻的；雕刻般的

83. spare

[spɛr]

adj. 空閒的；備用的；多餘的
n. 備用品；備胎
v. 騰出；空出；省去

Joyce likes to do a bit of gardening in her **spare** time.
Joyce 喜歡在空閒時從事一些園藝活動。

in sb's spare time　　　某人空閒時
spare tire　　　　　　 備胎；腰上的贅肉
spare parts/capacity 備用零件 / 容量
spare no expense　　　不惜一切代價

84. spectator

[spɛkˋtetɚ] / [ˋspɛktetɚ]

n. 旁觀者；(運動比賽的)
　 觀眾

⇨ -spect-「看」+ -ate「使…」+ -or「做…動作的人」，
　 做觀看動作的人就是觀眾

The overzealous **spectators** ran down onto the field to celebrate the team's victory.
過度熱情的觀眾跑到球場上去慶祝該隊的勝利。

a spectator sport　讓人觀賽的運動

同 viewer / watcher

中級

85. **stadium**

[ˋstedɪəm]

n. (周圍有座位的) 體育場；
競技場

同 gym / arena

★ 複數：**stadiums ／ stadia**

Hundreds of security guards are stationed all over the **stadium** to prevent violent incidents.

數百名保安人員駐守在整個體育場以防止暴力事件發生。

補充　a baseball/football stadium　棒球／足球場

初級

86. **stage**

[stedʒ]

n. 舞台；時期，階段

⇨ -sta -「站立」+ -age「名詞字尾」，讓表演者站立的
地方就是舞台

After the movie roles dried up, Marcie went back to her **stage** career.

在電影演出角色變少後，Marcie 回到她的舞台生涯。

補充
stage name　藝名
stage fright　怯場
take/occupy the center stage in N.
在 N. 中佔有重要地位
at this stage　在此階段、時期

中級

87. **statue**

[ˋstætʃu]

n. 雕像

Greg had such an impact on this town as a baseball player that they erected a **statue** of him in front of the stadium.

身為一位棒球選手，Greg 對這個城鎮影響非常大，所以他們在體育場前方豎立起他的雕像。

補充
a statue of N.　　　　N. 的雕像
put up/erect a statue　豎立一座雕像
Statue of Liberty　　　美國的自由女神雕像

中級

88. **stretch**

[strɛtʃ]

v. 延展；伸開；拉長
n. 舒展；延續的一段時間

stretcher n. 救護擔架
stretchable adj. 能伸展的

同 v. = extend

It's a good idea to **stretch** after a long drive.
在開了那麼久的車後，伸展一下蠻不錯的。

補充
stretch out　　　　　　伸展開來，躺下
stretch one's leg　　　　伸伸腳、走動走動
(work) at full stretch　　全力以赴

89. **stroll**

[ˋstrol]

n./v. 散步；閒逛

I prefer to take my girlfriend on a leisurely **stroll** through the park for most of our dates.
大部份的約會我都喜歡帶著我女朋友在公園裡悠閒地散步。

補充
take a stroll = take a walk 散步
stroll along/around N.
沿著 N. 散步 / 在 N. 附近閒逛

---

90. **stunt**

[stʌnt]

n. 特技表演；花招

The actor has performed his own **stunts** for the film, defying warnings from professionals.
那演員不管專家警告，親自上陣表演電影中的特技。

補充
a stunt man/pilot 特技表演者 / 飛行員
an advertising stunt = a publicity stunt
宣傳噱頭
do one's stunt　表演特技
pull a stunt　做愚蠢冒險的事

stun v. 驚訝，震驚

---

91. **surfing**

[ˋsɝfɪŋ]

n. 衝浪運動

⇨ surf「衝浪」+ -ing「名詞字尾」

Hawaii is known as the birthplace of **surfing** and has some of the best places to catch waves in the world.
夏威夷以衝浪運動的誕生地而聞名，且擁有數個世界最佳撲浪地點。

補充
channel-surfing = channel-hopping
不斷轉台、換電視頻道
surf the Internet 瀏覽網路
couch-surfing
沙發旅行，借住不同人家沙發住宿的旅遊方式
surf and turf = surf'n'turf 海陸大餐

surf n. 浪花 v. 衝浪

---

92. **symphony**

[ˋsɪmfənɪ]

n. 交響樂；和諧、一致

symphonic adj. 交響樂的

⇨ sym-「共同」+ -phon-「聲音」+ -y「名詞字尾」，
　所有樂器一起發出聲音就是交響樂

Listening to the **symphony** makes me feel relaxed.
聆聽交響樂讓我感到放鬆。

16 交通

17 社交與用餐

18 休閒娛樂

19 醫療保健

20 日常生活

初級

93. theater

[ˋθɪətɚ]

n. 戲院；劇場

★ 英：**theatre** ／ 美：**theater**

I always go to matinee shows at the **theater** to avoid the crowds and save some money.

我總是去戲院看日間場的表演以避開人潮並省錢。

 | go to the theater　去看電影
home theater　　 家庭劇院設備

theatrical adj. 劇場的；戲劇的；誇張的

同 cinema

中高

94. thriller

[ˋθrɪlɚ]

n. 恐怖小說，驚悚電影

⇨ thrill「使毛骨悚然」＋ - er「做…動作的事物」

The novel I'm reading is quite a **thriller**, and I'm dying to see who the killer is.

我正在讀的這本小說真是本驚悚小說，而我超想知道殺手到底是誰。

 a thriller writer 恐怖小說作家

thrill v. 使毛骨悚然；使顫抖

同 chiller

中高

95. time-out

[ˋtaɪmˋaʊt]

n. 暫停；休息時間

同 pause / break

The coach was forced to take a **time-out** to give his out-of-shape team a breather.

教練被迫得喊出暫停，讓他那打得荒腔走板的球隊能喘口氣休息一下。

96. to be sold out

[tə][bɪ][sod][aʊt]

phr. 被賣完；銷售一空

The show has **been sold out** for months, so your only chance to get tickets will be to find someone who is selling them online.

這場戲的票幾個月前就已經銷售一空了，所以你唯一可以取得門票的機會就是去看看有沒有人在網路上賣票。

 sold as seen 沒有保固，以現有狀況售出的

97. tournament

中高

[ˋtɝnəmənt]

n. 比賽；錦標賽

⇨ tour「巡迴，遊歷」+ - ment「名詞字尾」，錦標賽就是要不斷來回比賽

If I finish in the top 10 at this golf **tournament**, I will get a chance to play on the professional tour.

如果我在這次高爾夫錦標賽中能進前十名，我就有機會打職業巡迴賽。

> 補充　knockout tournament 淘汰賽
> a tennis/basketball/badminton/golf tournament
> 網球 / 棒球 / 羽球 / 高爾夫錦標賽

同 contest / game

---

98. trophy

[ˋtrofɪ]

n. 獎品；戰利品
adj. 用來炫耀的

Andy started compiling **trophies** when he was just four years old and now he has over one hundred.

Andy 從四歲開始就在累積他的勝利獎盃，到現在他已經有超過一百個了。

> 典故　來自希臘文 trope 指「擊潰敵軍」，古時戰士擊敗敵人後會將敵人的武器堆起並獻祭給天神，加上字尾 -phy 就是指獻祭的東西，也就是戰利品。

> 補充　a trophy cabinet 戰利品櫃
> a trophy wife
> 指嫁給有錢老男人的年輕女性 (做為標示成功的戰利品)

同 獎品：prize / award

---

99. tune

中級

[tjun]

v. 調 (收音機 / 電視) 頻率，調頻道
n. 曲調，旋律

Please stay **tuned** for the weather forecast coming up next.

別轉台，稍後將播出天氣預報。

> 補充　tune in to N.　收看或收聽 N.
> stay tuned to N. 繼續收看或收聽 N.，不轉台
> in tune with sb. 同意某人；和某人意見一致
> He who pays the piper calls the tune.
> [諺語]：付錢的是老大。

同 n. = melody / music

100. **usher**

[ˈʌʃɚ]

n. 引座員；招待員
v. 引領；招待；迎接

 v. = lead / guide

The **usher** will take you to the seat.
引座員將帶您到您的座位去。
This new era in product development will be **ushered** in by our best quality TV ever.
我們史上最高品質的電視將引領產品研發進入新紀元。

補充 to usher in N.　引進 N.
　　　to usher sb. in　引導某人進入

實力進階

Part 1. 常見電影分類的英文

動作片 action films	劇情片 drama
冒險片 adventure films	史詩片 epic films
藝術片 art films	恐怖片 horror films
喜劇片 comedy	歌舞片 musical films
紀錄片 documentary films	愛情片 romance films
西部片 western films	奇幻片 fantasy films
科幻片 science fiction films(sci-fi)	驚悚片 thriller
動畫片 animation	災難片 disaster films
戰爭片 war films	

Part 2. entertainment vs. amusement

entertain 和 amuse 都有娛樂、使人高興的意思，不過轉變爲名詞 entertainment 和 amusement 的時候，兩者的意思卻不完全相同：

entertainment	通常指娛樂節目或表演，尤其是影視娛樂，如：live entertainment 就是現場表演。
amusement	指能達到娛樂效果的活動，所以遊樂園就叫做 amusement park（如：迪士尼樂園）；amusement arcade 就是指有電子遊戲機的遊樂場。

隨堂練習

★ 請根據句意，選出最適合的單字

(　　) 1. Rising Asia-based design star Jason Wu will make a _____ at New York fashion week on Monday.
    (A) finale   (B) debut
    (C) lecture   (D) stage

(　　) 2. Robin Williams, American actor and comedian, was _____ for getting audiences to roll in the aisles and was regarded as a "national treasure" by the public.
    (A) renowned   (B) exhibited
    (C) culminated   (D) entertained

(　　) 3. A _____ will be held before the wedding to make sure everything goes right.
    (A) trophy   (B) landscape
    (C) symphony   (D) rehearsal

(　　) 4. The importance of preserving culture _____ cannot be overemphasized.
    (A) tournament   (B) spectator
    (C) journal   (D) heritage

(　　) 5. Erica used to spend most of her _____ time doing research in the library. Now she prefers to go mountaineering.
    (A) spare   (B) stunt
    (C) resounding   (D) intellectual

解答：1. B　2. A　3. D　4. D　5. A

Unit 19 醫療保健

中高

1. acute

[ə`kjut]

adj. 嚴重的；急性的；機靈的；
尖銳的

Brian thought he had just a touch of the flu, but it developed into an **acute** case of pneumonia.

Brian 原本認為他只不過是得了流感，但最後卻發展成急性肺炎。

補充
SARS = Severe Acute Respiratory Syndrome
嚴重急性上呼吸道症候群
an acute conflict/crisis　　嚴重的衝突 / 危機
have an acute sense of N.　對 N. 的感覺很敏銳

同 keen　adj. 極敏銳的

反 dull　adj. 鈍的；不鋒利的
chronic　adj. 長期的；慢性的

中高

2. addict

[`ædɪkt]

n. 沉迷、有癮的人

[ə`dɪkt]

v. 使沉溺；使成癮

⇨ ad -「to」+ -dict -「說」，一直說給你聽讓你漸漸被吸引而沉迷

It's a big challenge for nicotine **addicts** to quit smoking.

對尼古丁成癮者來說，戒煙是很大的挑戰。

補充
a cyber addict　　　網路成癮者
a selfie addict　　　自拍狂
a shopping addict　購物狂
be addicted to N.　　對 N. 上癮；沉迷於 N.
be highly addictive　容易上癮的

addicted adj. 沉迷的；入迷的
addiction n. 沉溺；成癮；入迷
addictive adj. 使人沉溺的；使人上癮的

中高

3. allergic

[ə`lɝdʒɪk]

adj. 過敏的

⇨ allergy「過敏症」+ -ic「形容詞字尾」

I didn't know I was **allergic** to pollen until I arrived in America in the spring.

我一直到在春天時到了美國才知道我對花粉過敏。

補充
be allergic to N.　　對 N. 過敏
an allergic reaction　過敏反應

allergy　n. 過敏症

---

4. alleviate

中高

[ə'livɪˌet]

v. 使減輕、緩和

⇨ al -「to」+ -levi -「拉起」+ -ate「動詞字尾」，把東西拉起來讓你感覺輕一點

This cream should **alleviate** some of those aches and sores.
這個乳膏應該能緩解一部份的痠痛。

[補充] alleviate sb's pain 減輕某人的痛苦

alleviation n. 減輕；緩和

[同] ease / relieve

---

5. antibiotic

中高

[ˌæntaɪbaɪ'ɑtɪk] /
[ˌæntɪbaɪ'ɑtɪk]

adj. 抗菌的

n. 抗生素

⇨ anti -「對抗」+ -bio -「生命」+ -tic「形容詞字尾」

Antibiotic drugs are ineffective for the flu.
抗生素藥物對流感沒有效。

[補充] be on antibiotics for N. 因 N. 而接受抗生素治療

---

6. appointment

中級

[ə'pɔɪntmənt]

n. 約會，正式會面；任命

 appoint「指派，指定」+ -ment「名詞字尾」

Walk-in patients are only welcome until 11:00 am, after which you will need to make an **appointment**.
臨時來現場的病人只能在上午十一點前掛號看診，在那之後你得預約才能看診。

[補充]
doctor's/dentist's appointment
醫師 / 牙醫約診
make/arrange an appointment 預約會面
by appointment 採預約制
an appointment letter （工作的）錄取通知函
an appointment book （工作的）行事曆

appoint v. 指派；指定

---

7. bacteria

中級

[bæk'tɪrɪə]

n. 細菌

★ 單數：**bacterium**

It is an illness caused by **bacteria** in drinking water.
這是由飲用水中的細菌所引起的疾病。

[補充]
bacterial infection 細菌感染
germ n. 病菌

bacterial adj. 細菌的；細菌引起的

中高

8. **biological**

[͵baɪəˋlɑdʒɪk!]

adj. 生物的；生物學的

⇨ - bio - 「生命」 + - logi - 「學說」 + - cal「形容詞字尾」

Studies have shown that the **biological** connection between twins includes both physical and psychological aspects.

研究已知雙胞胎之間的生物性連結包括了身體層面和心理層面。

補充

biological father/mother/parents	原生父母
biological weapons	生物武器
biological clock	生理時鐘
biological diversity = biodiversity	生物多樣性

biology n. 生物學
biologically adv. 生物學地

初級

9. **cancer**

[ˋkænsɚ]

n. 癌；惡性腫瘤

Avoiding foods with additives and various preservatives can reduce your risk of getting **cancer**.

避免食用含有添加物和各種防腐劑的食物可降低你罹患癌症的風險。

典故

cancer 來自拉丁文的 cancer，原指「螃蟹」。古希臘醫師希波克拉底發現惡性腫瘤上有多條血管，長得像螃蟹一樣，後人便以 cancer(螃蟹) 來稱呼這種身體內部的腫瘤疾病，也就是我們今天所說的「癌症」。

補充

breast cancer	乳癌
lung cancer	肺癌
skin cancer	皮膚癌

中高

10. **capsule**

[ˋkæps!]

n. 膠囊；小容器

adj. 濃縮的

⇨ - caps - 「盒子」 + - ule「表小東西」

Just take two **capsules** every eight hours with food and come back to see me if your condition does not improve within 72 hours.

每八小時在進食前後吞服兩顆膠囊，如果七十二小時內狀況沒有改善再來找我。

補充

space capsule	太空艙
time capsule	時空膠囊
capsule hotel	膠囊旅館
a capsule description of N.	N. 的簡要介紹

中高

11. carbohydrate

[ˌkɑrbəˈhaɪdret]

n. 碳水化合物；醣類

⇨ **carbo-**「碳」+ **-hydr-**「水」+ **-ate**「使變成」

Athletes need plenty of **carbohydrates** before doing rigorous exercise.

運動員在進行激烈運動之前需要大量的碳水化合物。

補充	low carbohydrate diet 低碳水化合物飲食；低醣飲食 high/low in carbohydrate 碳水化合物含量高 / 低

縮 carb

中高

12. cavity

[ˈkævətɪ]

n. 蛀牙；洞；腔

 cave「洞穴」+ **-ity**「名詞字尾，表性質」

Because you have been skipping out on brushing your teeth, some **cavities** have developed.

因為你一直都沒有刷牙，有些牙齒便蛀掉了。

補充	nasal cavity	鼻腔
	chest cavity	胸腔
	abdominal cavity	腹腔
	cavity wall	空心牆，夾層牆

同 tooth decay n. 蛀牙

中高

13. checkup

[ˈtʃɛkʌp]

n. 健康檢查

Your medical insurance will pay for one free **checkup** a year to promote good health.

你的醫療保險每年會提供一次免費的健康檢查以促進健康。

補充	annual checkup 年度健康檢查

中高

14. cholesterol

[kəˈlɛstərol]

n. 膽固醇

My **cholesterol** level was too high, so my doctor put me on a low-carb, high-vegetable diet.

我的膽固醇指數太高了，所以我的醫生要我進行低碳水化合物、大量蔬菜的飲食計劃。

★ low-carb diet = low-carbohydrate diet：低碳水化合物飲食

補充	HDL cholesterol	高密度脂蛋白膽固醇
	LDL cholesterol	低密度脂蛋白膽固醇
	high/low in cholesterol	膽固醇含量高 / 低

中高

15. **chronic**

[ˋkrɑnɪk]

adj. 長期的；慢性的

⇨ - chron - 「時間」+ - ic「形容詞字尾」

Bradley had **chronic** bronchitis, which makes it hard for him to do aerobic exercise for too long.

Bradley 有慢性支氣管炎，這讓他很難長時間進行有氧運動。

 chronic disease/pain　慢性疾病 / 疼痛
a chronic shortage of N.　長期缺乏 N.

chronically adv. 長期地；慢性地

反 acute adj. 急性的

中高

16. **cleanse**

[klɛnz]

v. 使清潔；清洗；淨化

⇨ clean「乾淨的」+ - se「動詞字尾」

This face wash cream can **cleanse** deeply into the pores of your skin.

這個洗面乳可以深層清潔皮膚毛孔。

 cleanse sb./sth. of N. 清除、淨化某人 / 某事物的 N.

cleansing n. 清洗
cleanser n. 清潔劑

同 clean / wash / rinse / purify

中高

17. **clinical**

[ˋklɪnɪkl]

adj. 診所的；臨床的

⇨ clinic「診所」+ - al「形容詞字尾」

In **clinical** trials, this new drug was found to have minimal side effects.

臨床實驗中發現這個新藥的副作用很少。

 clinical research/training 臨床研究 / 訓練
clinical trials of a drug 藥物臨床實驗
clinically proven 經臨床驗證

clinic n. 診所；臨床教學
clinically adv. 臨床地；透過臨床診斷地

中高

18. **comprehensive**

[ˌkɑmprɪˈhɛnsɪv]

adj. 全面的；廣泛的；
綜合的

 com-「一起」+ pre-「先」+ -hens-「拿」+ -ive「形容詞字尾」，把東西拿到一起就包含了很多、很廣泛

The premiums for your **comprehensive** health insurance plan will be sky-high.
你的綜合健康保險計劃的保費將會是天價。

補充 comprehensive insurance 綜合保險
a comprehensive survey 一項全面性的調查

comprehend v. 理解
comprehension n. 理解力

同 complete / full

初級

19. **concern**

[kənˈsɝn]

v. 關心；擔心
n. 關心的事；關切

 con-「和…一起」+ -cern-「篩選，詳查」，一起詳查表示很關切

I am **concerned** about your health. Please take care of yourself.
我關心你的健康。請照顧好你自己。

補充 concern about sth. 對於某事物的關心

concerned adj. 關心的；擔憂的

中級

20. **conscious**

[ˈkɑnʃəs]

adj. 有知覺的；意識到的；
清醒的

 con-「完整地」+ -sci-「知道」+ -ous「形容詞字尾」，能完整知道事物就表示是清醒的

Always be **conscious** of when you experience severe chest pain and notify your doctor immediately.
要注意當你意識到有嚴重胸痛時要立即通知你的醫師。

補充 be conscious of N. = be aware of N. 察覺到 N.
be conscious that 子句 = be aware that 子句
察覺到…

同 aware

反 unconscious adj. 昏迷的；無意識的

中高

21. **contagious**

[kənˈtedʒəs]

adj. 接觸傳染的

 con-「一起」+ -tag-「接觸」+ -ous「形容詞字尾」

The Ebola virus is not **contagious** as long as a person is not showing any symptoms.
只要一個人沒有顯現症狀出來，伊波拉病毒是不具傳染性的。

補充 be highly contagious 具高度傳染性的

中高

22. **coverage**

[ˈkʌvərɪdʒ]

n. 涵蓋範圍；保險項目

⇨ cover「涵蓋」+ -age「名詞字尾」

You only require basic insurance **coverage** since you are a young, healthy man.
由於你是年輕的健康男性，你只需要基本的保險涵蓋項目就好了。

補充		
	insurance coverage	保險涵蓋範圍
	market coverage	市場涵蓋範圍
	wide/in-depth coverage	廣泛 / 深度報導

cover v. 遮蓋；包含

中級

23. **decay**

[dɪˈke]

v. 腐蝕；蛀蝕

n. 腐朽；蛀牙

⇨ de-「分離」+ -cad-「掉下」

All that coffee you drink is causing your teeth to **decay** at an alarming rate.
你喝的咖啡已使你的牙齒以驚人的速度蛀蝕了。

補充		
	tooth/dental decay	蛀牙
	fall into decay	日漸衰敗、逐漸凋零

同 decline / rot

---

24. **dehydrate**

[diˈhaɪˌdret]

v. 脫水；使乾燥

⇨ de-「分離」+ -hydr-「水」+ -ate「使…」，使水離開就表示脫水了

In the desert heat, we **dehydrated** quickly and finished three liters of water in just two hours.
在沙漠般的炎熱中，我們很快就脫水了，而且還在兩小時內就喝光了三公升的水。

dehydrated adj. 脫水的
dehydration n. 脫水

同 dry up

中高

25. **dental**

[ˈdɛntl̩]

adj. 牙齒的；牙科的

⇨ -dent-「牙齒」+ -al「形容詞字尾」

You haven't had a **dental** visit for years, which explains your difficulty with chewing anything hard.
你已經好幾年沒去牙科看牙了，這也就是為什麼你無法嚼硬的食物的原因。

補充		
	dental decay	蛀牙
	dental treatment/operation	牙科治療 / 手術
	dental floss	牙線

dentist n. 牙醫

中高

26. **diabetes**

[ˌdaɪəˈbitiz]

n. 糖尿病

⇨ dia - 「通過」+ betes 「源自希臘文，表出去」

Cases of **diabetes** have risen along with high-sugar diets.

糖尿病人數隨著高糖份飲食而升高了。

> **典故** 糖尿病的病徵就是過度排水，**diabetes** 就是指水份過度排出。

> **補充** diabetic complications 糖尿病併發症
> a diabetic diet　　　　糖尿病飲食

diabetic adj. 糖尿病的 n. 糖尿病患

中高

27. **diagnose**

[ˌdaɪəgˈnoz]

v. 診斷；判斷

 dia - 「通過」+ -gnos - 「知道」

Your mixed symptoms make it difficult to **diagnose** what's wrong with you.

你的混雜症狀使診斷你的問題變得很困難。

> **補充** diagnose sb. with N.(病名) 診斷某人有 N.(病名)

diagnosis n. 診斷結果，診斷 (複數為 diagnoses)

中級

28. **disease**

[dɪˈziz]

n. 疾病

 dis - 「表否定」+ ease 「輕鬆舒適」

There is a new strain of this highly-contagious **disease** this year, so please protect yourself.

今年這種具高度傳染性的疾病出現了新型態，所以請保護好你自己。

> **補充** an infectious/contagious disease 傳染病
> a common/rare/fatal disease
> 普遍 / 罕見 / 致命的疾病
> heart/lung/kidney disease 心臟 / 肺 / 腎病

同 illness / malady

易混 decease v. 死亡

中級

29. disorder
[dɪsˋɔrdɚ]
n. 混亂；（身體）機能失調

⇨ dis -「表否定」+ order「秩序」，身體機能沒有秩序就是失調

Having social anxiety **disorder** forces me to avoid crowds of people.
由於我有社交恐懼症，這使我避免接觸人群。

補充
be in disorder	在混亂的狀態
sleep disorder	睡眠障礙
anxiety disorder	焦慮症
eating disorder	飲食失調
genetic disorder	基因性疾病；遺傳疾病

中級

30. drowsy
[ˋdrauzɪ]
adj. 昏昏欲睡的；睏倦的

Taking this cold medicine made me so **drowsy** that I fell asleep on my computer at work.
服用這感冒藥讓我昏昏欲睡，以致於我在工作時就在我的電腦上睡著了。

補充
a drowsy afternoon　令人昏昏欲睡的午後
N. cause drowsiness　N. 會產生睡意

drowsiness n. 睡意
drowsily adv. 昏昏欲睡地；想睡地

初級

31. drugstore
[ˋdrʌɡ͵stor]
n. (AmE) 藥妝店；藥品雜貨鋪

同 pharmacy / chemist's (BrE)

⇨ drug「藥品」+ store「商店」

During the flu season, you might wait thirty minutes to get your prescription filled at the **drugstore**.
流感季節時，光在藥房領藥可能都得等上三十分鐘。

中級

32. emergency
[ɪˋmɝdʒənsɪ]
n. 緊急情況；非常事件

⇨ emerge「浮現，出現」+ -ency「名詞字尾」，從水裡突然冒出來就是突發的緊急事件

After Craig's nasty fall on the ice, we whisked him away to the **emergency** room for stitches.
Craig 在冰上嚴重一摔，我們立刻飛奔送他到急診室縫合。

補充
the emergency room	急診室
the emergency exit	緊急出口
an emergency call/measure/meeting/landing	
緊急電話 / 措施 / 會議 / 迫降	
in an emergency	在緊急情況下
in case of emergency	以防萬一

中高

33. epidemic

[ˌɛpɪˋdɛmɪk]

n. 流行病，傳染病；盛行

adj. 流行性的，傳染的；
流行的

⇨ epi -「在…之間」+ -dem -「人們」+ -ic「形容詞字
尾」，在人們間傳來傳去的就是流行病、傳染病

The government was able to stop the spread of the
epidemic by quarantining patients.
政府將病患隔離就能阻止流行病的擴散。

 a flu epidemic　　　　流行性感冒
an epidemic of crime　犯罪盛行

同 widespread / prevalent　adj. 流行的

34. ergonomic

[ˌɝgəˋnɑmɪk]

adj. 工效學的，人體工學的

⇨ ergon「希臘文，工作」+ -nom -「規則」+ -ic「形容
詞字尾」，符合人體工作規則的就是人體工學

Great care has been taken at this office to give all
workspaces an **ergonomic** design.
這間辦公室特別關注要讓所有工作空間都符合人體工學設計。

 an ergonomic keyboard/mouse/chair/design
人體工學鍵盤 / 滑鼠 / 椅子 / 設計

ergonomics　n. 人體工學

中高

35. erupt

[ɪˋrʌpt]

v. (火山) 噴發；爆發；(皮
膚) 長疹子

⇨ e -「向外」+ -rupt -「噴出」

Tom's seafood allergy was so bad that a rash **erupted** all
over his body after just one bite.
Tom 的海鮮過敏狀況很糟，他才吃了一口全身就冒出疹子了。

 erupt from N.　　　由 N. 噴發出來
erupt into N.　　　爆發變成 N.
rash erupt on N.　在 N. 上長出大片疹子

eruption　n. 爆發；(熔岩) 噴出；(皮膚) 大片出疹

36. **excruciating**

[ɪk`skruʃʌˌetɪŋ]

adj. 極痛苦的

⇨ ex-「向外」+ -cruci-「嚴酷的」+ -ate「使…」 + -ing「形容詞字尾」，被殘酷對待，外表就會顯現極為痛苦的狀態

When I stepped on a nail, **excruciating** pain shot through my entire leg.

當我踩到一根釘子時，一股劇烈疼痛立刻穿透我整條腿。

補充
an excruciating pain 劇烈疼痛
excruciatingly painful/uncomfortable
極度痛苦 / 不舒服

excruciate v. 施酷刑；使痛苦

同 agonizing

中高

37. **faculty**

[`fækḷtɪ]

n. 機能，能力；(AmE) 學院；大學全體教職員

On suffering a concussion, Greg lost **faculty** of all his limbs.

在遭受腦震盪後，Greg 的四肢都失去功能了。

★ concussion：腦震盪

中高

38. **fatigue**

[fə`tig]

n. 疲勞；疲累

v. 使疲乏；使疲累

You have already run twenty kilometers this week, so take a day off to combat **fatigue**.

你這週已經跑了二十公里了，所以休息一天應付疲勞吧。

補充
chronic fatigue syndrome 慢性疲勞症候群
physical/mental fatigue 身體 / 精神疲勞
compassion fatigue 同情心疲乏

同 n. = tiredness / exhaustion

初級

39. **fever**

[`fivɚ]

n. 發燒；狂熱

Bobby's **fever** stayed at around 39 degrees Celsius all night.

Bobby 發燒，一整晚體溫都在攝氏三十九度左右。

補充
hay fever 枯草熱；花粉症
dengue fever 登革熱
a fever of N. 充滿對 N. 的狂熱

feverish adj. 發熱的；狂熱興奮的

中級

40. **handicap**

[ˋhændɪˏkæp]

n. 殘障；不利條件；障礙

v. 妨礙；使不利

Rachel has a severe **handicap**, which confines her to a wheelchair.

Rachel 嚴重不良於行，這讓她只能坐在輪椅上。

> **典故** 源自古時一種名為 hand in cap 的遊戲，後成為賽馬時在馬上加裝重物的規則，衍生出表不利的條件。

> **補充** mental/physical/visual handicap
> 心理 / 肢體 / 視覺障礙
> be handicapped by N. 受到 N. 的阻礙
> the handicapped　　　殘障人士

同 disability n. 傷殘，喪失能力

中高

41. **hygiene**

[ˋhaɪdʒin]

n. 衛生

The spread of the infection at this neighborhood is due to poor public **hygiene**.

感染之所以會在這個社區蔓延是由於不良的公共衛生。

> **典故** 源自希臘神話中掌管健康的女神 Hygieia。

> **補充** personal/public hygiene 個人 / 公共衛生

hygienist n. 衛生學者

中高

42. **immune**

[ɪˋmjun]

adj. 免疫的；可免除的；
　　 不受影響的

⇨ im -「表否定」+ munis「拉丁文，服役」，不用服役就是可免除服役、不會受到影響的

Once you receive this vaccine, you should be **immune** to contracting polio.

一旦你接種這個疫苗，你應該就不會感染小兒麻痺了。

> **補充** be immune to N. 對 (疾病) 免疫；不受 N. 的影響
> be immune from N.　　 避免 N.
> immune system/response 免疫系統 / 反應
> AIDS = Acquired Immune Deficiency Syndrome
> 後天免疫缺乏症候群

immunity n. 免疫力

43. **indemnity**

[ɪnˋdɛmnətɪ]

n. 保障；賠償金

 in - 「表否定」 + - demn - 「損失」 + - ity 「名詞字尾，表狀態」，讓你沒有損失的狀態就是提供你賠償金做為保障

The insurance company determined that no **indemnity** was owed the patient, as he had gotten hurt doing such a risky activity.

他因進行高風險活動而受傷，保險公司決議不給付賠償金。

補充
provide/offer an indemnity for/against sth.
提供針對某事物的賠償
double indemnity provision
（保險合約中的）加倍保障條款
Letter of Indemnity = L/I（貨運）賠償保證書

indemnify v. 保障；賠償

 compensation / reimbursement

中高

44. **infectious**

[ɪnˋfɛkʃəs]

adj. 有傳染力的；易傳播的
（通常為空氣傳染）

 infect 「傳染」 + - ious 「= - ous，充滿⋯的」，充滿傳染力的就是易傳染的

As he was highly **infectious**, Brad was told by the school to stay at home until his symptoms had subsided.

由於他的病有高度傳染力，Brad 被學校告知得待在家裡直到他的症狀消失。

補充
an infectious disease	傳染病
an infectious laughter	具傳染力的笑聲
be highly infectious	具極高傳染性的
be infected with N.	感染 N.

infect v. 傳染，使受感染，病菌污染
infection n. 傳染病，感染

中級

45. **inject**

[ɪnˋdʒɛkt]

v. 注射（藥劑）；注入

 in - 「進入」 + - ject - 「丟擲」

I'm going to **inject** you with a special serum which should help mitigate the symptoms of the disease.

我要幫你注射一種特別的免疫血清，它能幫助緩和你的疾病症狀。

補充
inject A into B	將 A 注入 B 裡
inject sb. with N.	為某人注射 N.
take an injection	接受注射

injection n. 注射；打針

中級

46. injure
[ˈɪndʒɚ]

v. 受傷；損傷

⇨ in-「表否定」+ -jur-「法律」，不守法會造成傷害

You'd better quit playing American football before you **injure** your legs.
在你雙腿受傷之前，最好停止打美式足球了。

| 比較 | hurt 著重帶來身體痛苦的傷害；injure 則強調因意外而造成的受傷。 |

補充	the injured	傷者；傷患
	be badly/seriously injured	嚴重受傷
	injure oneself/bodyparts	某人受傷 / 某部位受傷

injury n. 傷害；損害
injured adj. 受傷的

同 hurt

中級

47. insurance
[ɪnˈʃʊrəns]

n. 保險

⇨ insure「投保；承保」+ -ance「名詞字尾」

Without **insurance**, you'll need to pay a fifty-dollar fee up front before you are admitted to the emergency room.
沒有保險的話，你得預先付五十元的費用才能被安排到急診室。

補充	car/health/travel insurance
	汽車 / 健康 / 旅遊保險
	insurance policy	保單
	insurance payment/premiums	保險費
	take out insurance	買保險
	claim on the insurance for N.
	要求保險賠償 N. 的損失

insure v. 投保；承保

中高

48. intake
[ˈɪnˌtek]

n. 攝取量；吸收

⇨ in「進入」+ take「拿」，拿進身體裡就是攝取、吸收

Your daily **intake** of alcohol needs to be mitigated before your liver is totally destroyed.
在你的肝臟完全受損前，你應該降低每日的酒精攝取量。

| | daily intake of N. | N. 的每日攝取量 |
| | an intake of breath | 倒吸一口氣 |

49. irritate

中高

[ˈɪrəˌtet]

v. 刺激；使過敏，使發炎；激怒

Spicy curry **irritates** my stomach so much that I can't handle more than a few bites.
辣咖哩會大量刺激我的胃，只要多吃幾口我就受不了。

 補充

irritate sb.	激怒某人
irritate sth.	刺激某物
irritable bowel syndrome	腸躁症
cause skin irritations	造成皮膚刺激疼痛

irritated adj. 被激怒的；發炎的；疼痛的
irritating adj. 惱人的；令人不快的
irritation n. 發炎；疼痛

反 soothe v. 撫慰；緩和

50. isolate

中級

[ˈaɪsḷˌet]

v. 使隔絕；使孤立

 isolé「法文，與世隔絕的」+ -ate「使…」

The patient must be **isolated** in the room at the very back of the hospital for everyone's safety.
為了每個人的安全著想，該名病患必須被隔絕在醫院最後方的一個房間裡。

 補充

isolate A from B	將 A 與 B 隔開
isolate sb. from sth.	將某人隔絕於某物之外
be geographically/socially isolated	被從地理上 / 社會中孤立

isolated adj. 被隔絕的；孤立的
isolation n. 隔離；孤立

同 quarantine

51. keep in shape

[kip][ɪn][ʃep]

phr. 保持身體健康

I would rather run five kilometers a day to **keep in shape** than play a violent sport like hockey.
我寧可一天跑 五公里來保持身體健康，也不要從事像曲棍球之類的激烈運動。

 補充

in good shape	狀況很好
out of shape	狀況很差；變形，走樣

同 keep fit

中高

52. liable

[ˈlaɪəbḷ]

adj. 易於…的；傾向於…的；
有義務的

⇨ lier「古法文，綁住」+ -able「可…的」，綁住人的就是責任義務

The doctor told Kevin that he is very **liable** to have the heart disease.

醫生告訴 Kevin 說他很有可能會有心臟病。

As Emily's parents, you can be held **liable** for her criminal actions.

身為 Emily 的父母，你們對她的犯罪行為負有責任。

be liable to V.	有可能會做…
be liable to N.	有義務支付 N./負 N. 的責任
be liable for sth.	對某事負責
have legal liability	負有法律責任

liability n. 責任，義務；負債；傾向

中級

53. medical

[ˈmɛdɪkḷ]

adj. 醫療的；醫學的
n. (BrE) 體格檢查

Barbara was admitted to several **medical** schools, but she chose to attend the most prestigious one.

Barbara 獲准進入幾間醫學院，但她選擇其中最具威望的一所就讀。

medical care/treatment/advice
醫療照顧 / 治療 / 建議
medical certificate　　醫生證明
the medical profession 醫學界

中級

54. mental

[ˈmɛntḷ]

adj. 心理的；精神的

⇨ -ment-「思考」+ -al「與…有關的」，和頭腦思考有關的就是心理層面的、精神狀態的

Henry is in a bad **mental** state after witnessing a tragic car accident.

在目睹一場悲劇車禍後，Henry 的精神狀態就很不好。

mental health　　　　心理健康
mental age　　　　　 心智年齡
mental disorder/illness 精神疾病

mentality n. 心態

同 psychological

反 physical adj. 身體的

中級

55. **nutrition**

[njuˋtrɪʃən]

n. 營養

Good **nutrition** gives you the energy necessary to continue intense exercise.
良好的營養提供你做持續激烈運動時所需的能量。

nutrition facts/information	營養成份（食品標示）
nutrition consultant	營養顧問

nutrient n. 養分，營養物
nutritious adj. 營養的
nutritionist n. 營養學家

初級

56. **operation**

[ˌɑpəˋreʃən]

n. 手術；運作

⇨ operate「動手術」+ -ion「名詞字尾」
Steve will have an **operation** to remove excessive fat around his waist.
Steve 將動手術去除腰部的多餘脂肪。

perform an operation	執行手術
have/accept an operation	接受手術
operate on sb./body parts	
給某人動手術；在某部位動手術	

同 surgery n. 手術

中級

57. **organ**

[ˋɔrgən]

n. 器官

Thanks to an anonymous **organ** donor, Maria received her emergency kidney transplant.
幸虧有一位匿名的器官捐贈者，Maria 才能接受緊急腎臟移植手術。

典故 源自希臘文 ergon 表「工作」，在人體內工作的東西就是器官。

organ transplant	器官移植
organ donor	器官捐贈者
the sense organ	知覺器官

中高

58. **outbreak**

[ˋaʊtˌbrek]

n. (疾病或戰爭) 爆發

⇨ out「向外」+ break「破裂」
An **outbreak** of cholera swept through the village in a matter of weeks.
霍亂疫情爆發在幾週之內就橫掃整個村子。

the outbreak of N.	N. 的突然爆發

初級

59. **patient**

[ˈpeʃənt]

n. 病患

adj. 有耐心的

⇨ - pati - 「承受」 + - ent 「具…性的」，承受病痛的人就是病患

The **patient** screamed in pain after having his leg amputated.

該名病患在腿部截肢後痛得大叫。

補充	inpatient	住院病人
	outpatient	門診病人
	an emergency patient	急診病人
	be patient with sb.	對某人有耐性

patience n. 耐性

中高

60. **pharmacy**

[ˈfɑrməsɪ]

n. 藥房

The **pharmacy** can't fill your prescription without a doctor's signature.

沒有醫生簽名，藥房不能讓你領藥。

| 補充 | pharmaceutical | adj. 製藥的，藥品的 |
| | the pharmaceutical industry | 製藥業 |

pharmacist n. 藥劑師

中級

61. **physical**

[ˈfɪzɪkl]

adj. 身體的；實體的

⇨ - physi - 「自然；本質」 + - al 「形容詞字尾」

Bob is starting a **physical** fitness regimen of one hour per day of exercise.

Bob 每天規律運動一個小時鍛鍊體適能。

補充	physical examination	體格檢查
	physical fitness	身體健康；體適能
	physical science	自然科學
	the physical world/environment	
	真實世界 / 環境	
	physical price = cash price	
	實體價格，現金價格	

同 身體的：corporal / bodily

中級

62. **physician**

[fɪˋzɪʃən]

n. 醫生；內科醫生

 physic「古用法，醫術；藥劑」+ **-ian**「表專精某技術的人」

We are searching for a family **physician** who specializes in treating young children.

我們正在找一位精通治療兒童的家庭醫生。

| 補充 | resident physician | 住院醫師 |
| | primary care physician | 主治醫師 |

反 surgeon n. 外科醫生

易混 physicist n. 物理學家

中級

63. **pill**

[pɪl]

n. 藥丸

Taking this antibiotic in **pill** form won't be strong enough; you will need to get an injection.

服用藥丸形式的抗生素不夠強，你需要接受注射。

補充	a sleeping pill	安眠藥
	a vitamin pill	維他命丸
	a bitter pill (to swallow)	難以接受的事實
	to sugar/sweeten the pill	
	給藥丸加糖衣，將人不愛的東西變得容易接受	

---

64. **pollen**

[ˋpɑlən]

n. 花粉

All the grass **pollen** floating around in the spring gives me allergy attacks.

春天飄散在空中的雜草花粉讓我飽受過敏之苦。

| 補充 | pollen allergy 花粉過敏 |

pollinate v. 給(植物)傳授花粉

中高

65. **practitioner**

[prækˋtɪʃənɚ]

n. 開業者；執業醫生；執業律師

 practice「執行」+ **-tion**「= **-ian**，表族群」+ **-er**「做…動作的人」

Many health **practitioners** have to pay higher and higher costs for malpractice insurance.

許多醫療保健從業人員得付愈來愈高的費用支付醫療責任保險。

補充	a medical/legal practitioner
	開業醫生 / 執業律師
	general practitioner = family practitioner
	家庭醫生

practice v. 實行；開業執行 n. 業務；工作

66. **premium**

[`primɪəm]

n. 保費；獎金；
　額外費用

adj. 高價的；優質的

Health insurance **premiums** have increased by 20% in just the past two years.
僅過去兩年來健康保險費用就增加了百分之二十。

補充
a monthly/annual premium of (price)
每月 / 年 (多少錢) 的保費
pay a premium for N.　為 N. 付較高的費用
buy/sell... at a premium　以較高的價格買 / 賣⋯
premium price/quality　高價 / 優質

---

67. **prescribe**

[prɪ`skraɪb]

v. 開藥方，囑咐

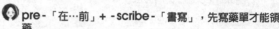 pre - 「在⋯前」+ - scribe - 「書寫」，先寫藥單才能領藥

This is the highest possible dosage of this painkiller that I can legally **prescribe** for you.
這是我可以合法開給你止痛藥的最高劑量了。

補充
prescribe N. for sb./sth.
對某人 / 某病症開 N. 的處方
prescribe sb. sth.　開某藥方給某人
prescription drug　處方藥

prescription n. 處方

---

68. **pulse**

[pʌls]

n. 脈搏

v. 跳動；振動

When we arrived at the scene of the accident, the victim already had no **pulse**.
當我們到達事故現場時，受害者已經沒有心跳脈搏了。

補充
take/feel sb's pulse 幫某人把脈
quicken the pulse　脈搏 / 心跳加快

---

69. **purify**

[`pjʊrəˌfaɪ]

v. 淨化；使純淨；提煉

⇨ pure 「純淨的」+ - fy 「使⋯化」
I have installed a high-quality machine under my kitchen sink to **purify** my water.
我在我家廚房水槽下方安裝了一台高品質的淨水機。

補充
purify the air/water 淨化空氣 / 水
purify sb's spirit of/from N.
淨化某人的精神使不受 N. 的干擾

pure adj. 純淨的；不摻雜的
purification n. 洗淨；淨化

同 refine / cleanse

16 交通

17 社交與用餐

18 休閒娛樂

19 醫療保健

20 日常生活

70. **recovery**

[rɪˋkʌvərɪ]

n. 恢復；復甦；重獲

⇨ re -「回來」+ cover「遮蓋」+ -y「名詞字尾」，把掉落的東西蓋回來就恢復原狀了

After your successful knee surgery, you will still have an expected **recovery** time of about five months.

在你的膝蓋手術成功後，預估你還有約 五個月的恢復期。

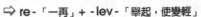

補充　the recovery room（手術後的）恢復室
make a full recovery (from...)
（從…中）完全康復

recover v. 恢復；復原；重新找到

---

71. **relieve**

[rɪˋliv]

v. 減輕；緩和

⇨ re -「一再」+ -lev -「舉起，使變輕」

I've tried many different ways to **relieve** the symptoms of cold.

我已經試過很多種不同的方法來緩解感冒症狀了。

補充　relieve sb. of N. 讓某人解除 N. 的束縛
relieve sb. of their duties/responsibilities
解除某人的義務／責任
relieve oneself 小便（禮貌說法）

relief n. 緩和；減輕

同 alleviate

---

72. **remedy**

[ˋrɛmədɪ]

n. 治療法；藥物

There are several home **remedies** you can try to stop the itch from your poison ivy rash.

要止住毒藤疹所引發的搔癢，有幾種民俗療法你可以試看看。

★ poison ivy rash：毒藤疹

補充　home remedy　民俗療法
a remedy for N. 解決 N. 的藥
beyond/without remedy
無可救藥的，無法挽回的
Desperate diseases must have desperate remedies.
[諺語]：絕症要用猛藥醫；非常時期要用非常手段。

11 製造

12 金融

13 科技技術

14 房屋地產

15 出差旅遊

中高

73. **sensation**

[sɛnˋseʃən]

n. 感覺；轟動

 sense「感覺」+ **-ate**「使…」+ **-ion**「表狀態」，使有感覺的狀態就是知覺

You will feel a slight tingling **sensation** all over your body when you first apply the ointment.
你第一次擦這個藥膏時全身會有輕微的刺痛感。

| 補充 | a sensation of/that...　…的感覺 |
| | cause a sensation　　　引起轟動 |

sensational adj. 轟動的

同 feeling n. 感覺

中高

74. **sensitivity**

[ˌsɛnsəˋtɪvətɪ]

n. 敏感性，敏感度

⇨ **sensitive**「敏感的」+ **-ity**「表狀態」

Alicia has an acute **sensitivity** to bright light, so she wears sunglasses almost everywhere.
Alicia 對光有極度的敏感性，所以她到每個地方都戴著太陽眼鏡。

補充	the sensitivity of sth.　某物的靈敏度
	the sensitivity to N.　　對 N. 的敏感度
	be sensitive to N.　　　對 N. 很敏感

sensitive adj. 敏感的

中高

75. **setback**

[ˋsɛtˏbæk]

n. (疾病) 復發；阻礙，挫折

 set「設置」+ **back**「後面」

Since her cancer went into remission almost two months ago, Katy has not suffered any **setbacks**.
由於 Katy 的癌症在約兩個月前已開始好轉，她已沒有疾病復發的問題了。

★ go into remission：(疾病) 好轉

| 補充 | suffer a (major/serious) setback |
| | 遭遇 (主要的 / 嚴重的) 困難、挫折 |

中級

76. **severe**

[səˋvɪr]

adj. 嚴重的，劇烈的；嚴厲的

Dana's migraine headaches are so **severe** that she has to put her head down on the desk.
Dana 的偏頭痛太嚴重了以致於她得趴在桌上。

補充	SARS = Severe Acute Respiratory Syndrome
	嚴重急性上呼吸道症候群
	a severe pain 劇烈疼痛
	a severe difficulty 極度困難

severely adv. 嚴苛地；嚴酷地
severity n. 嚴格；嚴厲

中高

77. **side effect**

[saɪd][ɪˈfɛkt]

n. (藥物的) 副作用

One **side effect** of taking this strong medication is drowsiness.
服用此強效藥物的其中一個副作用就是睏倦。

> **補充** aftereffect n. (藥物或疾病等的) 副作用，後遺症

中級

78. **sneeze**

[sniz]

v. 打噴嚏

n. 噴嚏

sneezy adj. 打噴嚏的；引起噴嚏的

I got sick after Tom **sneezed** into my face during PE class.
Tom 在體育課時打噴嚏到我臉上後我就生病了。

> **補充** give a violent sneeze 打一個大噴嚏
> not to be sneezed at (口語) 不可小看的

初級

79. **stress**

[strɛs]

n. 緊張；壓力；強調

v. 強調

stressful adj. 緊張的，有壓力的
stressed adj. 感到有壓力的 (= stressed out)

Greg is under quite a bit of **stress** to close the deal by the end of the weekend.
要在本週末前達成交易讓 Greg 感到相當有壓力。

> **補充** be under stress　　　　處於壓力下
> stresses and strains　　　緊張和壓力
> lay/put/place stress on sth. 強調某事，重視某事
> to stress the importance of N. 強調 N. 的重要性

中級

80. **stroke**

[strok]

n. 中風；突來的一擊

After suffering two **strokes**, Maria could no longer perform the daily duties of her office job.
在連續兩次中風後，Maria 就沒辦法進行她辦公室的日常工作了。

> **補充** have/suffer a stroke 中風
> heat stroke　　　　中暑

中級

81. surgery

[ˋsɝdʒərɪ]

n. 手術

Gary was told to eat nothing for several hours both before and after the **surgery**.

Gary 被告知在進行手術前後數小時內不要吃東西。

 補充

a major/minor surgery	大 / 小手術
have/undergo a surgery	接受手術
cosmetic surgery	美容手術
plastic surgery	整形手術
organ transplant surgery	器官移植手術

surgical adj. 外科的

surgeon n. 外科醫生

同 operation

中級

82. symptom

[ˋsɪmptəm]

n. 病徵；症狀；徵兆

⇨ sym - 「一起」+ -pto - 「掉落」+ -ma 「拉丁名詞字尾」，和疾病一起掉出來的東西就是病徵

Patients often do not exhibit any **symptoms** of the deadly virus until they get a sudden upset stomach and fever.

病患通常是到突然肚子不舒服和發高燒時才會有這個致命病毒的症狀。

補充

a symptom of sth.

某種疾病的症狀；某個問題的徵兆

symptomatic adj. 是…徵兆的

中級

83. syrup

[ˋsɪrəp]

n. 糖漿；糖水

Once you start coughing, drink some water instead of taking cough **syrup**.

你一開始咳嗽時要喝水，而不是喝咳嗽糖漿。

 補充

cough syrup	咳嗽糖漿
maple syrup	楓糖漿
corn syrup	玉米糖漿

syrupy adj. 糖漿狀的；太過甜膩的

中級

84. tablet

[ˋtæblɪt]

n. 藥片；匾額；一片…

⇨ table「桌子」+ -let「表小東西」，像桌子一樣平坦的一小片東西就是藥片

Be sure to take one **tablet** with plenty of water and food three times a day.

務必一天三次在進食前後喝大量水服用一錠藥片。

 補充

take a tablet of N.	服用 N. 的藥片
tablet (PC)	平板電腦
graphic tablet	電腦繪圖板

16
交通

17
社交與用餐

18
休閒娛樂

19
醫療保健

20
日常生活

中級

85. **therapy**
[ˈθɛrəpɪ]
n. 治療法

Tom will undergo five months of physical **therapy** to recover from the accident.
Tom 得接受五個月的物理治療才能從事故中復原。

補充
drug/gene therapy 藥物 / 基因療法
alternative therapy 替代醫療；另類療法
be in therapy 在接受心理治療中

therapist n. 治療師；某種療法的技師或專家
therapeutic adj. 有助於治療的；有療效的

中級

86. **thermometer**
[θəˈmɑmətɚ]
n. 溫度計

 thermo - 「熱的」+ meter「測量的儀器」
Theresa refused to stick a **thermometer** into her mouth to find out just how bad her fever was.
Theresa 拒絕含溫度計看自己燒得有多嚴重。

補充
clinical thermometer 體溫計
the thermometer reads... 溫度顯示為…度

中級

87. **throb**
[θrɑb]
v./n. 跳動；悸動

After two hours with a **throbbing** headache, I couldn't stand the pain and took a strong dose of aspirin.
在我的頭持續抽痛了兩小時之後，我受不了疼痛就服用了劑量很強的阿斯匹靈。

補充
throb with N. 伴隨著 N. 而顫抖
throbbing pain 抽痛

throbbing adj. 跳動的；抽動的
heartthrob n. 明星帥哥
同 pulsate v. 跳動

中級

88. **transplant**

[ˈtrænsplænt]
n. (器官) 移植；移植物
[trænsˈplænt]
v. 移植；移居

⇨ trans - 「橫跨」＋ plant「種植，放置」，把東西從這裡移到那裡放就是移植

It took a team of surgeons eight hours to finish the complicated heart **transplant**.
完成這個複雜的心臟移植花了外科醫師團隊八個小時。

 補充
to transplant N. (from A) into B
將 (A 的)N. 移植到 B 裡
a heart/liver/kidney transplant
心臟 / 肝臟 / 腎臟移植
organ transplant surgery 器官移植手術

transplantable adj. 可移植的
transplantation n. 移植法

中高

89. **trauma**

[ˈtrɔmə]
n. 外傷；心理創傷，痛苦經歷

★ 複數：traumas ／ traumata
The coroner determined that Mike died of blunt force **trauma**.
法醫判定 Mike 死於鈍器重擊創傷。

補充 the trauma of N. N. 所帶來的創傷

初級

90. **treatment**

[ˈtritmənt]
n. 治療；處理方式

⇨ treat「對待」＋ - ment「表手段」

There are various **treatments** for this condition.
這種症狀有許多種治療方法。

補充
a treatment for sth.　　對某疾病的治療
give/receive treatment 給予 / 接受治療
equal/preferencial treatment for sb.
對某人的平等 / 優先待遇

treat v. 對待；處理；請客

中高

91. **undergo**

[ˌʌndəˈgo]
v. 經歷；接受 (手術或治療)

⇨ under「在下方」＋ go「走過去」，從下方走過去表示經過、經歷了

The child had to **undergo** an emergency operation to remove a battery from his throat.
那孩子得接受緊急手術拿出卡在他喉嚨裡的電池。

 補充
undergo a surgery/operation 接受手術
undergo a trial/test　　　　接受審判 / 考試

同 experience v. 經歷

92. **vaccine**

[vækˋsin] / [ˋvæksin]

n. 疫苗
adj. 疫苗的；牛痘的

⇨ **vacc**「拉丁文，乳牛」+ **-ine**「表化學成份」，牛痘疫苗來自乳牛

Mike was ordered to get several **vaccines** before visiting several overseas clients.
Mike 被規定要先接種數種疫苗才能去拜訪一些國外的客戶。

| 典故 | 十八世紀時，英國醫生詹納察覺擠牛奶的女工沒有得到天花的病例，發現牛痘與天花病毒的相關性，便由乳牛身上取得牛痘病毒加以處理，成為能讓人體產生免疫力的「疫苗」。 |

| 補充 | a ... vaccine　　　　　…的疫苗
vaccination against N. 對抗 (疾病) 的疫苗 |

vaccinate v. 給 ... 接種疫苗
vaccination n. 種痘；接種疫苗

93. **vein**

[ven]

n. 靜脈

The nurse was having trouble finding a **vein** on the sickly man to tap her needle into.
那名護士沒辦法在那個病懨懨的人身上找到靜脈打針。

| 補充 | blood vessel 血管
artery　　　動脈 |

venous adj. 靜脈的

94. **virus**

[ˋvaɪrəs]

n. 病毒

With such a deadly **virus** making its way around the school, the administrators cancelled school for several days.
由於如此致命的病毒在學校裡到處流竄，主管單位將學校關閉了數天。

★ make one's way：前進；有進展

| 補充 | a virus infection　病毒傳染
the flu virus　　　流感病毒
computer virus　　電腦病毒
anti-virus software 防毒軟體
virus spam mail　　病毒垃圾郵件 |

viral adj. 病毒性的；由病毒引起的

中級

95. vital

[ˈvaɪtl̩]

adj. 生命的；充滿活力的；
極其重要的

⇨ - vit - 「生命」+ - al「有關…的」

Every few hours, a nurse checks on all my **vital** signs and administers more medicine if necessary from my IV drip.

每幾個小時，護士就來檢查我所有的生命跡象，如果有需要的話還會在我的點滴中加入更多藥劑。

補充		
	vital organs	重要器官
	be vital to N.	對 N. 是很重要的
	play a vital role	扮演重要角色
	of vital importance	至關重要

vitality n. 活力；(組織、國家的) 生命力

中高

96. vulnerable

[ˈvʌlnərəbl̩]

adj. 易受傷的，脆弱的；
易受責難的

⇨ - vulner - 「受傷；傷口」+ - able「易…的」

The football player was in a **vulnerable** position on the field when he was hit hard from behind without warning.

當那名足球員被從後方無預警撞擊時，他正在球場中一個容易受傷的位置上。

補充	be vulnerable to sth. 對某事很脆弱

vulnerability n. 脆弱；弱點
vulnerably adv. 脆弱地；易受傷害地

中級 🎧

97. ward

[wɔrd]

n. 病房

The maternity **ward** is filled to capacity at the moment, so some pregnant mothers will have to be assigned a room on the upper floors.

產科病房目前已經滿床，所以有些孕婦將被分配到樓上的房間。

補充	maternity/general/children's ward 產科／一般／兒童病房

98. **wellness**

[ˈwɛlnɪs]

n. (AmE) 身心健康；健康

⇨ well「健康的」+ -ness「表狀態」

There is a temporary **wellness** clinic being set up in the conference room for all employees to get free checkups.

會議室裡設置了一個臨時的健康診所，讓所有員工可以免費做健康檢查。

補充 | wellness program 健康計劃

well adj. 健康的，安好的

中高
99. **wheelchair**

[ˈhwiˈtʃɛr]

n. 輪椅

⇨ wheel「輪子」+ chair「椅子」

Every bathroom in your building needs to have at least one toilet stall that is equipped for **wheelchairs**.

你們大樓的每個洗手間都需配置至少一間輪椅可進入的廁所。

補充 |
be confined to a wheelchair 坐輪椅
wheelchair access　　　　　無障礙設施
wheelchair-accessible van　無障礙廂型車

中高
100. **wholesome**

[ˈholsəm]

adj. 有益健康的

⇨ whole「健康的」+ -some「形容詞字尾」

Sticking to a totally **wholesome** diet, Bob was able to lose ten kilograms without any exercise.

由於徹底堅持健康飲食，Bob 沒有做運動也能減十公斤。

補充 |
wholesome food　　　　　　 健康食物
wholesome entertainment 有益健康的娛樂
Bitter pills may have wholesome effects.
[諺語]：良藥苦口。

同 healthful

反 unwholesome adj. 不衛生的；有害身心的

實力進階

Part 1. 常見身體不適症狀的說法：

	sore throat	喉嚨痛		
	stuffy nose	鼻塞		
I have a:	cough	咳嗽		
	headache	頭痛		
	backache	背痛		
	pain in + 身體部位	（身體部位）疼痛		

	dizzy	頭暈	feverish	發燒的
	cold	畏寒	sleepy	想睡的
I feel:	sick	生病；不舒服	sweaty	多汗的
	nauseated	噁心的，想吐的	tired	疲勞的
	short of breath	呼吸困難	thirsty	口渴的
	light-headed	暈眩，頭昏眼花的	weak	虛弱的

Part 2. drugstore vs. pharmacy

drugstore 和 pharmacy 雖然都有賣藥，但是並非完全相同喔！它們的不同之處主要是從下列三大方面去區分：所賣的藥之種類、販賣對象、櫃台工作人員

1. drugstore: drugstore 一般販賣的藥是 over-the-counter medications (OTC)，也就是非處方用藥，換句話說，OTC 指的就是不需醫師所開的處方、一般民眾可自行購買的藥，當然在 drugstore 為您服務的人員也不需擁有專業相關藥師證照，他們的工作就只是幫助客人找到所需的藥品，沒有權利給予客人醫療建議。

2. pharmacy：pharmacy 其實就是藥局，所以醫生所開的處方藥 (prescription medications) 必須在 pharmacy 才可以買到或取得，當然在 pharmacy 為客人服務的都是具有專業藥師證照的藥師，他們的職責除了配藥、確保劑量的正確，當然還要清楚告知病人如何使用藥物以及藥物可能產生的副作用。

3. drugstore 和 pharmacy 還有一個很大的不同，就是 drugstore 除了賣藥，還兼賣很多日常用品或化妝品之類的商品，在台灣其實就是藥妝店。

隨堂練習

★ 請根據句意，選出最適合的單字

(   ) 1. My sister is _____ to cats; every time a cat comes near her, she just can't help sneezing.
    (A) severe   (B) allergic
    (C) immune   (D) liable

(   ) 2. David has been suffering from _____ back pain ever since he was injured in the car accident five years ago.
    (A) chronic   (B) wholesome
    (C) infectious   (D) biological

(   ) 3. It is surprising that this company is _____ to recession when most industries suffered great loss.
    (A) comprehensive   (B) acute
    (C) epidemic   (D) immune

(   ) 4. According to the initial investigation, the plane crash which claimed fifty lives last week is caused by metal _____.
    (A) stress   (B) hygiene
    (C) fatigue   (D) handicap

(   ) 5. Although this soldier finally goes home, he never recovers from the _____ of war.
    (A) trauma   (B) vaccine
    (C) therapy   (D) cavity

解答：1. B   2. A   3. D   4. C   5. A

Unit 20 日常生活

中高

1. absent-minded

[ˈæbsn̩tˈmaɪndɪd]

adj. 心不在焉的；健忘的

⇨ absent「缺席的」+ mind「心智」+ -ed「形容詞字尾」

Being **absent-minded**, it was no wonder that Robert had so many typos in his report.

Robert 老是心不在焉，難怪他報告裡有這麼多錯字。

補充　double-minded adj. 三心二意的

absent-mindedly adv. 不專心地，心不在焉地

同 distracted

反 attentive adj. 注意專心的
　　alert adj. 警覺的；機敏的

中高

2. accustom

[əˈkʌstəm]

v. 使習慣於…

⇨ ac-「to」+ custom「風俗習慣」，去使自己適應風俗習慣

Jake is **accustomed** to being the person who takes care of all the little things for the team.

Jake 習慣當個為團隊處理所有瑣碎小事的人。

補充　accustom oneself/sb./sth. to...
使某人（自己）/ 某事物習慣於 …
become/get accustomed to N./V-ing
變得對某事物習以為常

accustomed adj. 習慣的；通常的

同 adapt / adjust / be used to

中級

3. aggressive

[əˈgrɛsɪv]

adj. 有侵略性的；積極的；
　　有進取心的

⇨ ag-「to」+ -gress-「前進」+ -ive「有…性質的」，
　一直向前前進表示積極進取、很有侵略性

Sandy is a fairly **aggressive** salesperson, but she's not intelligent enough to put together a deal that customers might want.

Sandy 是個相當積極的業務員，但是她還沒聰明到到能搞定買賣雙方。

★ put together a deal：使雙方達成協議

補充　a violent and aggressive behavior
暴力且具攻擊性的行為
an aggressive campaign/strategy
雄心勃勃的宣傳活動 / 策略

aggressively adv. 侵略地；有衝勁地
aggression n. 侵略；侵犯行為

中高

4. anticipate

[æn`tɪsə͵pet]

v. 預見；預期

 anti - 「=ante - ，在前」 + - cip - 「拿取」 + - ate「動詞字尾」，事前先拿表示預見了未來的狀況

Bill made a great career out of **anticipating** the way the markets would go.

Bill 因為預見市場走向而創造了成功的事業。

補充 | anticipate N./V-ing　　預期、預料到某事物
It is anticipated that...　大家預期…

anticipation n. 預期；期望

同 expect / forsee

初級

5. apologize

[ə`pɑləˌdʒaɪz]

v. 道歉；認錯

★ 英：apologise ／ 美：apologize

 apo - 「脫離」 + - log - 「說」 + - ize「動詞字尾」，為了脫離錯誤而說出道歉

I want Barbara to **apologize** for her harsh comments before I agree to speak with her again.

在我同意再與 Barbara 說話之前，我要她為苛刻的評論向我道歉。

補充 | apologize to sb.　　　向某人道歉
apologize for N./V-ing　為某事道歉

apology n. 道歉；認錯

中級

6. astonish

[ə`stɑnɪʃ]

v. 使吃驚；使驚訝

 as - 「=ex - ，向外」 + - ton - 「打雷」 + - ish「動詞字尾」，外面突然打雷讓人嚇一跳

I admit that I am **astonished** to find that you have cleaned the house from top to bottom.

我得承認在發現你把房子徹底打掃乾淨時我感到很驚訝。

補充 | be astonished to see/find...　驚訝地看到 / 發現…
be astonished at N.　　　　對 N. 感到驚訝

astonishing adj. 令人驚訝的
astonished adj. 驚訝的；驚愕的

同 surprise / shock / amaze

中級

⇨ attract「引起注意」+ -ive「有…性質的」

7. **attractive**

[əˋtræktɪv]

adj. 有吸引力的；引人入勝的

Ms. Hudson is quite **attractive**, but she needs to have a stronger work ethic if she wants to be an actress.

Hudson 女士相當迷人，但是如果她想成爲女演員，她需要擁有更強烈的工作使命感。

補充 an attractive offer 很誘人的機會
find sb. attractive 發現某人的迷人之處

attract v. 吸引；引起…的注意
attraction n. 吸引力

同 appealing

反 unattractive adj. 不具吸引力的

8. **avid**

[ˋævɪd]

adj. 熱切的；渴望的

Steve is an **avid** sports fan who never misses watching his favorite team's games.

Steve 是個熱情的運動迷，他從未錯過他最愛球隊的比賽。

補充 an avid reader/listener/collector
狂熱的讀者 / 聽衆 / 收集迷
be avid for N. 很想得到 N.
take an avid interest in N. 對 N. 很感興趣

avidness n. 渴望；熱心

同 eager / keen

9. **brag**

[bræg]

v. 自誇；吹噓

Don't **brag** about how many sales quotas you will meet; just work harder.

不要吹噓你會達成多少銷售數字；你只要更努力就好。

補充 brag about N. 吹牛，自誇
brag (to sb.) about sth. 向 (某人) 吹噓某事

同 boast

中級

10. clash
[klæʃ]
v./n. 衝突；分歧

Although they **clash** on political views, Martha and Andy still have a lot in common.
雖然 Martha 和 Andy 在政治觀點上有所衝突，但是他們還是有很多共同點。

 補充
to clash with sb. over/on sth.
為某事與某人衝突
a clash of opinions/cultures
意見／文化上的衝突
a personality clash with sb.
和某人性格上有衝突
a clash between A and B
A 與 B 之間的衝突

同 conflict

中高

11. collector
[kəˋlɛktə]
n. 收藏家；收稅員

⇨ collect「收集」+ -or「做⋯動作的人」
Ashley's hobby as a **collector** of antiquities is expensive to maintain.
Ashley 作為古董收藏家的嗜好要靠著昂貴的花費來維持。

 補充
a coin/stamp/art collector
錢幣／郵票／藝術收藏家
a ticket/tax collector 收票員／收稅員

collect v. 收集
collection n. 收藏品

中高

12. columnist
[ˋkɑləmnɪst]
n. 專欄作家
column n. 專欄文章

⇨ column「專欄」+ -ist「專精⋯的人」
The **columnist** wrote about the government's abuse of power.
這名專欄作家寫了篇關於政府濫用權力的評論。

11
製造

12
金融

13
科技技術

14
房屋地產

15
出差旅遊

13. **combative**
[kəmˋbætɪv]
adj. 好戰的；好爭鬥的

⇨ com - 「一起」 + bat 「打」 + -ive 「具…性質的」

It is better not to get too **combative** during a debate so you can appear calm and in control for the judges.
辯論中最好不要太好鬥，這樣你在裁判的眼裡看起來就是冷靜且能掌握局面的。

補充 in a combative mood/spirit 處於準備應戰的情緒

combat v. 戰鬥，搏鬥

中高
14. **compassion**
[kəmˋpæʃən]
n. 憐憫；同情

 com - 「一起」 + passion 「拉丁文，受難」，看到別人難過好比和他一起受苦就是同情

I have **compassion** for the poor because I used to be one of them.
我對窮人有同情心，因為我過去也曾經和他們一樣。

典故 compassion 中的 passion 一字原指耶穌在十字架上受難的意思，後才引申為狂熱而強烈的愛恨情感表現。compassion 就是有一起受難的感受，也就是同情、憐憫。

補充
feel/show compassion　　　　感到同情
be filled with compassion　充滿同情
compassion fatigue　　　　　同情心疲乏

compassionate adj. 富有同情心的

同 mercy / sympathy

中高
15. **conceive**
[kənˋsiv]
v. 構想；想像；懷孕

 con - 「一起，表加強語氣」 + -ceive - 「拿取」，把想法拿來放一起就形成構想

How did you ever **conceive** of the ridiculous idea of shutting down the factory for two days?
你怎麼想想得出關掉工廠兩天這種荒謬的點子啊？

補充 conceive of V-ing/N. 想像出…

conception n. 概念；想法

中級

16. **congratulate**

[kənˈgrætʃəˌlet]

v. 祝賀

 con - 「一起」+ gratulari「拉丁文，開心高興」，與對方一起開心就是在祝賀對方

I wish to **congratulate** you on your new appointment as the CEO.
我要恭喜你當上新執行長。

補充 congratulate sb. on sth. 祝賀某人的某事

congratulation n. 祝賀；慶賀

中級

17. **considerate**

[kənˈsɪdərɪt]

adj. 體貼的

 consider「考慮，認為」+ -ate「形容詞字尾」，考慮很多就是體貼的

It's very **considerate** of you to wait for us.
你等我們真的好體貼。

補充 It is considerate of sb. to V. 某人很體貼會做⋯

consideration n. 考慮

易混 considerable adj. 相當大的；相當多的

中高

18. **contentment**

[kənˈtɛntmənt]

n. 滿足；滿意

 con - 「一起」+ -tent - 「持握」+ -ment「名詞字尾」，喜歡的東西都一起拿著就會感到滿足

You should feel at least some **contentment** at your job or you should resign.
你至少要對工作有感到些許滿足，不然你就該把工作給辭了。

補充 a look of contentment 看起來很滿足的樣子

content adj. 滿意的，滿足的

中高

19. **curriculum**

[kəˈrɪkjələm]

n. 課程

 -curr - 「跑動」+ -culum「拉丁名詞字尾」

I would like my son to study at a school with a rigorous **curriculum**.
我想讓我兒子在一所課程嚴謹的學校就讀。

典故 來自拉丁文的 curriculum 原意指以跑步進行的課程或職業，也指競賽用的車或快馬車。1630 年代時，蘇格蘭的格拉斯哥 (Glasgow) 大學引用這個拉丁字來稱呼他們的課程，隨後用 curriculum 指課程的習慣便在歐洲各地流行起來。

補充 CV = Curriculum Vitea 簡歷；履歷書

curricular adj. 課程的
extracurricular adj. 課外的

中級
20. **defeat**

[dɪˈfit]

v. 戰勝；擊敗
n. 失敗

⇨ de -「表否定」+ -feat -「做」，把別人做的結果打回原來的樣子就是擊敗他了。

There is so much pressure for our team to **defeat** our greatest rival and take home the trophy.
要將我們最大的對手打敗並帶回勝利獎盃，對我們團隊來說有很大的壓力。

補充
to defeat N. by (points)	以…分擊敗某人 / 某隊
a serious defeat	嚴重受挫
admit defeat	認輸

同 v. = beat / overcome

中級
21. **defence**

[dɪˈfɛns]

n. 防禦；防護

★ 英：defence／美：defense

⇨ de -「離開」+ -fen -「擊打」，把人打離開、打回去就是在防禦。

When Emily criticized me at the meeting, my supervisor came to my **defence**.
Emily 在會議中批評我的時候，我的上司幫我說話。

補充
come to sb's defence	幫助某人；保護某人
in defence of...	為保衛…；為…辯護

defensive adj. 防禦的；保衛的
defend v. 防守，防衛

反 offence / offense n. 冒犯，進攻

中級
22. **despair**

[dɪˈspɛr]

n. 絕望；使人絕望的事物
v. 感到絕望

 de -「表否定」+ spair「拉丁文，希望」

The farmers felt great **despair** because there was another drought this year.
農夫們因為今年又有乾旱而感到十分絕望。

補充
in despair	絕望地
drive sb. to despair	使某人絕望
N. be the despair of sb.	N. 讓某人失望
to sink into despair	徹底絕望

despairing adj. 感到絕望的；無望的

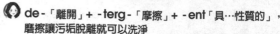

16 交通

17 社交與用餐

18 休閒娛樂

19 醫療保健

20 日常生活

中級

23. detergent

[dɪˋtɝdʒənt]

n. 洗潔劑；洗衣粉
adj. 有清潔力的

 de-「離開」+ -terg-「摩擦」+ -ent「具…性質的」，磨擦讓污垢脫離就可以洗淨

After switching laundry **detergent** brands, Amy broke out in hives.
在換了洗衣粉的牌子後，Amy 突然長出了蕁麻疹。

補充 laundry detergent 洗衣精，洗衣粉

---

24. detest

[dɪˋtɛst]

v. 憎惡；痛恨；嫌惡

detestation n. 憎惡；嫌惡
detestable adj. 令人厭惡的
同 hate / dislike

I **detest** cleaning up after other people's messes.
我痛恨清理別人留下來的髒亂。

補充 detest N./V-ing 痛恨…

中級

25. devoted

[dɪˋvotɪd]

adj. 忠實的；摯愛的

 devote「致力於…」+ -ed「形容詞字尾」，因為熱愛就會致力專注

Marcia is such a **devoted** fan of the famous singer that she attends her concerts in other countries.
Marcia 對那名歌手實在太死忠了，以致於她還去參加那名歌手在國外的演唱會。

補充 be devoted to N. 熱愛 N.

devote v. 奉獻…；致力於…
devotee n. 熱心之士，愛好者
同 忠實的：loyal / faithful

中級

26. discard

[dɪsˋkɑrd]

v. 拋棄；丟棄

 dis-「離開」+ card「紙牌」

Items that are unclaimed after 15 days will be **discarded**.
十五天後還是沒人認領的物品將會被丟掉。

典故 discard 源自撲克牌遊戲，紙牌離開了你的手，就表示你不要這張牌了，也就是「拋棄、丟棄」了。

同 throw away / get rid of

中級

27. **disgust**

[dɪsˋgʌst]

n. 作嘔；反感

v. 作嘔；厭惡；導致反感

Stacy expressed her **disgust** at the nasty smell by a lot of complaints.

Stacy 以許多抱怨表達了對這股惡臭的反感。

 補充
in disgust 　　　　　　　　厭惡地，生氣地
be disgusted at/with/by N. 對 N. 感到噁心

disgusting adj. 噁心的，令人想吐的

中高

28. **disposition**

[ˌdɪspəˋzɪʃən]

n. 性格；傾向

⇨ dispose「配置；安排」+ -ition「名詞字尾」，人的性格是天生就被配置好的

It is said that people suffering from stress may be born with a nervous **disposition**.

據說壓力大的人可能天生就有緊張的性格。

補充
have a cheerful disposition　性格開朗
people with a … disposition　有…個性的人
have/show a … disposition to/toward N.
有…傾向

dispose v. 配置；安排

同 temperament n. 性格
　 inclination n. 傾向

中級

29. **dispute**

[dɪˋspjut]

n./v. 爭論；爭議；爭執

⇨ dis-「分開」+ -pute-「想」，各自有不同的想法就會產生爭議

With a diplomatic attitude, Sara helped settle the trade **disputes** to prevent them from escalating.

Sara 以圓滑的手法協助處理貿易糾紛，以避免衝突擴大。

 補充
settle/resolve the dispute　　　解決爭端
trade/labor dispute　　　　　　貿易 / 勞資糾紛
a dispute over N.　　　　　　　對於 N. 的爭議
be in/under dispute
有爭議，處在爭議中
beyond dispute = undoubtedly　無庸置疑地

同 n. = conflict / disagreement

30. distress

中高

[dɪˈstrɛs]

v./n. 悲痛；苦惱

⇨ dis - 「分開」+ - tress - 「拉緊」，用力拉使人離開所愛就造成痛苦

Tom feels so **distressed** at having to work so many hours just to make ends meet.

Tom 對於只是要為了求得溫飽而必須工作這麼多時數而感到痛苦。

補充　in distress 在痛苦中

distressed adj. 痛苦的；悲傷的

31. dreadful

中級

[ˈdrɛdfəl]

adj. 糟透的；可怕的

dread n./v. 害怕，恐懼

dreadfully adv. 恐怖地，非常地

同 awful / terrible

⇨ dread 「害怕」+ - ful 「充滿…的」

After years of neglect, the house looks absolutely **dreadful**.

經過這麼多年的荒廢，那棟房子看起來真是糟透了。

32. drop off

[drɑp][ɔf]

phr. 讓…下車；下降，減少；打盹

drop v. 掉落

Daisy has to **drop off** her kids at school every day before going to work downtown.

Daisy 每天到市中心上班前要先送小孩到學校。

補充　drop sb. off　讓某人下車
drop off point　下車點

33. **elegant**

[ˈɛləgənt]

adj. 典雅的；有品味的；巧妙的

elegance **n.** 典雅，優雅

同 graceful / tasteful

Francine is wearing an especially **elegant** dress to the fundraiser dinner tonight.
Francine 今晚穿了一件特別高雅的洋裝出席募款晚會。

補充　an elegant solution to the problem
解決問題的巧妙方法

---

34. **engagement**

[ɪnˈgedʒmənt]

n. 約定；婚約；訂婚

⇨ engage「訂婚，約定；從事」+ -ment「名詞字尾」

The whole family was shocked to hear of Emily's sudden **engagement** to a man she had just started dating.
聽到 Emily 跟一個才剛開始交往的男人突然訂婚了，所有家人都好驚訝。

補充
a prior/previous engagement
已定好的約定、約會
an engagement letter = a letter of engagement
僱用信
without engagement 非約定的

---

35. **enthusiastic**

[ɪnˌθjuzɪˈæstɪk]

adj. 熱心的；狂熱的

⇨ en-「進入」+ -thus-「神」+ -iast「做⋯的人」+ -ic「形容詞字尾」

Jason is not very **enthusiastic** about going to parties. I suggest that you invite someone else.
Jason 並不熱衷去派對。我建議你邀請別人。

典故　原意指神跑到人的裡面，心靈受到神靈啟發而進入狂喜狀態，引申為對某事物很熱衷、很熱情投入。

補充
be enthusiastic about N./V-ing 對⋯很熱衷
an enthusiastic welcome　　熱烈的歡迎

enthusiast **n.** 熱心者；狂熱者
enthusiasm **n.** 熱情；熱忱

36. **esteem**

[ə`stim]

n. 尊敬

v. 尊重，視為

Professor Jones, I hold you in such high **esteem** for your contributions to the conservation of wildlife.
Jones 教授，我非常尊崇您對保護野生動物的貢獻。

補充
sb. be held in high esteem by N.
某人受到 N. 的高度推崇
be highly esteemed　　極受敬重
the sense of self-esteem　自尊心

self-esteem n. 自尊

同 n. = respect / regard

---

37. **exclaim**

[ɪks`klem]

v. 呼喊；大聲說出

⇨ **ex-**「向外」**+ claim**「宣告」

All staff **exclaimed** in delight when they heard of the good news.
全體員工在聽到這個好消息時都開心地尖叫。

補充
exclaim in delight　開心地尖叫
exclamation mark　驚嘆號

exclamation n. 驚叫；感嘆句

同 cry out / shout

---

38. **exert**

[ɪg`zɝt]

v. 用力；發揮；盡力

⇨ **ex-**「向外」**+ -ert -**「附加，加入」，加入你們一起用力向外推

Gina **exerts** quite an influence on her husband's decisions.
Gina 在她丈夫所做的決定上發揮很大的影響力。

補充
exert oneself　某人盡全力

exertion n. 努力；用力氣；花心思

---

39. **expected**

[ɪk`spɛktɪd]

adj. 預期會發生的；預料中的

⇨ **expect**「預期；預料」**+ -ed**「形容詞字尾」

Your daughter is **expected** to make a full recovery from the virus by the end of the week.
你女兒預計這個週末前就能從病毒感染中完全康復。

補充
as sb. expected　　　如同某人所預期的
sth. be to be expected　某事很可能發生

expect v. 預期；預料

反 unexpected adj. 意外的；想不到的

初級

40. fail

[fel]

v. 失敗，不及格

Although Sherry **failed** in her quest to become an entertainer, she went on to become an excellent physician.

雖然 Sherry 在追求成為藝人的路上失敗了，但是她繼續努力成為一名優秀的醫生。

fail to V.	無法做到…
fail in sth.	做某事失敗了
never fail to V.	從來不會沒做…；一直會做…
sth. fail sb.	某物使某人失望；某人因缺乏某物而無法做…

failure n. 失敗

同 flunk

反 pass v. 通過

初級

41. fancy

[ˈfænsɪ]

adj. 花俏的；別緻複雜的；豪華的

After a hard week at the office, you deserve to be taken out to a **fancy** restaurant for dinner.

經過一週辛苦的工作之後，到一家高檔的餐廳享用晚餐是你應得的。

fancy decorations	花俏的裝飾
fancy words	花言巧語
fancy restaurants/ hotels	豪華餐廳／旅館
fancy prices	昂貴的價格

反 plain adj. 樸素的

中級

42. fascination

[ˌfæsn̩ˈeʃən]

n. 入迷；著迷；魅力

Rebecca has a peculiar **fascination** with Christmas decorations, spending thousands of dollars on them each year.

Rebecca 對聖誕裝飾特別感興趣，每年都要花上數千元。

典故 fascinate 來自拉丁文 fascinare，意思是施魔法、說咒語使人迷惑、蠱惑他人，加上名詞字尾 -ion 就是 fascination，指使人著迷的魅力。

have a fascination for/with...	對…十分感興趣
hold a fascination for sb.	對某人很有吸引力
in fascination	著迷地

fascinate v. 迷住、吸引，使著迷
fascinating adj. 迷人的；引人入勝的

16 交通

43. **fondness**

['fɑndnɪs]

n. 喜愛；鍾愛

⇨ fond「喜愛的」+ -ness「名詞字尾」

Our client, Mr. Newman has a **fondness** for whisky.
我們的客戶 Newman 先生喜歡喝威士忌。

 a fondness for N.　對 N. 有所愛好
be fond of N.　　喜愛 N.

fond adj. 喜歡的，喜愛的

同 love / liking / affection

17 社交與用餐

44. **frustrated**

['frʌstretɪd]

adj. 挫敗的；失意的，沮喪的

⇨ -frustr-「徒勞的」+ -ate「使…」+ -ed「形容詞字尾」

Tammy was **frustrated** that her boss didn't promote her.
Tammy 很沮喪她的老闆沒讓她升職。

 get/feel frustrated at/with N. 對 N. 感到灰心沮喪

frustrate v. 使挫敗；使沮喪
frustration n. 失敗；挫折

同 disappointed / discouraged

18 休閒娛樂

45. **gloomy**

['glumɪ]

adj. 陰暗的；憂鬱的；令人
　　沮喪的

⇨ gloom「黑暗」+ -y「多…的」

I don't understand why you have such a **gloomy** outlook for your job search.
我不了解為何你對於找工作這麼悲觀。

 gloomy weather　　　陰暗的天氣

gloom n. 黑暗、陰暗

19 醫療保健

46. **go through**

[go][θru]

phr. 通過，經歷；從頭到尾
　　（演出、討論、進行流程）

Hans has **gone through** a job loss and a home foreclosure this year.
Hans 今年經歷了失業，以及房屋抵押贖回權遭取消。

 go through sth.
經歷某事；將某事從頭到尾進行一次
go through with N.　　完成 N.，實行 N.
go through a bad patch 處於困境

同 experience / go over / work through

20 日常生活

中級

47. **grain**

[gren]

n. 穀物；顆粒

This country's economy depends a lot on **grain** exports.
該國經濟主要倚賴穀類出口。

補充
grain prices/production/market
穀類價格 / 產品 / 市場
a grain of N. 一點點的 N.（常用於否定句）

中級

48. **grateful**

[ˋgretfəl]

adj. 感激的；感謝的

⇨ grate「= 拉丁文 gratus，感謝的」+ - ful「充滿…的」
I am **grateful** to you for so many years of guidance and
support.
我非常感謝你多年來的指導與支持。

補充
be grateful to sb./for sth.　感激某人 / 某事
be grateful to V.　　　　　爲能做…覺得感謝
be deeply/eternally grateful 非常感謝、感激

gratitude n. 感激之情
gratefully adv. 感激地；感謝地

同 thankful

反 ungrateful adj. 忘恩負義的；不領情的

初級

49. **habit**

[ˋhæbɪt]

n. 習慣

Dr. Johnson just published an essay on how our eating
habits affect our health.
Johnson 博士剛剛發表了一篇關於我們的飲食習慣如何影響
健康的論文。

典故
英文的 habit 源自法文 habit，原意表「宗教團體
成員所穿著的服裝」，到 14 世紀時，habit 用來指
要穿著宗教服裝執行的慣例儀式或活動，後來 habit
便衍生出指慣例的行為或習慣。

補充
be/get into the habit of N./V-ing
有 / 養成…的習慣
have a habit of V-ing　　有做…的習慣
break the habit of V-ing　擺脫…的習慣
out of habit　　　　　　出於習慣

habitual adj. 習慣的；已成習慣的

中高

50. **handicraft**

[ˈhændɪ͵kræft]

n. 手工藝；手工藝品

handcrafted adj. 手工製作的
craft n. 工藝；手藝

回 handiwork

⇨ **handy**「巧手的」+ **craft**「技藝」

Stephanie bought some traditional **handicrafts** as souvenirs from her holiday in Australia.

Stephanie 從澳洲度假回來買了些傳統手工藝品當紀念品。

---

51. **hectic**

[ˈhɛktɪk]

adj. 忙亂的，繁忙的

If you continue with such a **hectic** schedule, you'll be burned out in no time.

如果你繼續過著這麼忙亂的生活，你很快就會筋疲力竭。

典故　hectic 來自希臘文，原指結核病產生每日頻繁發燒和畏寒不斷交替的狀態 (hectic fever)，後來就以 hectic 表示這種忙亂的交替，也就是繁忙的、忙亂的。

補充　a hectic day/week 忙亂的一天／一週
hectic lifestyle/schedule/pace
忙碌的生活方式／時程／步調

回 busy / chaotic

---

52. **hideous**

[ˈhɪdɪəs]

adj. 極醜的；極難看的

hideousness n. 極醜；駭人聽聞
hideously adv. 可怕地；非常討厭地

回 ugly

The novel is interesting; however, the book cover is **hideous**.

小說很有趣；然而，書的封面好醜。

補充　a hideous face/dress 其醜無比的臉／服裝

11
製造

12
金融

13
科技技術

14
房屋地產

15
出差旅遊

53. hostile

[ˋhɑstl]

adj. 敵方的；不友善的

⇨ host「主人，（古）軍隊」＋ -ile「有…傾向的」

Eric's bad attitude provoked a **hostile** response in return.
Eric 的惡劣態度引來對方的惡意回應。

典故　host 是主人，在舊時的用法也指「軍隊」，hostile 就是要動用到軍隊、有用兵的傾向，就是面臨敵意、不友善的情形，所以 hostile 就是敵對的、不友善的。

補充　a hostile takeover/acquisition/deal
充滿敵意的接管／併購／交易
be hostile to N. 對 N. 持敵對態度

hostility n. 敵意；敵對態度

同 unfriendly

---

54. hybrid

[ˋhaɪbrɪd]

adj. 混合的；雜交的
n. 混合物；雜交物種

This type of **hybrid** car is known for its great fuel efficiency.
這款油電混合車以其絕佳燃油效能而聞名。

典故　hybrid 來自拉丁文 hybrida，原指雜交所產下的動物，現在則用來指混合兩種以上不同能源或系統的機械、設備或電腦。

補充　a hybrid car/engine　　油電混合車／引擎
a hybrid between/of A and B　A 與 B 的混合物

同 mixture n. 混合體

---

55. illusion

[ɪˋluʒən]

n. 幻想；假象，錯覺

⇨ il-「= in-，進入」＋ -lus-「戲弄」＋ -ion「表狀態」，會戲弄人的就是假象

These name-brand clothes create the **illusion** that Amy is wealthy, but she is far from it.
這些名牌衣服創造了一個 Amy 很富有的假象，其實她一點都不富有。

補充　be under the illusion that...
誤以為…；有…的錯覺
have no illusion about N. 對 N. 不存幻想
create the illusion of N.　創造出 N. 的錯覺

illusive adj. 假象的，幻覺的

56. impartial

[ɪmˋpɑrʃəl]

adj. 不偏袒；無偏見的；公正的

➡ im - 「表否定」 + part「部分的」 + -ial「有關…的」，不會只重視局部就是公正、不偏袒的

You are supposed to be **impartial** as a chairman.
你作爲主席應該要公正無私。

補充 impartial advice/judge 公正的建議 / 評斷

impartiality n. 公正
impartially adv. 公平地

同 unprejudiced

反 partial adj. 不公正的，偏袒的

中高

57. implicit

[ɪmˋplɪsɪt]

adj. 含蓄的；絕對的

➡ im - 「進入」 + -plic - 「摺」 + -it「形容詞字尾」，把東西摺進去不讓人直接看到就是含蓄的

There is an **implicit** moral message in every one of this author's books.
這個作者的每一本書裡都有一個隱含的道德寓意。

補充 A be implicit in B　　B 裡隱含著 A
implicit trust/faith　　絕對的信心

implicitly adv. 含蓄地；暗示地

反 explicit adj. 清楚明確的，直截了當的

中高

58. impulsive

[ɪmˋpʌlsɪv]

adj. 衝動的；草率的

 im - 「進入」 + -puls - 「推動」 + -ive「有…性質的」

Kathy tries to stay away from shopping malls because she is such an **impulsive** buyer.
Kathy 試著遠離購物中心，因爲她是個衝動的購物狂。

補充 an impulsive buyer 衝動購買者

impulse n. 衝動；推動
impulsively adv. 衝動地

同 impetuous

11 製造

12 金融

13 科技技術

14 房屋地產

15 出差旅遊

59. **indigenous**
[ɪnˈdɪdʒənəs]
adj. 土生土長的；本地的

⇨ indi-「= in-，在內」+ -gen-「產生」+ -ous「有很多…的」，在內部產生的就是本地的、土生土長的
The government should set aside more land for **indigenous** people.
政府應該要撥出更多的土地給原住民。

| 補充 | be indigenous to N. | 是 N. 土生土長的 |
| | indigenous firm/business | 本土公司 / 行業 |

同 native / aboriginal

中級
60. **instinct**
[ˈɪnstɪŋkt]
n. 本能；直覺

 in-「在內」+ -stinct-「刺，戳」，受到刺激而產生的衝動行為就是直覺
Birds are born with the **instinct** to migrate.
鳥類生來就有遷徙的本能。

補充	have an instinct for N.	對 N. 很有天份
	herd instinct	群體直覺
	killer instinct	頑固的本性；執意要做的個性

instinctive adj. 本能的；天性的
同 intuition

初級
61. **jealous**
[ˈdʒɛləs]
adj. 嫉妒的；唯恐失去的

⇨ jeal「熱情」+ -ous「有很多…的」，投入很多情感以致於害怕失去就是嫉妒
Don't be **jealous** of others' success.
不要嫉妒他人的成功。
We are very **jealous** of our good reputation.
我們非常珍惜我們的好名聲。

| 補充 | be jealous of... | 對…感到嫉妒；很珍惜… |

jealousy n. 嫉妒
jealously adv. 嫉妒地
同 envious adj. 嫉妒的

62. literate
['lɪtərɪt]

adj. 有文化素養的；能讀寫的

n. 有文化素養的人；能讀寫的人

 littera「拉丁文，字母」 + -ate「有…性質的」，有懂字母、認得文字的性質就是有文化素養的

The children in this town become **literate** at such a young age thanks to our great preschool programs.
這個城鎮的小孩在這麼小的年紀就能讀寫，這都要歸功於我們絕佳的學前教育課程。

| 補充 | computer literate 精通電腦的；懂電腦操作的
financially/technologically literate
懂財務/科技的 |

literacy n. 讀寫能力；知識
literature n. 文學

反 illiterate n. 不識字的人；文盲　adj. 不識字的；文盲的

中級

63. nasty
['næstɪ]

adj. 糟糕的，令人不悅的；嚴重的

Lisa and Joe had a particularly **nasty** fight in the meeting room.
Lisa 和 Joe 在會議室裡吵得很兇。

| 典故 | nasty 來自荷蘭文的 nestig，以英文來看就是 nest（鳥巢）+tig（小樹枝）組成，因鳥巢裡還會有羽毛和鳥的排泄物，看起來總是很髒，所以荷蘭文的 nestig 除了指「像鳥巢的」，也指「骯髒的」，進入英文這個字的拼字就變成了 nasty 指骯髒的、令人討厭的意思。 |

| 補充 | get/turn nasty　　變糟、變亂
cheap and nasty　廉價又劣質的
nasty injury　　　嚴重的傷害 |

nastily adv. 嫌惡地

中級

64. offensive
[ə'fɛnsɪv]

adj. 冒犯的，唐突的；攻擊性的

n. 進攻

⇨ offense「侵犯，冒犯」 + -ive「有…性質的」

I find it very **offensive** that you don't respect my culture!
我覺得你不尊重我的文化是很冒犯的！

| 補充 | be offensive to sb.　　冒犯某人；對某人無禮
an offensive weapon 攻擊性武器
take the offensive　　先發制人 |

offend v. 冒犯，侵犯
offense n. 侵犯，冒犯

反 defensive adj. 防禦的；防衛的

中高

65. optimistic
[ˌɑptəˋmɪstɪk]
adj. 樂觀的

⇨ optimum「最理想的」＋ - ist「人」＋ - ic「似…的」

Even with all the bad blood between us, I am still **optimistic** that we can reach a compromise.
即使我們之間存在著嫌隙，我還是樂觀的認為我們能夠和解。

★ bad blood：嫌隙；仇恨

 be overly optimistic/over-optimistic 過度樂觀
be optimistic about sth. 對某事很樂觀

optimum adj. 最理想的，最佳的
optimist n. 樂觀主義者，樂天派

同 positive

反 pessimistic adj. 悲觀的；消極的

中高

66. outgoing
[ˋaʊtˌgoɪŋ]
adj. 外向的，好交際的；外
出的，離開的

⇨ out「向外」＋ going「走」

You're so **outgoing** that it's no wonder you are the best salesperson in this company.
你這麼善於交際，難怪你能成為本公司的最佳業務員。

 an outgoing personality 外向的個性
an outgoing call 外撥電話
outgoing flights 出境航班

同 sociable adj. 好交際的

反 incoming adj. 進入的；到達的

中高

67. overwhelming
[ˌovɚˋhwɛlmɪŋ]
adj. 壓倒性的；勢不可擋的

⇨ over「超越」＋ whelm「壓倒」＋ - ing「形容詞字尾」

The **overwhelming** number of attendees shows that the topic fits people's interests.
龐大的出席人數顯示這個主題切合人們的興趣。

Some people find performing in front of 20,000 people to be **overwhelming**, while others just can't get enough of it.
有些人覺得要在兩萬人面前表演會很令人難以招架，而有些人卻覺得游刃有餘。

 overwhelming majority 壓倒性的多數
be overwhelmed by... 被…壓垮而感到茫然

overwhelm v. 壓倒，戰勝；使不知所措，難以承受
overwhelmingly adv. 壓倒性地；無法抵抗地

中級

68. **panic**

[ˋpænɪk]

n. 恐慌
v. 使恐慌

★ 動詞變化：**panic, panicked, panicked, panicking**
Be careful with how you word the announcement so as not to cause a **panic**.
謹慎注意你宣佈時的用詞，以免造成恐慌。

 panic 來自希臘神話的牧神 Pan，Pan 掌管樹林與原野，同時據說也是在牧群或森林中發出神祕聲響及帶來傳染病的來源，所以 Pan 的出現就會造成 panic 恐慌。

cause/trigger panic	造成 / 引起恐慌
There's no panic. /Don't panic.	不用 / 別慌張。
in panic	恐慌地；慌張地
panic buying/selling	恐慌性搶購 / 賣出
press the panic button	按下緊急求救鈴

panic-stricken adj. 驚慌失措的

同 n. = fright

中高

69. **passionate**

[ˋpæʃənɪt]

adj. 情感強烈的；熱情的

⇨ **passion**「熱情」+ -**ate**「有⋯性質的」
Debra has a **passionate** interest in buying stocks.
Debra 對買股票有強烈興趣。

 be passionate about sth. 對某事物很狂熱

passion n. 熱情
passionately adv. 熱情地

同 zealous / enthusiastic

中高

70. **perceive**

[pəˋsiv]

v. (以某些方式) 理解；察覺，感知

 per-「徹底地」+ -ceive-「拿」，徹底拿到心中表示你察覺到了、感知到了
I **perceived** a note of unhappiness on the manager's face.
我察覺到經理臉上的不悅。

perceive sb./sth. as sth.	認為某人 / 某物是⋯
perceive sb./sth. to be/have sth.	
認為某人 / 某物有⋯	

perception n. 感知能力；洞察力
perceptive adj. 觀察力敏銳的

同 notice

中高

71. prejudice

[ˋprɛdʒədɪs]

n. 偏見；歧視

 pre-「在…前」+ -judi-「判斷」+ -ce「名詞字尾」，在事前就先做判斷就是偏見、歧視

Despite Karen's father's **prejudice** against her boyfriend, in the end he gave his blessing to their wedding.

儘管 Karen 的父親對她的男友有偏見，他最終還是贊成了他們的婚禮。

補充 prejudice against... 對…的偏見

prejudicial adj. 不利的；有損害的

中級

72. preserve

[prɪˋzɝv]

v. 維護；保存；醃製

n. 蜜餞；果醬

 pre-「在…前」+ -serv-「保護」，事前先保留守護起來就是保存

Every effort must be made to **preserve** the traditions of our ancestors.

我們必須盡力保留祖先的傳統。

補充 preserve sb. from... 保護某人使免於…
sb. be well-preserved
某人保養得很好，看起來很年輕

preserver n. 保護者
preservation n. 保護；保持
preservative adj. 保存的；防腐的 n. 防腐劑

中高

73. profound

[prəˋfaʊnd]

adj. 學識淵博的；強烈的，深刻的

 pro-「向前」+ -found-「= fund，基金」

Henry made such a **profound** statement that no one could utter a single word in disagreement.

Henry 發表了如此有深度的言論，以致於沒有人能提出一丁點兒反對的意見。

典故 found 是來自 fund 表基金，原指生意人做生意的資本、放口袋底的本金，引申有底部的意思；profound 就是一直往底部前進、愈往底部前進就愈深入、感受也愈深刻；愈深入知識之海，學問就愈廣博，因此 profound 也有表「學識淵博的」意思。

補充 profound insight 深謀遠慮
a profound book 深奧的書

profundity n. (知識的)深度；(學識)淵博

反 superficial adj. 表面的；膚淺的

初級

74. **propose**

[prə`poz]

v. 提議，建議；求婚

 pro - 「向前」+ -pose - 「擺放」，將我的提議往前放

I'd like to **propose** a toast to the bride and groom- may you live long and prosper.

我想要向新郎新娘敬酒致意，祝你們幸福長長久久。

補充	propose V-ing	提議做…
	propose sth. to sb.	向某人提出…建議
	propose to sb.	向某人求婚
	to propose a toast to sb.	向某人敬酒致意

proposal n. 建議；求婚

 suggest v. 建議

中級

75. **province**

[`pravɪns]

n. 領域；省；州

 pro - 「在前」+ vince 「拉丁文，戰勝、掌控」

Lauren posed a question that was far outside the **province** of the technician.

Lauren 提出的問題已經遠遠超出這位技師的專長領域。

典故	province 在古時指羅馬的官員依羅馬法律來代表政府掌控、管理的區域，後來衍生爲我們現在所稱的省或州，抽象涵義則表示某個領域。

補充	sb's province	某人的專精
	within the province of N.	涵蓋在 N. 的範圍內

provincial adj. 省的，在首都圈外的；外省的；鄉下的

中高

76. **provoke**

[prə`vok]

v. 引起；激起；激怒

 pro - 「向前」+ -voke - 「 = -voc - ，表召喚」，往前大叫就會引起注意

The policy changes **provoked** a storm of protest.

政策改變引發了激烈抗議。

補充	provoke sb. into V-ing	激怒某人去做…
	sb. be easy provoked	某人很容易被激怒

provocation n. 挑釁，激怒
provocative adj. 挑釁的，煽動的

中級

77. **quarrel**

[ˈkwɔrəl]

n./v. 爭吵；爭執

The team members had a **quarrel** about the budget.
團隊成員爲預算問題而爭執。

quarrel with sb. over/about sth.
和某人就某事物爭執
patch a quarrel up = patch up a quarrel
弭平爭執
It takes two to make a quarrel.
[諺語]：一個巴掌拍不響。

quarrelsome adj. 愛爭吵的；動輒吵架的

中高

78. **reckon**

[ˈrɛkən]

v. 認爲

Possessing such size and strength, Tim is a force to be **reckoned** with on the football field.
Tim 擁有這樣的體型與體力，是足球場上一股不可小覷的力量。

be reckoned to be... 被認爲是…
be a force to be reckoned with
成爲不可小覷的力量
a name to reckon with 鼎鼎大名的人

中級

79. **recognize**

[ˈrɛkəɡˌnaɪz]

v. 認出；識別

★ 英：**recognise** ／ 美：**recognize**

⇨ re - 「再次」+ co - 「一起」+ - gn - 「知道」+ - ize「動詞字尾」，兩相比較再看一次就會認出來、辨識出來

I could hardly **recognize** George after he lost 10 kilos on an extreme diet.
George 在劇烈節食後瘦了十公斤，我幾乎快認不出他了。

recognize A by B 透過 B 辨識出 A
recognize A as B 將 A 視爲 B

recognition n. 認出；承認
recognizable adj. 可辨認的；可識別的

同 identify

80. recycling

[riˋsaɪkḷɪŋ]

n. 資源回收，回收利用

⇨ re -「一再，返回」+ cycle「循環」+ -ing「名詞字尾」

The **recycling** truck only comes around once a week in my neighborhood, so many people throw their bottles out with their regular waste.
我這個鄰里的資源回收車每週只來一次，所以很多人都將瓶罐與一般垃圾一起扔掉。

 a recycling center 資源回收中心
waste/metal/plastic recycling
廢棄物 / 金屬 / 塑膠類回收
3R = Reduce, Reuse, Recycle
減量、重覆使用、再利用

recycle v. 再回收，使再利用

初級

81. refuse

[rɪˋfjuz]

v. 拒絕

[ˋrɛfjus]

n. 廢料；廢棄物

⇨ re -「回來」+ - fuse -「傾倒」，把你倒過來的東西再倒還給你表示拒絕、回絕

I simply **refuse** to be a part of this illegal business operation anymore!
我拒絕再參與這個非法事業的運作！

Bottles and cans can be recycled and should be separated from household **refuse**.
瓶罐可以回收再利用，應該要與家中廢棄物分開來。

 to refuse sb. sth. = to refuse sth. to sb.
拒絕提供某物給某人
refuse to V.　　拒絕做…
a refuse dump 垃圾場

refusal n. 拒絕；謝絕

同 decline / reject v. 拒絕
waste / garbage n. 廢棄物

82. repulsive

[rɪˋpʌlsɪv]

adj. 使人反感的；令人厭惡的

⇨ repulse「使厭惡，使反感」+ -ive「有…性質的」

Though many people find insects **repulsive**, they are considered a delicacy in my hometown.
雖然很多人覺得昆蟲令人厭惡，但是牠們在我的家鄉卻被視為美味佳餚。

repulse v. 使厭惡，使反感
repulsion n. 反感

同 disgusting

中高

83. **retaliate**

[rɪˈtælɪˌet]

v. 報復

⇨ re-「返回」+ talis「拉丁文，以同樣方式」+ -ate「使…」，以同樣方式還回去就是報復

When you are outnumbered, it's best not to **retaliate** when others insult you.

當你們在人數上居於弱勢時，最好不要在別人侮辱你們時反擊。

補充
retaliate against sb./sth. with N.
以 N. 來報復某人／某事物
retaliate by V-ing　　　　透過做…來報復
impose retaliatory tariffs　徵收報復性關稅

retaliation n. 報復
retaliatory adj. 回敬的；報復的

同 revenge

中高

84. **rigor**

[ˈrɪgɚ]

n. 嚴格；嚴謹

★ 英：**rigour** ／ 美：**rigor**

⇨ -rig-「堅硬的」+ -or「= -id，表性質」

The overall **rigor** of the workflow is what sets us apart from others.

工作流程整體的嚴謹度就是使我們和別人與眾不同的地方。

補充　the rigors of the winter　冬天的嚴寒

rigorous adj. 嚴密的；嚴厲的

中高

85. **ripple**

[ˈrɪpl]

n. 漣漪；細紋；水波

v. 起漣漪；使呈波狀

The stock market crash in Europe caused a **ripple** effect on the entire world economy.

歐洲股市崩盤對整個世界經濟產生連鎖反應。

補充
ripple effect　連鎖反應
ripple of N.　一波波的 N.

86. scandal

['skændl̩]

n. 醜聞

After only one year in office, the mayor resigned amid an embarrassing **scandal**.

就任僅僅一年後，那名市長就在一件尷尬的醜聞中辭職下台了。

典故 scandal 來自拉丁文 scando 指「跳」，原指遇到絆腳的障礙要跳起來的動作，後來指會絆到人的障礙，之後衍生出讓人在人生路上跌一跤、會名譽掃地的東西，也就是不光彩的「醜聞」。

補充
create/cause a scandal	造成醜聞
a scandal erupt/break	醜聞曝光
be caught up/involved in a scandal	捲入醜聞中

87. sentimental

[ˌsɛntə'mɛntl̩]

adj. 感情用事的，多愁善感的；感傷的

sentiment n. 情緒；感傷

➪ -senti- 「感受」+ -ment「名詞字尾」+ -al「形容詞字尾」

Don't make any reply for **sentimental** reasons.

不要因為情感因素而做出回覆。

補充
sentimental value 情感價值
popular sentiment 民意

88. skeptical

['skɛptɪkl̩]

adj. 懷疑的

skeptically adv. 懷疑地
skepticism n. 懷疑論

同 doubtful

★ 英：sceptical／美：skeptical

 -skept- 「= -scept- ，觀看審視」+ -ical「關於…的」，會一直觀察審視就是因為存有疑慮

We remain **skeptical** about what they have promised.

我們仍對他們所承諾的事抱持懷疑的態度。

補充 remain skeptical about/of sth. 對某事存疑

89. species

中級

[ˈspisɪz] /[ˈspiʃɪz]
n. 物種

💡 -spec- 「觀看」+ -ies「名詞字尾」，天地間可觀察到的各種東西就是不同的「物種」

Contrary to popular belief, there are actually hundreds of **species** of insects living in the so-called "lifeless" desert.

有別於一般人的認知，的確是有上百種的昆蟲物種生活在所謂「無生命的」沙漠中。

補充　endangered species 瀕臨滅絕的物種
a rare species of N.　N. 的稀有品種

90. spouse

中高

[spaʊs]
n. 配偶

He is so supportive of his **spouse** that he stayed at home to take care of the kids while she pursued her career.

他非常支持他的另一半，所以他在太太追求事業的時候，留在家中照顧小孩。

典故　源自字根 -spon-「發誓」，透過發誓、承諾誓言的人，就是指結婚的新郎新娘。

補充　office spouse 關係密切的辦公室異性伙伴

同 better half

91. startle

中高

[ˈstɑrtl̩]
v. 使驚嚇

💡 start「突然開始」+ -le「表反覆的動作」，頻頻做出突然開始的動作讓人嚇得不知所措

The negative news about food safety **startled** many people into changing their eating habits.

有關食品安全的負面新聞使人們震驚，使許多人開始改變飲食習慣。

補充
be startled to see/hear/learn
驚訝地看到 / 聽到 / 知道
startle sb. into V-ing　使某人震驚而變得…
It startles sb. to do sth.　做某事使某人感到震驚。

startled adj. 受驚嚇的
同 surprise /shock

310

中高

92. **stern**

[stɝn]

adj. 嚴苛的；嚴格的

同 severe / strict

Ms. Stone is quite **stern** with her subordinates.
Stone 女士對她的屬下相當嚴苛。

補充 a stern face/expression/look
嚴厲的臉 / 表達方式 / 樣子
sb. be made of sterner stuff 某人非常堅強、強勢

中級

93. **surrender**

[sə'rɛndə]

v./n. 投降；放棄；屈服

⇨ sur - 「越過」+ ren - 「= re - ，返回」+ - der - 「給予」，東西都交付過來就是投降了
The negotiation failed because neither side was willing to **surrender** any of their claims.
因為沒有一方願意放棄自己的主張，所以談判破裂了。

補充 unconditional surrender 無條件投降
to surrender to sb. 向某人投降
to surrender sth. to sb. 將某物交付給某人

同 v. = give in / yield / submit

中高

94. **tailor-made**

['telə‚med]

adj. 特製的；適合的

⇨ tailor「裁縫師」+ - made「由…製作的」，由裁縫師特製的表示十分適合的
This position at the company is **tailor-made** for you-you'll be traveling ninety percent of the time.
公司的這個職位是專為你量身訂製的，你將有百分之九十的時間都在差旅中。

補充 be tailor-made for sth. 正好適合從事（某工作）

95. **take up**

[tek][ʌp]

phr. 討論，處理；
開始從事；佔用

You need to **take up** your complaint with the manager instead of the clerk.
你需要向經理提出申訴，而不是店員。

補充 take up V-ing 開始做…
take up office 到任；就職
sb. be taken up with N.
某人的時間或精神都被用在 N. 上

takeup n. 使用度，購買率

同 discuss v. 討論

11
製造

12
金融

13
科技技術

14
房屋地產

15
出差旅遊

96. **thrift**

[θrɪft]

n. 節儉；節約

By adhering to a policy of **thrift**, the Jones family was able to buy a house with cash after only five years.

藉由堅守節約的策略，Jones 家能夠在僅僅五年就以現金買下一棟房子。

 典故 thrift 來自動詞 thrive「興旺、繁榮」，因興旺繁盛就會有多餘的物資得以儲存，到十六世紀時就以 thrift 表存錢的習慣，也就是「節約」。

補充 thrift shop 慈善義賣商店
spendthrift n. 揮霍無度的人

thrifty adj. 節約的

同 economy / frugality

---

97. **tranquility**

[trænˈkwɪlətɪ]

n. 平靜；安寧；穩定

★ 英：tranquillity ／ 美：tranquility

 ➪ trans -「遍及」+ -quil -「安靜的」+ -ity「表性質」

Nothing compares to the **tranquility** of staring at miles of cornfields as the sun slowly sets.

沒有什麼能比得上在太陽緩慢落下時凝望延伸數英里玉米田的寧靜感。

補充 the tranquility of N. 寧靜的 N.

tranquil adj. 平靜的；平穩的

中高

98. **tuition**

[tuˈɪʃən]

n. 教學；學費

 tuit「源自拉丁文，表看管」+ -ion「名詞字尾」

One year of **tuition** at the state's most prestigious boarding school is ten times the annual salary of the average working man.

那州最有名望的寄宿學校一年的學費，是一般勞工階級年收入的十倍。

補充 tuition fee　　　　　　　學費
receive tuition in (subject) 學習…（科目）

tutor n. 家教

中級

99. **upset**

[ʌpˋsɛt]

adj. 攪亂的；心煩的

v. 攪亂；使心煩意亂

★ 動詞變化：upset, upset, upset, upsetting

⇨ up「向上」+ set「擺放」，把東西底部翻轉過來向上放 就會攪亂事物、讓人心煩

Kim was **upset** that she never got the chance to compete after her season-ending injury.

Kim 對於沒機會在季末受傷後再度比賽感到很不開心。

 補充
upset the apple cart　製造麻煩；破壞某人的計劃
upset sb's stomach　　讓某人想吐

初級

100. **value**

[ˋvæljʊ]

n. 價值

v. 評價；重視

Unless you have something of **value** to add to this conversation, stay out of it.

除非你對於這個會談能加點甚麼有價值的東西，否則離遠一點。

 補充
core values　　　　　　核心價值
culture/social values　　文化 / 社會價值
go up/down in value　　價值增加 / 減少
to value sb./sth. for N.　因 N. 而珍視某人 / 某物

valuable adj. 值錢的，貴重的
valueless adj. 無價值的，毫無用處的
values n. 價值觀

實力進階

Part 1. 實用動詞片語

日常生活情境常伴隨許多動詞片語使用，常見的有：

動詞	片語	例詞 / 例句
drop	drop off 減少；讓…下車	Sales dropped off last month. 上個月的銷售額下滑。
	drop out 退出，休學	drop out of school 輟學
	drop by 順道拜訪	drop by for a cup of coffee 順便來喝個咖啡
	drop in on sb. 臨時造訪某人	drop in on you 臨時來拜訪你
get	get to 到…	get to the airport 到機場 get to Fifth Avenue 到第五大道
	get rid of 擺脫	get rid of the headache 擺脫頭痛 get rid of the meeting 從會議中脫身
	get back to 回電，回覆	I will get back to you later. 我等一下回電給你。
go	go through (1) 經歷； (2) 從頭到尾看一次	(1) go through a surgery 經歷手術 (2) go through the file 　　 將文件從頭到尾看一次
	go along with N. 贊同，意見一致 [比較]：get along with sb. 　　　　　 和人相處融洽	We don't go along with your idea. 我們不贊同你的想法。

動詞	片語	例詞 / 例句
take	take part in 參加	take part in the game 參與遊戲 take part in the ceremony 參加儀式
	take care of 照顧，負責	take care of the kids 照顧小孩 take care of the finances 負責財務事宜
	take on 承擔	take on the extra work 承擔額外的工作
	take up (1) 開始從事； (2) 佔用	(1) The mayor took up office last month. 市長上個月剛上任。 (2) The couch takes up too much space. 沙發佔了太多的空間。
	take over 接管，掌控	take over the company 接管該公司
	take off 起飛	The flight will take off in five minutes. 班機將於五分鐘後起飛。

16 交通

17 社交與用餐

18 休閒娛樂

19 醫療保健

20 日常生活

隨堂練習

★ 請根據句意，選出最適合的單字

(　　) 1. After learning that the rainy weather will last for days, all the kids feel great _____ since the picnic might have to be put off.
    (A) illusion   (B) despair
    (C) compassion   (D) prejudice

(　　) 2. My parents often tell us to be _____ about the advertisements and commercials since they tend to hype up the products which they promote.
    (A) skeptical   (B) dreadful
    (C) hideous   (D) repulsive

(　　) 3. It is beyond _____ that advances in technology have made people's lives easier and more comfortable.
    (A) defence   (B) instinct
    (C) thrift   (D) dispute

(　　) 4. The rumor of an outbreak of the deadly Ebola virus causes _____ in this country.
    (A) panic   (B) ripple
    (C) fancy   (D) engagement

(　　) 5. Because she is highly computer-_____, she has a better chance to be hired.
    (A) hostile   (B) literate
    (C) optimistic   (D) hectic

解答：1. B　2. A　3. D　4. A　5. B

附錄－常見易混字比較

1. infer vs. imply

infer [ɪnˋfɝ] v. 推論

infer 是聽話者從說話的人所說的內容衍生或推論出想法。

常用句型：infer... from sth. 從某事物推論出…

例 It is difficult to infer anything from such evidence.
從這些證據中很難得出任何想法。

imply [ɪmˋplaɪ] v. 暗示

imply 是說話者說的話裡隱含其他意思。後方直接加上所暗示的想法。

例 Eric never meant to imply any criticism.
Eric 沒有任何批評的意思。

? Are you [a. implying / b. inferring] that I am wrong?
你是在說我是錯的嗎？

2. consult vs. counsel

consult [kənˋsʌlt] v. 商量，諮詢

consult 是去請教別人意見。

例 consult your doctor 就醫
consult a map 查地圖

counsel [ˋkaʊnsl] v. 建議　n. 建議；律師

counsel 是給予別人建議。

常用句型：counsel sb. to do sth. 建議某人去做某事

例 counsel them to give up the plan
建議他們放棄這企劃

? You'd better [a. counsel / b. consult] your supervisor before you submit the proposal.
你在上呈提案前最好先問過你的主管。

解答：1. a　2. b

3. agree / approve / consent

agree [ə`gri] v. 同意，應允

agree 表示同意某事進行時，常用句型：agree to V./N.

例 agree to cooperate 同意合作
agree to a request 同意一項請求

approve [ə`pruv] v. 同意，批准

approve 表示正式批准時，為及物動詞，句型：approve N.

例 approve the plan 批准該計畫

consent [kən`sɛnt] v./n. 同意，允許

句型：consent to N./V.

例 consent to the merger 同意此併購案
consent to sell 同意出售

? The committee unanimously [a. consented / b. approved / c. agreed] the proposal.
委員會全體同意這項提案。

4. oppose vs. object

oppose [ə`poz] v. 反對

oppose 是及物動詞，一定要有受詞表示所反對的人事物。

句型：sb. oppose sth. 或 sb. be opposed to sth./V-ing

例 oppose the idea 反對這個想法

object [əb`dʒɛkt] v. 反對

object 是不及物動詞。object 一字本身就表示反對。

句型：sb. object to sth./V-ing 反對(做)某事
sb. object that... 表示提出反對的理由

例 I object. 我反對。

? Most of us are [a. opposed / b. objected] to the budget plan.
我們大多數反對這個預算案。

解答：3. b 4. a

5. survey vs. research

survey [ˋsɝve] n. 調查

survey 通常以詢問、觀察動作或行為的方式加以記錄或進行。survey 是可數名詞，進行調查可以說 carry out/conduct/do a survey。

research [ˋrisətʃ] n. 研究

research 通常會包含 survey 的過程，有時會加上對標的物進行實驗、測試。research 是不可數名詞，進行研究要用 carry out/conduct/do the research。

? I'm doing some [a. research / b. survey] on renewable energy sources.
我正在做可再生能源的研究。

6. obtain vs. attain

obtain [əbˋten] v. 獲得

obtain 的 -tain- 來自拉丁文 tenēre，字面上表「to hold」，就是握有、持有某樣東西或職位。

例 obtain the information 獲得資訊
obtain the scholarship 獲得獎學金

attain [əˋten] v. 獲得

attain 的 -tain- 來自拉丁文 tangere，字面上表「to touch」，就是去碰觸、去接觸，較強調透過一連串努力所達成、達到的目標或取得成功的地位。

例 attain a high mark in the exam 考試獲得高分
attain excellence within the field 在該領域達到極致

? Only a few candidates will [a. obtain / b. attain] the chance to interview with the manager.
只有少數應徵者會獲得與經理面試的機會。

解答：5. a 6. a

7. material vs. ingredient

material [məˋtɪrɪəl] n. 原料，材料

material 指塑膠或木頭等工業用原料。

例 building materials 建築材料。

ingredient [ɪnˋgridɪənt] n. 原料；成分

ingredient 常指烹飪用的材料，也就是食材；也指組成物質的成分，特別是食物的營養成分，所以像食品包裝上列出的內容物成分，就是 ingredient。

? Many household cleaning [a. materials / b. ingredients] are highly toxic.
很多家用清潔材料都非常的毒。

8. individual / personal / respective

individual [͵ɪndəˋvɪdʒʊəl] n. 個體 adj. 單一的

individual 強調單一個體在一個群體中所具有的獨立性。

例 an individual case 單一個案
an individual account 獨立的帳戶

personal [ˋpɝsn̩l] adj. 個人的；私人的

personal 表示與群體無任何關聯的個人、私人。

例 personal matter 個人事務
personal life 私生活

respective [rɪˋspɛktɪv] adj. 各別的

respective 強調和群體間有所關聯的各別個體

例 our respective rooms 我們各別的房間
their respective roles in a play 在戲裡他們各別的角色

? Obviously, Pete got more [a. personal / b. respective / c. individual] attention in the team.
顯然 Pete 在團隊中得到了較多的個別關注。

解答：7. a　8. c

9. complement vs. supplement

complement [ˋkɑmpləmənt] n. 補充

complement 是指原本已經有東西了，然後用 complement 與之相搭配、互補，讓事物的結果更完美。

例 The good wine is a complement to a good meal.
加上美酒能讓這頓美食更臻完美。

supplement [ˋsʌpləmənt] n. 補充，增補

supplement 是指原本的東西有所欠缺，加上 supplement 才能補足缺乏的東西。

例 vitamin supplements 維他命補充品（因為攝取的維生素不足所以要用補充品補足）

? This document is a [a. complement / b. supplement] to the main report.
這份文件是用來補充主要報告的。

10. spend vs. expend

spend [spɛnd] v. 花費

spend 最常表示花費金錢或時間，後方常加上一筆金額或一段時間當受詞。
句型：spend sth. on sth./ spend sth. V-ing
例 spend $50 on the bread 花 50 元買麵包

expend [ɪkˋspɛnd] v. 花費

expend 通常指為某一專門目的而花費大量金錢、時間或精力，是較正式的用字。
句型：expend sth. on sth./ expend sth. V-ing
例 expend too much time and effort on the project
花費太多時間力氣在這專案上面

? She usually [a. expends / b. spends] one hour calling her clients every day.
她通常每天會花一小時打電話給客戶。

解答：9. b　10. b

常見易混字比較

11. confirm vs. conform

confirm [kənˋfɝm] **vt. 證實；確認**

confirm 包含 firm「堅固，堅定的」，表示確認事實堅定不變，去證實的意思。
confirm 是及物動詞，後方一定要有受詞表示被證實或確認的事情。

例 Five people have confirmed that they will attend the meeting.
有五個人確認會出席會議。

conform [kənˋfɔrm] **vi. 遵守，遵照；按規矩行事**

conform 包含 form「形式」，表示讓大家的形式都一樣，因此是指按規矩行事，
遵守規定的意思。

常見用法：conform to sth. 遵守，遵照（規定、模式等）

例 conform to the safety standards 符合安全標準
conform to the model 遵照範例

? The plans were officially [a. conformed / b. confirmed] yesterday.
這些計畫昨天經過官方證實了。

12. installation vs. installment

installation [ˌɪnstəˋleʃən] **n. 安裝；裝置**

installation 包含名詞字尾 -ation，表示動作的過程或狀態，因此 installation
是指去安裝的動作，也指安裝好的裝置。

例 installation of the new system 安裝新系統
a heating installation 暖氣設備

installment [ɪnˋstɔlmənt] **n. 分期付款**

名詞字尾 -ment 通常表示行為的結果，installment 是把每一筆錢分別安置在不
同的位置上，就是分期付款。

例 pay for the car by installments 分期付款買車

? Do you have to pay extra for (a. installation b. installment)？
你需要額外付安裝費嗎？

解答：11. b   12. a

13. transition / transaction / transmission

transition [trænˋzɪʃən] n. 轉變

transition = trans- + -it- + -ion，字根 -it- 表「行走」，transition 字面上表示 go through，走過去到另一邊，經歷轉變和過渡。

transaction [trænzˋækʃən] n. 交易

transaction = trans- + act + -ion，字面上的涵義是「drive/carry through」的狀態，彼此帶來、送過去，也就是商品和金錢進行交換的「交易」。

transmission [trænsˋmɪʃən] n. 傳送

transmission = trans- + -miss- + -ion，字根 -miss- 表「寄送」，transmission 字面上的涵義是「send across」，就是把東西、資訊送過去的「傳達、播送」。

? The company was slow to make the [a. transaction / b. transition / c. transmission] from paper to computer.

這間公司很慢才從文書作業轉變成電腦作業。

14. assure vs. ensure

assure [əˋʃur] v. 向…保證

assure 指向人保證，使人安心。

常用句型：assure sb. that... / assure sb. of sth.

例 We can assure you of our full support.
我們向你保證會全力支持你。

ensure [ɪnˋʃur] v. 確保

ensure 是確認某事保證發生，常指確保人的安全或確保事物的品質。

常用句型：ensure sth./ ensure that... / ensure sb. sth.

例 Necessary steps were taken to ensure their safety.
採取了必要措施以確保他們的安全。

? Using the shipping labels can [a. assure b. ensure] that your packages stay upright.
使用這些出貨標籤能確保你的包裹維持在直立的狀態。

解答：13. b 14. b

15. publication vs. publicity

publication [ˌpʌblɪˋkeʃən] n. 出版；發表；出版物

publication = pūblicāre「拉丁文，使公開」+ -ion「名詞字尾，表動作的過程或結果」。publication 強調使人事物公開的動作，就是去出版、發表；而出版的結果就是出版物，publication 指出版物時是可數名詞。

例 The magazine has ceased publication.
該雜誌已經停止出版。

publicity [pʌbˋlɪsətɪ] n. 關注，名聲；宣傳

publicity = public「公開的」+ -ity「名詞字尾，表狀態」。publicity 字面意思是公開的狀態，公開的人事物會得到關注，公開的狀態也表示一種宣傳。

例 The case has generated enormous publicity.
這宗案件已經引起了大眾高度關注。

? The company had received bad [a. publication / b. publicity] over a defective product.
這公司因為瑕疵產品的緣故得到了壞名聲。

16. intense vs. intensive

intense [ɪnˋtɛns] adj. 極度的，劇烈的；（活動）緊張，激烈的；（人）情感強烈的

intense = in-「在裡面」+ -tens-「用力拉」，在心裡用力拉使人產生強烈的感受，因此 intense 強調人的內在感受很強烈，形容事物時則表示事物或活動是緊張、激烈的。

例 intense pain 劇痛
intense competition 激烈的競爭
intense debate 激烈的辯論

intensive [ɪnˋtɛnsɪv] adj. 集中的，密集的

intensive = intense + -ive「有…性質的」，intensive 強調外在事物的性質是集中深入的，通常是指在短時間內投入極大的努力或行動。

例 intensive training 密集訓練
intensive bombing 密集轟炸
intensive care 特別護理

? Hearing about the news, he could not help feeling [a. intense / b. intensive] disappointment.
聽到那個消息時，他不禁感到極度失望。

解答：15. b　16. a

17. favorable vs. favorite

favorable ['fevərəbl̩] adj. 贊同的；適合的；討人喜歡的

favorable = favor「偏愛；支持」+ -able「能夠…的」，能讓人支持就是贊同的，能讓人偏愛的就是討人喜歡的。

例 Luckily, the clients are favorable to this proposal.
幸運地，客戶贊成這項提議。

favorite ['fevərɪt] adj. 最喜愛的 n. 特別喜愛的人或物

favorite = favor「偏愛」+ -ite「形容詞字尾，有關的」

例 Blue is my favorite color.
藍色是我最喜歡的顏色。

? Mark's ideas met with [a. favorite / b. favorable] response.
Mark 的主張反應很好。

18. adapt vs. adopt

adapt [ə'dæpt] v. 使適合，適應；改造；改編

adapt = ad-「to」+ apt「適合、恰當的」，改變使人事物達到適合的狀態就是適應、改編。

句型：adapt to sth. 適應某事物
　　　be adapted for... 改編成…

例 We need to adapt to the new system quickly.
我們需要快點適應新系統。

adopt [ə'dɑpt] v. 採用（意見，方針）；收養

adopt = ad-「to」+ -opt-「選擇」，做出選擇表示採用，選擇了某人就是指收養。

例 adopt a different method 採用不同的方法
adopt a child 收養孩子

? The camera has been [a. adapted / b. adopted] for underwater use.
這款相機已經改造成在水裡也可以使用。

解答：17. b　18. a

19. temporary vs. tentative

temporary [ˋtɛmpəˌrɛrɪ] adj. 暫時的，臨時的；短期的

temporary 來自字根 -tempor- 表時間，因此 temporary 是指時間短暫、臨時，不會持續。常用來形容 job, position, employment 等。

例 temporary work 臨時工作
temporary accommodation 臨時住處

tentative [ˋtɛntətɪv] adj. 暫定的，不確定的

tentative 原意指嘗試，因此是強調事物的不確定性，常用來形容 plan, agreement 等。

例 tentative arrangement 初步協議
tentative conclusions 初步結論

? The plans are [a. temporary / b. tentative] and have to be finalized by June 30.
這些計畫是暫時的而且必須在六月三十日前定案。

20. attribute vs. contribute

attribute [əˋtrɪbjut] v. 歸因於

句型：attribute A to B/ A is attributed to B 將 A 歸因於 B

例 The study shows that childhood obesity can be directly attributed to fast food.
研究顯示孩童肥胖可以直接歸因於速食。

contribute [kənˋtrɪbjut] v. 貢獻；導致

句型：A contribute to B A 導致 B

例 The study shows that fast food directly contribute to childhood obesity.
研究顯示速食直接導致了孩童肥胖。

? His bad temper is [a. attributed / b. contributed] to his ill health.
他的壞脾氣要歸咎於他身體不健康。

解答：19. b　20. a

常見易混字比較

21. offer / provide / supply

offer [ˋɔfɚ] v. 提供，主動提出 n. 提議

offer 來自字根 -fer-「帶來」，強調是主動給予的動作。

句型：offer sth. to sb. = offer sb. sth. 提供某物給某人

例 She offered drinks to her guests.
她提供飲料給客人。

provide [prəˋvaɪd] v. 提供，供給

provide = pro-「向前」+ -vid-「看」，預先看到需要而做準備去供給，因此 provide 強調準備充分而提供的意思。

句型：provide sth. for sb. = provide sb. with sth. 提供某物給某人

例 provide readers with the latest information
提供讀者最新資訊

supply [səˋplaɪ] v./n. 供給，給予

supply 原意指從下方往上填滿使其完整，表示供應所需，因此常指提供食衣住行等民生用品，而且是較長期且大量的供應。

句型：supply sth. to sb. = supply sb. with sth. 提供某物給某人

例 a list of foods supplying our daily vitamin needs
供應每日所需維他命的食物清單

? This organization [a. offers / b. provides / c. supplies] people on low incomes free legal advice.
這機構為低收入者提供免費法律諮詢。

解答：21. a

327

22. accept vs. receive

accept [əkˋsɛpt] v. 接受；同意；採納；接納

accept 是指開心樂意的接受，因此也有同意的意思。

例 accept the advice 接受建議
accept the job 接受這份工作
be accepted to the school 被這所學校錄取
credit cards are accepted 接受刷卡

receive [rɪˋsiv] v. 接受，收到；迎接

receive 指收到送來的東西，也有迎接客人的意思。

例 After Betty accepted Bill's apology, she received a bunch of roses the next day.
Betty 接受了 Bill 的道歉之後，她就在隔一天收到了一束玫瑰花。

? Check your account to make sure you have [a. accepted / b. received] their donation.
核對你的帳戶確認你有沒有收到他們的捐款。

23. damage vs. harm

damage [ˋdæmɪdʒ] v./n. 傷害

damage 常用於指無生命事物的損傷，指傷害事物使其失掉價值、用途或外表，而這些損害在未來是可能修復的。damage 當名詞為不可數，字尾加 s 的 damages 則指賠款或賠償金。

例 He damaged my car with a stone.
他用石頭損壞我的車。

harm [hɑrm] v./n. 傷害

harm 指傷害一個人心智、健康、權利、事業等；名詞時為不可數。

例 The scandal has harmed the reputation of the company.
醜聞傷害了公司的聲譽。

? The building was badly [a. damaged / b. harmed] by fire.
這棟大樓因為火災受到嚴重的損害。

解答：22. b　23. a

24. price / value / worth

price [praɪs] n. 價格 v. 給...定價

price 是加諸於物品的外在價格，指支付的金額，常與動詞 pay 連用。

例 pay a high price 付高價
at half price 半價

value [ˈvæljʊ] n. 價值，價格；重要性 v. 估價；重視

value 指金錢上的價值，也指人事物的重要性。當動詞時表示估價，與 at 連用。

例 The painting was valued at $2000.
那幅畫估價為 2000 元。

worth [wɜθ] n. 價值 adj. 有...的價值；值得的

worth 可指金錢上或精神上的價值，和 value 意思雖相近但用法不同。

句型：金額 + worth + of sth. 值某金額的東西

例 $200 worth of gifts 值兩百元的禮物

句型：sth.+ be worth + N. 金額某物有某個特定價值

例 The house is worth about 20 million dollars.
這房屋大約值兩千萬元。

? The foundation offers scholarships [a. valued / b. worth / c. price]
$10000 to graduates from poor families every year.
這個基金會每年提供價值一萬元的獎學金給來自清寒家庭的畢業生。

解答：24. b

25. arise/raise/rise

arise [əˋraɪz] vi. 發生，產生（動詞變化 arise-arose-arisen）

不及物動詞，常指問題或困難發生。片語 arise from 表示「由…引起」。

例 potential problems that may arise
可能會發生的潛在問題

例 Accidents arise from carelessness.
疏忽大意往往會引發事故。

raise [rez] vt. 舉起；提升；提出 n. 加薪 (AmE)

及物動詞，表示具體舉起某物或是抽象意義上使某事物提升增加。

例 raise your hands 舉手
raise taxes 增稅
raise a question 提出疑問

rise [raɪz] vi./n. 上升；增加（動詞變化 rise-rose-risen）

不及物動詞，常表示人事物具體地往上移動或數量增加。

例 Sales are rising by 2% a month.
銷售量一個月增長 2%。

? The bank will (a. rise b. raise c. arise) interest rates to 3 percent.
銀行將會提高利息至 3%。

解答：25. b

字彙索引

字彙索引

字彙索引

字彙索引

字彙索引

國家圖書館出版品預行編目 (CIP) 資料

徐薇教你背新多益單字 / 徐薇編著 . -- 臺北市：
　碩英，2015.05
　　冊；　公分. --
　　　ISBN 978-986-90662-2-8（下冊：平裝附光碟片 ）

1. 多益測驗 2. 詞彙

805.1895　　　　　　　　　　　　104001171

徐薇教你背新多益單字（下）

發行人：江正明

發行公司：碩英出版社

編著者：徐薇

責任編輯：賴依寬、黃怡欣、黃思瑜、王歆

英文編輯：Jon Turner、Paul Deacon、Sherry Wen

美術編輯：陳爾筠

錄音製作：風華錄音室

地址：106 台北市大安區安和路二段 70 號 2 樓之 3

電話：02-2708-5508

傳真：02-2707-1669

出版日期：2015 年 08 月

定價：NT$450